Mink Elliott is a journalist who has worked on many magazines in both the UK and Australia. She is author of *The Pissed-Off Parents Club*, also published by Sphere.

Just Another Manic Mum-Day

MINK ELLIOTT

sphere

SPHERE

First published in Great Britain in 2012 as a paperback original by Sphere

A CIP catalogue record for this book
is available from the British Library.

ISBN 978-0-7515-4615-6

Typeset in Caslon by M Rules
Printed and bound in Great Britain by
Clays Ltd, St Ives plc

Papers used by Sphere are from well-managed forests
and other responsible sources.

MIX

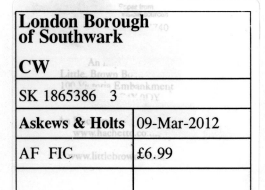

To Samantha and Maximilian

Chapter 1

'Watch out!' I shriek as a globular white wodge seems to come out of nowhere, hurling itself down straight towards the top of Jack's baseball-capped head.

Things go all slow motion, the screeching seagulls the only sound I can hear as Jack stops dead in his tracks, looks over his shoulder at me and then up into the bright blue sky.

SPLAT.

'Ooh.' I wince. 'Bullseye.'

Joey looks up at her daddy, her concerned mouth open wide.

'Uh-oh,' she says. 'Are you OK, Daddy?'

Jack laughs his manly, confident laugh and ruffles Joey's hair with one hand while the other wipes a small speck of seagull poo off his cheek.

'Not to worry,' he chirrups, whipping off his baseball cap to inspect it. 'Most of it's on this old thing. High time I binned it anyway. And luckily, I just so happen to have *this* on me . . .'

He pulls another cap with BONDI emblazoned across it out of his jeans' back pocket, arranges it on his head, gets Joey's beaming seal of approval and turns to face me.

'Anyway,' he flashes me a disarming grin, 'having a bird poo on you is good luck, you know.'

'Well, we're going to need every bird in Sydney to poo on us in that case. *Daily*.' I grin back as we walk down Didgeridoo Drive to get to the big grassy verge overlooking Bondi Beach.

'I promise you it'll be different this time, Roxy,' he says, grabbing Joey's hand again so they can carry on with their synchronised skipping, laughing and squealing as they go. 'This time moving will be the best thing we've ever done!'

Well, things certainly feel different. For a start, it's like the footpath is virtually *melting* beneath my flip-flopped feet on this blisteringly hot Australia Day bank holiday, and I look around me, a little stunned and self-conscious at the staggering amount of tanned, firm flesh on show.

And even though I'm quite covered up by comparison in long shorts and a T-shirt, at least I've abandoned my usual suspicion of shoes that *expose* rather than *hide* your feet and put on the appropriate casual footwear for The Big Aussie Day Out Down The Beach: bright white Havaianas flip-flops – or *thongs* as they call them here. You can imagine my surprise and creeping horror when the surfwear-shop assistant said I didn't need a changing room, I could try on a thong right there by the checkout.

I spluttered at the suggestion. Me? In a G-string? In broad daylight? Completely sober on the shop floor? Oh, the humanity.

But because my toes haven't seen daylight for yonks (and *I* haven't seen my toes for ages, either, come to think of it), now I feel strangely ... *liberated*. Maybe it's also got something to do with my brilliant all-white outfit. I decided this morning to do away with my usual head-to-toe all-black ensembles and instead opt for white, as a sort of sartorial nod to optimism and looking on the bright side; my newly adopted attitudes. I sigh and wonder whether this is the beginning of a beautiful new friendship with white. And my feet.

My feet, Jack, Joey and I find a relatively uncrowded spot of grass to sit on and gaze at the sea and sand, drinking in the holiday, fun atmosphere, the hot sun beating down on us.

There are happy, laughing families playing Frisbee with their excited, barking dogs; the far-off sizzle of sausages, steaks and onion rings cooking on industrial-sized barbecues mingles with the soothing sound of waves crashing ashore; the heady smell of good times and salt and vinegar chips fills the thick, humid air.

'Isn't this beautiful,' Jack states, rather than asks. 'Come on, Joey, let's go and get some food!'

I watch them gambol off into the haze and stretch my legs out in front of me. I lean on my elbows, close my eyes and gently ease my head back, pointing my smothered-infactor-150-seriously-wilting-English-rose face to the Australian sun.

Taking a long, deep breath in, I try to clasp my hands together over my stomach, but I can't – there's simply too *much* of me to get my hands around.

Because, unfortunately, I'm just not like those women who *snap* back into shape, squeezing into their size 6 jeans five minutes after popping a baby out. *My* genes – and sweet shops and supermarket pastry aisles – have always had it in for me, I'm afraid. So after I had Joey, there was no snapping, no bouncing and certainly no *pinging* back into my pre-pregnancy shape. More like *blancmangeing* back.

Which I've been trying to rectify (with very little success) ever since the last time we moved – from London to Riverside, a small village in Berkshire, when Joey was ten months old. I ended up feeling so isolated, so lonely and so frustrated with Jack that I was fairly *forced* to set up the Pissed-Off Parents Club at the local pub, where like-minded souls struggling with the whole parent thing would meet once a week.

My shoulders slump at the memory.

But this time moving will have been the *right* thing to do and we will have moved to the *right* place, I tell myself, putting my shoulders back and pointing my face towards the sun, thus assuming a more upbeat, positive pose. This time things will be totally different because … um … well …

I hear Joey and Jack approaching and open my eyes, just in time to see a massive hot dog being thrust in my face.

'For you, Mummy,' says my sweet little girl, settling herself on the grass next to me.

'Thank you, darling.' I sit up, crossing my legs.

I glance over at Jack and, despite the fact he's seriously eyeballing the *Sports Illustrated* bikini-clad supermodel beach volleyball team bouncing about in front of us on the sand, I smile. Because I love his outlook, his enthusiasm and his certainty, I really do. That's what persuaded me to move here, after all – the infectious excitement of Jack in Big Plan mode.

It's just that we've been here for nearly a month and I'm still not convinced. I don't feel at home here yet.

I need a sign, positive proof that everything's going to be great, something solid to suggest that things will be different from now on. I squint as I stare at the glaring sun, to let it know I mean business, and say softly, quietly: 'Go on, sun or universe or whoever's in charge up there – give me a sign.'

Nothing happens, so I look back to my lunch and take a big sniff of sausage, two sauces and white bread roll. My mouth starts to water – blimey, even my *eyes* start to water. Its deliciousness just about totally takes over all my senses and I close my eyes to really savour the moment. I open my mouth wide and take my first delectable bite.

A microsecond later, I hear the unmistakeable spurt

and splodge of tomato sauce being fast ejected all down my front and even on to my feet. I stop mid-mastication and open my eyes.

And there they are, bright red and dark brown blobs of barbecue and tomato sauce spattered all over my top, my shorts and my brand spanking new trendy white flip-flops.

'Oh, great,' I groan.

'Hoo!' Jack hoots, nudging Joey, pointing at me. 'Hot dog POO!'

'Yucky!' shouts Joey, joining her dad in laughing at the latest misfortune to befall Mummy.

The more I grimace, the more they fall about cackling hysterically, clutching their stomachs for fear their ribs will break. Eventually, I manage to wipe myself down with about a hundred tissues and wonder whether this is it – whether spilled hot dog sauce is the sign I've been looking for.

And as the seagulls swoop and squawk overhead and the sound of children's laughter fills my ears, I can't help muttering to myself, 'Thanks, universe. Thanks a bunch.'

Chapter 2

I've never really been one for astrology. Not seriously, anyway. Of course, when I was younger, I'd check out my New Year predictions in the January issues of my favourite magazines. And maybe, once in a while, I'd glance at a newspaper's daily stars to check that disaster wasn't going to dog me on that night's hot date or anything. These days, though, I haven't got time for all that zodiac stuff (or NAB – New Age Bollocks – as Jack would call it), and anyway, it just seems so unlikely, so far-fetched. But today something happened that just might make me think again.

There we all were – me, Jack and Joey – frolicking in the sand and surf. Well, to be totally honest, Jack and Joey were larking about in the water while I was sitting under an umbrella in my baseball cap, sunglasses and black burkini, when suddenly, out of the blue, came a friendly and familiar, but impossible to place, voice.

'Roxy! Is that you under there?'

I looked up and squinted into the blazing sun, wondering who this wetsuit-wearing, ridiculously fit and fabulous twenty-five-year-old could be. And who on earth could have possibly recognised me in my brilliantly sun-repelling, body-hiding, pale-complexion-protecting, hopelessly unflattering all-in-one giant romper suit?

'Yes?' I replied warily.

'It's meeee!' the voice squealed. 'Jasmine! Jasmine Lucy? From uni – remember?'

I squinted even harder, desperately racking my brains, my head hurting a little with the strain of trying to think that far back.

'Umm.' I stalled for time, trying to stand up in the dry sand, which is difficult enough at the best of times but when you're as hefty and uncoordinated as me, well, I imagine it's like watching a hippo slipping about on a banana skin.

'Rox! You haven't changed a bit!' she said, making me splutter with disappointment.

'Oh! Don't say that! Surely I wasn't this ... well, um, I didn't have all this baby weight hanging around when we were at uni, did I?' I objected, perhaps a little too defensively.

'Still as feisty as ever.' She laughed, nudging me in the general rib area. '*Plus ça change!*'

It must have been twenty-odd years since we last saw each other. Twenty years since I was twenty-two, at university, hell-bent on having the time of my life.

But things have changed *a lot* since then. *I've* changed a lot since then. It's having Joey that's done it.

Where I was once feisty, as Jasmine put it, I suppose I'm now more, well, *fusty*. You might have described me as bolshie back in the day – but now belchy would be more accurate. And I used to be wild, but now I'm mild. Pneumatic? Rheumatic. Hot and horny? A bit chilly, actually – now where did I put my favourite cardie ...?

Not that I mind so much, really – I've always kind of looked forward to the time in my life when I can potter about in the garden, looking gorgeous like Felicity Kendal in *Rosemary & Thyme*, doing a bit of weeding in a baggy old jumper as opposed to getting mashed and going clubbing in a boob tube, Kylie hotpants and sky-high stilettos.

As Jasmine took my hand and helped me up, she shook her head and said *Plus ça change* again and then, suddenly, DING! So *that* was where I knew her from – second-year French. My attendance in those days was *très pauvre*, at best, so no wonder my memory of her was hazy.

'What have you been up to for the past God knows how many years?' I said, trying to play down the decades that have flown by since we last saw each other.

'Twenty!' she gasped. 'Twenty years! I can't believe it!'

'All right, all right – keep your voice down,' I whispered, looking around furtively. 'We've just moved here from the UK and I don't want the whole of Bondi to know I'm old enough to be its mother.'

She looked like she was about to say: '*Grand*mother,

9

more like!', but she didn't. She simply smiled, making me wonder whether I'm just too paranoid about this whole age thing.

'So, still searching for a home, then?' She asked.

'Eh?' I replied, a little taken aback.

'Some things never change,' she continued. 'You were never settled at uni – always had an air of the temporary about you.'

'I did? Well, how about you?' Quickly I switched the subject. 'You still into all that astrology, clairvoyant, mystic stuff?'

'*Bien sûr!*' She grinned. 'I make quite a tidy living out of it, too. Keeps a roof over me, the hubby and the kids, anyway.'

She went on to tell me she's got four kids, a wonderful husband-manager, and is a very well regarded, well known astrologer, with a stall at the Bondi markets on a Sunday, a website, astrology and clairvoyance columns for several magazines and newspapers, and even a regular Friday spot on *G'day!*, the most popular morning TV news show in Australia. I'm impressed.

'Still building your family, then?' She smiled, her eyes twinkling as she stole a lightning-fast glance at my stomach.

'No, no, no.' I shook my head and patted my tummy. 'Just eaten too many pies. We've only got the one – Joey, my daughter. And she's enough for us – *too* much most of the time!'

Jasmine regarded me quizzically and I felt a sudden, strange urge to offload, as if she was my closest friend and I simply *had to* divulge all my secrets.

'And anyway,' I began, 'it's too late for me now – I'm convinced I'm starting The Change. Apparently, brain fog and mood swings are two of the top symptoms of early menopause – and I've got them both in spades, lately, let me tell you.'

'Hmm.' She hummed sagely. 'So, new country, new life, then?'

'I hope so,' I said, looking at Jack and Joey larking about in the foamy, frothy waves.

Jasmine followed my gaze out to sea and we stood there in silence for a few minutes. I wasn't sure what to say to fill the dead air – and this only served to highlight my fish-out-of-water feelings. I was so obviously out of place here in Oz – I didn't look like everybody else, I didn't sound like everybody else, I didn't worship the sun like everybody else and ... I felt utterly disconnected.

Looking off into infinity, it occured to me that this was the first time I'd indulged in some quiet contemplation for ... ooh, let's see ... three-and-a-bit years? I hadn't felt so alone with my thoughts since Joey first crash-landed into our lives.

Of course, I love her to bits and wouldn't change her for the world, but she is what's known in parenting circles as 'a handful'. Roughly translated, this term is usually used for a child who: is in your face 24/7; is incapable of playing alone, demanding your constant attention while simultaneously revealing your embarrassingly remedial arts and crafts skills; refuses to leave your side, even when you need to go to the loo so you end up pleading with her for a little privacy; insists on sleeping with you, her feet in your face as she takes over, upside down and diagonally across your bed.

Which would be all right if I got a *break* every now and again. Not to sit around, my feet up on a bar stool as I sip pina coladas with male models or anything (although ...), but if I had some Joey-free time, I could make money – maybe even finish a cup of tea for once. Then I could afford to put her into day care, where my adorable little muck spreader could run some other poor (but paid) soul ragged.

I was getting excited at the thought, remembering I have an interview for a full-time job tomorrow. And then slowly, like I was coming back into the room after being hypnotised, that familiar refrain started running through my head, getting louder and louder: *I need more time and money, I need more time and money, I need more time and flipping money!*

'Penny for your thoughts,' said Jasmine warmly.

'Oh.' I sighed. 'I just wish I had more time. I never get *half* the things done that I intend to, and yet I'm always exhausted.'

'Know what you mean.' She nodded. 'I'm always running around like a chook with its head cut off, putting out

12

little fires and playing peacemaker to my warring kids. Honestly, if it's not one, it's the other three. Maybe we both need to do a course in time management—'

'HA!' I scoffed. 'I haven't got *time* for time management!'

'Or . . .' she whirled round to face me and grabbed hold of both my elbows, a mischievous glint in her eye, 'you could try your hand at some New Moon Wishing – only takes a tick. And it's nearly 100% guaranteed to sort you out. There's a new moon tonight at a quarter past eight. Figure out what it is that you really want, what would really make you happy, make your wishes out loud and write them down, too. Keep them brief, to the point—'

I snorted a little bit, just enough to show Jasmine that I'm a tad sceptical about all this sort of stuff.

'Non-believer, eh?' She smiled. 'Look it up on my website and have a bash at it. You've got nothing to lose by giving it a try. And you never know, you just might get something out of it.'

She began jogging on the spot and consulted her sports watch.

'Oh! I really must fly, now. Lovely to see you again, Roxy – do take care, won't you?'

And off she trotted, bounding gracefully over the dry sand as she glanced enigmatically over her shoulder at me, and winked.

So here I am, the evening sky presenting itself in all its multi-coloured glory just outside our flat's bedroom window. I've come in here by myself, ostensibly to prepare for tomorrow's interview at an online publishing company (considering what I know about websites and blogs you could write on a gigabyte), but also to get away from a tantrumming, recalcitrant, refusing-to-go-to-bed Joey.

I start my research with Jasmine's site and, slowly but surely, the wails and foot-stamping coming from the front room are drowned out by the beauty spa panpipe sounds seeping soothingly out of the laptop.

I look at the desktop clock. 8.13 p.m. Hmm. Well, there's no harm in making a few wishes, is there?

I tear off a piece of A4 from the notepad and grab a pen. I'll write as I talk, just like Jasmine said, thus saving time as well as making it clear to the cosmos exactly what I'm wishing for, so that there are no cock-ups at Dreams Come True HQ or whatever.

Right. So. Now. What do I want, what do I really, really want?

1. To Get My Dream Job – actually, any old paying job will do
2. To Get Skinny – starting tomorrow, obviously
3. To Get Intimate With Jack More Often – we had sex three weeks ago, but that was the first time in . . . God, I can't even remember
4. To Get Organised – so the only things getting ticked off are items on my never-ending To Do List (i.e. not me, Jack or Joey)

5. To Get Settled – give Sydney a really good go for six months and see whether it feels more like home or whether I still miss Blighty.

'ROX!' Jack bellows from the front room. 'Come and HELP! *NOW!*'

I jump out of my seat and look around, feeling startled and guilty.

'Er ... coming!' I shout back as I fold up the New Moon Wish List and put it into the zip pocket inside my handbag.

I get up and head for the door, pausing to turn round dramatically and stare down the bright new moon.

'And could you please, please, PLEASE get Joey to calm down? Do as she's told once in a while?' I clench my teeth a little and whimper as I make my last wish.

I'm sure my *cri de coeur* has fallen on deaf ears though. I mean, it's not like I *believe* in any of this cosmic claptrap or anything.

Chapter 3

'Nanny!' squeals Joey and tugs at my arm when we hear the front door buzz. 'Mummy! Let Nanny in!'

'OK, OK.' I head towards the entry phone and buzz her in.

Good old Anita. She was one of the main reasons I agreed to the move to Oz – she'd promised us she'd babysit Joey whenever we needed her to. And because finding childcare in Bondi is nigh on impossible when you haven't had your kid's name down on the waiting list three years before they were even conceived, I would've been well and truly stuck up a certain well-known creek in a barbed wire canoe without a paddle today if she hadn't been available.

Not that there isn't a sometimes rather hefty price to pay for her help. Like right now, when I'm in dire need of some quality ego-boosting, some gentle, motherly confidence-bolstering, she cuts me to the quick.

'Thanks so much for doing this, Anita,' I say, making sure she knows how much I appreciate her help.

'It's fine – just make sure you're back in time for me to

go to my Sexy Septuagenarians salsa class after lunch,' she says sternly.

'No worries.' I smile sweetly at the thought. 'Sounds like a lot of fun. Must be great being seventy-five years *young* these days . . . '

'Oh, please,' she rasps, looking me up and down. 'Is it? You tell me, dear – is being seventy-five years young just like being twenty stone *slim*?'

Ooh, she's harsh when she wants to be, that Anita.

She chuckles and says, 'Sorry, darl, couldn't resist. I saw Joanie Rivers on TV the other night and she was saying how much she hates that expression. So, anyway – how *is* that diet going, hmm?'

I grimace by way of answer. It's fantastic that Anita moved to Bondi to be nearer to us, but it doesn't half send your self-esteem plummeting sometimes. And when I ask her whether she wouldn't mind bunging the sheets into the washing machine while I'm at my interview she nearly bites my head off.

'Darling, I don't *do* domesticity – life really *is* too short from where I'm standing! You know, now the internet's opened things up, there are a million men out there just waiting for me. So many men, so little time. Come on, Joey! Let's see which gorgeous grandfathers we can meet at the playground today!'

So . . . nanny by name, but definitely not a nanny by nature. Joey joins in the merriment and off they trot, holding hands and laughing all the way.

All of a sudden I feel butterflies in my tummy. Must be the excitement I feel at the possibility of re-entering the workforce.

But, God! What will I do with Joey if I get the job? Maybe I'll have to take her to work with me. Or I might have to work from home – be *forced* against my will to work from beachside cafes ...

I'm getting ahead of myself, here. I haven't even GHDed my hair super-straight for the interview, yet, let alone got the job.

Now, let's see ... trackie-daks? No. XL 'menopause' blue fleece bought from Sainsbury's a hundred years ago? Um ... no. Massive shapeless black-velvet maternity dress and Blundstone boots? Don't be ridiculous! It's all so ugly and old and there's no way anyone with even a shred of human dignity would ever wear something like that. Not to their professional office, at any rate. And anyway, it's late January in Sydney – which means it's as hot and humid as buggery, to use a tried and true Australian phrase.

I haven't got a wardrobe full of great gear, designed to show off my fabulous figure at every turn, it's true. But I *do* have some old clothes from the UK, like my fur-trimmed Jigsaw wool coat, my Hobbs knee-length boots and a little brown and cream floaty floral number from Zara which, when teamed with black 40-deniers, should cover up my body nicely. Well, cover up my body, at least. A British winter does those prone to chubbing out no favours. And I, unfortunately, fall with a great big fahlump into that fat camp.

But I can't wear that stuff – it's far too hot. There's nothing else for it, it's going to have to be flip-flops, three-quarter-length black leggings and an oversized white shirt with ruffles down the front, a bit like the shirt a man would wear under his tuxedo and bow tie. I straighten my hair, which is a bit silly in this humidity, really, but you've got to at least *try*, haven't you? Because as far as I'm con-cerned, I look like two completely different people depending on the state of my hair. Straightened? Competent, reliable, almost pretty. Left curly? Fugs.

As I walk to the station, I wonder what I can expect when I get to the office, based on what little I know about the company.

I applied for this job with 'new, young, funky, relaxed online publishing group, Maverick Media'. Now, being neither new nor young nor remotely funky, and definitely anything but relaxed, I figured it was a long shot. And even though the ad specified 'no time wasters, please', I still went for it. Well, I'm trying to be optimistic, remem-ber? And my new attitude must be paying off because, lo and behold, I got called in for an interview.

God. Work. I can't *wait.* Just imagine – witty banter ricocheting off the walls, as opposed to toast soldiers and soft-boiled egg; a radio blaring out all the latest Top 40 hits, instead of The Wiggles mind-meltingly droning on about fruit salad; and, speaking of which, lunches and train trips unencumbered by a whiny three-year-old who's hot/tired/hungry and about to go into tantrum over-drive.

And I'd get paid! I'd be able to buy myself some clothes, get my hair cut and coloured, and not be accused of sponging off Jack. Which he's never actually come right out and said, but it doesn't stop me feeling in my bones – *in me water*, as my gran used to say – that that's exactly what he is, indeed, thinking. Adult company all day, doing something I love *and* getting paid for it . . .

I'm beside myself at the prospect.

But then, quick as a flash, I revert to type and forget about my new upbeat demeanour. I frown and think how out of the loop, how out of practice I am at this whole work malarkey. And I'm completely and utterly *rubbish* at interviews – especially when I'm nervous, and today the prognosis is not good because I am, as they say, *totally bricking it*.

With good reason, I might add. I mean I've had some *disastrous* interviews over the years. One in particular still haunts me in times of severe stress. Like now.

I cringe momentarily as I remember when I was working at TVText in London, desperate for a real job on a magazine, and going for an interview at a teen mag. Now, this was years ago – the Spice Girls and Take That were huge (this was the first time around), *Smash Hits* was massive and *Top of the Pops* was still on. So there I was, sitting in a small, stuffy room with a man called Harvey and a woman called Sophie grilling me about bands, *Grange Hill* plotlines and what I thought your average twelve-year-old girl was into.

'So who would you have as the major pin-up if it was up to you?' asks Harvey.

'Um,' I reply, unable to stop myself thinking about how drop dead gorgeous this Harvey guy is.

'It could be someone from a band, a TV show ...' Sophie tries to help me out.

'Ah, uh,' I stutter, breaking into a sweat. The pressure's mounting and my silence is only making things worse, until ...

'Harvey!' I squeal.

'Who?' they chorus.

'Um, you know, that guy in East 17 ... whatshisname ... Harvey something, isn't it? Harvey, um ...'

'Oh,' says Sophie, disappointed. 'You mean Brian Harvey?'

'Yes! Yes – that's him! Brian Harvey.' I squirm in my seat.

The dead air between us is so uncomfortable, I see no other option than to render my own name mud in teen mag circles forever more with an ill-advised: 'Although Harvey here would make a pretty great pin-up, too! Don't you think, Sophie?'

I fake laugh, pathetically.

Harvey and Sophie swap half pitying, half should-we-call-security glances and before you can say, 'I'll get my coat, then – know where the nearest dole office is?' I'm shown the door.

I could just imagine them talking about me after I left the building.

Sophie: 'Don't think she really knows her teen stuff.'

Harvey: 'And she's not much chop as a flirt, either. I mean, who tries to chat someone up in an interview? Next!'

I'm thinking about this, biting my bottom lip, feeling a bit nauseous with nerves (and, perhaps, the memory of Brian Harvey) and positively *baking* in my leggings as I walk towards Maverick Media when an old derro sees me perspiring profusely as I walk past and says, 'Hot enough for ya, darl?' in that typically dry Aussie way.

At once, this makes me smile and remember that millions of people have it worse than me. And in these days of jobs being thin on the ground, I should be thankful that one almost-perfect-for-me exists. And how lucky am I to have been asked in for an interview? Well, even seasoned optimists must be struggling to stay positive in this heat, I think to myself, and take a deep breath, pushing on through the haze.

Once at the street entrance to the top floor office, the same voice that called me in for an interview last week buzzes me into the building. I wait for the lift. And wait. And wait some more. By now I'm about ten minutes late and getting really flustered.

The fire stairs beckon, winking at me in their wicked,

steppy way, and even though I know my carefully-put-together professional look will be ruined, I begin my journey walking up ten stiflingly hot flights of stairs.

By the time I get to the top, I'm dripping. My nerves, plus the unbearable heat mixed in with my suspected perimenopausal state cruelly conspire against me and I'm sweating like a stuck pig. Not glowing – or even perspiring – but full-on fountaining-forth-from-the-forehead soaking wet, like a sprinkler, a tide that no amount of Kleenex can stem. And when I think about all that time spent drying and GHDing my hair straight . . .

'Sorry I'm so late,' I splutter. 'I think the lift might be broken.'

'No dramas,' says the twenty-four-, twenty-five-year-old (tops) MD of Maverick. 'Phil. Phil Nelson. Nice to meet you, Roxane, thanks for coming in.'

Uh-oh, I think. Isn't that the standard kiss-off line interviewers use? Like, thanks for making the effort and coming in and all, but we've already given the job to someone far younger, taller, prettier and with much more *naturally* straight hair than you. So thanks – but no, thanks.

'Now,' Phil goes on, 'let's dive straight in, shall we? Tell me. Why do you want to be editor of Kidding Around?'

'Um,' I reply, my rehearsed, well-thought-out answer deserting me. 'Well . . . '

I resist the temptation to say what I've always wanted to say in interviews before – 'Because I need a bloody job!' – and realise my nervousness has also legged it, most probably because they're all so young in here. No one's over twenty-five – it's like walking into the babies' room at a nursery. Without that sickly whiff of poo and bleach, obviously.

So, relaxing somewhat and settling in for a bit of a chat, I start by giving Phil my potted work history.

'Well, I used to work at *Positive Parenting!* in London, before I had my daughter, Josephine, and ever since I left to go on maternity leave, I've really missed it.'

'Missed what, exactly?' Phil enquires, raising an eyebrow.

'Er, the camaraderie of your colleagues, the creative fulfilment, the fact that you're, um, talking about babies and kids and great products, and you're surrounded by adults who you can have a laugh with and . . . '

Phil's not looking too inspired by this (after all the crap interviews I've had, I can read interviewers' faces pretty well now), so out of thin air I muster up the courage to lie my little heart out, bleating on about readership numbers, advertising revenue and circulation figures, the thrill of a challenge and the warm satisfaction of victory when your triumph has trounced your main rivals.

Phil perks up at this, as though now I'm talking his language. Clearly, this is the sort of thing he wants to hear.

'So what was your proudest moment at *Positive Parenting!*, then?' he asks, all wide-eyed and practically panting like a puppy.

'Umm.' I stall for time, frenetically sifting through my mental portfolio, scraps of work I've done over the past twenty-odd years of writing for magazines.

'Ah,' I continue, my eyes jumping about like a drug-runner's at Customs. I'm desperate for inspiration, my brain whirring as I try to remember something, *anything*, I've done that I've been really proud of.

'Um,' I say again, wiping my forehead with the back of my hand.

And then it comes to me.

'Actually,' I smile, straightening up, 'I once wrote this quiz called "Yummy, Slummy or just plain Ummy?"'

Phil raises the left half of his mouth into a lopsided smile. 'Go on.' He nods, as if giving me permission to speak.

'And it was all about how these days there are so many books and magazines around telling you the right and wrong ways to bring up your kids, we've totally lost sight of our own, innate parenting abilities. Like, it's all got way out of hand and far too prescriptive, so even if you *think* you might have some mothering instincts, you certainly don't trust them. So we came up with a new type of mum – the mum who checks what the so-called experts say and then dithers about, being indecisive, hesitant, insecure and unsure until the storm blows over and things sort themselves out. The Ummy Mummy is someone who's overly dependent on self-help for the petrified parent, and *still* hasn't got a clue what to do. Which is pretty much all of us, I think.'

Phil turns his mouth down and studies my CV as he ever so slowly nods.

'Um,' I carry on, 'we had questions like: "Your seven-month-old baby is crying. You a) can't hear him – your nanny's looking after him at home, so she can deal with it. What possible use could you be? You're dressed head-to-toe in Chloé, lunching with your lady friends in Notting Hill, and you've got Pilates in an hour . . . b) don't care – you've got a stonking headache after last night's debauchery and you've got to get to the shop for some ciggies anyway, so he'll just have to wait for his Cheesy Wotsits. Who knew weaning on to solids would be so cheap, easy and orange? Or c) flap about like a headless chicken, call all the women in your mother and baby group, consult Gina Ford, then the Baby Whisperer, then *Positive Parenting!* until finally you settle on Annabel Karmel. But she can't help – she's all about food! Um . . . um . . . Oh, I don't know! What would *you* do?"'

Phil looks at me blankly.

His eyes are glazing over – you're losing him, you're losing him! Reel him back in somehow! Quick!

'Anyway, the thing I'm most proud of is the mail we got in response – it was phenomenal. Women all over Britain felt vindicated in that they weren't alone and they weren't mad, it was just that in the absence of family being close, they had no guidance, no help. They'd lost the ability to think for themselves and trust their decisions when it came to being a mother. We even got news items – free publicity to you and me – on morning TV and in the papers and the editor did some radio interviews based around it. It was as though we'd isolated a new gene, dis-covered a new strain of Mummy DNA or something. We became our readers' new best friend.'

'That's what I like to hear. And the readership figures?'

'Went through the roof. Subscriptions flew out the door. It was quite amazing.'

'Sounds awesome,' says Phil, grinning like his life depends on it. 'Got one last question for you then, Roxane. How soon can you start?'

Chapter 4

My last few days of freedom before I get back to the coal-face and start work again – and here I am stuck in a doctor's surgery.

But this place is nothing like its UK counterparts. For a start, there's an ultrasound and X-ray section all its own. I mean, you don't have to go anywhere else to get those things done; it's like a one-stop-pre-op-shop.

And everyone's so chirpy. The ladies behind the reception desk, the GPs who quickly pop out, trilling their patients' names ... even the patients themselves seem to be enjoying the experience. It makes such a pleasant change from the soggy, germ-infested walls of GPs' surgeries I have known back home.

And it seems that every male in here is fit, too. But maybe that's just Bondi. Or maybe it's the new me, looking at the world with fresh, positive eyes, seeing the good-looking in everything. Then *again*, perhaps it's because Jack and I had our once-yearly shag four weeks ago.

Ever since that fateful night, my saucy senses have been well and truly awakened. So much so that I see sexy guys everywhere – especially where they just don't exist: in fat, sixty-year-old bus drivers pinned to their seats by big steering wheels that cut into their fleshy bellies; spotty teenaged pizza delivery boys in baseball caps; Ben 10. I know, I know, it's getting out of control – which means it must have been one hell of an earth-shattering shag to shake awake my libido. It's lain dormant for . . . God, um, *centuries*, it feels like.

'Mu-um!' Joey's siren call cuts through my reverie like the sound of a mosquito *eee*ing around your ear on a silent, boiling hot night.

'What, darling?' I enquire absent-mindedly, trying to tear my eyes away from the gaggle of bleached-blond, mahogany-tanned surfers sitting together in their wet-suits, boards up against the wall, laughing about a busty girl in some celebrity magazine.

'I've always wondered what you call a group of surfers.' I strike up a conversation with the elderly lady next to me. 'What do you reckon, then? A swell? A current? A rip? Board members?'

'Sexist pigs, mostly, in my experience.' The woman turns her mouth down as she looks over her glasses at the group of young men, pointing to them with the spine of her newspaper. 'Probably all here to get their crabs seen to after their latest spit roast conquest.'

I nod and imagine she's right, if the things you hear

about Aussie sportsmen in the news are anything to go by. This makes me avert my adoring gaze and finally turn my full attention to Joey.

'Hmm? What is it, sweetie?'

'Where are the crabs? Is there a fish tank?'

I consider her questions carefully and answer thus:

'Ooh, look! There's a Thomas the Tank Engine railway set by the reception desk – shall we go and play with it?'

Joey's eyes light up and we run (well, *she* runs, I'd say I sort of canter, if I was being kind to myself – half lope/half waddle, if dealing with the facts) to the reception desk.

We only just sit down when my name is called.

'Oh! That's me!' I say, standing up, quite taken aback at how swift the service is here.

'You can leave the beautiful little kiddie with us, darl – just while you have your check-up,' chirrups one of the ladies behind the desk.

'If you're sure that's OK.' I raise my eyebrows, surprised by this outward cheerfulness and desire to help.

'No worries, love. We'll have lots of fun while Mummy sees the doctor, won't we?' The same lady addresses a delighted Joey.

As I follow the young woman (she looks no more than thirty to me – and that is still virtually an infant in my eyes) into the ultrasound wing of the surgery, I'm amazed to see such white, gleaming, clean and new-looking equipment. So much so, I actually gasp when I spy what appears to be an overgrown overhead projector near the bed.

'How ya goin', Roxane? My name's Narelle,' the sonographer tells me gleefully.

'Hello there,' I say, unsure whether I'm supposed to shake her hand (God knows – and I'd hazard a pretty good guess, too, where *that's* been), so I settle on a very English, very stiff-upper-lipped nod.

This embarrasses me somewhat, considering she's being so open and friendly and is about to take a good look at my insides. So I up the ante and have a stab at small talk. When in Rome and all that . . .

'It's a bit of an . . . er . . . ' I struggle to find the right word as I hoist myself up on to the examination table.

'High bed?' offers Narelle.

'No. Well, yes, it is, but that's not what I mean. I mean it's a bit of an . . . '

'Undignified position for a lady to find herself in?' She chuckles as I lie down, bend my knees, take a deep breath as I try to hold my tummy in, and shut my eyes tight.

I guffaw slightly and try again to finish my sentence.

'Yes! But it's also a bit of a *bugger*, actually.'

'What is?' Narelle counters as I hear two thin latex gloves snap on to her hands.

'The fact that I might be pregnant. Now. When we've only recently arrived in Australia. I start my new full-time job on Monday, see.'

'And not only that,' she says with a giggle, as I hear a third rubber thing snap, 'but I'm going to have to do an internal if your dates are correct – we won't be able to see anything through your stomach, through the transducer.'

'Too fat?' I ask, screwing up my face.

'No!' She laughs. 'It's probably too early to show up yet, that's all.'

I open my eyes to see her unrolling what looks like a condom on to some kind of Ann Summers love tool. No, really – it even looks ribbed, *for her pleasure.*

I groan. But not in a good way.

'It won't take a sec,' Narelle reassures me, 'so if you don't mind, take your undies off, sit up in this chair, pop your knees up against these pads and open wide, as they say! Now, let me take a look, see what we're dealing with here . . .'

I follow her instructions and tell myself there's no *way* she could be enjoying this, she's simply trying to make the best of another dreary day probing about inside poor, possibly pregnant women.

Which is, for me, I suspect, highly unlikely. Not just because of my advanced age, where the odds are so severely stacked against my getting up the duff in the first place (apparently, your chances of falling pregnant after the age of forty are one in a hundred, according to that great internet know-all Dr Google and his Band of Merry Medical Statistics), but even if I had been *with child*, it's bound to have deserted me by now, given my track record in miscarriages.

I've had three, so far, you see – three that I've known about. Two before Joey was born and one since, shortly after my fortieth birthday.

And even though I'm aware that my period is late, I put it down to things going awry due to early-onset menopause. Really, if the alarming regularity of my inner grumpy old lady surfacing is anything to go by, it's *got* to be menopause. Like, whenever I hear a leaf blower strike up its annoying little lawnmower engine lately, I can't help but shake my head, tut and mutter, 'What's wrong with a *rake*, for goodness' sake?'

Honestly, sometimes I feel like I'm turning into Jasmine or Prudith off *Sorry, I've Got No Head*. *A thousand pounds*, I say to myself, and let out a little giggle. Or, more accurately (and rather less elegantly), snort.

'Sorry. Am I hurting you?' asks Narelle.

'No, no. No. Not much . . . ' I wince.

And then I close my eyes and begin mentally preparing a list of pregnancy pros and cons to pass the inordinate amount of time this examination's taking. I start with the cons:

WHY IT'D BE A BAD THING

1. I'm forty-two – far too old to be a new mum! At this rate, I'll get my free bus pass before I get the kid off to Reception

2. We've only just – JUST – finished all that baby stuff with Joey. Why on earth would we want to do it all over again?

3. I've got the organisational skills of a kidney bean at the best of times, so God knows how I'd cope with *two*

4. I'm about to start a great new job! I can't go around pouring milk on my keyboard and shoving Weetabix into the floppy disk slot every morning

5. We've only just arrived in Sydney – what'll happen to socialising? Being with child means no alcohol or cigarettes for nine months, remember

6. And there goes that diet and exercise regime I was just about to throw myself into with gusto. No, really, I was – any minute now

7. Did I already mention I'm too old?

WHY IT'D BE A GOOD THING

1. Um … it might be nice for Joey to have a little brother or sister?

2. Er …

3. ???

'A-HA!' shouts Narelle enthusiastically. 'There it is! One strong little heartbeat.'

'Really?' I open my eyes and peer down, first at Narelle's arm between my knees and then to the screen she's kindly turning towards me.

'Yep. See?' she says proudly, chuffed with her handiwork.

'Um, not really,' I answer. I can never make out anything in these grey, fuzzy pictures. Always looks to me like someone's turned the TV on to a non-existent channel, black and white dots flitting about furiously on the screen.

Narelle punches some keys on the scanning machine's computer keyboard thingy and zooms in.

'Oh! Yes!' I squeal.

'Going by the size and the dates you've given me, I'd say this little tacker was about forty-two days old. You're at the end of your sixth week of pregnancy!'

My head swims – and not just because she's talking in numbers and I am ridiculously rubbish at maths. Jack says I'm not so much mathematically *challenged* as mathematically *beaten* before I even begin, no contest.

But I've only just this second finished convincing myself that I couldn't *possibly* be pregnant, making a list whereby there would only be one good thing about it if I was. One!

'So . . . I've been pregnant for six weeks?' I ask incredulously.

'Yes.' She takes the condom off the scanning dildo and throws it in the bin. 'Well, yes and no. We count the first day of your last period, your LMP, as the first day of your pregnancy. Even though your egg was only fertilised approximately two weeks after you started bleeding.'

She motions at me to get dressed and pull myself

35

together as she snaps the rubber gloves off her hands and shuts down the machine.

'So I'm *four* weeks pregnant, then?'

'No,' she says, starting on her paperwork, 'six weeks. Thirty-four to go.'

'Ah, the old forty weeks of pregnancy.' I nod, like all this long-lost knowledge is coming back to me now.

'Yep,' she says, not looking up. 'Nine months.'

Which really throws me. Always has. I've never been able to make any sense of the way they work this stuff out.

'Hang on,' I frown, pulling up my knickers, 'nine months – at four weeks per month – is thirty-six weeks, right? So forty weeks must be ten months . . .'

Ten months? Ten months is nearly a whole year! A whole year of no going out, no drinking, no eating pâté . . . Well, I can do without the pâté, but no ice-cold Coronas with a wedge of lime on a meltingly hot day? No catch-ups with old friends over ice-cold or even lukewarm Coronas? No Coronas?! That's . . . that's just so *unfair*.

I get some sort of a sense of how those convict Brits sent out here 220-odd years ago for stealing a loaf of bread must have felt. I mean, ten months? Now *that's* punishment.

Narelle throws me a look that, if I'm not mistaken, says something along the lines of 'Don't bother your pretty little head with the details, darl' and stands up, handing me my notes and ushering me out of the examination room.

'You have done this before, haven't you? I mean, you

already have one child, right?' she asks. 'And how old are you again?'

'Forty-two,' I mumble into my chest.

'Forty-two, eh? So far, so good, then! Gooood on ya, Mum!' She sings that last bit, giving me the old thumbs-up for added emphasis.

I must be looking confused, because she then says, 'It's a line from an old ad. For bread, as I recall. I can remember it from when I was a baby.'

'Oh, right.' I nod.

I do understand this affliction, after all. I know only too well what it's like to get an advertisement's jingle stuck in your head – happens to me all the time. In fact, there's this particularly annoying one I've seen quite a lot lately, for relationship counsellors, and the bit that I can never get out of my head, the bit that sometimes even makes an appearance in my dreams, goes, to the tune of Rod Stewart's 'I Don't Want To Talk About It': *Yes we wanna . . . talk about it, how to save your rel . . . So come and see us we are just round the corner, come and see us and we'll listen . . . to your har-ar-ar-art . . . woe is your heart . . .*

It's typically Australian in that they seem to shorten every word they utter (hence 'relationship' becomes 'rel') and I find myself singing it a lot – so much so that Joey often joins in. Except she substitutes 'heart' for 'fart' most of the time, scrunching up her face and waving her hand in front of her nose shortly before she falls to the floor laughing.

'Make an appointment at the GP's desk over there for a check-up in six weeks' time.' Narelle smiles at me.

In a daze I wander over to the GP's desk. Joey barely acknowledges my return, save for a whiny 'Ohhh! I don't want to go now!' and I book an appointment for six weeks hence.

On our way home, I call Jack.

'Guess what,' I say, instead of the more traditional, 'Hello.'

'What?' he says. 'Make it quick, Rox – I'm about to go into a meeting.'

'We're pregnant,' I say, cupping my hand around the receiver so that Joey doesn't hear.

'What?'

'P-r-e-g-n-a-n-t.' I spell it out.

'We're . . . What are you on about, Rox?'

'Listen, silly! I'm *pregnant*.'

Nothing. He says absolutely nothing.

'Jack? Are you there?'

'Ah, yeah, yeah. That's great, darl. Look, I've got to go. I'll call you later, OK?'

'OK, Daddy-to-be for the second time—'

And the line goes dead.

Hmm. Not exactly the reaction I was expecting. Still, it is a bit of a shock for both of us. And he *was* just about to go into a meeting, so . . . he'll come round. By the time he gets home tonight, he'll be punching the air and praising his God-like baby-making abilities. We're both going to have to adjust, though: thankfully we've got nine, ten, eight – whatever, *loads* of months to get used to the idea.

Back at home, I plonk Joey in front of *Home and Away* (the cheapest, least-hassle babysitter at my disposal) and stand in the kitchenette, holding the phone.

Now, who else can I call? Who will want to revel in my good (if not slightly unsettling) news? Charlie, my best friend back in the UK? Yes, of course! *She'll* want to yammer on for hours about the baby!

'What's Bondi like, then?' sighs Charlie over the phone. 'Bet it's gert lush.'

'Yeah, I suppose it is,' I reply. And then I cup my hand over the receiver when I say, 'But it's horrendous being *pregnant* in this heat . . . '

There's a pause from both our ends.

'Sorry, it must be a dodgy line or something, because I could've sworn I just heard you say you're PREGNANT!' She shrieks.

'I know, I know!' I squeal back.

'But *how*? I mean, you're practically *post*-menopausal and you and Jack *never* have sex . . . unless it's . . . have you been shagging someone else? Have you got some hot Hugh Jackman-type toy boy out there already?'

'I wish.' I giggle.

'Oh. My. *GOD*. Roxy! That is amazing! How do you feel?'

'A bit shell-shocked, actually.'

'I bet. How far gone are you?'

'Six weeks.'

'What did Jack say? Bet he's over the moon! Bet he didn't know there was any life left in the old dog . . . '

'Yeah.' I laugh nervously.

'Oh my God – I can't believe it! You've only been there five minutes and already you've got a bun in the oven, a pad by the beach, a fab new job. Bet you're wondering why it took you so long to make the move out there, eh? It was soooo the right decision. Anything's got to beat the cold, grey, bleak, freezing pouring rain you get here,' she says flatly.

'But I love the cold. Autumn's my favourite season. All those red and orange leaves in the trees, the fantastic boots in the shops, the cosy jumpers and coats. And all those great old pubs with roaring fires to snuggle up next to.'

'Yeah, right.' She sniffs, and through a particularly soggy-sounding nose-blowing, says in her stuffed-up voice, 'When was the last time you went to a pub with a blazing fire and got cosy with some gorgeous man?'

'Well,' I begin, 'not for ages, obviously. Years, in fact. But—'

'Just kiss the good times goodbye, sister – those days are long gone and they're never coming back.'

There's quiet for a few seconds, and then she speaks again.

'Sorry, Rox,' she sniffs. 'Congrats. I'm happy for you.

No, really I am. It's just … it's just … It's boyfriend trouble.'

'You and John rowing or something?' I ask.

'No. Not yet, anyway. Thing is, Rox, I think he's cheating on me.'

'John? Cheating on *you*? No way – he's far too into you! Why? What makes you think he's pashing someone else?' I ask as I stare at two youngsters kissing on a beach at sunset in *Home and Away*.

'*What*-ing someone else?' she says impatiently.

'Pashing,' I say, shaking my head and thus my gaze free from the Aussie soap. 'You know, kissing. Snogging. Copping off—'

'All right, all right, I get it.' She sounds irritated. 'I haven't actually *seen* anything, haven't caught him in flagrante or anything yet – it's just a feeling. He seems distracted, not as keen to sit in watching *Come Dine with Me* as he used to be.'

'Well, it can get a bit boring after a while,' I say, nodding.

'That's not the point, though, is it? It's about being together, sharing the experience, creating and nurturing that bond between you.'

'You're right,' I agree. 'Jack and I would be lost without our daily dose of *Corrie* – it's a couple of months behind, but now we've got Oz Tube, we can watch UKTV and the BBC. We get *Gavin and Stacey* and *Miranda*—'

'Brilliant,' she huffs. 'I'm glad you're sorted for decent telly.'

'Well, we had to go for the cable, didn't have much of a choice—'

'I was being sarcastic!' she yells down the line.

I jump and the jolt must knock some sense in to me, because suddenly I remember how supportive and brilliant Charlie was to me when I was so upset, thinking that Jack was having it away with someone else back in Riverside.

'I'm sorry, Charlie, really I am. Tell me more, go on.'

'Oh, I haven't got time now – I've got to get to bed. Just promise me you'll have a think and tell me what to do about John's affair.'

'Course I will, Hon,' I say in hushed, soothing tones, my comforting noises being transmitted down the line in the nick of time. 'But don't worry, I'm sure it's just your imagination playing tricks on you. John would never do anything to hurt you, Charlie. Charlie? Are you there?'

I get my answer when I hear a click and one long, lonely, continuous dial tone.

Chapter 5

Like most put-upon parents of precocious pre-schoolers out there, the only way both Jack and I can do full-time, nine-to-five jobs even halfway decently is to put Joey into a local day care centre. But can we find one that isn't already chockers in Bondi?

Can we bollocks.

Until, that is, in a last, desperate bid, I phone up the twenty-eighth place on my exhaustive, both-sides-of-A4-using-teeny-tiny-writing list – a place called Shalom! Baby, a Jewish nursery in North Bondi.

'Yus, you're in luck, one of our girls has just moved back to Israel, so we do have a slot for a three-year-old,' says the South African accent over the phone.

'Oh, that's great!' I nearly faint with relief. 'But Josephine isn't ... we aren't, um, we're not Jewish – or religious at all, for that matter, so would we still be allowed to—'

'Of course!' comes the reply. '*We* don't discriminate.'

I nod as an image flashes into my head of Jewish Aussie

mums on sports day, cheering on their offspring: *Aussie, Aussie, Aussie! Oy vey, oy vey, oy vey!*

And so, regardless of the exorbitant $90-a-day fee, on my first day at my new job, at 7.30 a.m., I walk a particularly dawdling and let's-stop-here-and-wonder-at-the-beauty-of-the-humble-ladybird-for-half-an-hour Joey to her new pre-school. No, no, no, I'll rephrase that: I *try* to walk her to pre-school. After, of course, the de rigueur tantrum she throws at home when I tell her she can't wear the little girl's Fairy Princess outfit that Charlie bought for us as a going away present – a hers 'n' hers, mother-and-daughter twin-set of matching pink satin tops and light pink netting and tulle ballerina skirts.

Charlie said she couldn't resist it when she saw it and laughed herself stupid imagining Joey and me traipsing around Bondi Beach in our identical, super-girlie gear.

I assured her that, of course, that was *never* going to happen and Joey'd be lucky if I ever let her wear it at all. Oh no, you won't catch me Disney-princessing my little girl into a neat fairytale gender stereotype. Ha! No way.

'Mean Mummy!' Joey cries.

'Yes, yes,' comes my reasoned reply as I fish a dark denim skirt/pink halterneck top combo out of a suitcase full of her clothes.

'I want Daddy,' she blubs.

'Well he's already gone to work. And I'll be late for my first day if you don't *help* Mummy and get your *skirt* on,' I say, not quite so reasoned this time.

'DADDY!' she shrieks.

'For Christ's SAKE, Josephine!' I bellow, as I feel a big drop of sweat trickle off the end of my nose and land on my bended knee. 'JESUS!'

'It's *my* choice what I wear because *I* have to wear it!' screams Joey in response, making some sort of sense.

Did I mention before that she's only three years old? *Three?*

'OK, OK!' I calm down, impressed with her logic. 'Keep your Lola knickers on. You can wear what you want, sweets – I've got to sort myself out now. Big day for Mummy, today!'

I leave a delighted Joey to her own devices and haul everything I own, clothes-wise, out of the cupboard. The small mound it creates makes me want to cry, because there's nothing – not *one* thing – that I would feel comfortable or cool in on this scorchio thirty-seven-degree day.

It's all full-on wintry stuff, and while it's not mumsy per se – I mean, it's not like I've raided Ann Widdecombe's wardrobe or anything – it's all drab and drear and old and worn out. Definitely *not* the garb befitting an editor at a new, young, funky online publishing house.

On the floor, about to throw the mother of all tantrums myself, fairy princess Joey skips into my bedroom and points her Tinkerbell wand at me.

'I put a spell on you, Mummy,' she says sweetly. 'So you can find something pretty to wear to work.'

'It better be a good one, then, baby – because I'm going to need all the help I can get.'

'I know!' she squeals, chuffed to bits with herself. 'Why don't you wear the mummy's fairy princess dress?'

'Ho! Good thinking, gorgeous, but I don't really think . . . '

Hang on. Wait a minute. Wait just one cotton-pickin' minute, here. It's not such a bad idea, you know. Yes, yes, I realise what I said before, but desperate times call for desperate measures.

I pull the top and skirt out of my half-unpacked suitcase, lay them out on the bed and sigh.

I couldn't. Could I? Well, let's see . . .

Is it new? Never been worn before . . . Is it young? You don't get much younger than a three-year-old's favourite outfit, and Charlie only bought it recently, so yes. Is it funky? You-hoo-hoo-betcha.

'Oh, go on, then,' I say, making Joey jump up and down like she's on an invisible pogo stick.

'My magic works!' She giggles.

There's no way, though, that I'm wearing the sleeveless tank top. Not with my flubbery upper arms. So I settle on one of Jack's light pink business shirts and don the skirt. It's a bit short for me (i.e. a good inch or so above my knee), but with my little electric-blue pixie boots that I've had since 1985, some heavy makeup, dangly crystal earrings and lightly teased 'do, I feel . . . faintly ridiculous, yes. But I just about manage to convince myself I'm a

46

dead ringer for Demi Moore in *St Elmo's Fire* if I squint a lot and only look at myself from certain angles, so I give Joey a well-deserved hug.

We brush our teeth side by side, two minty-fresh fairies getting ready to go.

'Lean over the sink, Joey!' I nag through the bubbly toothpaste froth.

'Hmm?' She looks up at me, toothpaste running down her chin.

'Don't let the ... lean over or ... YOU'LL GET TOOTHPASTE ON YOUR OUTFIT!' I gargle, frustrated.

Joey spits into the sink, wipes her chin with her hand and looks down at her chest.

'No toothpaste, Mummy,' she says, looking up at me, all wide-eyed and innocent.

'Good girl,' I say, relieved, and spit the last of my toothpaste out.

Joey starts giggling uncontrollably.

'What, sweetie?' I smile.

She points up at me. 'Toothpaste all over Daddy's shirt!'

I check my chest and, sure enough, there's one large, long, bright white stripe of paste down my front.

'Typical,' I mutter as I try in vain to dab it off with a wet towel.

'Silly Mummy.' She beams at me.

'Yes, well,' I can't help but smile back, 'just you make sure you do as Mummy *says*, not as she *does*, OK?'

Popping her Tinkerbell wand in my handbag, we set off for Shalom! Baby, all candy-pink and laughing, skipping and holding hands. No, really. As unlikely picture-perfect as it sounds, it's true. For about a block, anyway.

We stop when we get to the kerb, look both ways and cross the wide, bubbling tarmac of the road. It's boiling out here and only now do I remember that I forgot sunscreen for the both of us as well as hats. Bugger.

Right on track for being late for my first day, I desperately try to chivvy a reluctant, obstinate Joey along.

'Come on, sweetheart. We're going to be so late!' I say, as if she a) understands and b) gives a toss.

'Look, Mummy!' she squeals. 'A ladybird!'

'Wowsers,' I say, deadpan. 'We'll look at her later, shall we? But now, *let's move*!'

And so it goes for the best part of the next hour. By the time we're on the home straight and I've got her new pre-school in my sights, Joey demands a Caramello Koala and when I say no, decides to chuck a tanty the likes of which I've only ever seen on *The House of Tiny Tearaways* – right out the front of The Stupid Bloody Galah, our local pub where rough tradies enjoy their beers and ciggies on the footpath at 8.45 a.m.

Joey's screaming at the top of her lungs, tears streaming down her face as she stands her ground firmly. No amount of my cajoling, bribery or manhandling will make her budge. So there I am, Joey's Diego rucksack in my hand, my oversized Tardis handbag falling off my sloping, battle-weary shoulder, a crowd of buffoons laughing heartily at my pathetic attempts at getting Joey to do my bidding, a stonking headache and, after five minutes or so, bereft of the will to live.

Just then, Joey's Tinkerbell wand falls out of my bag and drops to the ground, which looks like a good idea to me, so I follow suit, fahlumping my bum on the ground. I'm surrounded by past and present punters' dog ends and spilled ale, but I don't care.

'Cop an optic on the sugar PLUMP fairy,' guffaws one of the blue-vest, black-short-shorts, dusty-beaten-up-Blundstone-boots-wearing punters.

Joey stops for a nanosecond in surprise and then starts up again, wailing as if she's experimenting, seeing which registers her voice can handle – sort of like a yodelling banshee – and then I join in.

The pair of us are bawling our eyes out like it's some kind of competition, until I grab her little arms hanging forlornly by her sides and pull her down to the ground with me, hugging her tightly to my sore early pregnancy bosom. I stroke her crazy little-kid hair (going more and more ringletty as the humidity rises) and we rock back and forth until eventually we've both calmed down sufficiently to stand up, walk away and stop making a show of ourselves.

'I know a fairy and her name is nuff.' The same old bloke laughs behind us. 'Fairy nuff! Geddit? Fairy NUFF!'

The rowdy throng slaps its collective, hairy thigh and I roll my eyes. This is not how I'd planned my return to normal life after three years in the child-rearing wilderness. Not even remotely.

'I'm sorry,' I say to her as we near her pre-school, exhausted already.

'I'm sorry, Mummy,' she says softly, looking up at me with her huge blue eyes, her face still wet and red from the tears. She even manages a small, hesitant smile.

Which, of course, in turn, makes me a little bit teary. My darling. And we haven't even got to the painful saying-goodbye-at-the-gate bit yet.

So anyway, when we get to the pre-school, and I'm signing her in, amidst all the Isaac Cohens and Hannah Goldsteins, she suddenly drops my hand and I hear a high-pitched squeal. She darts off, running straight up to a little girl in a scarily similar fairy princess outfit (complete with plastic shiny silver tiara) who screams at her on approach. Joey shrieks in delight and they take each other's hands, turning in a circle as they jump up and down like a pair of candy-pink lunatics.

'She's going to be just fine, Mum,' says a South African voice into my ear, the same voice I spoke to on the phone belonging to Leah, the manager. 'Wise choice of outfit for the first day, by the way.'

I self-consciously swipe my hand over my bum, as if to dislodge any fag ends that may have stuck to my netting during our little contretemps outside the pub. And make a mental note that all these layers of netting do absolutely nothing for the size of one's bum. I mean I can *feel* my huge hips jutting out either side of me, covered in pink netting – talk about a wide load. I feel as though I'm dressed like a Tudor queen – all pale-faced and shelf-like of hip.

'Oh, thanks, Leah,' I say, relieved that Joey's already making friends. 'Actually, it was her idea – I wanted her to wear this great Baby Gap navy blue dress that's got three-quarter-length sleeves and flowers and the cutest little—'

'I meant you, actually.' She smiles. 'But, yus, sometimes our babies know what's bist for us, too.' She winks as she pats my shoulder reassuringly and turns to greet another mum.

I stare at Joey playing with her new friend until my proud gaze is interrupted by a pained cry. But it's not a toddler, this time – it's a mum.

'Get OFF her, Gila,' the mum shouts as she tries to pull out a little girl who's leaning into a baby buggy.

'Let GO! No! Naughty girl. You do *not* strangle your baby sister. EVER!'

The poor red-faced woman pulls a kicking and screaming little girl out of the buggy and hands her to Leah, who calmly and expertly takes her inside for some professional distraction tactics.

'Crikey,' is all I can manage to say, as if I'm channelling the Crocodile Hunter, blending in beautifully with my surroundings and the local wildlife. 'Are you OK?'

51

'I'm fine,' she says, placing the baby on her shoulder and straightening up. 'But this poor little one! Her big sister's madly in love with her, really, but ... I'm Shoshanna, by the way.'

I introduce myself and we both watch Leah marching a 100%-cheered-up Gila towards us.

'What do you say?' Leah gently prods the little girl.

'Sorry, Samia. Sorry, Mummy.'

'OK. Give us all a hug,' says Shoshanna and bends down to pull the little girl to her free shoulder.

Leah looks at me, thins her lips into a smile and cocks her head to the side, her eyes twinkling. I try to do the same, forcing my face into what I think is an 'Isn't that simply *too* adorable?' expression. But when I glance at my reflection in the glass front doors, I realise I look more constipated than empathetic, and I reel back in horror.

'Argh! I'm so late,' I gasp. 'Joey! Joey? Come and give Mummy a kiss goodbye!'

Weirdly enough, for the first time ever, she does exactly as she's told. She runs up to me, throws her arms around my neck and plants a big, fat, wet kiss right on my lips.

'Bye, Mummy!' She beams as she wheels around and disappears in a flash of fairy froth and princess pink.

Leah gives me that look again. Shoshanna does, too.

I swell with pride, bid them both farewell and then hightail it out of there, wrestling with the child-proof gate for a few minutes, making me miss the bus in fine style, running after it, yelling at it to wait, my arm outstretched to the heavens.

I slow my loping to a full stop and look around me dejectedly, breathing hard and pouting. Catching my reflection in the rapidly disappearing bus window, I'm instantly reminded of Sarah Jessica Parker in the opening credits of *Sex and the City*, what with that mess of curly hair and that cute pink tulle tutu . . .

And even though I find the resemblance rather uncanny, I bet no one else does.

'What are you doing for lunch?' Kylie, the receptionist, asks me.

'Hadn't thought about it yet,' I reply. This is a lie, of course. Truth is, I've thought of little else since I polished off that sausage and egg McMuffin for breakfast this morning.

'There's an awesome little cafe round the corner,' she says quietly, and stretches her mouth into a dazzlingly white, perfectly straight-toothed smile worthy of a *The Price Is Right* prize model, waving her hand in front of her balletically as if to reveal a state of the art washer/dryer or speedboat or something. 'I'll give you the goss on all this if you like. It's *fairy* juicy stuff!'

'Yep, good one.' I smile, nodding emphatically. But then I see Phil looking at me over the partition wall and quickly swivel my chair back to face my computer.

Already I'm in Phil's bad books. I was heinously late, in this ridiculous get-up – then I showed myself up by asking what html stood for (I still haven't got a clue, even though he did actually tell me – I really must remedy that small eyes-glazing-over-when-bored-stupid problem I've got) and then I had to enlist the help of the friendly receptionist to log on.

'First, turn your computer on.' She giggled, glancing around to see if anyone else was watching. They weren't, thankfully. There's only so much humiliation a girl can suffer in one morning. And there are just nine of us in here anyway; six of us huddled over computers, quietly beavering away.

The first email I got was a directive from on high stipulating that there will only be any working from home in extra-special circumstances and that all editors must be at the office by 8.30 a.m., leaving for home no earlier than 5.30 p.m. every day. Turns out, before last week, everyone was working away from home quite happily – and far too frequently. Now, however, they're all forced to physically come in to work and are severely cheesed off about it, silently seething over their laptops. Which is *another* reason why it's so quiet in here (the other reason being that, as far as I can see, my fellow three blog eds are clones of Professor John Frink, the dweeby, bespectacled scientist from *The Simpsons*, blogging about cars, gadgets and computer games throughout their whole solitary day).

There are three self-proclaimed 'high-powered sales

execs' (two men and one woman) sitting round the side that Phil's on, loudly braying about their deal-cutting prowess. Or laughing uproariously at YouTube clips of old ladies' teeth falling out as they rap or kittens chasing balls of wool from *Australia's Funniest Home Videos*. Or shouting down the phone, banging on about how Maverick's going to be one of the big boys any day now, because Bill Gates has indicated that he's interested in all our world-beating, award-winning blogs.

The other three eds are so ticked off about their cosy work-from-home set-ups being busted, they threw me filthy looks when I said what a bummer it was having to come all the way into work.

'Don't get anyone started,' said the gadget guy, in a surprisingly deep voice.

But Kylie, who had no excuse to work from home and was getting quite jack of sitting in this office all by herself all day, is actually quite chuffed she'll have some company from now on.

'Ooh, no,' I say loudly, forgetting again that I'm in the Silent Office. 'I can't today – I've forfeited my lunch hour, being so late in and all—'

'Shh.' Kylie looks at me crossly and puts an acrylic-nailed finger up to her plump, bee-stung lips. Then she traces an 'S', an 'M' and another 'S' in the air with said finger.

My mouth must be hanging open, making me look as dim and confused as I'm feeling, because she leans in to me, bending low so that her boobs are level to my face, her head just beneath the boss's eyeline. She says:

'SMS. That's how we communicate here.'

I do my best not to stare at her unfairly pert breasts creating the perfect cleavage in her tight low-cut scarlet T-shirt and drag my eyes up to hers.

'What's that?' I whisper.

She straightens up a bit and signs the same letters again, air-alphabet-style. But I'm still drawing a blank.

'SMS?' she asks, wrinkling her forehead and widening her eyes.

Obviously she thinks the mnemonic is enough, but it's absolutely meaningless to me.

'I'll sort you out later. Shh.' She shushes me again and then turns round to sit with her back to me for the next seven long, almost eerie, excruciatingly quiet hours.

'Not bad.' I answer Jack when he walks through our front door that evening, asking how my first day at work went. 'Not bad, but not great, either.'

'All first days are like that,' he says soothingly. 'And you've not been working for such a long time, now; it's only natural to feel nervous for a little while. It'll get better. I promise. And if it doesn't, just think of the money!'

I tell him all about me and Joey crying out the front of The Galah in the morning and The Quietest Office On Earth while he flings Joey up in the air, like he's tossing a caber, until they both collapse on the couch in fits of laughter.

'I don't think we have any readers, though – or, if we do, they never send comments in. The more comments your posts get, the better you look in the boss's eyes, apparently. And the more controversial you can be, the better, maybe garner some publicity. But the site looks so awful! It badly needs a redesign. And I doubt anyone knows it even exists – either readers or advertisers.'

'Try to keep positive, babe – think of it as a challenge, a new adventure,' he continues. 'Like your fashion sense. I mean, what the ... what *are* you wearing?'

'Don't.' I shake my head and close my eyes. 'Shopping for new clothes for me as soon as, yeah?'

'Hoo! Can't wait!' Jack claps his hands together in mock-glee.

'That's Daddy being sarcastic, Joey, sar-ca-stic. It's when you *say* something, but you actually *mean* the opposite. Like, when Daddy belches after dinner and Mummy says "nice". I'm being sarcastic then, because it's *not* very nice, burping, is it?'

'Can you burp the alphabet, Daddy?' an excited Joey asks.

'Of course,' Jack replies proudly and starts with the letter 'A', faltering on the 'C' a little, but regaining his composure all the way to the alphabet's natural conclusion, in an American-sounding 'Zeee'.

'Again! Again!' Joey jumps up and down like a Teletubby.

'You're going to have to give me a crash-course in

57

computers and computer jargon, too, Jack, because I sound like a moron, asking Kylie what things mean every five minutes. And I can't even ask her properly – I have to do it by M&M's or something.'

'Now you're talking – any treats? Come to think of it, what's for dinner?' He carries Joey over to the fridge and peers in, holding the door open.

'Um.' I hum and haw, stalling for time. It's my fault – I was supposed to pick something up for us on our way home from the pre-school this afternoon, but I completely forgot.

'Bugger-all from the fridge at any rate,' he announces. 'Who's up for Chinese, then?'

'Yay! Fried rice!' yells Joey.

'Yeah, why not?' I sigh, rubbing my paunch that still looks just like a fat tummy as opposed to a pregnant belly. 'I'm going to get massive again any day now, anyway. So what's on telly to go with our takeaway?'

'Usual crap,' says Jack. 'Thank God for Oz Tube.'

I couldn't agree more.

However, in an effort to assimilate, acclimatise to and familiarise ourselves with Aussie popular culture (and, as a result, make me feel less homesick), we've promised ourselves we'll watch terrestrial TV for one hour every night. And tonight we manage to sit through a whole episode of *In the Family Way*, a super-popular Aussie drama series that makes *Skippy* sound like Shakespeare.

But at least it gives me an idea for a regular spot on KiddingAround.com.au – it could be a potential magnet for comments, too, so Phil's going to love it. I get quite animated, explaining it to Jack:

'Pretty simple, really,' I say, 'it'd just be a review of the previous night's telly every weekday. We could call it "Last Night's TV" or "What We Watched on TV Last Night". Or something . . . '

'Catchy,' Jack says.

'Because we all know that when you become parents, you don't get out much any more, so you're stuck in, watching crap on TV every night.'

'"Crap On TV" – there's a better title.' Jack nods.

'What does "crap" mean, Mummy?' Joey pipes up.

'Um, rubbish. It's not a good thing to say, though, Joey. Strictly for grown-ups. OK?'

Joey shrugs her shoulders and immerses herself in her mermaid puzzle book once more.

'But there might be something good once in a while, too,' I say, as balanced as ever. 'People will write in with their opinions about the state of the telly here – we'll get so many comments, it's going to be great!'

'But not everyone's as addicted to TV as you,' Jack says, pressing the 'up channel' button on the remote every two seconds.

'Everyone watches telly, though – and never more than when you can't afford a babysitter or are so tired you can't face the thought of going out. It's the nation's favourite hobby.' I point at Jack, then to the TV, then back to Jack. 'See?'

'No, it's not – that's barbecues,' says Jack, not taking his eyes off the screen. 'But what do I know? I'm sure it's a great idea.'

'You could be a bit more supportive, you know.' I sigh.

'I'm sorry,' he says. 'If I get time – work is full-on at the mo – but if I get time, I'll make sure I leave a comment. Make you look good for the boss. How do you like them apples?'

'That'd be great. Oh, Jack, it really could be the beginning of something quite beautiful. You know, I can see it now – loads of readers' comments, me being blogger of the month at Maverick.' I make a sweeping gesture with my arm, narrowing my eyes as I stare dreamily at the brick wall just beyond the kitchenette's windows.

'Yeah, yeah, great. Now shh.' Jack shushes me impatiently. '*MythBusters* is on.'

Chapter 6

So we've made it past the twelve-week mark (just), and I'm now in my thirteenth week. So far, so good. Not that that means we're in the clear, not at all, not by a long shot. Dr Google says that women can suffer miscarriages all the way up to twenty-two weeks and beyond. So I'm not getting cocky or anything – in no way relaxing about the whole thing yet.

But I do feel so different this time. Now, I know that probably means nothing and you shouldn't ever count your chickens until they've actually hatched – and I'm not saying that I have the smallest intuitional-type clue as to whether this one's more viable than the last one or my body's more capable of holding on to it than last time – but I definitely feel different.

I don't remember feeling quite so disgustingly sick all the time when I was pregnant with Joey, for a start. I mean, this time it's really vile. I can't walk down the street without grimacing and giving people dirty looks as if the hair conditioner they're using, the sausage roll they're munching, the perfume they're spritzing or even the laundry powder they're using is bringing an olfactory Armageddon down upon me. Going to work is like being trapped in an underground, overflowing sewer in mid-summer, even if I'm walking past a florist.

Still, I think of the money and the fact that I actually *have* a job as I close Shalom! Baby's front gate behind me. I click my tongue on the roof of my mouth and wince when I look across the road and see the snaking queue of weary workers waiting at the bus stop.

That bit in 'Manic Monday' that goes on about not being able to make it into work on time even if Susannah Hoffs had an aeroplane blares out of the cafe near the bus stop. Honestly, you can't move in Bondi for hearing that song. Someone must've got a job lot on *The Best of the Bangles* CD or something, because it's incessant.

I heave a humongous sigh.

'Can't be that bad,' says Shoshanna's cheery voice behind me, making me jump.

'No, no – course it isn't,' I say.

'Got time for a quick coffee?' she asks, her voice wavering ever so slightly. I look into her eyes and see that she's not merely asking, she's pleading with me, begging.

'I can't,' I say sulkily. 'I'm late already.'

'Oh, go on.' She pouts, raising her eyebrows. 'Just one teensy, weensy coffee. You could be late in, say you were interviewing someone.'

We've had coffee together several times since the first day I saw her dropping off her daughter. And now that Joey and Gila have become good friends, we'll usually meet up on the weekend so the girls can play in the sand and we can sit in the shade under the promenade, commenting on the bodies and fashion choices of all those who present before us on the beach.

I know, I know – glass houses and all that – but it kills time and keeps the kids happy. And Shoshie's excellent company. Reminds me of Charlie in some ways, but sunnier, more positive. Just the tonic to keep the Monday morning blues at bay.

'I really shouldn't,' I say.

'Goody-goody,' she teases. 'You haven't chucked one sickie yet – and you've been there, what? Three months?'

'Nah, it's only been seven weeks or so,' I say, opening my eyes wide in surprise at my late onset of apparent jobsworthiness.

'Oh, come on! First one's on me ...' She dangles a carrot.

'I ca-hah-hah-han't,' I whine.

'No dramas.' She smirks. 'I mean, if you haven't got time for a friend in need ...'

And there it is. Right there. It doesn't take much – just a bit of emotional blackmail and the promise of a free drink – and I'm skiving off work.

'You're right, Shoshie. I'll just text the boss and tell him Joey's feeling poorly so I won't be coming in today. I'll soften the blow by saying I'll work from home. That sounds plausible, doesn't it?'

'Sort of – except if he knows anything about trying to work when you've got kids under your feet, he'll know you're telling porkies.'

'A-ha! But he doesn't. I'd buy it if I were a childless young man. Just like male PE teachers at school always used to let you off doing stuff when you said it was that time of the month.'

I text Phil and get a swift reply, saying no worries and hoping that Joey's OK. Phew. That was easier than I thought it would be.

And with that, we walk back down to South Bondi, and then up the hill to our favourite air-conditioned cafe on the corner, Serenitea.

We're high on the hill now, overlooking all those silly sods who insist on burning themselves to a crisp on the beach, but we can't tear our eyes away from a badly behaved boy kicking chairs and screaming the cafe down.

This little boy – must be about two-and-a-half, three – is completely tearing the place apart. His mum is falling over herself apologising to her fellow coffee drinkers and the waiter, but the boy has gone berserk. Eventually, the manager asks her and her son to leave, indiscreetly pointing out that the kid's antics are keeping potential punters at bay – and making existing ones bail out in their droves.

'Madam!' says the haughty manager. 'Either control

that child or I'll have to ask you to vacate the premises. You're driving my customers away!'

'I'm trying!' snaps the hapless mum. 'He's got ADHD and I'm at the end of my tether – but thanks for your help,' she adds sarcastically.

'Can I help?' says Shoshanna, making her way towards the other side of the caff.

'No, we've got to go now, anyway,' says the harassed mum. 'But thanks for asking.'

'Anytime,' says Shoshie with her spectacular sunshiny smile that can light up even the dimmest of dark, cool cafes. 'In fact, next time, do join us, won't you?'

'Don't think we're welcome here any more,' says the mum, shooting the manager daggers. 'But maybe we'll see you around sometime.'

And off they go, the mum saying sorry to everyone sitting at the outside tables as her little boy kicks over the Specials blackboard in a final act of defiance.

'Can't take 'em anywhere,' I venture as Shoshie sits down.

'I know how she feels,' she says.

'Yeah, what's up?' I ask. 'You're awfully keen for a coffee this morning – more so than usual. Is everything OK?'

'Yeah, fine,' she says, staring into the chocolate swirls she's making in her skinny-cappuccino foam. 'Just didn't fancy being cooped up at home alone with this one all day again.'

We both look down at her baby girl, Samia, sleeping sweetly in the buggy with her little fists clenched up by her ears.

'Yeah, it's good to get out if you can.' I nod sympathetically. 'Make the most of her not being able to walk, Shosh – and hey! At least you aren't getting kicked out of cafes. Yet!'

'I bet we would if Gila was here, too,' smiles Shoshie. 'I mean, I know she loves her little sister to bits – but she can get carried away with the hugs and kisses sometimes, it's like she doesn't know her own strength. Look at those red marks around her neck. That's where Gila was cuddling her a tad too emphatically yesterday. Poor little mite.'

I inspect the marks and run my finger along a particularly nasty-looking red welt. Cuddling? Yeah, right. Whenever I see Gila, she's positively *mauling* her baby sister. And it doesn't look too friendly or loving to me – more like she wants to kill her.

'Are you sure it's a love thing with Gila? Sure she's not just insanely jealous?'

'Well, maybe a bit. But it's normal, totally normal. And anyway, I don't want to make a big thing of it, make it even more obvious to Gila how she can grab the spotlight. It's tricky with two, very tricky.' Shoshie sighs.

'I really worry about that,' I say, looking down at my swelling, but beautifully camouflaged in a rip-off Pucci-print, stomach. 'What if Joey does her nut out of jealousy

and resentment? What if she becomes a monster because it's the only way she can get some attention? What
if she tries to do away with the baby when I'm not looking?'

'You're worrying needlessly – Joey's a lovely kid and
she'll be thrilled when the baby comes along. And in the
long term, Rox, so will you, honest. Just look at my two –
with any luck, yours will love each other just as much as
mine and be great friends. Joey's old enough to actually
help you out with the baby, too, just like Gila does. For
the most part, she's absolutely wonderful with Samia. For
the most part . . . '

We sit and gaze at the waves for a while until a gorgeous surfer runs slowly past the cafe window. You can
hear a pin drop as the whole of Serenitea, now empty save
for us, the manager, the waiter and a few elderly ladies
who lunch, follows him with their eyes. A woman behind
us even mutters, 'Phwoar!' and we nod in agreement.

'Always running,' I offer, smiling. 'Down to the beach,
back from the beach – guys in wetsuits carrying surfboards
under their arms. You can't take a walk in Bondi without
being run over by surfies!'

'At least they have a place to go,' says Shoshie, standing
up to get a better view of the surfer's bum in his board
shorts as he disappears down the hill. 'Somewhere he
knows he and his board are welcome. Somewhere they'll
have fun together, have a break from the real world, lose
themselves at sea.'

'*Where everybody knows his name . . .*' I sing that bit from the *Cheers* theme.

Shoshie doesn't flinch.

'Bit early for such wistfulness, isn't it?' I try again.

Shoshie sits down just as 'Manic Monday' is piped through the cafe.

'Ooh, I love this song.' She sways in her seat and we sing along with The Bangles in unison, chortling.

'God, I miss work,' says Shoshie.

'Ugh, don't remind me,' I grunt. 'And anyway, what do you mean, "miss work"? You work like a dog, bringing up two kids with no help – *and* you don't get paid for it!' I've said this so many times in my own defence when arguing with Jack about money, the words fairly trip off my tongue.

'You know what I mean.' Shoshanna tuts. 'Having to be accountable to someone, think about something other than feeding and sleeping routines. I miss solving problems, using my brain. I don't have a bad one, you know, and I was once quite well respected as the senior nutritionist at catering college. All my years of training and working in nutrition haven't been for nothing now I'm a mum, have they?'

'I know. It's as though the minute you have a baby, you're not taken seriously any more,' I say. 'It's like there's so much involved with looking after kids, you couldn't *possibly* get your head around anything more challenging than finding a good nappy-rash cream.'

'All washed up, with nowhere to go.'

'Shoshie, are you OK? Is that what's getting you down? Want to talk about it?'

'No, not really,' she patently lies, staring distractedly out of the massive wall of a window in front of us.

I study her eyes for any clues as to what's bugging her, but they just look blank, empty, as she stares longingly out at the sea.

Never one to let an opportunity to bang on pass me by, I see an opening, take a deep breath and leap into it.

'Well, mind if I get something off my chest?' I go on, without waiting for her answer. 'Jack's only gone and got a loan out to add to our massive debt in the UK – and guess what it's for? You'll never guess . . . a sodding motorbike! Unbelievable. Talk about rebel-without-a-clue mid-life crisis – just as he's about to become a father for the second time. *And* he broke our promise to each other that we wouldn't do anything on credit ever again – if we wanted something we'd have to save up for it and pay for it in cash. I'm so pissed off with him.'

This shakes Shoshie out of her reverie.

'Maybe you should set up that Pissed-Off Parents Club you're always talking about again, then – right here in Sydney.'

'Hey, yeah! Except I'd call it the Pissed-Off *Partners* Club this time – I think some people got the wrong end of the stick with the name. I mean, it was never about being annoyed with kids – it was about how hard it is adjusting to your new role as a parent and kissing goodbye to your old life as someone only ever responsible for themselves. It's not easy, letting go of your selfish ways.'

'Almost impossible for blokes – much more so than for us women.'

'Well, to be fair, we have so much longer to come to terms with it – our lives change irrevocably the minute we find out we're pregnant, but guys carry on, business as usual, for ages.'

'Long after the child is born, usually. So how much did Jack spend on his mid-life crisis machine, his MLC?'

'Seventeen-and-a-half grand,' I say, indignant. 'But that's not all – there's pricey insurance, leathers – the helmet alone cost $900.'

'You've already got a car, what do you need a bike for?' she asks. 'And didn't you notice a large amount of money missing from your joint account?'

'What joint account?'

'You're married, with one kid and another one on the way and you don't have a joint account?' Shoshie's incensed.

'Um, no. Should we?'

'Damn straight you should! How do you get food and petrol and coffees in cafes?'

'With my money.'

'*Your* money? How ridiculous! Whatever you earn combined with whatever Jack earns is the *family* money.

You're not single any more, selfishly pursuing your own individual interests – you're a family. How weird.'

'Well, how do you and your husband organise the finances?'

'What's Isaac's is mine – I'm not earning any more, but I'm raising his two kids, so his salary goes straight into our account. We pay for groceries, petrol, bills and the mortgage, and, if there's anything left, we divvy it up between us.'

She looks at me like I'm a complete idiot, like it's obvious, like everyone in the whole world operates this way.

'Sit down with him and draw up a budget. You must get this sorted out before the baby arrives. Money troubles split the vast majority of couples up, you know. And one in three marriages ends in divorce, so fix it fast or you'll be arguing through your respective lawyers before you know it.'

Ouch. Much as I'm cheesed off with Jack, I don't want us to break up over it. I just wish he'd spoken to me about it first, wish he'd given me a chance to rant and rave about what a stupid idea getting an MLC was.

Of course, I finally realise, that's exactly why he *didn't* talk to me about it. Maybe that's why he doesn't talk to me about much in general – he thinks I'll pooh-pooh everything, put the kybosh on all his ideas, be a big handbrake on fun.

The radio's still playing 'Manic Monday'.

'Manic Monday? Yeah, right – this is so fraught and

frenetic, isn't it?' I smile at her over the top of my over-sized coffee cup.

'Yeah. Lounging about in a cafe overlooking one of the most beautiful beaches in the world – this is the life.'

'Mind you,' I frown, 'I'm not moaning or anything, but it's not like we do this every day, is it? Work is totally stressful – I don't get a lunch hour because I have to leave early to go and pick Joey up. And I always get in late because we've had tantrums on the way to pre-school—'

'*Blame it on the train but the boss is already there …*' Shoshie sings along with the Bangles.

And I'm glad she does – for years I've been singing the wrong words, thinking that Prince must have been off his head when he wrote it, because it didn't make sense to me. I thought it was 'blame it on the train but the *bus* is already there'. Super-rich megastar musicians, I used to think, wouldn't have a clue about going to work nine-to-five on rubbish public transport, having to come up with new excuses for serial lateness. No wonder he got it wrong.

And then I remember I was just in the middle of a moan. No, sorry – not a moan, really – more an interesting discourse on women's roles as wives, workers and home-makers in the twenty-first century …

'Where was I? Um, yeah. And when I leave Joey there, for ten hours or whatever it is, I miss her like crazy. Seems I let everyone down – her, work – I can't do any of it prop-erly, you know? You just can't win.' I smile, sensing that Shoshanna knows exactly what I'm on about.

72

'And the money you make goes on the childcare anyway,' she agrees, 'so you're in negative equity before you've even begun. That's why I quit my job at the college – something had to give. But by crikey I miss it. Or at least I miss getting my teeth into something other than making Annabel Karmel pies.'

I nod supportively, despite the fact I have never, *ever* managed to make an Annabel Karmel pie. Or anything Annabel Karmel, for that matter. Fish fingers are the peak of my culinary imagination – and even they can be a bit of a test sometimes.

A couple of young mums enter the cafe and cause a commotion, banging chairs with their buggies, shouting at their toddlers and ineffectually trying to soothe their bellowing babies.

One little boy has a red football shirt with the number 10 and the word 'Messi' on the back; the other has the same in blue but with the word 'Dirti'. They come tearing towards us, weaving in and out of tables and knocking over chairs.

'Ahem!' stage-coughs the young, stoned-looking waiter who's suddenly appeared at our table. 'Are you ladies going to order anything to eat?'

He bends down and whispers to us, 'You could sit here all day with your kids and your pushchairs on just one coffee for all I care – but my manager wants a higher turnover of covers. Reckons mums and kids are killing his business. He's on my case and I really need this job. So what's it gonna be?'

I can barely hear him over the cacophony the kids are making, so Shoshie just shakes her head no, while I shout in reply.

'Nothing more for me.' I cover the top of my cup with my hand and accentuate my mouth movements to help him lip-read, in case he can't hear over the terrible noise either.

'Suit yourself,' I think he says and he disappears back into the kitchen.

'I'd better get home and see if I can do some work,' I yell into Shoshie's ear. 'The boss is bound to be checking the site and he'll know I haven't put anything new up there today. Which is a bit of a bummer – I could really do with an all-dayer in here!'

Suddenly the music is turned off, we hear the sound of smashing crockery and out from the kitchen marches a portly, mid-fifties guy with greasy black hair and steam coming out of his ears.

Clearly a man on the edge, he pulls a chair from one of the tables and stands on it.

'RIGHT!' he shouts, flinging his arms out to the side like he's an American baseball umpire declaring someone out. 'That's IT! All people with children must leave my cafe. ASAP. PRONTO. RIGHT BLOODY NOWWWWW!'

He glares in our direction and eventually we realise he's talking – OK, *shouting* – at us.

'Well! Turns out *we're* not welcome here, either. I'll

74

walk you back,' says Shoshie as she bangs the wheels of her buggy into every table as we make our way out.

And as we trudge slowly up the steepest hill in Christendom, up Ridgey Didge Road to our flat, it occurs to me that, unlike the surfers and their boards, the mums and toddlers round here have nowhere they can call their own – nowhere just for them, where they're welcome and, indeed, *encouraged* to hang out, where they can sit on one measly coffee all day.

'You know, if I owned that cafe, I'd make it totally mum-friendly,' I say, panting. 'There are so many women around here toting babies and toddlers, but you never see them in the cafes, do you? It's like they've been ostracised since they had kids, forced to skulk about on the fringes of cafe society.'

'True,' agrees Shoshie, not even puffing. 'As if it wasn't bad enough that you don't have your own money or career, your figure's gone to pot, you're up half the night, every night, tending to your kids and trying to ignore your husband's snores – now you're not even allowed the sanctuary of a skinny-cap in your local caff any more.'

I stop, put my hands on my hips and grimace when I realise we're not even halfway up the hill yet. 'I know. It's – *huff* – madness!'

'Kids, eh? They'll ruin your life if you're not careful,' Shoshie turns and shouts, looking back down the hill at me.

I garner all my strength and catch up to her. But this is

no mean feat – I'm walking practically perpendicular, here.

When I reach her, I put one hand on Shoshie's shoulder and bend over, on the verge of hyperventilating I'm so out of breath. Sweat drips from my red face on to the footpath.

Eventually, Shoshie breaks the coronary-any-second silence.

'I'm sorry if I'm a bit of a misery today, Rox. I just need something to do with my life. I need to dedicate myself to something other than the kids . . . '

'Love 'em to bits and wouldn't change 'em for the world,' we say together and laugh, echoing every mum's favourite preface to '*but* . . . '

We lock arms and continue walking, Shoshanna's toned, brown biceps dragging me up the hill as well as pushing Samia in her buggy. Put you to shame, these Bondi yummy mummies – they're worse than the ones in the UK – all bronzed, fit, trim and never out of breath.

And just then, a woman pushing a Phil&Teds pram with a baby and a toddler in it runs past us. *Runs* past us. Uphill. Up this ludicrously steep hill. We both watch after her, me in awe, Shoshanna proudly.

'Is it just me or is this whole kids business so much easier if you're twenty-five?' I squint, pinching the fat under my bra in an effort to alleviate the pain of a stitch.

'That's Tania,' says Shoshie. 'She's forty-eight. Local legend. Used to be a little, well, *width-challenged*, shall we say – until she became one of my private clients and I sorted her out. '

'So it is just me, then. Talk about being an unfit mother!'

'You know, if I devised a nutritionally balanced diet for you, I'd have you running up this hill effortlessly, too. You should watch it at your age, you know.'

'Thanks, thanks a bunch. I'm pregnant, remember, so I'm eating for twelve. If I can't drink anything any more, I might as well munch and be merry – and there are some fab caramel slices with my name on them at that cafe … up there, near … the bus stop …'

I trail off. I don't know whether I've just suffered a stroke or a heart attack what with all this physically debilitating exertion, but a flash of inspiration hits me like a bolt out of the blue. It just comes to me and, all of a sudden, I can picture the future perfectly.

'Hey, Shosh,' I say slowly. 'Why don't we open up a cafe for mums?'

She looks at me like I've just suggested harakiri.

'Well, for mums *and* dads, really – but ostensibly for mums. And their kids. If normal cafes won't take them any more, why don't we create a place solely for them? Why don't we just do it? Me and you. A mums' cafe.'

'Duh! You're joking, right?'

'No, seriously. Think of all the mums with nowhere to go round here – they're everywhere! The Tanias of Bondi could all cool off there after their runs, so to speak. And you could be the nutritionist at large – make extra money doing consultations and working out diets for mums and mums-to-be while they catch up on the goss over a coffee. You could even do special diets for kids!'

'Hmm, caffeine – one of the worst toxins known to—'

'Whatever, Shosh!' I dismiss her, my heart racing once again. 'It would get you working; give you something to do other than look after your kids.'

'But aren't small businesses recipes for disaster in a recession?'

'No better time for a cafe to flourish – it's cheap, quick entertainment, perfect for cash- and time-strapped mums, where they can pop in and out or sit on one coffee all day and not be booted out for their badly behaved sprogs!'

Shoshanna looks a little less appalled now – even as though she might be considering the idea.

'And hey! We could have a *House of Tiny Tearaways*- or *Supernanny*-type person there, solving behavioural problems on site!'

Shoshanna raises her eyebrows and I take it as encouragement, so I go on.

'We could have an area for babies to just sit or crawl about in, a buggy shelter out the front, babysitters on tap, all sorts of services on a cork noticeboard ...'

'But how?' Shoshie frowns. 'Costs a fortune to set up a business like that – and most cafes and restaurants fall by the wayside within six months of opening. I know this because most catering college students go on to open restaurants after graduating, and nearly all of them fail dismally. Apparently, 89% of restaurant start-ups are doomed to close before they've even been open a year.'

She's making it up as she goes along, I think to myself. Even so, it's enough to dampen my enthusiasm.

We both stare at the ground and 'hmm' a bit.

'Well, are you even remotely business-minded?' she asks me. 'Have you got a good head for figures?'

I suddenly come over all Melanie Griffith in *Working Girl*, put my hand on my hip, toss my hair and say huskily: 'I have a head for business and a bod for sin.'

'Yeeaah,' says Shoshie, missing the reference and forcing an uncomfortable smile. 'Sooo ... could you do up a cracking business plan and then get the bank to lend us the necessary loads of money?'

My face falls.

'No. I am *so* rubbish at maths – I still use my fingers to count and I can barely work a calculator, let alone a cash register.'

'Me too,' says Shoshie. 'Suppose that's that, then.'

We walk in silence for a bit. This immediately reminds me of work and makes me feel that all-too-familiar stab of guilt for shirking.

'I'd better get home, do some work.' I sound defeated.

'Hang on – what about Isaac?' Shoshie pulls my elbow back. 'I didn't tell you earlier because I was, well, a bit embarrassed, I suppose. But he's, ah ... he's just been sacked.'

'Oh, poor Isaac,' I say unconvincingly. I'm not exactly what you'd call sympathetic to the plight of greedy money-makers – Isaac's a banker, I think Shoshie said. Or something ending in *anker*, anyway, by the sounds of him.

'Yeah, well, hedge fund managers everywhere are feeling the pinch,' Shoshie goes on, with not a hint of sarcasm or irony. 'They're the ones who have to take the blame for this God-awful worldwide financial crisis – even though it's not strictly their fault. There always has to be a scapegoat, I suppose.'

'Hmm.' I bite my tongue.

'But anyway, he's free now, so he could sort out the financials for us, deal with the money side of everything. And we'd be in really safe hands, he almost never takes risks – that's probably what he was sacked for!'

'Would he be interested, though? In a cafe? For mums?'

'Oh, yes,' says Shoshie, raising one eyebrow in a slightly scary way. 'He'll do exactly as he's told from now on. Be a good little boy.'

'Brilliant! Course, I'll have to leave work, dedicate myself to the cause 24/7 before Junior comes along. And when it's born, I'll be able to bring it to work with me! Ooh, I've always fancied myself as the perfect hostess – sorry, front of house – meeting and greeting, setting the warm, friendly atmos. Ever watched *Ramsay's Kitchen Nightmares*? I know exactly what to do because of that show – it'll be a doddle! Pity I can't cook—'

'That's what Jack always says.' She elbows me right in my stitch, throws her head back and laughs, looking the happiest I've seen her all day. 'But first things first – what are we going to call this fantastic new place?'

Chapter 7

Because Phil was really nice about me working from home the other day, I text him the truth, this time, and tell him that I have a hospital appointment for a small procedure. I've got a lot on today, see. I've got to get Joey off to Shalom! Baby, draw up a business plan with Shoshanna at my place and, later on this arvo, I'm having a CVS to check for chromosomal abnormalities in the baby. So, really, I have no other choice than to take today off as well. Sorry, *work from home* today.

'Right. So. Where do we start?' Shosh asks, as she arranges three different fluoro pens (yellow, pink and green), two biros and two sharpened pencils into a neat row at the top of her spiral-bound notebook.

Honestly, she is so organised and tidy, she makes Mr Sheen look like Worzel Gummidge. When I comment on this, she snorts and says:

'Well, you *have* to be organised when you've got *two*

kids! Otherwise it all goes to hell in a handcart. And anyway, the cafe will be perfect practice for you.'

Baby Samia's gurgling contentedly on the Persian rug in front of CBeebies while Shoshanna and I sit at the kitchen table, waiting for inspiration to strike. I've never even thought about doing a business plan before and Shosh got Isaac to do hers for her, when she went briefly into business on her own as a nutritionist.

'Why don't we work out what we want the cafe to be and then we can Google what exactly to say, how to format it and then put it in a presentable style so that the bank manager can see what a guaranteed success it'll be?' I suggest.

So we do. And it's a real eye-opener. Who knew there was so much to consider?

The first website we come across says you have to decide what you can promise to the customer.

'Like a manifesto,' I murmur as we both peer into my laptop.

'A mission statement, yeah.' Shoshie nods slowly. 'So what do we promise we'll do for our customers?'

'What would make the perfect cafe for a mum just like you?'

'That's easy.' Shoshie sighs. 'To be cooked for and cleaned up after – without me having to lift a finger.'

'And to know the kids are being looked after while you take it easy,' I offer.

'You know, if we can't sell it to ourselves, we've got

Buckley's of selling it to a bank manager. Or our clientele, for that matter,' Shoshie ventures.

'Well, let's start selling – we know what we want, we're mums, exactly the people we're targeting, so let's sell it to ourselves!'

Shosh grabs her pink fluoro pen and draws a big oblong on her pad. And after half an hour of us shouting things out and her scribbling away like mad, she shows me this:

WE PROMISE WE WILL ALWAYS –

* Pamper knackered parents and carers – you're number one in our book, and you deserve the best!

* Look after your kids while you relax – our registered childminders know how to keep the little ones occupied and happy

* Treat you, your noisy bent-on-destruction toddlers, your prams and your pooey babies with respect. We welcome families of all shapes and sizes and consider it an honour to be in your (sometimes whiffy, often witty, but always wonderful) presence

* Provide sanctuary and shelter from the child-rearing storm – because we know that sometimes it can all get a bit overwhelming and you just have to take a break before you explode

* Let you sit on one coffee for hours and hours on end – but ... ouch! We'd prefer it if you sat on a chair – much more comfy

* Make scrummy, nutritious food for you and your brood, making life easier for you – and a whole lot more fun!
* Be on your side and never, ever, ever judge you. We've been there and we know that what you need is support and a shoulder to cry on – not criticism
* Be open early! We'll always be here for you whenever you need us, just like family – but better.

We work out how we're going to do this (we'll provide childminders, toys, a baby area, a barista, a licence to serve alcohol), how much we reckon it'll cost to do this (nothing too outrageous, but if we're going to do it, we're going to do it right, as Wham! might say), and how much we think we'll make in profit month-by-month in the first, second and third years (absolutely *heaps*).

'We'll have to advertise for staff,' Shoshie says, flipping the pages of her pad over and clicking the pen lid on to her biro.

'Yep. And I've been thinking – maybe only single mothers should be allowed to apply. Positive discrimination, yeah? And their kids, depending on how old they are, could be looked after in the supervised crèche. What do you think?'

'I like it,' she says. 'I'll put an ad in *Sydney Mums*, that free magazine you see in cafes and chemists.'

'Good idea. I'll put an ad up on KiddingAround, too, advertising for waiting staff and plugging the cafe at the same time.'

'Great,' she says, writing on her pad furiously.

'How much do you think we should pay ourselves, Shosh?'

'I dunno. Isaac would have more of a clue about that sort of stuff than me.'

'But we should find out, we should know. I don't want Isaac to be in control of too much – it's our cafe. And, I don't know whether I should say this, but, well, I don't know if I trust Isaac. With my future, I mean.'

'I know, Rox, and you're right to say it. I've got something to say, too, because I think we should begin as we mean to go on – with honesty and trust at the heart of the business.'

'Sounds ominous,' I say. 'Go on.'

Shosh takes a deep breath and tickles Samia's chubby cheeks.

'When I first met Isaac, I was a little kid,' she begins.

'Is this going to be your whole life story? Because we haven't got that long, you know.' I nudge her in the ribs.

'I'm only thirty-four! *Your* life story would take … well, anyway. Just a bit of background to help you understand where I'm coming from, that's all,' she says, sitting up straighter.

'Zac was the singer in my older brother's band and his best friend. They modelled themselves on Duran Duran, all billowy romantic Lord Byron white shirts, blow-dried burgundy hair dos and tight leather trousers. Although sometimes it was too hot for the leather pants and they'd end up playing in brightly coloured board shorts. They toyed with calling themselves DuBeau DuBeau for a while, but it just sounded too feminine and not Aussie enough. So they settled on Dubbo Dubbo.'

'Pffftht!' I laugh.

'No, don't – they were very cool at the time. Anyway, I idolised Isaac, thought he was to die for. So well dressed! And he was such a gentleman. When I was a teenager, in my last year of high school, I went to a gig of theirs. They were still doing the pub circuit in Sydney and still attracted a modest crowd. I remember one night, me and a couple of my friends – as well as some really young girls from the convent school next to ours – jumped into the back of the band's Tarago, you know, those minivan things, and headed off back to their hotel. But before we got there, Isaac made the driver turn round and take me and my friends home. He said he didn't want to take advantage of his rock star status, wanted to do the right thing by his best friend. So we got out and then they took the convent girls home. I'll never forget that – honourable.'

'How do you know he didn't just take the convent girls back to the hotel after he'd got rid of you?'

'Because … well, he wouldn't have. Although, now you mention it … ' Shoshie squints and thins her lips.

'Sorry to interrupt.' I pat her on the knee. 'Nasty habit of mine. Do go on.'

Shosh shakes the unpleasant vision out of her head and coughs daintily.

'Right. Yes. Well, fast forward several years and we've fallen in love. We get married, buy a house together and then decide to have the kids. When I got pregnant with Gila, Isaac and I were so in love, so full of optimism and hope for the future. Of course, when Gila came along, our worlds were turned upside down. And not always in a good way. But mainly in a good way – for me, anyway. Isaac, on the other hand, felt surplus to requirements, as lots of men do. Gila unwittingly drove a wedge between us, both of us grappling with our constant desire for independence coupled with the crushing weight of responsibility. I soldiered on, as you do, but, before too long, he was having an affair. When I eventually found out, I was devastated. But not quite as devastated as I was when he suggested he carry on with this woman, who just so happened to be his boss. He wanted to stay married to me, coming to some kind of arrangement, like an open marriage. He said I was free to have someone on the side – a part-time lover, he nauseatingly called it – as if I was in any way "free", trying to look after a baby 24/7.'

'Blimey,' I murmur encouragingly.

'Quite. So what could I do? I no longer had any income, I had Gila who totally relied on me and the family unit I'd held so dear was fast becoming farcical. It was as though

Isaac thought he was some French boulevardier, entitled to the missus at home and countless mistresses dotted about the place. So I made the best of it and found solace in the shape of Rabbi Goldman, often talking to him late into the night, when Gila was asleep and Isaac was out. Then . . . ' She pauses. 'Then I got pregnant with Samia.'

'And she's the rabbi's, right? She's not Isaac's!' I squeal and slap my thighs.

'Calm down.' She looks cross. 'It's not *Days of Our Lives*. No, she *is* Isaac's. But when I found out, I had a break-down. I couldn't go on in our open marriage – I was constantly having my heart broken, feeling like second-, third-, even fourth-best, the downtrodden little woman, keeping the home fires burning and keeping the kids fed and watered – but somehow losing herself in the process and being constantly humiliated by her husband. I was a wreck. I'd become a hollow shell and I was desperate for an out. So desperate, I even contemplated suicide – but I just couldn't do it to the kids.'

I'm genuinely shocked. I don't know what to say. I put a hand on Shosh's knee.

'I'm so sorry,' I manage.

'Let me finish,' she says calmly. 'Rabbi Goldman knew all about it and brought me out of my depression. Thanks to him and our long talks, I was able to find the strength to go through with the pregnancy, give birth to the healthy and gorgeous Samia here and, a few weeks ago, tell Isaac that an open marriage wasn't for me. If he wanted to be with his other women, he could – but he couldn't expect me to be waiting for him at home. I was going to leave him. I demanded a divorce, took the kids and went and stayed at Mum's.'

'This was just a few weeks ago?'

'Yes. But then he bombarded me with flowers and chocolates and texts and phone calls – and begged me to come back. We met, talked about everything and he promised his long-standing affair with his boss was over. So, rightly or wrongly – well, most probably wrongly – I agreed to go back to him.'

'Gosh,' I mutter inadequately.

'Yeah, I know. But the worst part is, when he told his mistress I'd left him, *she* called the whole thing off. Turns out the most attractive thing about Isaac, to her, was me – me and the kids; his unavailability. The minute he was single and free to do whatever she wanted him to do, whenever she wanted him to do it, the fire went out for her. She dumped him and sacked him, both in the same meeting. Just like that.' She clicks her fingers.

'So it wasn't his burning love for you that made him beg you to come back?'

'No, not entirely. But, for better or for worse, we're now back together. And he's promised me no more affairs, no more open marriage garbage.'

'But now he hasn't got any income, either.'

'That's right. Which makes him all the more committed to the cafe. If we can work together, as a couple, and make some money for ourselves, as a family, we just might be able to survive, marriage and kids intact.'

'So the cafe is marriage counselling of sorts for you?'

'Oh no!' She laughs. 'We tried that crap years ago – waste of time and money.'

Talk about a rotten reputation – poor old counselling's got a really bad name.

'Yeah.' She sighs. 'We went every week for four years. Until I found out Isaac was sleeping with the counsellor. Had been for three of those four years.'

'Oh,' I say and look at the beautifully behaved Samia. 'Last of the red-hot lovers, your Isaac.'

'Hooh!' exclaims Shoshie. 'Anyway. I feel so much better now I've got all that off my chest. Now. The caff. Where were we?'

'Staff. And hey! If relationships are so strained when you become parents, why don't we get a counsellor on board? Someone who counsels couples with kids as a specialty.'

'Brilliant!' Shoshie looks vibrant and young and full of beans again. 'And what about a *Supernanny*-type, too?'

'Yes! God knows Joey and I could use some time with her. And maybe I could get some tips to nip the newborn baby's inevitable bad behaviour in the bud before it really takes root.'

'It'll be the best thing that's ever happened to you, this baby. Honestly, Rox. You and Jack will be better and

91

stronger and Joey will be a fabulous big sister. And you'll be part-owner/manager of the first cafe for mums and kids in the world! What more could you want?'

'For Isaac to concentrate on what he's doing and not shag every woman that comes into his eyeline?'

'Yes, well ... It's our last-ditch attempt at making it work – he knows the stakes are high. And I just *feel* he's going to be faithful, strong, a fantastic provider, a whizz with the financials and the perfect family man from now on. You just wait and see.'

'Hmm.' I'm unconvinced. 'He jolly well better be.'

'And maybe,' she picks Samia up and rocks her gently side to side, 'we could make it a real family business. Maybe Jack could get involved, too. He's in IT, isn't he? He could set up a website and we could do e-newsletters for our members.'

'We'll need a Twitter account, Facebook ...'

'Yep. And now all we need is to secure that $100,000 loan, a decent name, the perfect premises and we're away!' Shosh sighs happily.

I can't help feeling as if my heart's going to pop, as Jack used to say, with the sheer joy of knowing we're creating something fantastic for the exhausted, cranky, fed-up and ostracised parents of Bondi.

'Bring me your tired, your poor ...' I declare, standing up, hand on heart, my eyes fixed on a point somewhere in the middle distance.

'You're nuts!' Shoshie laughs. 'Oh, Roxy. Do you think

it'll work? Think it'll make a difference? Make us some money – make us all happy?'

'You betcha!' I beam at her.

Because it could, it really could. It could take off in a big way. It could be massive. Huge. Couldn't it? It's possible. More than possible. *Likely*. Most likely. Probable, even.

'It's almost a dead cert!' I say.

Now, how's *that* for positive thinking?

When I was pregnant with Joey, I opted to have an amniocentesis at Queen Charlotte's in London. It was pretty awful, but over fairly fast. And the best thing about it was we knew there'd be no surprises when she was born other than learning her sex. But now, nearly four years on, the hospital in Sydney is recommending I have a CVS because I'm so old. I'm practically Jurassic in their eyes, it seems.

Jack was with me for nearly every antenatal appointment then – and especially when I had the amnio, holding my hand. But this time round, this is the first time he's accompanied me to the hospital.

I ask the receptionist whether it's going to be transvaginal or abdominal. And guess what? Yep, all that pain of a bikini wax for nothing – the needle's going through my stomach.

'Don't be such a big wuss,' says Jack to calm my nerves.

'I'm not! How would you like it if they stuck a massive needle in your tummy?'

'I wouldn't make a song and dance about it like you're doing. Stoic, me – I take my pain like a man.' He smiles, thumping his fist on to his chest like Tarzan.

'Like a man?' I say. 'You mean whinge and cry and moan and start mumbling about making a will as though you're at death's door when you've only got a cold?'

'It was flu,' he says indignantly. 'Swine flu, probably. But anyway, they give you an anaesthetic—'

'Which in itself is horrendous! And it just shows you how painful the CVS is if they have to numb you first.'

'Roxane Carmichael?' asks a woman in a white coat.

'That's us!' I shoot out of my chair and grin at her like a loon.

'This way, please,' she says, guiding us down the corridor.

They tell me what they're going to do, get me to sign some forms and eventually start. They squeeze gel on to my tummy and do a scan.

'We don't want to know the sex by the way,' I say, distracted from the imminent pain by the grainy picture on the screen of what I guess is our baby.

'Our lips are sealed,' says the female doctor. 'But we won't know, either, unless he – or she – moves away from there ... Come on, Baby, move!'

She pushes down hard on the transducer into my flesh and tries to make the baby shift its position. For about twenty minutes.

'If it doesn't happen in the next ten minutes, I'm going

to have to go and pick Joey up,' says Jack, looking down at me.

'Oh no! Move, Baby – get a wriggle on!'

But it doesn't. So Jack kisses me, tells me I'll be fine and leaves me alone with the doctors.

'At last!' says the female doctor, smiling at me. 'Thank you, Junior! He's ... it's moved! Now, let's do this thing. Roxane, you will feel a slight sting, more of a scratch, really – that's the anaesthetic – and then nothing, but a tiny bit of pulling from the inside.'

'Great,' my mouth twitches, 'I can hardly wait.'

Eventually, I dare to open my eyes and exhale.

'Is that it?'

'Done,' she says. 'All over, now. Are you OK?'

'Hoo. Relieved that's finished. Can you tell anything from what you've seen so far? Does everything look all right?'

'I can't tell you much until we get the results. But it all looks good to me. Don't worry so much. Chromosomal abnormalities are very rare and it's a good sign that you've made it past twelve weeks without incident, so fingers crossed it will all be OK.'

They make me lie there for about ten minutes, until I feel ready to get up and go into another room, where they give me Panadol, a cup of tea and a biscuit. I ask for more biscuits and they happily oblige (they're Tim Tams, a particularly moreish Aussie biscuit, sort of like a Penguin – always difficult to have just one). They say I'll probably get cramps, like period pain for a short while, and that's normal. So, too, is getting a tiny bit of spotting. They're all very reassuring and motherly and that cuppa is the best one I've had for ages. Probably because it's not decaf.

Left alone in the room, I notice there's music playing softly, barely audibly. It's that Bangles 'Manic Monday' song again. What's the story with Sydney's love affair with this song? It seems to be on high rotation everywhere – everywhere *I* go, anyway. And even if it's not on, it's playing repeatedly in my head, on a loop with whatever ad jingles I can't shake.

I look around at the posters adorning the walls about post-natal depression and breastfeeding being best. I clutch the side of my stomach when I feel the dull ache of the cramps and remember the ordeal both Joey and I went through trying to get the hang of breastfeeding. And the way I was made to feel like a total failure as a mum when I made the decision to feed Joey exclusively with formula.

I check my phone. Jack's texted telling me that Joey's fine and to text him when I'm on my way home.

And get a taxi – I'll pay 4 it, he writes.

'My hero,' I say out loud.

Bleep! Another text from Jack.

> Only because I have to make Joey's
> dinner, get her in the bath and put her
> to bed – otherwise I'd be there to pick
> you up! Xxx

Awww.

Bleep!

All of a sudden it's like Piccadilly Circus on my phone. It's a text from Shoshanna.

> What about Mums Aloud? For the
> cafe? Or should that be Allowed?!?!

Like it! I text back.

Or The Kids' Cafe? She texts again.

Not so much, I answer, humming The Bangles' tune.

'*It's just another manic mum-day, whoa, whoa,*' I hear myself singing.

I sit bolt upright, ignoring the cramps.

'Manic Mum-Day! Instead of Monday, Mum-Day. Would that work? Manic Mum-Day. As a name for a cafe? What about the full bit? Just Another Manic Mum-Day. Hmm. Bit long, isn't it? Signwriter'll cost a fortune. We'll need a jaunty font ... I like it, though. It's got a certain ring to it. What if we shorten it? Just go with the acronym – JAMM? Well, it's just how we mums feel most of the time, in a jam. And how cosy and sweet and safe and warm and comforting does JAMM sound? Yes. Just Another Manic Mum-Day. I LOVE it!' I shriek out loud.

'You all right in here?' The concerned-looking receptionist sticks her head round the door.

'Yes! Sorry – just a bit excited,' I answer.

'Take it easy, now, won't you?'

I nod emphatically while my fingers fumble with my phone.

Call off the dogs! I text Shoshie. *I've got it!*

Chapter 8

Jack's back from an obviously exhausting ride on the MLC and is now ensconced in the front room, watching *Air Crash Investigation* while Joey and I rummage about in the kitchen, finding things to put in the fruit salad she's desperate to make.

'Fruit salad, fruit salad,' she sings. 'Yummy, yummy.'

'No – you promised me you wouldn't sing that again if I helped you actually make one, now, didn't you? Hmm? That's enough Wiggles, thank you.' I point my index finger at her and raise my eyebrows higher and higher until I can feel the wrinkles carving ever-deepening crevices into my forehead.

'Sorry, Mummy.' She laughs.

'That's OK,' I respond wearily. 'Now, what next?'

She grabs a handful of blueberries – the furry ones having already been chucked out by me seconds earlier – and says:

'I'm sprinkling blueberries over strawberries and it

looks like big, fat, navy blue raindrops plopping on to a red, freckly face.'

She casts me a sideways glance and smiles coyly. Who says she's watched too much Nigella with her mummy?

'What do you know about running a cafe?' shouts Jack from the front room. 'Or any business for that matter?'

'Nothing much,' I bellow back. 'But it's a great idea, don't you think?'

No reply comes, save for a 'Dohhh! That's gotta hurt!' a few seconds later.

'Have we got any icing sugar, Mummy?' Joey asks. I've figured out that she only calls me 'Mummy' when she wants something – and 'Mum' when she's coming over all stroppy-teenager and is annoyed with me. Not surprisingly, I hear 'Mum' the most.

'No – and you don't need it on fruit salad, it's sweet enough,' I say, firmly but fairly. 'Just like you.'

'But you are going to keep your real job, aren't you?' It's Jack, re-joining our conversation after being diverted by a particularly nasty air disaster.

'Um … yeah, I suppose,' I answer. 'Until it takes off and I go on maternity leave, anyway. Not that I get any maternity leave, having only been there five minutes.'

'Seems like a pretty stupid time to start up a business, doesn't it? GFC and all that? Will Shoshanna work there full-time?'

'Can Gila come for a sleepover, Mummy? Pleeeeease?' Joey pipes up.

'Yeah, she will.'

'YAY!' Joey does a little jump up off the kitchen chair she's standing on.

'No!' I grab her and steady her on the chair. 'No, that's dangerous, Joey. And I mean Shoshanna will work at the cafe full-time – not that Gila can come for a sleepover.'

'But Mummy!'

'I said no, Joey. Now just accept it.' I try my best authoritative voice but it wavers a bit, betraying my guilt. Guilt about not being there for her all day every day and then denying her something she really wants that would be a load of fun for her. And a wrecker's yard to tidy up for me.

'You're too young,' I add.

'YOU are a meanie, Mum.' She almost explodes with rage and jumps down off the chair, running out of the kitchen into her bedroom.

'That went well,' I mutter to myself and finish off making the fruit salad.

'Squirt half a lemon over it to stop it going brown,' I hear my mum say, and so do exactly as I'm told, just before I put the big glass bowl in the fridge.

I walk into the front room and flop on to the couch. It's this great big chocolate-brown thick corduroy number which has a 'chaise' bit. Jack's commandeered this bit as his permanently, so I prop myself up with cushions at the other end, in a corner, and stretch my legs out that way.

'Ugh,' I groan. '*Air Crash Investi*-blimmin'-*gation* again, is it?'

'You love it,' he responds, not taking his eyes off the screen.

We sit there, physically – and, dare I say it, emotionally – miles away from each other, watching dodgy re-enactments of horrific plane crashes and I wonder what he's thinking.

'How's work?' I venture.

'Busy,' he answers.

I want to know how he feels about the baby. There's only twenty-five weeks to go now … *only* twenty-five weeks? That's forever! But we haven't really discussed anything baby-related yet – the most we've said is when I mentioned maternity leave just now.

'I should feel the baby move soon, in a few weeks,' I say brightly.

'Uh-huh,' is the best he can do.

I give it up as a bad job. I mean, if he wanted to talk, he would. It's just a pity that when I want to chat, feel closer to him, he's so distant from me it sometimes makes me feel like he doesn't care.

Still, at least this gives me something to bung up on the website tomorrow, in the bit about what we watched on TV. How many more women out there are just like me, having to suffer through their husbands' questionable viewing choices? In reverent silence? Must be millions.

'Ugh, adverts,' he grunts as he gets up to go to the kitchen to get a cold glass of water. 'Want anything?'

'No, I'm OK,' I say, as that all-too-familiar tune starts up on the telly.

Yes we wanna ... talk about it ...

The song fades into the background and a friendly, good-looking older man in a white coat perches on the end of a desk and speaks ever so sincerely to the camera:

'If you're in the rel from hell, don't dwell waiting for the death-knell – gi's a bell and run pell-mell down to your local Rels 'R' Us!'

He laughs, his eyes creasing up at the sides, making crow's feet look sexy all of a sudden.

'We're the relationship experts and we've never met a problem we couldn't fix. We specialise in couples counselling and, for couples with kids? We know you've got it tougher than most. So before you front up to divorce court and break up your happy home, come and see us for a chat. We promise we'll listen – if you promise you'll talk ... from the heart.'

Woe is your heart ...

A blonde girl in a dazzling white sundress laughs as she runs slo-mo through a daisy-studded green meadow. A dark-haired man in a white shirt and trousers chases after her and then it cuts to the pair of them lying under a willow tree, holding buttercups under their chins and then collapsing into each other's embrace, snogging the other one's face off. Next thing you know, two white-haired twin five-year-old girls in mini versions of their mum's white dress gambol into view and jump on their apparent parents, all of them tumbling about in bliss. It's the picture of perfectly happy family life. Something stirs in my heart and I realise I badly want a piece of that action.

Jack walks back into the front room and plonks himself down on to his bit of the couch, the memory foam yielding to his shape.

'Hey! Maybe we should go to counselling,' I say excitedly, like I'm suggesting we go to Alton Towers or hot air ballooning.

'What?' Jack splutters on his water. 'Individually or together?'

'Together. As a couple.'

'Why? We're all right, aren't we?'

'Well, yeah, I suppose. *All right* . . .'

'Only all right?'

'Well, yeah. I mean we're not exactly setting the world alight, are we? And we can do better than all right. We rarely talk about important things – you know, like how we feel about each other and Joey and—'

'Yes, we do – that's *all* we talk about!'

'But not in any *real* way. You'd always rather watch *Air Crash Investigation* or *MythBusters* – or go for a ride on the MLC than talk to me.'

'That's not true! It's just that at the end of a day we're both so knackered, all we can do is watch five minutes of telly before we pass out.'

'But I'm always up for talking – much more than watching telly.'

'Hmm.' He sounds as though he just might be coming round to the idea. Or, at least, he's not as totally opposed as he was a few seconds ago. Then again, maybe he's just biting his tongue, deftly avoiding a row.

'Listen, there's a time and a place and I'm willing to admit that sometimes – rarely – I may go a bit overboard and talk too much, but you never listen, you just hear background noise, me blathering on.'

He looks at me, surprised to hear this, and half smiles.

'So, yes, maybe, on occasion, I do go on a bit. And we definitely have money issues—'

'I won't be able to carry us all on just my salary when the baby comes – not when redundancies are rumoured and we could be well and truly rooted any day now—'

'Speaking of, that's another thing – maybe counselling would help us communicate better in the ... ah ... in the *bedroom*.' I wink awkwardly at him.

'Normally I'd say we can't afford it, but you'd jump down my throat about the bike if I did.' He sighs like a beaten man. 'And I'm as up for some rumpy as the next bloke, so instead I'll say yes. Go on. Let's do it.'

Just then, Joey comes back into the room, stands in the doorway and stares at the TV.

'Not FAIR!' she squeaks, stamping her little foot. 'You've had your TV on all day! I haven't seen any kids' TV for *aaaages*!'

She's right about the first part, but the second bit's an out and out lie.

'That's not true, Jo—' I start.

'It IS! It IS true. You are ruining my whole LIFE!' And she finishes it.

'Come on, now, honey. Do you want CBeebies? Shall we put that on for you? Only if you stop shouting and crying, though. Do you want CBeebies?' Jack talks her down with his dulcet tones.

She nods her head slowly and deliberately and climbs on to the couch, snuggling up to Jack, who's making busy with the remote.

'Pots and pans will start to smell, if we don't wash them really well,' sing *Big Cook, Little Cook*.

'They're right, Joey – want to come and help me do the washing up?' I ask her, remembering I read somewhere that getting older kids to help around the house makes them feel special when lots of family attention is being focused on an impending new baby.

'No, thank you,' she chirps sweetly.

Ask a stupid question . . .

Jack's taken Joey to the park, so I seize the day and jump on the Skype to Charlie.

'He said that? Really? He voluntarily, of his own volition, no bribery or beer involved – he said he'd go to *counselling* with you?'

'Yup.'

'Unbelievable.' Charlie screws up her face, as if she's in pain.

'So we're going to do it!'

'God, how ... how grown up of you.'

'Yeah.' I giggle at the thought of me acting like an adult. 'I just want to get him talking more, before the baby comes. Iron out a few of our rougher edges. Hopefully the counsellor will be able to convince Jack that it's good to bang on and we'll learn how to talk to each other properly, without everything turning into a huge argument or a few days of no speaks.'

'Wow. Good luck with that. Make sure you get a man, though. Men have a tendency to run off with their female therapists. Just look at Tony Soprano and Doctor Melfi.'

'He fancied her, but she was having none of it. And anyway, totally different scenario. Tony was a killer, remember – a Mafioso.'

'Whatevs.' She yawns. 'So what else is happening?'

'Um ... apart from my silent worlds of work and home and getting really, massively fat, you mean?'

Charlie smiles wanly.

'But jeez, Charlie – how much weight have you lost?'

'Dunno. Didn't think I'd lost any.' She looks down at her chest and arms and pats her stomach with her scrawny right hand.

'God, yeah, you better be careful – I know you love your skinny jeans and everything, but the Biafran, size-zero look is so unattractive. Particularly on us women of *un certain ahhj*,' I say, trying to sound French.

'You're right. I'm forty-five! I'm too old for all this!' She waves her hand at the screen, overreacting a smidge, if you ask me.

'All this new-fangled technology? Know what you mean!' I say. 'You should try uploading images and downloading html thingies. It's a complete mystery to me. I'll be sacked for total incompetence any day now.'

'You won't be able to work when you've had the baby, anyway. Will you?'

'Um ... yes, I will!' I sit on my hands, getting all excited. 'Me and another mum from Joey's pre-school are going to open a cafe!'

Charlie doesn't look up from her probably concave stomach.

'A cafe for mums and their kids!' I squeal. 'We're going to be mumpreneurs!'

'Oh yeah?' She looks up at me, raising one perfectly sugared eyebrow.

'Yeah ... What's wrong, Chuck? Are you OK?' I ask.

'Oh, I don't know. Sorry, Rox. I just can't keep anything down. Even the thought of a bacon sarnie makes me gag,' she says, holding her throat as if she may just throw up right here and now.

'How are things with John? Caught him at it yet?'

'It's not some playground game, you know, Roxane,' she snaps. 'This is not some idiotic trifling gossip on *Neighbours*.'

'No, no, I'm sorry – I didn't mean to—'

'It's worse than that,' she says tightly.

'What could be worse than *Neighbours* – utter tosh.' I smile, hoping to see her lighten up as I steer her into familiar waters, calmer seas.

'Now, don't laugh, don't tell me you told me so and definitely, DEFINITELY do not say "Congratulations".'

'What is it, Charlie?'

Suddenly her image disappears. But there, in the inky blackness on the screen, I hear a small, weak, scared and lonely voice – a voice barely recognisable as Charlie's – say:

'I'm ... oh, God ... I'm pregnant.'

'You're WHAT?' I bark.

'You heard.' She sniffs.

'But I thought you and John were ... estranged.'

'We're going through a bit of a rocky patch at the moment, but we're still on shagging terms.'

'Wow. Jesus. How do you feel?'

'Wiped out. Sick. Tired. And terrified.'

'Welcome to my world.' I smile.

'What are we like, Rox? We're too old to be new mums. *Again!*'

'Tell me about it.'

'Well, how are you feeling now? How are you coping?'

'I'm making a lot more lists, getting a lot more sleep, I've totally axed the cigarettes, there's definitely no drinking and I've pretty much come round to the idea. I'm even almost looking forward to it,' I say, surprising myself with how far I've come. 'And you will, too, Chuckie. You might be freaking out now, but you'll soon get used to it. What did John say when you told him?'

'I haven't told him yet. Thought I'd figure out how I felt about the baby first and then deal with him. I'm only five weeks.'

'But you will tell him soon, won't you? Before you do anything rash. He has a right to know. Chuck? Charlie? Hello?'

The words 'call dropped' flash on to the Skype screen. I quickly try her mobile and her landline, but I'm met with her voicemail at every turn. I send her an email, letting her know of my concern and imploring her to call me as soon as she can.

Charlie and I have always enjoyed a close, symbiotic relationship, you see, and now I can really feel Charlie's pain – her fear, anxiety and loneliness – even all these millions of miles away from each other.

I rub my fast-swelling belly and forage in the fridge for something sweet – anything to get rid of the bad taste in my mouth and the uneasy feeling I'm left with in the pit of my stomach.

Chapter 9

At the sides of the escalators at Kings Cross station in Sydney, there are adverts that you can look at (as opposed to staring at the arse two steps ahead of you) during your journey to the outside world or the platform below. Just like in London on the Tube.

I often marvel at the ads for the railway system itself: I mean, did you know that a train can not only take you home after a hard day's graft, it can transport you to the Blue Mountains, too – or even Dubbo Zoo for a great day out? It's amazing – a train can take you almost anywhere you want to go!

Well, *duh*, as they say round here, usually in a particularly dumb, drongo-ish drawl to accentuate the stupidity of stating the absolutely bleeding obvious.

But only this morning do I notice how patronising these ads are.

The one that really takes the biscuit is a big blown-up photo of a woman pushing a pram. Emblazoned across said pic are the words 'Travelling with a PRAM?' with 'pram' all bold and extra-big like this is the most dramatic thing to ever even *think* about doing.

In smaller type underneath the probing question, it says:

'Remember to hold on to your pram.'

And underneath *that*, in smaller type, the phone number you can call to get your eager hands on the railways' free pram safety DVD.

Really – how dim do they think mums are?

I say this out loud, I'm so incensed, as I walk to the ticket barriers. And then inspiration hits.

Phil's been on at me to localise the website's content a bit more (as opposed to simply ripping off US site BabyCenter.com, he intimated) and this would be perfect! If I could just take a quick photo of this ad, stick it up on the website under the heading 'How Dumb Do They Think Mums Are?', the comments will come flooding in and the site will instantly have a more local, immediate and Australian feel to it. Two birds, one stone. Brilliant.

I whip the camera out of my bag and take several photos of the poster before the security guards begin to get suspicious and, pleased with myself that I've nearly completed an excellent bit of blogging and I haven't even got into the office yet, I skip off to work.

After I've asked Kylie to transfer the photo to the system, read over the post to ensure there are no heinous typos and put it up on to the site (I still don't know how to do any of this), I ask her if we've received any comments about 'What We Watched Last Night' or any of the other new things I've worked on. As per, her answer's in the negative. So I put on the headphones and have a good old trawl around YouTube for songs about kids and being a kid that are guaranteed to make you cry. I was exceptionally teary today as I left Joey at Shalom! Baby and feel like indulging myself. And I'm going to turn it into a Top Ten list for our Friday Fun Day page/blog/bit, too, so it counts as work.

There's Cat Stevens' 'Father and Son', Harry Chapin singing 'Cat's in the Cradle', Stevie Wonder and 'Isn't She Lovely', John Lennon doing 'Beautiful Boy' ... God, there are loads out there, designed purely to make your mascara run.

I must be crying buckets and sniffing loads, because Kylie taps me on the shoulder, mouthing a concerned, 'Are you OK?'

Wiping my eyes, I tell her it's the songs, pointing at YouTube with my thumb, like a hitchhiker. She doesn't flinch. Doesn't she know Loudon Wainwright singing 'Daughter'? Nup. Surely she knows that really old Australian band, Axiom, doing 'A Little Ray of Sunshine'? Nope. Gilbert O'Sullivan and 'Clair'? *Any* of the classics I've got lined up for my list? Not a single one. I laugh and tell her she's too young, that's her problem. But to myself I'm thinking it's really me who has the problem. I mean,

I'm just too flaming old. Chances are, neither of our two readers will recognise any of these songs, either.

And then we discuss – via internal email, of course, even though she sits right next to me – my plans for the KiddingAround site.

'Once we've redesigned it,' I write, 'it'll get loads more readers. It should look much more feminine, bright oranges and pinks and light greens and loads more white space – assuming that the majority of our readers is female – and we should really calm down on the US content. I'm going to try to get more local news stories about parents up there.'

'Hence the train poster, I see,' Kylie writes back. 'And what about advertising?'

'I imagine once the site looks and sounds loads better, advertisers will be begging to give us their money. Keen as. What do you think?'

'Sounds awesome.'

'Kyles,' I type, 'do you think anyone reads KiddingAround? Do you have access to readership figures? And be honest – I can handle the truth!'

'Oops – got to go. Phil wants me to get him a sandwich.' I can hear her tapping furiously away. 'Want me to pick you anything up while I'm out?'

'Yes, please! Could you grab me a double cheese and tomato toastie with onion and mayo? And a big packet of cheese and onion crisps? Box of Maltesers wouldn't go astray, either, now I think about it … Thanks, Kyles – you're a legend!'

'Crikey – R U pregnant or just hungover?'

She doesn't know, does she?

She can't have guessed.

Can she?

'Chance'd be a fine thing!' I write back. 'Neither – just starving!'

The afternoon passes pleasantly enough, with me stuffed to the gills, 'sharing' a jumbo box of Maltesers with Kylie (who only gets to eat about three, while I greedily scoff handfuls of four at a time) until 4.30 flashes at me from my computer's clock and I get ready to make my exit and get back to North Bondi, where I'll meet Shoshanna and we'll present our business plan for JAMM to the manager of the You Beaut Bank.

Anita's picking up Joey for me this afternoon, which is great, as long as I collect Joey from hers by six-thirty this evening. She's off to a Perky Pensioners poker night at the North Bondi Returned Servicemen's League Club. She says it doesn't start till seven-thirty, but she needs plenty of time to spruce herself up, if she's going to be in with a chance with Ray, an elderly gentleman she's got her eye on.

'Or Tom or Wayne or Alan,' she chuckled down the phone at me. 'Any of 'em'll do. In fact, come one, come all! They can all put their teeth on my bedside table tonight if they play their cards right.'

I try to close my mind's eye to the image of all these

gummy old blokes padding around Anita's bedroom in their Y-fronts, but it's not easy.

Neither has it been easy learning the lines Shosh has given me for our showdown at You Beaut Bank. She says I have to sound confident, pretend to know what I'm on about.

The twelve-year-old manager (Troy, he says his name is in his high, unbroken voice) plays with our professionally printed, colour-coded four-page business plan, flipping pages over and back every few seconds. He says, distractedly, while he reads, that now is the perfect time to launch great business ventures. And if an idea is really good – like ours – they may, indeed, feel compelled to put up the finance.

We sit there while he reads, Shosh concentrating on her posture, correcting her shoulders, straightening her back and placing her cupped hands in her lap. I try to do the same, but I can't get my hands to meet underneath my belly, so instead I rest my hands on the top of my tummy, fingers crossed.

Eventually, Troy looks at me and asks about football.

'Oh, I don't know much about the beautiful game – the "you beaut" game, you might say.' I chuckle, my staccato laugh betraying my nerves.

'Not football, the *footfall*.' He giggles, stealing a swift glance at my tummy.

'Oh! Um, well, I'm still pretty steady on my pins, don't plan to be falling over much for a long time to come, so ...

I won't be carrying plates much as front of house, but will help out when needed, obviously. I will take some time off to have the baby, though—'

'Ha ha! Awesome. No! Foot*fall*, the amount of potential customers passing by your premises every day!'

Shosh and I swap concerned glances.

'We haven't exactly found any premises yet, Troy.' Shosh smiles. 'But we know we want it to be in Bondi where there are hordes of parents, millions of mums, just like us, who are crying out for their own place to go, a place for them to call their own.'

'Yeah,' I join in, 'if we could get somewhere on the main strip, someplace on Didgeridoo Drive, with a view of the beach, it would be amazing. Awesome, I mean.'

'Awesome and way beyond your budget.' Troy titters.

'Well, even in the well-heeled back streets there are plenty of places that you could turn into cute little cafes. You wouldn't get so much of the tourist trade there, but definitely a steady flow of lucrative local parents and carers,' Shosh says, sounding as though she knows whereof she speaks.

'Awesome, awesome. Now, how does your marketing and advertising pan out?' Troy asks with a grin.

'We've got some online ads all ready to go, we'll get on Facebook and Twitter and we'll have the usual sandwich boards out the front. But we know our market and we know that word of mouth is stronger in the parenting community than anything else. So hopefully, once people have sampled our wares, word will spread around the pre-schools, day care centres, schools, mother and baby groups, et cetera, and profit will come calling in no time,' I say confidently, as per Shoshanna's instructions.

'Awesome. Would you pay yourselves a wage?'

'Yes,' I say – at exactly the same time as Shosh says a louder, more assured, 'No.'

'How will you two live, then? I don't want the deaths of two families from starvation on my conscience!' Troy smiles.

'What we mean,' Shosh goes on, 'is that *initially* we won't receive a wage. But my husband, Isaac, will be the general manager, so our family will be fine. And Roxane's husband has a good job in IT, so no one's going to starve.'

'Not with the amount of pies and pastries the cafe will be producing,' I say, mouth starting to water at the prospect. 'Our pastry chef will see to that.'

'Which brings me to one of my major concerns about your cafe.' Troy clears his throat and goes all deadly serious. 'The number of staff. Is it really necessary to have a pastry chef? As well as a barista? Seems to me you've got a rather large payroll for such a small business, what with childminders and managers, chefs and waiting staff, too ...'

Hearing Troy say it *does* make it sound a little over-indulgent – maybe just a little bit too ambitious for us, two rookie mumpreneurs in their infancy. But Shosh holds firm.

'Well,' she sits up even straighter, 'maybe we could lose the pastry chef. But we've been through it several times and we believe that the only way to make our cafe a success, to make it stand out, is to do it this way. We envisage paying 25% of our revenue to rent, a further 25% to the payroll, 35% to supplies and the maintenance and the last 15% we will see as profit – but place in a separate account for contingency money.'

Troy nods slowly, Shosh looks pleased with herself and I look up at the ceiling, trying feebly to add up all those percentages in my head, see if they come to a hundred.

'Once we start turning a profit, Roxane and I will look at paying ourselves a wage – but in the interim, we're both more than happy to take the hit and plough whatever we can straight back into the business.'

Troy clasps his hands together, turns his two forefingers into a steeple, taps his chin and leans his elbows on the desk.

'Let's get down to tin tacks, here – how much profit do you hope to make on a monthly basis in the first year?'

'All things taken into consideration – staff, overheads, unforeseen circumstances – we guesstimate $1000-a-month pure profit,' says self-assured Shoshie.

'Ooh, guesstimations make me nervous.' Troy winces. 'But, well, if we *were* to lend you the money, when would you be able to pay us back?'

'If we could negotiate nothing to pay for the first year,

119

0% interest for the second and the APR for the third, would you feel comfortable with that?' I say, coming over all *Dragons' Den* hardball, but not having the faintest clue what any of it means.

'I'm not sure about paying absolutely nothing for the first year – but 0% interest is something we could look at if you started paying us back immediately.' Troy smiles. 'Look, I think you've really got something here. I told my mum about it last night and she thinks it's a fantastic idea. She loves it. She says that even though you two don't have any real business experience, managing a family and little kids is exactly the same and the best practice there is.'

Aww. A boy who loves his mummy. And listens to her. Because she's right! Shosh and I can't help ourselves and, like a synchronised sighing team, we cock our heads to one side and smile at him, looking like his bursting-with-pride aunts or something.

'Ah, what the heck.' Troy beams. 'Let's do it!'

Shosh and I both shoot up out of our seats.

'Woohoo!' whoops Shosh.

'Yay, JAMM!' I shriek.

Troy darts out from behind his desk and we both give him a hug. His glasses end up a little skewiff and he emerges blushing, looking a tad more dishevelled than he did when our meeting began, but he seems happy.

'The only fly in the ointment,' he coughs, straightening up his glasses, 'is that we can't take as big a risk as we'd like to on you. So, for the time being, would $75,000 be enough to get you started?'

'Yes,' Shosh and I say swiftly, in unison, lest he change his mind.

'I've got a feeling about this cafe. And my feelings are rarely wrong. But do take some advice, please, ladies,' he says sternly. 'Expect the unexpected, *listen* to your customers, keep your staff in the loop with regular updates so that you're always, always on the same page and, last but not least, *enjoy* yourselves. Follow those four rules, keep your fingers crossed and I'll see you on the cover of *Business Review Weekly* in no time.'

Gor – Troy has single-handedly, in only thirty minutes, completely changed my mind about bankers. Turns out they *do* care. They *are* human. Well, this one is, anyway. And even though I'm sure his bottom line is still profit, profit, profit, at least he's had the imagination, the foresight, the *cojones* to see what a winner our cafe will be. What a man!

'Tell your mum she can come in anytime for free coffees,' I say, delirious with delight.

'*Discounted* coffees,' Shosh smiles, 'it's business, after all.'

'Awesome,' squeaks Troy. 'To the power of a hundred!'

On our way through the front door to our flat, my mobile bleeps, letting me know a message has just landed in my inbox.

It's a text from Kylie.

> You have GOT to watch the news!
> 6 p.m., Channel 9 x

Joey jumps on to Jack, who's lying on the couch, watching, fortuitously, the Channel 9 news.

'Every mother's nightmare nearly came true for a Melbourne woman today as she let go of her pushchair for just one second, only to watch it career on to the train tracks, right in front of an oncoming train.'

Oh, God. How awful!

'This CCTV footage shows the dreadful moment when a young mum, waiting on a railway platform, let go of her pram to [slight pause for effect] *fix her hair.'*

The grainy CCTV pictures on the screen render me speechless.

'Miraculously, Baby is unhurt and doing well. Mum, on the other hand, is understandably shaken and says she will always use the pushchair's brake from now on. A spokesperson for In Train, the New South Wales branch of the national railway network told us that they are not responsible for this accident and will not take any blame as there are warnings everywhere on their railway system, urging mothers to always hold on to their prams.'

Up flashes an image of the poster.

'A cautionary tale for all new mums out there, to be sure. And on a lighter note, the YouTube clip of this potentially

devastating accident has had the most viewings of any Australian clip on the international video-uploading site ever, and it's only been up live for three hours. So, it's another worldwide first for Aussies. Oi, oi, oi! Now, what's happening with the weather, Sam? Is it going to be another perfect day here in paradise tomorrow?'

'Oh no,' I murmur.

'You've got to get over all this whingeing about the weather, Rox – it's getting—'

'No, no! It's not that!' I spin round and tell Jack all about the poster at Kings Cross and the genius idea of putting it up on the website and taking the mickey out of it.

'What was the heading?' he asks, with a slight smirk.

'Um,' I wince, '"How Dumb Do They Think Mums Are?"'

'Well, there's your answer right there.' He points at the TV.

'Still, at least it's home-grown and topical,' I say, trying to look on the bright side. 'And it's already had one comment. Quite funny it was, too – it said: "That railways pram safety DVD sounds like a riot – even more laughs than an episode of *In the Family Way*!". So at least it's controversial, sparking debate and opinion and comment with our readers.'

'Rea*der*, singular.' Jack grins. 'That was me!'

'What? I thought you were too stressed and crazy-busy at work to look at silly parenting sites.'

'I was being supportive!' he hoots.

My phone beeps. It's Kylie texting me again.

> HA! I wouldn't worry about it – no
> one reads KiddingAround anyway! X

Chapter 10

When I finally arrive at work the next day, I'm greeted by a few sheets of paper sitting on my keyboard.

On the fluoro-yellow Post-it note stuck to the front, it says:

Detailed instructions for all commands on the system! Online for dummies – easy! K x

She must be getting sick of doing all the posting and everything technical for me. And who can blame her?

'Oh, great!' I say.

'Shush!' she replies.

'Oops – sorry,' I whisper as I carefully place my handbag on the floor and tiptoe over to the kettle to make a cup of dreary decaf tea. I nod good morning to the boss, who's staring at me unnervingly and leaning back in his leather office chair.

Is it my imagination, or is he looking at my tummy? Uh-oh. He knows. He must do, what with all the food I'm putting away, and never going to the after-work drinks.

Then again, he might think that's what parents are like: unsocial teetotallers whose idea of fun is a sausage and egg McMuffin – without the hangover.

Nah, he knows. He definitely knows I'm pregnant.

'Ah, Roxane,' he says, making me jump.

'Oh! Morning!' I say, trying to come across as breezy but simply sounding guilty.

'Can I borrow you for a moment?' he asks, jutting his chin out as he straightens his tie. 'Just a quick word . . . '

Oh, great. Here we go. Nothing good has ever followed those two phrases in my extensive experience of working in offices. Ever. A sacking or a verbal warning, maybe – but never praise or a promotion, that's for sure.

Painfully aware of my swelling stomach, I sit in the interview room – sweltering just as I did the day of my interview – and proceed to get a rollocking about yesterday's railway-poster-post debacle.

'It's this kind of thing that could get us taken off the air entirely!' he says.

'I'm sorry, I . . . ' I'm lost for words a bit now, possibly because I'm so relieved he wants to tear strips off me for something other than being pregnant. Maybe he doesn't know, maybe he hasn't twigged yet.

'I mean, it's a parenting site, for Christ's sake! You can't call our readers dumb! Or dim!'

'But I didn't! I said it was the *railways* who must think—'

'Exactly!' he squeaks.

I sit back further in my chair, surprised by his outburst.

'OK, OK,' he says, calming down a bit. 'Thing is, Roxane, I'm new to this, too. I'm the youngest MD in Sydney business history and I don't want to cock it up. This could be the beginning of great things for me – and you – if we play our cards right and, well, I don't want to pile on the pressure, but KiddingAround needs to start doing a whole lot better if it's going to survive and I need to start acting like a proper MD. So I'm going to have to come down on you pretty hard.'

'Like, how hard?' I wince.

'Look,' he leans in, speaking quietly, 'I like what you're doing with the site – I don't have kids yet, so I don't know about lots of the stuff you're posting, but I do know that you can't go around insulting your readership.'

At this Kylie knocks on the door, comes in, hands a document to Phil and backs out, closing the door behind her.

'And I've already had the CEO of Maverick on the phone to me this morning – who had the Chief of Railways on the phone to him last night, rousing on him about this. So I suggest you fix it up ASAP. Or you might find KiddingAround and yourself offline for good!' Phil shouts loudly enough for anyone – nay, *everyone* – outside the room to hear.

Jeepers. No need for him to go so over the top just for appearances' sake. Everyone knows I'm new to this whole website, online malarkey.

Luckily it only takes me a few seconds (I'm getting really quite good at this upbeat, optimistic thinking now) before I manage to find and grab hold of the one and only positive I can see in this whole shambles.

'At least we know we have a reader.' I smile tentatively. 'The Railways Chief, I mean.'

'Just sort it out.' He smiles back. 'But Rox? No more working from home. Not even if Joey's sick. I'm sorry, but them's the rules.'

Bloodied, but unbowed – well, not exactly *bloodied*, and only the teensiest bit bowed (Phil's not really scary management material) – I follow Kylie's excellent instructions and put up the YouTube clip of the woman on the train platform, turn the story into a warning for all pram-pushers using public transport out there and leave the railways poster up there, commenting on their responsible, timely advertising.

Then, the bit truly between my teeth, I put up an ad for Just Another Manic Mum-Day, Sydney's Premier Cafe for Parents and Carers.

Overtired? Overstressed? Over it?
Sounds like you're having ...

JUST ANOTHER MANIC MUM-DAY!

But don't drop your bundle just yet,
strap the kids down and come on over to the
coolest new cafe in town. Grab a cake and a
coffee and take a load off with our –

* Fab food

* Registered childminders

* Sympathetic ear and liquor licence!

Address and phone numbers TBA. All enquiries to
Roxy@MaverickMedia.com.au

JUST ANOTHER MANIC MUM-DAY!

It's the cafe you've been dreaming of,
where taking it easy is always
the order of the day.

Watch this space!

An email from Kylie pops up as soon as I've finished.

'What was that chat with Phil all about?!?!' she asks.

'The pram on the platform post – tell you more later!'
I type back, knowing full well that I won't have a chance
to go into it before the day is over.

'BTW, there's a comment about "What We Watched
Last Night" waiting for you in the queue,' she writes.

I gasp excitedly, saying, *I knew it! I knew it!* to myself,
and check the list of instructions she's written for me so I
can find my way around the indecipherable system and
get to the comments bit.

I quickly click on the comment pertaining to my 'What
We Watched Last Night' post about *In the Family Way*,

hoping against all hope that it's not Jack being supportive again, but a real live reader. Imagine!

My eyes nearly pop out of my head as I read it.

'*Who gives a FUCK what you watched last night?!*'

The second Joey sees me, she throws the Barbie doll she's playing with to the ground, like a baseball player flinging his bat to the side after hitting a potential home run, and bounds full-pelt straight into my groin.

'Mummee!' she shrieks as she flings her arms around my hips.

'Well, hello, gorgeous!' I say and pat the top of her head, stroking her blonde ringlets.

'I missed ya, Mummy!' she says, looking up at me with her massive turquoise-blue eyes.

My heart melts right along with the rest of me.

'I missed you, too, petal.'

'No!' She starts crying, her eyes filling up with water. I knew it was too good to be true. Talk about capricious!

'What? What's wrong? You *didn't* miss me?'

'I mitzvah!' she says.

'Now, just because there are some younger kids here, it doesn't mean that you can speak like a baby. Use your words in a full sentence,' I say.

She harrumphs and stamps her foot, the usual precursor to a mega-tantrum.

'I need a MITZVAH note from YOU. You DIDN'T

write me a MITZVAH NOTE!' she shouts angrily through clenched teeth.

I look pleadingly at one of her teachers, Morah Dinah. 'Mitzvah note?' I ask.

'It's for when Josephine has done something well, helped you or done something all by herself, like getting herself dressed in the morning or tidying her room or helping with the washing up. You tell us about something she's done that makes you proud and we'll read out the notes in class. Then she'll get a sticker!' Morah Dinah says, smiling and ruffling Joey's hair.

'Oh!' I look back down at Joey, who's looking so hard-done-by, so dejected and cruelly neglected that I can't help feeling really sorry for the poor little mite. Even if, simultaneously, I can't think of one single thing she's done lately that's been in any way helpful. I wonder what the word for 'massive hindrance' is in Hebrew.

'I'll write one for you tonight and put it in the box tomorrow morning,' I placate her. Somewhat.

She's obviously totally ticked off with me about this whole mitzvah note farrago and shoots me daggers while grunting and curling her hands tightly into little fists of pent-up fury. I sometimes forget that she's only three and prone to irrational outbursts of frustration, although God knows where she gets her theatrical, over-the-top mannerisms from.

And just as I start thinking about getting a taxi home to nip in the bud any screaming fits and fists-pounding-pavements that might be brewing – I don't think I could cope with that on top of the day I've had – a piercing cry cuts through the cacophony of kids.

'Rox-eeee!'

It's Shoshanna.

'Wanna go to Serenitea?' she says as she prises Gila off her baby sister.

'Not now, Shosh – it's the witching hour. Joey will go nuts if I don't have her dinner ready soon. And I'll go super-nuts if I don't have her in bed, fast asleep, by seven-thirty.'

'No, no – obviously not now! What are you doing later on?'

'Passing out on the couch halfway through *Everybody Loves Raymond*. You know, the usual.'

Joey wails.

'And writing mitzvah notes! Mitzvah notes all night long!' I trill.

Shoshanna snorts and puts her fists on her hips. I've seen her do this a thousand times before, whenever she's talking to Isaac on the phone. She goes quite serious and school marmy, incredulous at the incompetence she has to deal with.

'Of course, of course,' she says quickly. 'How about the weekend, then?'

'Yeah, you betcha!'

'Well, you can't!' she splutters, waving her hands about like she's a sped-up black-and-white minstrel singing

'Mammy'. 'It's closed down, Rox – all boarded-up and everything.'

'No!'

'Ho-ho-ho-ho yes! And guess what?' she adds breathlessly.

'What?'

'We're going to put in an offer!'

'What?'

'We're putting in an offer right now, as a matter of fact – I got Isaac on to it as soon as I saw the For Lease sign on my way here.'

'Oh my God! This is incredible!'

'Don't you worry about a thing, Roxy – with Zac as our finance man, it's all under control.'

'Yeah,' I say, deadpan. 'What could possibly go wrong?'

Shoshie ignores me.

'I'm expecting to hear back from him, saying our offer's been accepted, any minute now.'

'Ooh – it's just like *Location, Location*!' I squeal. 'You know, when Kirstie or Phil phones the estate agent and—'

Shoshanna's mobile beeps.

'That'll be him,' she says and fumbles with her phone. 'Yep, it's him and he says . . .'

'What? What? Quick! What does he say?' Anxiously I rub my tummy.

'YAY! What does he say?' Joey and Gila shriek in

unison, holding hands and jumping up and down.

'And he says ... ' She looks up from her mobile and stops, like she's just about to say the name of the winner for this year's Best Film at the Academy Awards, but is pausing to maximise the tension.

'And he says? What, Shosh?' I cry, the suspense killing me.

'And he says ... '

'It's all yours, ladies,' says a short, dark, curly-haired guy, smugly swinging on the Shalom! Baby child-proof gate.

'Oh!' cries Shosh. 'Isaac! Are you serious? Have we really got Serenitea?'

'Yes, you have. Serenitea is now officially yours.' He beams, bowing his head and pulling his hands into a prayer pose. 'Yeah. Landlord's an old mate of mine from the music biz. Let me have it rent-free for the first three months to give you girls a chance to get the cafe on its feet. It'll be a reduced rate for the second three months, but, after that, full whack for such prime real estate – $1000 a week.'

I don't believe it. It sounds too good to be true.

'Isaac! You're a star!' I shake my head in disbelief and hold out my hand for him to shake.

He kisses it and looks penetratingly deep into my eyes.

'You can thank me later.' He smirks. 'By the way, I've sorted out all the health and safety certs, got your liquor licence in train and all the furniture, equipment and fittings come with the caff as a job lot. Including the head chef and a waiter.'

We all stand there in stunned silence. Even Joey and Gila are quiet, mouths agape.

'Ah, it was nothing. All in a day's work. But right now, let's celebrate. For you, Foxy Roxy, along with my lovely, good lady wife Shoshanna, are now the proud owners of the finest coffee house in the land. Serenitea is dead – long live Just Another Manic Mum-Day!'

And no truer words were ever spoken. Not by Isaac, anyway.

Chapter 11

'Total waste of time and money,' whispers Jack as he flicks through a well-thumbed copy of *Scientific American.*

'Just give it a go.' I elbow him gently in the ribs. 'It's a man, so you won't feel ganged-up-on or intimidated. And I am really impressed that you're doing this with me, by the way.'

'We should be able to sort this out between us at home, by ourselves – not have to pay some jumped-up creep an extortionate amount of money just so he can tell us we need to communicate better. But I am an impressive guy, so . . . ' He half smiles.

Not as stonkingly impressive as the vision I see before me, though, as a tall, dark and unfeasibly handsome George Clooney-alike leans on his office's door jamb and speaks in a voice like cream.

'Roxane? Jack? Do come in. I apologise for the delay – just catching up on some paperwork.'

It's the same guy off the ad for Rels 'R' Us and his

warm smile and firm but friendly handshake make me instinctively fan my face with my hand, like a *Deal Or No Deal* contestant, as we sit down.

'I'm Tarquin and I'll just turn the air-con up,' he says in that deep voice you'd happily drown in.

All this and thoughtful, too.

'Now,' he grins, pulling his chair out from behind his desk and sitting in front of us, his cords shortening considerably to the length of ankle freezers, exposing his mismatching business socks and beaten-up old desert boots, 'first off, before we get down to tin tacks, I'd like to start with a few trust exercises.'

Jack and I swap concerned glances.

'Come on, now, it won't hurt, promise.' Tarquin smiles. 'Stand up, Roxane, in front of Jack. Jack? Hook your arms under Roxane's and stand steady. Roxane? Close your eyes and, when you're ready, fall into Jack's arms. Really let yourself go. Relax. And trust that Jack will catch you.'

The pair of us stand and assume our positions. Jack slides his really rather muscly arms under mine and I close my eyes.

I wait for the feeling of trust to wash over me. To *know* that Jack will catch me.

'I can't!' I open my eyes, laughing nervously. 'I don't want to break his arms with my bulk or anything – maybe he's not strong enough!'

'Of course I am!' Jack's affronted. 'Now stop faffing around and get on with it.'

I close my eyes, but a broad grin comes over me and I open them again.

'I can't do it.' I giggle.

'Don't you trust me?' asks a wounded-sounding Jack.

'Of course I do! I just . . . I'll try again.'

I take a deep breath, close my eyes and try to stop being so silly, only emitting small yelps of hysteria every few seconds.

What's come over you? This is for the good of your marriage! If you have no trust in a relationship, what have you got? Stop being such a wally. Go with the flow, relax and gently fall back . . .

'If you're not going to take this seriously—' Jack whips his arms out from mine and steps to the side just as I come crashing down on to the floor.

I muster a small laugh, but I'm really a bit embarrassed, falling on my bum like that in front of Tarquin.

Jack's breaking ribs, he's howling so hard with laughter, and even Tarquin's sniggering silently, his shoulders shaking as he turns his back to us and shuffles some paper on his desk.

'Sorry about that, Rox.' Jack extends the hand of friendship between sobs of laughter. 'But I thought you weren't going to do it.'

'I'm not a buffoon, you know! Not here for your amusement. And in my condition. Honestly!'

'Sorry, Rox. Really.' He crouches behind me, puts his arms under my armpits and lifts me up effortlessly, helping me regain my ladylike countenance with a guttural 'Oomph' as I land squarely on my feet.

'Oopsy daisy – there you go,' he chirps. 'Honest, Rox, you sounded like you weren't going to do it.'

'I trusted you, didn't I?' I brush myself down. 'Trust*ed*, mind, past tense.'

Tarquin turns round and wipes a tear of mirth from his eye. He sits down in the chair opposite us and clears his throat.

'Don't worry about that,' he reassures us. 'It happens all the time. Doesn't mean much, really – except that it's a good way to break the ice, help me get an idea of the dynamics of the relationship and ease into the nitty gritty of why you're here. And it's good to laugh. No, honestly – what a marriage needs to succeed is love and laughter. And wiv a little bit o' *blooomin'* luck, you should be fine.'

His thumbs stretch out some imaginary braces from his shirt as he puts on a terrible Cockney accent for that last bit.

'So, ah ... would you like to start the talking, Roxane? Ladies first.'

It takes a rather large effort not to swoon at Tarquin – despite the fact he's just been laughing at me – and re-focus on the matter at hand: my and Jack's rocky marriage.

'Um, I dunno,' I say warily, careful not to look to my left and catch Jack's eye. 'I suppose that maybe there's a chance I'm still a teensy bit miffed with him for a few things that he did when we lived in England.'

The air between us fizzes and crackles as Jack bristles.

'Oh yes?' says Tarquin, crossing his long legs and leaning his chin on his right hand, his elbow on the chair's arm. 'Can you expand on that? It's important you tell me everything so I can work out a way to help get your relationship back on track.'

Both Jack and I cross our respective legs at this, our feet pointing away from each other. Tarquin clocks this and scribbles something in his pad.

'Well, Joey was only ten months old when we moved to this village an hour and a half out of London. And I knew no one there, had no friends, didn't get on with the local mum and baby groups … and Jack worked up in London – sometimes staying the night – so I was often completely alone for days on end. I was miserable.'

'No change there, then,' Jack says under his breath while coughing, trying and failing to disguise what he's saying.

'Not true.' I shake my head. 'See? That's another thing that really gets on my wick. I was hopelessly miserable in Riverside, yes, but since we moved to Sydney – which, I might add, I didn't really want to do in the first place, but agreed to if it would make Jack happy – I think I've been much better. Despite the heat and the raging hormones.'

'Ah,' sighs Tarquin in his deep voice, 'another one on the way, eh? I didn't want to say anything, in case … sometimes you can't … anyway, that would explain away some of the tension here.'

'Hey!' I butt in. 'Don't hang all of this on me and my hormones! Whether I'm pregnant or not, Jack's always rubbish at sharing his feelings. I thought maybe getting away from Riverside and coming to the wide open spaces of Australia would get *him* to open up, too.'

'But you do know that wherever you go, there you are, don't you? I mean, the problem is not Sydney or London or Riverside – it's you. One, I mean. It's not *where* you are, it's *who* you are. That's why I always tell my clients that wherever you go, there you are. Worth remembering, that one,' he says, pleased with himself for sounding like such a wise old sage.

Jack and I swap quick glances and I bet he's thinking what I'm thinking – for a professional, fully-qualified guy, Tarquin doesn't half come out with some bumper-sticker philosophy. I wonder where he got his degree – a Kinder Egg?

My eyes are drawn up to something framed on the wall, which is, I imagine, his degree – there's a large red wax-look stamp on it at the bottom – but I can't make out anything more than that. Great, I think to myself, now my eyes are going – yet another old person's medical affliction rearing its ugly head. It'll be cataracts next.

'So obviously you're still intimate with each other – things haven't *completely* broken down in all aspects of your relationship, have they?' Tarquin carries on regardless.

Jack and I look at each other and force a smile.

'Twice,' says Jack quietly and shifts in his seat.

'Yes,' I say, trying to sound confident. 'Twice. We've done it two times since we got here – both on the same night if you must know—'

Tarquin shakes his full head of salt and pepper hair and stares at his pad.

'And one of those times got me pregnant.'

Tarquin nods. Jack studies the door.

'So how often do you two talk, then? *Really* talk?'

Jack and I answer at exactly the same time.

'Constantly,' he says, rolling his eyes.

'Never!' I nearly shout. 'I try, but always get short shrift. There's always something much more important to do, like play *World of Warcraft* or watch football or clean the loo – anything rather than talk to me.'

'Rubbish,' says Jack, waving his right hand past his ear.

'See what I mean? I talk to his hand more than I ever talk to him!'

'OK, OK,' soothes Tarquin, his thick, tanned, manly-but-sensitive-looking hands bouncing slowly, masterfully, on the air in front of him. 'Now let's all take it easy and calm down a bit.'

I take a deep breath. Jack sniffs.

'What about now? Are you annoyed about anything in the here and now?' Tarquin addresses me.

'No, not really. Just a bit, um, disappointed in our relationship,' I say, feeling a stab of sadness. 'I feel like a kept woman, doing the lion's share of looking after Joey, our daughter, and working, too – but still not being kept in the loop about our finances. And sometimes I feel as though we don't know each other very well at all. It's like the lack of communication between us makes me feel like we had a one-night stand and now we've come face to face in a packed work lift or something – small-talky, awkward and uncomfortable.'

I steal a glimpse at Jack, who's looking blankly at Tarquin.

'I just wish we could be a happy family,' I continue. 'A proper unit with a real sense of togetherness. I hope that soon, Jack and I will return to our before-kids mindset in a way and just be nicer to each other. Kinder. You know?'

'You've come to the right place, then. I'll give you two the tools, the techniques, to make that happen. Now. What about you, Jack?'

'I'm a decent, happy guy. Nothing really gets me down. Except her negativity sometimes,' he says, jerking his head in my direction.

'I'm not negative any more,' I plead my case, 'I'm really trying not to be. I think I've come on in leaps and bounds. How can we move on, as a couple, though, if you won't let go of all that?'

'Good point, Roxane,' Tarquin says.

Maybe now we're getting somewhere. Maybe now Tarquin will see how difficult it is to have a relationship with someone who is completely un-self-aware, doesn't

143

like to nut things out and analyse our respective thoughts and feelings. Maybe now Tarquin will say:

'Well, Roxane, the trouble here lies squarely on Jack's shoulders – he is rubbish, you're right. And it's all his fault. Now, what are you doing after this? Fancy getting a bite to eat at Beau Thai with me? You know, I found you irresistible the minute I laid eyes on you, when you walked in here. By the way, have I mentioned that I'm a multi-millionaire? And that I only do these counselling gigs every now and again simply because I'm an excellent listener and I love nothing more than to chat, dissecting relationships?'

Unfortunately, he doesn't say this. Instead, he says:

'It's important for both of you to let go of the past and come together. Inhabit a good place, share the loving space.'

Jack and I look at each other and manage tentative smiles.

'Let's talk money, now, hmm? Do arguments about money seem to crop up an awful lot?' Tarquin asks.

'God, yeah!' I say, edging my bum towards the front edge of my seat. 'You know, he's only gone and bought a motorbike. Sorry, took out a *loan* to pay for a motorbike.'

'I can afford it!'

'If you have to take out a loan, you *can't* afford it! And anyway, it's so selfish! What do Joey and I get out of it? Nothing, that's what! So we've gone even further into debt – *as a family* – purely so you can indulge your own ridiculous Marlon Brando fantasies.'

'I like motorbikes, that's all. Always have. And I needed a way to get to work so you can have the car – particularly for when the little one's born.'

Put like that, it sounds like getting a motorbike was this considerate, thoughtful, perfect family man's only real option.

There's silence for a bit.

'What this is all about, the point of all this, Jack, is to get your gripes about each other out into the open, so that, with my help, we can come to some kind of resolution. But you do have to be a little forthcoming and open to the idea,' Tarquin goes on. 'Do you think, with the motorbike, you're trying to escape the responsibilities and burdens of fatherhood? What would you say to the idea of taking public transport to work? And, being brutally honest with yourself, do you think you might be having *Rebel Without a Cause* fantasies?'

'Marlon Brando,' I interrupt. 'In *The Wild One.*'

Jack opens his hands, palms-up, and raises his eyebrows at Tarquin in a 'See what I mean? See what I have to contend with?' kind of way.

Tarquin closes his eyes in an exaggerated, extra-long blink and, when he opens them, nods and smiles at Jack encouragingly.

'Ah, let me see ... no, no and, er, no,' Jack says. 'I'd talk more if I thought she'd listen – but she constantly interrupts me and pooh-poohs everything I say. And if you want to talk about fantasies, what the hell does she think

145

she's doing, opening up a cafe? In a recession? When she can't even boil an egg? Now who's delusional, eh? She thinks she's flaming Nigella Lawson, I tell you.' He grins at Tarquin.

I blush at this. If *only* I had an ounce of Nigella in me, all coquettish and full-bosomed, obscenely wealthy and effortlessly sexy. Which reminds me – I must get the ingredients for her brownies and remember to take out the lamb mince to thaw, so I can make that Rapid Ragu I never get around to.

Tarquin's voice oozes thickly into my domestic goddess dream.

'First off, I'd suggest a joint bank account for all things kids and household, as well as your separate accounts for your own things. Obviously, when the baby comes, Jack, you will have to put in a bit more to cover Roxane's drop in earnings – but, until then, what would you say to, um, 25% of both of your monthly wages going into a joint account? Sound fair?'

I'm speechless. So's Jack.

Could it be that easy? Could it be that simple a solution to one of the biggest problems we've faced as a couple since Joey was born?

'OK,' says Jack finally, looking pleasantly surprised.

'Great. Now. Moving swiftly on from the money issue, do you find much to laugh about these days? Together, I mean.'

'I think we share a sense of humour,' I say hopefully, looking at Jack.

'Well, I have a sense of humour,' Jack beams at Tarquin, 'and I share it with her sometimes.'

Tarquin throws his head back and laughs a throaty, lustful ha ha. Jack chuckles at his own comic genius and snorts as his shoulders shake.

'So what do you think, then?' I cut in on their private joke.

'Right, yes,' Tarquin says, coughing and sitting up straighter in his chair. 'Well, the good news is I don't think you two are heading for divorce court anytime soon. Your problems seem to be standard common-or-garden men versus women stuff – with the added pressure of parenthood thrown in for good measure. Trust me, it's nothing too complicated. And the only slightly bad news is it's going to take a bit of work, a bit of effort on all our parts to set this thing right again. So. Are you committed?'

We both wait for the other one to speak. Tarquin looks expectantly from me to Jack, Jack to me, me to Jack – like he's watching client tennis or something.

'Ye-e-e-es,' we eventually say in unison, smiling nervously.

'Right!' Tarquin slaps his hands on his thighs. 'Here's a little exercise I want you two to try and do every day.'

'Oh, no! Not more trust exercises,' I groan.

'No, no – these are different. I want you to sit down at a table, facing each other, with no other distractions, and while one talks, the other listens. You get five minutes each – five minutes of *uninterrupted* talking about you:

147

your day, your thoughts during the day, how you felt about everything yadda yadda yadda. And the other one has to listen. Maintain eye contact with each other and, after the five minutes, the listener has to ask three questions about what the talker's said. Once that's done, swap. Easy. What do you think?'

'Five minutes?' Jack winces.

'Yeah,' I join in. 'It's not long, is it?'

'It's waaay too long,' whines Jack. 'Couldn't we make it *two* minutes?'

'Whatever works for you. As long as you take some time and do it, you'll see benefits immediately,' Tarquin says, looking at his leather-strapped watch. 'Time's up for this week. We'll see how you've got on next week. You can make an appointment online or over the phone. If you think this has been valuable, of course. No pressure.'

We come out of the Rels 'R' Us building and walk down Ridgey Didge Road towards home, where Anita's looking after Joey, desperate for us to return so she can get off to her Speed Dating for the Over-Seventies night.

A propos of nothing, Jack puts his arm round me. For the first time in ... God, I don't know how long.

'That wasn't half bad, you know,' he says. 'Yet another brilliant idea of mine ...'

'Total waste of time and money,' I say, smiling up at him, just as he looks down and winks at me.

'Yeah – I thought he had tickets on himself at first, but old Tarquin seems all right.'

And then it starts to rain lightly and Jack – without my even asking or making any kind of sarky comment about chivalry being dead or anything – offers me his jacket to put over my head, to protect my straightened hair from the frizz-making drizzle.

'It's PISSING down out there!' Jack declares as we come through our front door, creating puddles on the polished floorboards.

'Daddy!' squeals Joey, running towards us.

'How was she?' I ask Anita.

'Good as gold as always,' she answers, smiling at Joey.

What is it they say about kids being devils at home and angels away? Well, whatever it is, I'm about to say it when my mobile rings. I wander into our bedroom and answer it.

'Hello? Roxane Carmichael?' says a solemn voice.

'Yes,' I say.

'I've got your CVS results here in front of me,' says the voice, sounding even more morose.

I cross my fingers and shut my eyes tight. Because if the tone of voice is anything to go by, it's not good news.

It takes approximately a hundred years before the voice speaks again.

'And everything is fine – all chromosomes present and accounted for. Just letting you know.'

'Really?' I open my eyes in shock.

'Yes.'

'Nothing untoward at all?'

'No.'

'That's amazing!'

'Indeed. Now I must go – I have other, not-so-happy calls to make.'

'Oh, of course. OK,' I beam at the white wall in front of me, 'well, thanks! Bye. And thanks again!'

I let out a huge sigh, rub my tightening tum and fairly skip into the front room. Jack's got Joey on his shoulders as he does the washing up.

'I hate coming home to dirty dishes in the sink,' he says.

Usually, this would really get my back up, and we'd probably end up having a huge row about it – because I know what he's *really* saying here: he's having a go at me, having a dig about my housekeeping abilities – but tonight, I don't rise to the bait. I don't know whether it's Tarquin or the good CVS news or my new positive outlook, but I let it go. Just like that.

I run my fingers through my almost-straight hair and take a deep breath, slowly letting the narkiness and negativity out as I exhale.

And then I throw myself on the couch, swollen feet up on the cushions down my end, reach for the remote and turn on the telly only to see that Rels 'R' Us advert again. Now must be prime time for the broken-hearted and miserable to be watching the box.

And the lusty and desperate, because once that's over, on comes a Man Power ad. I look at the muscly bodies on screen and surreptitiously compare them to Jack's form. Hmm. Not bad. Nothing that laying off the beer for a while and lifting some weights wouldn't fix . . .

'Daddy, yuck! Look!' says an excited Joey.

Jack screams and jumps back from the kitchen sink. He's all man, my Jack. Talk about Man Power.

'Jesus CHRIST!' he shouts, carefully extricating Joey's legs from his shoulders. 'That's not a cockroach – it's a bloody lizard. A farking Komodo dragon!'

'Language, you big wuss,' I say.

Joey cackles maniacally, wetting herself in the excitement. Literally.

'It's winking at me!' Jack shrieks, as he throws a telephone book into the sink. 'It's pushing the far— the flamin' sink strainer up by its own head!'

I grab Joey and we confidently march over to said sink. And all three of us watch in disbelief as one side of the telephone book raises to reveal two thick long antennae waving about and then, slowly but surely, it rears a small, but perfectly malformed, ugly head, followed by a spiky, dark brown, multi-jointed, muscly insect leg. It cocks its head to one side and smirks.

'EEEEEK!' all three of us scream.

I take off out the front door with Joey clinging to me for dear life while Jack legs it down to the back of the flat. Safely in the vestibule, Joey and I giggle and put our ears up to the front door to hear Jack take on the cockroach in a clash of the titans.

Pots, pans and crockery clatter, bang and break as we hear '*Argh!*' and '*Oof!*', unsure if it's Jack or the roach making those sounds. Then begins the high-pitched squealing, like an audience of three-year-olds at a Dora the Explorer on Ice show. We're quite sure that's Jack.

He's spraying something and then stamping his foot on those poor floorboards repeatedly, which makes it sound like he's playing a particularly painful and heavy-footed game of Twister. This goes on for about ten minutes until finally he shouts:

'The dragon is dead! You can come back in now!'

Gingerly, we open the door and peer round it, taking in the scene of carnage and destruction. And there's Jack, standing proudly over his kill, one foot covering a tiny black dot on the floor.

'Quick! Take a photo, Rox,' he says, so chuffed with himself, he can barely get the words out.

'Of, ah, what?' I ask him. 'Um, you big strong hero.'

'Hercules! Hercules!' yelps Joey, jumping up and down and clapping her hands together. 'My Daddy's Hercules!'

'Yes,' says Jack, 'strong and protective, that's me. You know, I swear at one point he laughed at me. A real mocking, bullying laugh.'

'That might've been us, by the front door,' I suggest.

'Oh,' he says, deflated.

'But look at it – what a monster.' I wink at Joey and walk over to Jack, giving his biceps a good squeeze.

'It's so bloody huge, I could've put a saddle on it and rode it like Phar Lap!' Jack grins.

Later that evening, once we've all recovered from the marauder and Jack's testosterone-fuelled display of strength (which sees him flaked out on the couch by seven p.m.), I get Joey out of her bath, tuck her into bed and, at her request, start reading *Puff, the Magic Dragon* to her.

The book is beautifully illustrated and sumptuous to look at, but when we get to the bit about dragons living for ever, but not so little boys, I lose it. My face scrunches up and I can't help crying.

'Then one day it happened ... (sniff, blub), *waaah!*'

'What's wrong, Mummy?' says a concerned-looking Joey. 'Mummy?'

'Nothing [sniff] ... I just, um [snort] ... '

'Snorter McPhail!' She smiles at me. 'Are you snoring like Snorter McPhail, Mummy?'

'Ooh, sorry about that, Joey. Just came over all emotional.'

'Are you sad for Puff? Or the cockroach? I'll put my feet on your fat tummy, just like Daddy did to the cockroach!'

'No!' I say a tad too loudly, making Joey jump and start crying, too.

'Oh, sweetie.' I hug her tightly to me. 'Sorry to scare you like that. It's just, well, try not to touch Mummy's fat tummy for a while because ... because ... '

'You've ate too much ice cream again?'

'Yes. Sort of. Well, no, not really,' I say, confusing myself. 'No, peaches, the thing is [deep breath] there's a baby growing in my tummy.'

'There is?' She's all wide-eyed and sitting up now.

'Yup.'

'Really?'

I nod.

'How did it get there?' she asks.

'Daddy gave Mummy a very special kiss on my belly button.'

'You and Daddy do that to me sometimes … Oh! Do I have a baby in my tummy, too?'

'No.' I smile. 'But it means you will be a big sister in a few months. The best big sister in the world!'

This totally delights her.

'And I'll need you to be really helpful from now on, babycakes. I will get fatter and fatter and I won't be able to do everything that I do now, such as it is, so I can count on you, can't I? You will help me lots and lots, won't you?'

'I'll start right now, Mummy. Shall I put you to bed and read you a story?'

'No, it's OK.' I study her eyes, glad that she's received the news so well.

She stares back at me, all full of wonder and amazement and – as strange as this may sound – admiration. Or maybe I'm reading it all wrong. But something's changed in the way she looks at me. Something's different. All of a sudden, the little girl who's only ever had eyes for her daddy and barely concealed contempt for me is looking at me as though I'm a bit of a Hercules, too.

'Let's just have a snuggle and listen to the rain outside because it's . . . because it's . . . ' I trail off, misty-eyed, lost in the magic of the moment.

She kisses me on the mouth, squirms down under her sheet, turns on her side, places her hands together prayer-style and puts her head on them, on the Disney Princesses pillowcase Charlie sent over. I stroke her hair and tuck her curls behind her ear.

'Because it's . . . ' And I'm buggered if I can remember what I was going to say.

God. Imagine. Imagine if she went to bed every night like this – no tears, no tantrums, no running all over the flat screaming and jumping up and down on her bed. Imagine if she did become really helpful and we didn't go through trauma every day on the walk to pre-school. Imagine if she started to respect me a bit more and was no longer just Daddy's Girl. I know I'm getting carried away, but imagine if she wanted to emulate *me*, really listened to *me*, copied what I said and didn't mimic her dad so much, especially when he doesn't stop himself swearing in time or is just coarse and crass.

'Because it's really PISSING down out there!' she cackles.

Chapter 12

'I'm really sorry, Roxy, but we're going to have to let you go,' says Phil, all sad and forlorn.

I shift in my seat, an involuntary, unwelcome nervous smile spreading across my face. 'Is it because Joey was sick and I had to work from home? If so, it won't happen again, I promise.'

'No, no, it's not because of that.' He looks into my eyes for the first time since we sat down in the tiny interview room.

'The no comments for my posts? I can fix that, get all my friends to—'

'No, it's not the lack of comments or ... readers ...'

'I know – it's because I used the site to plug my own personal business venture?'

'You did?'

Oops.

'You didn't know?'

'No, I didn't. Not that it matters now. I'm so sorry, but—'

'It's because I come in late and leave early, isn't it? But I have no choice about that, Phil! You know Jack can't pick her up and the only way I can—'

'Look, it's nothing to do with any of those things, nothing to do with you at all.' He shakes his head, his eyes now stuck on a particularly hideous-looking stain in the middle of one of the Heuga carpet tiles. 'We're all going. The company's sold us – for a song, I'm told – and we're no longer needed, none of the sites, none of the editors, none of the management – none of us has a job any more.'

'As of?'

'As of right now.'

Bloody hell, I think.

'Bloody hell!' I say.

'I know,' he agrees, and runs a hand through his thick, no-signs-of-grey-or-receding-yet hair.

'When did . . . why . . . what did . . .?'

'It's irrelevant.' He sighs. 'We're all rooted. It's down tools and off to the pub as soon as everyone's cleared their desks, I'm afraid. My shout.'

'But—'

'Look, I've got to tell the others now, so can you start sorting your stuff out? Go and get a coffee and we'll reconvene at The Squatters' Arms at noon, all right?'

Usually I'm first in the queue for a boss-subsidised drink or twelve – and even if it's bad news and we're all commiserating down the pub, I'm normally there with bells on. And when I worked on a (very successful)

157

weekly men's magazine in the nineties, as one of only two women on the editorial team, we were rarely out of the pub. Lunchtimes would signal the end of the working day and the start of the well-oiled creative process of getting lathered and coming up with ever more ridiculous ideas for stories. It was hugely alcoholic – and massive fun – but that was then and this is now.

Now, I'm no longer twenty-three, I'm married, I have a three-and-a-half-year-old daughter, I'm eighteen weeks gone and I've just lost my job.

And anyway, I'm steadfastly sticking to my no booze rule. I don't even really want to be in pubs – they just remind me of what I can't have and what I'm missing a bit. A fair bit, come to think of it. Quite a lot, actually. A humongous amount, to be honest. Oh, all right, all right. I put my hand up. I'm missing a chilled glass of Chardy something severe.

Still, I think, getting made redundant will really give me something to fill the Tarquin-advised two-minute talk Jack and I are supposed to be having this evening. The talking/listening chats meant to be teaching us how to communicate properly, how to understand each other more.

'Bit of a shocker or what?' I say, wide-eyed, to Kylie. She's sitting at her desk, staring at her screensaver of Lady Gaga, mouth agape. That's Kylie's mouth that's agape, not Gaga's.

I sit down at my desk and swivel my chair round to face her back.

'Kyles?'

'Double cheese, large packet of cheese and onion, yes, I know,' she says in a monotonous robot way.

'Kyles? Are you all right?'

I stand up and sit on her desk, so I can see her face.

'Hmm,' she says, not looking up.

'Kylie, you're scaring me. Are you OK?' I shake her shoulder.

'Uh, yeah. What?' she barks, snapping out of her dream-like state.

'I was just saying,' I begin, relieved, 'that all of us being made redundant is a bit of a shocker, isn't it?'

'And the rest.' She purses her lips.

'What do you mean?'

She looks behind her, to her side and then beckons me to lean in, like she's got a secret.

'I'm twelve. Weeks. Pregnant,' she whispers.

I gasp, reeling back as though the sheer force of what she's said just hit me in the chest. And now my mouth's agaping all over the place, too. Which is unfortunate, because my reaction only serves to upset Kylie further. So much so, her carefully made-up face and perfect posture collapse simultaneously and she starts sobbing her little heart out.

'Mum and Dad are going to kill me and there's no way we'll be able to get married now and I'll be homeless and abandoned and I'll have to give it up for adoption and—'

'Marry who? Why will you be homeless? What the—'

'Phil,' she whispers wetly, her voice sodden with saliva and salty tears.

I reel back again. She slaps my knee and tells me to stop it.

'Come here, you,' I stretch my arms out and give her a massive hug until, eventually, she calms down a bit.

'Well, guess what?' I say cheerily.

'What?'

'So am I! Pregnant, I mean.'

'Oh, *duh*,' she sniffs, 'I know.'

'You do?' I ask, shocked and surprised for the fourth time this morning – and it's only nine-blimmin'-thirty.

'Everyone does!' she says. 'But you're an old hand at this – you've already had one, you're married and you don't live at home with your olds.'

'You still live at home with your mum and dad?'

'Yeah.' She smiles faintly. 'It happened when they were in South Africa on a rugby tour. And they are gonna *kill* me. They're strict Greek Orthodox. Oh, Roxy, I am *so* for it. And now I don't even have a job!'

'What about Phil? What does he say? Can't you move in with him?'

'He doesn't know.'

Just then, the man in question, Phil, comes out of the interview room, following the gadget site's über-geeky editor.

'OK, everyone,' he says, clapping his hands together once, making a hollow sound similar to that one you hear

160

when you hit a tennis ball in the exact right place, in the middle of the racket head where the strings are at their most melodic. 'Let's get trashed!'

'Right, missy,' I say to Kylie, echoing my own mum again, 'you're coming with me. Let's go to that chichi cafe you're always banging on about. The one round the corner. Just you and me, yeah?'

'The Bijou? Oh, great.' She sniffs and puts on her coat with lightning-speed, just like Joey does after I've made her take it off for the umpteenth time because I think she must be hot, like me, even though it's mid-winter now.

And when we get to The Bijou, I can see why Kylie's so keen on it. It's like an Egyptian belly-dancing cushion room, with loads of deep red and purple cushions laced with gold scattered about large benches. Instead of ordinary tables and chairs, they're all mismatched and higgledy-piggledy. And there are two Chesterfields guarding a long, low coffee table, making me feel like sinking into them on the spot. Big old-fashioned teapots are on every table (complete with hand-knitted tea cosies), the lights are low and there's soft music playing – nothing too obtrusive or anything that could get on your nerves. It feels as warm and comforting as you'd like your own kitchen to be, the smell of toast and coffee taking you back to those favourite after-school snacks of your childhood. The waitress is attentive but not too in-your-face and the cheesecake? Don't get me started. It's almost

161

unbearably delicious. So much so, I'm forced to have two slices. Well, you've got to support your local independent cafes, don't you? Just doing my bit.

Only once I've scraped the last lovely crumbs off my second plate do I finally notice that it's a child's Corningware Peter Rabbit plate, just like the ones I had when I was a nipper. And it gives me an idea.

'Eclectic, different cutlery and crockery for the kids,' I say out loud.

'Eh?' says Kylie, daintily sipping her peppermint tea.

Suddenly I realise I haven't told Kylie about my other business venture. Maybe it's time to let her in on it, try to take her mind off her considerable troubles.

'Just an idea for the caff. I'm opening up a cafe with a friend of mine, you see. In Bondi. A cafe for mums.'

'You are? How wonderful,' she says, her eyes twinkling. 'You know, it's always been a dream of mine, to one day have my own cafe. How exciting! What's it called?'

'Just Another Manic Mum-Day,' I say proudly. 'Didn't you see the ad for it on KiddingAround?'

'Um, no,' she says sheepishly. 'But what a great name! And you can always shorten it to JAMM, which sounds wonderfully warm and cosy and sweet. And mums are always finding themselves in one jam or another, what with all the millions of things they're juggling, aren't they?'

Either I've been given a massive dose of déjà vu with my cheesecake, or Kylie's so on the money, so on the same page as me, getting the whole idea of JAMM in a flash, that I'm a teensy bit gobsmacked.

'Ah ... too right they are,' I agree. 'There's usually far too much going on. You misplace and forget things all the time, stumble over your words like a ... like an ... um ... '

'When are you going to open?' Kylie says, putting me out of my tip-of-my-tongue misery.

'Six weeks. The loan comes through in four, and our first three months are rent-free, which is brilliant. Got to get all the staff together for a meeting soon, before the Grand Opening.'

'So you're all tooled up, I suppose. Don't need any waitresses?'

'Actually, we do. We've got one young waiter from JAMM's previous incarnation as a cafe that virtually *excluded* mums – but every time I saw him, he was stoned out of his tree. We could definitely do with another pair of capable hands ... Are you offering your services, Kyles?'

'Well, for a decent price, yes.' She beams.

'You're hired!' I point my finger at her, like Lord Sugar on *The Apprentice*.

We both stand up and lean over our small table for a mum-to-be hug – you know, where your arms entwine and your heads are close, but you stick your bum right out so that there's no danger of your tummies touching.

'Wow! Wait till I tell Phil!'

'About the baby?'

'No, no – not yet. I've got to get *my* head around it first. No, about your cafe. He thinks I'm a bit silly, sometimes, with all my ideas about my own cafe, but I always say as one door closes, another one opens, so ... '

'Positive thinking, Kyles. That's what I like to hear.'

'And now he'll be able to do that artisan bakery course, Strictly Knead To Know. He's been dying to do it for ages,' Kylie goes on.

'Really? I'd never have thought of Phil as the type.'

'Oh, he's a fantastic cook – and he bakes like a dream. Honestly, the first night we spent together he made Beef Wellington and apple turnovers. Pastry's his thing, really. No wonder I've put on ten kilos since we started seeing each other. But I found all that scrummy food and Phil himself impossible to resist!'

'Obviously,' I smile, glancing at her stomach and remembering when Jack used to seduce me with his culinary prowess. No one can order a Chinese and sprinkle salt and vinegar on chips quite like my Jack.

'Great idea, by the way, a cafe for mums. But hasn't it been done before? I can't believe they don't already exist,' says Kylie.

'If they do, they're not like this one. We're going to have childminders, a kids' play area, cut-price babysitting services ... '

'Pregnant waitresses,' says Kylie wistfully.

'Oh, Kyles,' I sigh. 'Everything's going to be fine, you'll see. The sooner you tell Phil, though, the sooner you two can get excited together and start planning for your new arrival. I bet he'll be over the moon.'

Kylie's eyes widen in a hadn't-thought-of-that kind of way and she nods slowly, as though considering this option carefully.

Just then, a woman, struggling with a wilful toddler, leaves the cafe with one of those beige/brown cardboard takeaway coffee cups and Kylie grabs my forearm excitedly.

'We have got to have them with the JAMM logo on. Great for mums on the school run, looking cool in the playground sipping from a pink, white and orange cardboard cup with JAMM emblazoned across it. I take it they're the cafe's colours? Like you wanted for KiddingAround?'

'That's a brilliant idea, Kyles. It could cost a bomb, though.'

'Nah, I'll get them for us on the cheap. My brother works at a printer's in Parramatta. He owes me a favour or two, considering what *he* got up to in the house while my parents were away on that rugby tour ... '

'Great!' I say, bowled over by Kylie's wily ways.

'Awesome,' she agrees. 'You know, JAMM could be just what I need – it could be the best thing to happen to me right now.'

And Kylie could be the best thing to happen to JAMM since ... well, since hot buttered thick-sliced white bread.

Several hours later, Jack and I settle down to start our two-minute talk. But not even thirty seconds in it goes all pear-shaped with him interrupting and not listening and getting narked and … and my day seems to go from merely bad to woeful.

It's my go to talk first.

'Today Phil told everyone they'd been made redundant. Kylie told me she was pregnant and we went to a cafe while everyone else went to the pub. I hired her as a waitress, and now I feel – well, apart from the fact I can't *wait* to have this baby so I can have a glass of wine again – strangely *relieved*. It wasn't exactly me, online publishing. And every cloud, right? It's a good thing, really, because now I can concentrate on the cafe—'

'Sacked?!' Jack croaks.

'No,' I say, 'made *redundant*. Like everyone else at Maverick. Whole thing's been sold. We're all out of a job – not just me.'

'As of today?'

'Yep. He said—'

'So no more money from you. That's it. I'm the sole breadwinner in the family now? *Again?*'

'Until the cafe starts making its million-dollar turnover, yes.'

'Great,' he looks skywards, 'just *great*.'

He runs a hand through his rapidly receding almost-white-it's-so-grey hair and grimaces. He looks at me, his eyes watering. Then he puts his elbows on his knees and his head in his hands.

'But babe?' I say. 'It's all going to be OK. We're going to

open the cafe in six weeks and I'll be able to devote all my time to it – up until the baby comes – and we've got some great plans and the place is looking fab and ... babe? Are you all right?'

Slowly he stands up, walks into the hallway, grabs his motorbike helmet – his $900 motorbike helmet, I might add (but don't, sensing it would somehow make things even worse) – and slams the front door behind him.

One minute later I hear him roaring off down the street on his bike, and, in my mind's eye, I imagine him popping a wheelie à la Tom Cruise in *Top Gun* when he takes off, all frustrated with Kelly McGillis while Berlin sing 'Take My Breath Away'. Without any of the homoerotic undertones, that is.

I suck at my tightly shut lips through my teeth and go in to check on Joey, who's out like a light, softly snoring under her Dora duvet cover. Satisfied she's OK, I head for the couch and lie down on it, preparing to make the most of the cable TV while we can still afford it. I turn on *Wife Swap*. Just in time for the ads.

That cheesy couple are prancing about in the golden meadow again, Tarquin's deep, lustrous voice making it all sound so easy, so quick to fix. The woman, who looks like a young Agnetha from Abba, stares deeply, meaningfully, into the man's eyes and runs her hands through his dark, thick blow-wave as they fall gently to the ground in their lovers' embrace.

And suddenly I burst into tears, gushing forth great

gusts and howls of pent-up emotion, rage and anxiety. I sit up, hang my head and blub for all I'm worth until slowly I become aware of something stirring inside. All this heaving must have woken the previously slumbering baby and, as if in celebration, it commences a particularly energetic game of keepy-uppy with its umbilical cord. Which makes me completely forget about Maverick and stroppy old Evel Knievel and my mouth opens in astonishment.

I grab either side of my bump. Looking down and grinning in anticipation of feeling the baby move again, I say to my unborn child:

'Don't you worry about a thing, Baby. Because everything's going to be fine. Just fine.'

And then my inner Ummy Mummy surfaces and voices her uncertainty, with a small, rather quavery, 'Isn't it?'

Chapter 13

So there I am, on the slightest of slight inclines, stopped at the traffic lights at Sulphur-crested Cockatoo Crescent, trying to turn right into Wobbegong Way, taking Joey to pre-school. And suddenly I start tearing at my own clothes, hot and sticky, desperate for some cool air.

I fumble for the switch on the inside of the door to undo my window, but only manage to roll every window in the car down except my own and I accidentally toot the horn and turn on both the radio and the windscreen wipers simultaneously. I can feel the sweat pricking my forehead and try to take deep breaths, while keeping my eyes on the lights, my left hand gripping the handbrake, white-knuckled. I check the rear-view mirror and see, just past Joey's head, an absolute behemoth of a bus right up my arse. There's no room for rolling back even a smidge in this scenario and my heart nearly comes through my chest as the panic attack reaches its zenith.

'Actually, Mummy, I think I *do* like Dora more than

Diego. But, Mummy! Mummy! I also like Diego more than Dora. I like them both more than each other, really, but—'

'Shut UP!' I snap, blinking the stinging sweat out of my eyes.

The lights turn green and I bet I do, too.

This is it. Do not muck it up. You've got precious cargo in the back – do NOT show yourself up to be the worst driver in Sydney. Even if you are. Come on. COME ON!

I feel the biting point and let the handbrake off while slamming my terrified foot down too hard, too fast, on the accelerator. The tyres squeal, we smell burning rubber briefly, I hold my breath, wincing – but we make it across and around without reversing into the bus or smashing into the car in front. Disaster is averted for one more day. Well, vehicular disaster at any rate.

'What's up, sweetie?' I ask, as I slowly become aware of sobbing from the back seat. 'Hmm? What's wrong?'

'You shouted at me! And didn't even say sorry!' she bawls.

Bugger. She's right. As always.

'Oh, I'm sorry, sweet pea! It's just that you know Mummy has to concentrate very hard when she's driving. She gets very nervous, doesn't she? And there was a big bus behind us, so I was scared—'

'That we'd crash in his face?' She sounds delighted at the thought.

'Well, yes.'

170

'Are you a rubbish driver, Mummy?' Her reflection grins at me in the rear-view mirror.

'Well, I wouldn't say that exactly—'

'And Daddy is the best driver in the world!' she declares.

'Yes, yes.' I concede defeat. 'Daddy is the best at everything.'

'He's even the bist Mummy?' She does that Aussie inflection thing again and mimics all the South African accents she hears at Shalom! Baby.

'No, you silly-billy! Mummy's the best Mummy!'

But she's already lost interest and is looking out her window.

We get to pre-school in under ten minutes door to door and despite our tiny altercation, which was so small it didn't even register on the Richter scale of tantrums, I am overjoyed. So overjoyed that I forget to be frightened at the intersection on the way back (there's no incline at all when you're going in the other direction) and congratulate myself on a job well done. I finally want to thank Jack, at this moment, too, for insisting we get a car when we first moved to Sydney, to hell with the debt.

I didn't want to get one, you see. I figured:

a) I need all the exercise I can get

b) so does Joey

c) we couldn't afford a car – even an old banger

d) cars are merely metal death machines – rubbish

for the environment, quite literally. And

d) in case you hadn't noticed, I don't exactly enjoy driving. In fact, it scares the living daylights out of me.

But Jack argued that a car would make everything so much easier. For all of us. I'm all for easy, me, so we bought a second-hand manual Mazda 3 shortly after we arrived. And I've been in a right two and eight about it ever since.

I know, I know – pathetic, isn't it? Bricking it at my age. I'm too old to be such a panic-attack-prone driver, who couldn't even drive to work on my first day because I was too nervous; too old to be a new mum again … too flaming old full stop.

In truth, I didn't seriously set about the task of getting my licence until shortly after my fortieth birthday. And it's all thanks to Jack because he bought me a whole load of driving lessons with the local Riverside instructor who specialised in nervous drivers.

A beaten-up old Nissan Micra would stop out the front of our house at seven-thirty every Monday evening (once Jack had got home, so he could look after Joey – or 'babysit', as he'd maddeningly call it, given he *is* her father) and we'd drive around for an hour. Or, to put it more accurately, I'd stall, forget to indicate, ride the clutch, roll backwards on hill starts, drive through roundabouts, convert three-point turns into twelve-point turns and generally make *other* drivers nervous for an hour every week.

I eventually did get my licence, though. And it only took me eight embarrassing goes.

I smile to myself as I remember joking with Charlie about our both being utterly *pants* at parking, her saying to a decidedly unimpressed Rose, her daughter, every time she'd parked atrociously:

'Don't worry – we can walk to the kerb from here' – one of our favourite lines from *Annie Hall*. And God, I realise I miss her so much. There simply aren't enough hours to maintain your personal relationships these days, let alone have a laugh, a bit of respite from all the frantic to-and-froing.

Well, usually that's the case. But before I head off back out to the caff for our first ever staff meeting, I'm going to indulge myself and wallow in my newfound lady of leisure status. I'm going to be good to myself, take it easy, put my feet up and Skype Charlie.

'Thank God you're looking a bit healthier than last time I saw you, Chuck,' I say when her grainy image appears on the laptop screen.

But even though it's not the best picture in the world, I can still make out that her hair's greasy and she's returned to her natural colour, rat-brown. Must not have had a chance to put in one of her burgundy rinses or get to the hairdresser's lately for some blonde highlights. She looks like she's put on quite a bit of weight, too – and for a slim, trim, thank-God-I'm-done-with-all-that-new-motherhood-stuff woman like Charlie, who prides herself on her immaculate appearance and boundless energy, it comes as a bit of a shock.

'I am feeling better, morning-sickness-wise,' she agrees. 'But the whole thing with John has gone totally belly-up.'

'How? Does he know about the baby? Are you going to split up?'

'Yes, he knows about the baby and no, we're not going to split up. Not yet, anyway.'

'What do you mean?'

'He says he needs some time to sort his head out. I said he's got approximately six months. He said he'll do whatever I want him to do for the baby, but he can't guarantee he'll be there for me.'

'Ooh, sounds grim.' I frown. 'But he will be there for his fancy-woman, I take it?'

'No, well, he's still denying he's having an affair. Says there isn't anyone else. He reckons we just don't have that much in common any more.'

'Apart from a whole new life.'

'I know, I know. But he's got a point, Rox,' she says, looking sad and resigned. 'I mean, when we met it was all pubs and clubs and cigarettes and beers and fun times. But ever since I got knocked up, I don't do any of that. *Can't* do any of it. Don't even want to. Particularly the fun bit, apparently, according to him.'

'But that's hormones, it'll pass. And when you have the baby, you can go back to doing what you did before.'

'But that's the thing,' she sighs, 'I don't *want* to go back to doing all that. It's boring. And it's time I grew up. Time he grew up, too.'

'There's nothing like a new baby to make you grow up quickly – for us women, of course. As for the men, it takes them much longer. *Years*. If, indeed, they ever manage it at all.'

'It's not fair, Roxy!' She sniffs.

'No,' I agree.

'Here I am with child! At my age! Oh, it's such a mess!'

She pushes a big fat brownie up close to the screen and says through her tears: 'Wanna bite?'

I'd love one and my mouth starts to water. Well, it's only been about an hour since I last shoved something down my throat. Amazingly enough, though, we do have some leftover pizza in the fridge, so I grab a couple of slices and join her in a feeding frenzy.

'I'm dreading it, Rox – all those insecurities, all those feelings of failure rearing their ugly heads again. Then yesterday I went to watch Rose play football. It was the weirdest thing – and don't scoff when I say it – but it was like an epiphany.'

'Ha!' I scoff through a mouthful of ham and pineapple pizza.

'Let me finish, Rox, this is serious,' she says, looking all solemn. 'I watched her dart in and out, bending it like Beckham all over the shop, and when she scored a goal, she was ecstatic. I wanted to run on to the pitch with my jumper over my head. I wanted to grab her and hug her tightly. I wanted to squeeze her to within an inch of her life. But *she* ran to *me*. She ran straight to me and nearly knocked me over with her embrace. I was so proud. She was so proud. And her first port of call was *me*.'

Charlie pauses as though she's waiting for me to get it, to understand what she's saying. I stare blankly back at her.

'Don't you see? It finally came to me, like a thunderbolt. That's what we're all here for – that's what it's all about. I stumbled upon the meaning of life.'

'What? Football?'

'Kids! Our kids. Somehow, in those moments when Rose scored a goal, I realised that that's the point. *She's* the point. I don't need John anymore – I only need Rose and the new baby. And even though I'm scared, I'm going to do my best to enjoy it more this time, now that I have more of a clue about what I'm doing.'

'Blimey,' I say. Mainly because I can't think of anything else – but also because I'm a bit taken aback. It's not like Charlie to be so reflective, so soft. And so positive.

'You're right,' I eventually manage. 'And you sound so healthy, in such a good place.'

'I'm getting there, Rox, I can feel it. Now what about you?'

I tell her all about getting retrenched from Maverick, the imminent opening of JAMM, Jack and I going to counselling and our first attempt at doing the exercises even though we're both, I suspect, hyper-apprehensive about it all.

Because what if, I explain to Charlie, the more we do those two-minute talks, the more we realise *we* haven't got anything to talk about any more, either?

'Waste of time and money.' Charlie grins. 'No, good on you, Rox – keep going to the counselling. What does Woody Allen say about therapy? Something like he's been going for fifteen years and is only going to give it fifteen more before he gives it up?'

Charlie starts to laugh, but then looks off-screen and groans.

'I'd better go – that's John's keys in the door. Don't be a stranger, Rox, OK?'

We say our reluctant farewells and I click on the red Skype button, making Charlie disappear from view.

I put on *Annie Hall* and after about an hour into the movie, I drift off into a deliciously deep sleep and have one of those weird, surreal, super-vivid pregnancy dreams . . .

Something stirs me and I sit up from my prone position on the couch as Joey walks in our door with Jack behind her (he's picked her up from pre-school – this is a dream, remember). But she looks different; she's changed. Gradually I realise that her cute blonde curls have gone ringletty in the heat, and now they've turned into just two long, single ringlets either side of her head and she's wearing a black hat. She's gone all Hasidic Jew on me – just like Woody Allen in that scene where he's eating dinner at

Annie's parents' place and Grammy Hall is peering at him, picturing him in all his Orthodox get-up.

I giggle out loud at this, waking myself up.

And then my mobile bleeps, rousing me for real and making me manoeuvre myself slowly into a sitting position to read the text. It's from Shosh:

> See you in 10!
> Sooooo excited!!!!

I get there late, of course, a tad discombobulated, but I'm filled with joy as I hand out the JAMM manifesto and watch the staff – *our staff*! How mad is that? – devour the principles and intentions at the very heart of the cafe.

In the middle of the table is a massive plate of pastries, tarts and sweet treats – at the very heart of my own personal interests at this point, I must say.

As I sit down, Kylie nudges me and whispers: 'They're a part of Phil's course – dig in!'

I don't need to be asked twice and nearly get whiplash, I reach out so fast for two pains au raisin and a brownie, placing them on the plate before me.

'Hi, hello, hiya, everyone,' I say as I scan the table, drinking in our motley crew of JAMMers.

First, my eyes land on the stoned-looking waiter, Luke, who we inherited from Serenitea. He looks just as dopey-eyed and super-relaxed as he did before, which is nice, actually – provides a bit of balance to Shosh and myself, who've become overnight Energizer bunnies, bouncing about in our seats with anticipation.

Our chef, another ring-in from Serenitea, seems like a really nice guy, despite having delusions of grandeur and insisting we call him 'Chef'. He's in his mid-thirties, is married, has two kids at primary school and a four-bedroomed mansion, complete with pool and tennis court in one of the outer-outer-*outer*-most suburbs of prohibitively expensive Sydney. He reckons only the mega-rich can afford to buy in Bondi – or even rent – and that couples with kids have to make that decision: beautiful beach, poncy cafes and bars on your doorstep, or pools and national parks in your very own detached house's backyard? He says the outer suburbs are crawling with kids and mums, desperate for a cafe like ours, and asks whether we have the funds to franchise.

'Give us a chance!' I laugh. 'We haven't even opened yet! Let's see if we can really make a go of it here, in poncy Bondi, and then we'll think about branching out.'

'She's right,' agrees Shosh. 'One thing at a time. Now, first up – what does everyone think of the manifesto?'

Eagerly checking the countenances on the mainly cheery-looking crowd, I'm surprised when Chef is the first to speak.

'This would look great on a sandwich board out the front,' he says, flicking the manifesto with his finger. 'Just the highlights, not the waffle. For example, "We promise we'll always ... pamper knackered parents and care for your kids while you relax." We could lure the punters in with this and then, once they're inside, they'll stay for the fantastic food and welcoming atmosphere.'

'How about one side of the blackboard for the manifesto and the other for the specials?' says creative genius Kylie.

'Inspired!' I cheep, rising off my seat a bit and looking at Shoshie. 'Why didn't we think of that?'

'So, these specials ... any ideas?'

'I make a fabulous mushroom risotto, if I do say so myself. Perfect. Every time,' Chef says modestly.

'Shall we keep it generic?' I wonder out loud. 'Until we really know what we excel in and what our customers like the most?'

'Yeah,' says Isaac, taking a break from his near-incessant texting. 'Let's play to our strengths, keeping in mind our mission statement. What can we offer our clientele that no one else does?'

'We could just call it Relaxation Risotto, then.' Chef grins.

'And Transcendental ... no, no, Take It Easy ... no, Time Out Tea!' shouts Kylie.

'Yeah! And how about Keep Your Cool Coffee?' I chip in.

'Pure Heaven Pastries?' Zoe, one of the twenty-year-old registered childminders, smiles.

'Chill Out Chardonnay,' Sophie, the other childminder, gets into the swing of things, 'and a Feel-Good Fruit Platter!'

'Brilliant.' Shoshie beams. 'Should keep us going for a while. But what about our look? As you can see, we haven't changed this place much at all. We plan on a paint job and some battered old leather couches a little further down the track, and some other small tweaks, but, right now, what you see is what you get. Unless any of you have some suggestions ... some cheap or, preferably, *free* suggestions?'

'I think it would be a nice touch to have our children's artwork on the walls. And not just in the crèche and the play area – but behind the bar on the mirror tiles ... all over every blank space,' Zoe says confidently.

'I agree,' nods Sophie, 'they don't need to be framed, just loads of them, brightly coloured and happy-looking.'

Just like you two, I think, congratulating ourselves on choosing wisely from Shalom! Baby's files of child-minders looking for work. They've both got long blonde hair, twinkly green eyes, small noses, big busts – and they're impossibly smiley, giving off an air of fun, warmth and competence. The perfect pair to look after your kids.

'Beautiful,' says Isaac, looking Zoe and Sophie up and down as he gnaws on one of the well-chewed arms of his Ray-Bans. 'And brainy, too.'

Shosh pokes Isaac with her pen.

'Darl?' she says softly.

'Ah, yes, yes.' Isaac shakes himself out of his dream-like state. 'Now didn't you have a cracking nutritionally sound idea you wanted to share with everyone?'

181

'Yes, I did.' Shosh blushes ever so slightly. 'I thought we could produce a few different well-balanced organic meals every day, for babies as well as kids. Maybe we simply purée the kids' meals and put them in jars, ready to sell to mums panicking about what to feed their babies. And I think we should have a kids' menu – but instead of the usual frozen fish fingers and chips, we could give them really good stuff. Proper food – well made and tasty.'

'I like it,' says Chef. 'But organic can get pricey. Why don't we go half and half. I'll draw up the menus tonight, email them to you and we can go to the market together on the first day. I might need some help in the kitchen, too, so . . .'

'Can we stretch to another member of staff, Zac? Isaac!'

Isaac's slumped down in his chair (not so as you'd notice, really, he's only a bit taller than me – five-foot-three? At a push? Shosh says what he lacks in stature he makes up for in charisma. I keep my own counsel when-ever she says this and flash her a sympathetic smile), but sits bolt upright when he hears Shoshanna.

'I'm not sure about more staff,' he says. 'We're close to busting our budget as it is, so, no. Not yet. Let's see how we go with the staff we have already.'

'I can help, I don't mind,' says Shosh. 'I'd love to get my hands dirty in a kitchen again.'

'They won't get dirty in *my* kitchen,' warns Chef warmly.

Jemima shifts in her seat, looking uneasy. She's the barista Isaac roped in. But she's got a face you could crack nuts on – she must make a fantastic cup of coffee, then, for Isaac to have hired her, if you know what I mean.

She coughs pointedly.

'I'm not used to working in a place where money's so tight,' Jemima says haughtily. 'I mean to say, all good cafes need baristas. And all good baristas need space and top equipment and time to create . . . '

My back's up immediately.

'I think you'll find all the equipment is in perfectly good working order – if not exactly state of the art—'

'I suppose they're only mums in a hurry – probably wouldn't know a really good blend if they fell over it.'

Well, now, that's torn it. What's she doing here? If she has no respect for our deserving clientele? I shiver in reaction to the icy aura surrounding this young, probably childless woman. She's so cold, I swear I saw a little light come on inside when she opened her mouth.

'She's very talented,' says Isaac apologetically. 'Give her a chance.'

Shosh and I swap concerned glances and then Kylie steps in to calm and soothe the suddenly frosty waters.

'Have you sorted out our logo? And what about the awning out the front there – want my brother to print the logo and tagline on it? I'm sure he'll get it done fast . . . '

'Oh yes!' I yelp. 'I asked an old friend of mine from the

Pissed-Off Parents Club to design it for us and he's done a wonderful job – I'll email it to you as soon as I get home. And we'll need the menus done up, too. Chef, will you also email Kylie the opening week's menu? And Kyles, can we get your brother on to it straight away?'

'Done,' says Kylie. 'So what is our tagline?'

'What about, "Where guilt-free good times are always the order of the day"?' I suggest.

Kylie chews her bottom lip, considering it carefully. 'How about, "For a guilt-free good time"?'

'Or just "Good times – guilt-free"?' chimes in Shoshanna.

We all nod to indicate that's the one and Kylie jots it down.

'Dude,' drawls Luke, making me jump – I'd almost forgotten he was there, he's been so quiet. Maybe he just woke up. 'Will we be allowed to smoke on our breaks? And where?'

God, ex-smoker that I am, I'm surprised I hadn't even thought about this.

'There's a space in the alley out past the kitchen where you can go, if you don't want to go for a walk,' I say.

'Definitely not out the front in your uniform, though,' says Kylie. 'I mean, it's such a dodgy look – and we're supposed to be family-friendly, after all.'

'Uniform?' asks Sophie. 'I haven't got a uniform.'

'Just wear something smart,' I say.

'In any colour, as long as it's black.' Shoshie smiles.

'Black shirt and trousers for the guys and black shirts and trousers or skirts for the girls.'

'And it may be beneficial to bear in mind that I like my uniforms just like my coffee.' Isaac nods at Sophie and Zoe. 'Short and black!'

Everyone groans.

'And Luke?' Shosh opens her eyes wide. 'We are just talking about tobacco, here, aren't we?'

Luke smiles enigmatically, his eyes closed. Or maybe he's just fallen asleep again.

'Luke? LUKE!' shouts Isaac. 'No dope on the premises, OK?'

Luke hauls himself up so he's sitting straight-backed and salutes.

'Yes, *sah*! No dope, *sah*!'

'Speaking of drill sergeants, I've yet to organise the JAMM supernanny, but I'm getting close,' I say, sitting on my hands, lest they betray my enthusiasm for this idea by waggling about too much. 'She'll be on board by the time we open. Oh, and I'm pretty confident if I ask Tarquin he'll offer his services on the same basis – i.e. privately, not funded by us. I'm sure having those two will really help set us apart from the competition.'

'You know, I've been thinking,' Kylie cuts in. 'How about our very own cookbook, too?'

'Yes!' hisses Chef, punching the air. 'Well, what chef doesn't want to be the next Jamie Oliver or Gordon Ramsay?'

'And,' Kylie goes on, 'what if we did some catering? Just small stuff – for school functions and pre-schools. And kids' parties . . .'

'Whoa! Hold your horses, Tonto,' says Isaac. 'Let's learn to walk before we run.'

'Can we have lots of toys for the kids?' asks Zoe. 'Any old stuff you don't want, please bring in.'

'Books, too,' adds Sophie. 'We need books for all ages, from baby cardboard books to *The Tiara Club* series and *Harry Potter*.'

'And what about a few computers or at least a laptop?' I say. 'So the parents could catch up on emails, do the online shop or even do some work.'

'Film nights!' Shoshie blurts out. 'Once a month? Where we can show a particular film that we all want to see, have a few glasses and enjoy getting out and about while the kids are safely tucked in bed at home?'

'Maybe we could organise cut-price babysitters,' I suggest.

Isaac claps his hands three times.

'All right, all right,' he says cheerfully. 'That's enough for one day, don't you think? I'm going to have a hell of a time sorting all this out before we open, so . . . Can I call this meeting to a close?'

'Just quickly, Isaac, before you go.' I point my pen at him, like Columbo interrogating a recalcitrant suspect, as I read off my list. 'I just want to make sure that you'll sort out a couple of Chesterfields? And the maternity/paternity policy, staff contracts, job descriptions ... '

I look up and notice Isaac's turning a rather sickly shade of beige. He nods, though, which I take as a yes, before he grabs his man-bag and makes a break for the door.

So we haven't painted the walls pink and orange. We haven't got the mismatched chairs or Chesterfields or, indeed, the low coffee tables to go with them. And no, we haven't even got round to getting the Peter Rabbit kids' crockery and cutlery sets yet ... but it looks great, just as it is. And with kids' paintings and drawings stuck up on the walls, it'll have that real cosy, cluttered family-kitchen feel to it in no time.

After everyone else has gone, I look around proudly, taking it all in. Eventually I remember I have to go home and, as I slide the front doors shut and lock them, I turn to see a beautiful wintry beach vista.

A chilly wind whips past me and I hunch my shoulders up to my ears. I marvel at the moon and how unbelievably bright it is tonight. It almost looks fake – like one huge, powerful floodlight has been suspended in the sky.

Its beams reflect on the sea, shimmering and sparkling, like the greeny-blue sequins on the tail of the Little Mermaid outfit Joey's got her eye on, and I feel as though my heart is going to pop – as Jack used to say, when he thought about me in the early days. I can't help myself,

187

giggling and beaming right back at that big old marvellous moon. Until at last I become aware of how mad I must look.

'Silly Mummy,' I say, as though Joey was here, and I face the wind, heading for home.

Chapter 14

We're due to open in an hour and, all of a sudden, Isaac's bolting for the front doors, mumbling something about the cash and carry and coffee supplies.

'Hurry back, will you?' Shoshie shouts at his fast disappearing form. 'We need you to sort out the float for the cash registers and ... oh, what's the point? I'll do it myself.'

She resignedly trudges over to the ludicrously expensive – but fabulously decadent – Victorian cash register she 'snapped up' at an auction last week ('$700 is a steal for something as beautiful as this!' It's certainly got something to do with robbery, I'd muttered under my breath) and studies its façade lovingly.

'Gorgeous. I'm going to have to put little sticker dots on the keys for dollars and cents – can't be doing with all this shillings, pence and whatnot. I can't even find the sale button!' She presses all the shiny silver and ivory keys.

Ding! Out pops the cash drawer, hitting her in the tummy.

'Hoo! Found it!' She giggles.

'Where's Isaac off to?' I ask, wandering over.

'It's just as well *he's* looking after supplies – I had no idea we were short of coffee. What a disaster it would've been if we'd opened to the caffeine-hungry hordes and ran out of it within an hour!'

'Blimey,' I say, 'I could've sworn we had … Oh well – thank God for Isaac.'

'My sentiments exactly.' Shosh smiles.

'Deep breaths, everybody,' says Shoshie as she and Isaac prepare to open the massive all-glass doors.

'Tits and teeth!' a grinning Isaac adds.

'Bumps and rumps!' Kylie sticks out her bum and elbows me in the tum.

'Come on,' I smile, 'get on with it! I'm parched as it is – bet there are billions of mums spitting feathers out there!'

And so, as 'Manic Monday' blares out of our huge speakers, they slide the doors open, letting in a small but perfectly warmed wave of humid, salty air.

It's one of those gorgeous days – bit hot for me, but everyone else assures me it's just perfect. So even if it is a Monday, Bondi is rammed and it shouldn't be too long before our cafe is, too.

We bustle about, trying to make ourselves look busy, wiping down tables, straightening our kids' artwork and wondering why the hell we haven't been overrun by snotty-nosed toddlers and frazzled mums.

'Give it a chance,' says Jack over the phone. 'You've only been open for five minutes!'

'Two hours, you mean,' I grumble back. 'There's only one person here, looking down her nose at us and pretending she's reading *The Contented Little Baby*. Just looks weird to me.'

'Maybe she's doing Michelin stars for mum cafes. Maybe she's a cafe critic for a newspaper. How does the place look?'

'Great!' I enthuse. 'Much better than it did, that's for sure. It's got an air of positivity and fun about it now. At least I think it has. But anyway. How are you going in there today? Everything all right?'

'Same old, same old.' He sniffs. 'Except the rumours are true – they *are* going to cull 25% of their staff. Only problem is, we don't know who and we don't know when. I do know that it's last in first out, though – so you'd better get some punters into that caff quick-smart if we're going to be able to pay the rent next month.'

He sounds cheery enough – a million miles away from the mean 'n' moody man on the verge of a nervous breakdown who took off on his motorbike the other week when I told him I'd lost my job.

Not that I blame him for reacting badly. It would be horrendous if he got made redundant: the way things are going so far, I wouldn't be able to support all three of us.

And now, 24 weeks gone, with the baby due in 16 weeks, exactly 112 days (I worked it out a second ago, going by the old 40-week rule. Well, there's nothing else to do – and with my remedial maths, my calculations took some serious time), we're going to be totally stuffed.

'Well, don't panic, Jackie. Have you started to look around for anything else yet? Contacted any recruitment agencies?'

'Yeah, yeah,' he sighs, 'did all that last week. There's just nothing out there. Big businesses are crumbling and small businesses ... well, you know what I think about small businesses. Especially start-ups in this climate.'

'It is a bit warm, you're right,' I say, waddling over to one of the tables directly under a slow-moving, Somerset Maugham-esque ceiling fan.

'But then again,' he says, 'maybe *you're* right. Maybe now's the time to take a risk, take a punt. I suspect we haven't got much choice in the matter, anyway.'

'Hmm.' I'm distracted by the cute, bouncy twin boys who've just bounded into the cafe. They're both white-haired, tanned-skinned and aquamarine-eyed. Your average surfie kids. Gorgeous. 'Bet their dad's not too bad, either.'

'What?'

'Um, not too bad, we're not doing too badly when it comes to dads – one's coming in right now. I better go, Jack – call you later.'

A shadow appears in the bright sunlight and, as it gets

closer, I see it belongs to a fine figure of a man – handsome, smartly dressed, with a confident stride as opposed to an aggressive swagger, his skin rugged, hardened by constant exposure to the elements but begging to be touched, it looks that silken. He extends his right hand to mine and is so surprisingly soft-spoken, he almost purrs. I close my eyes and I can picture all that testosterone ricocheting off his vocal cords, creating one hell of a super-sexy voice as he says:

'Ah, Roxane. This place looks amazing. Roxane? Are you all right?'

My eyes flip open. I put my right hand up to my forehead as a makeshift sun visor, so I can see properly – and be sure this Marlboro Man in touch with his feminine side is who I think it is.

And it is. It's Tarquin.

'Oh, hi, Tarq.' I blush, all disarmed by his hunksomeness. 'How's it going?'

'Not bad, not bad at all.' He smiles, making himself look all the more like *Magnum, P.I.* 'I know I'm not due till this afternoon, but I've got the kids all day today and we decided to come down to the beach early, so I thought I'd pop in, see how it's all going.'

'The kids?' I ask.

'Yes,' he says, sticking his hands in his pockets and swivelling from the hips. 'They're around here somewhere ... yeah, there they are, christening your chalk board.'

'They're yours? Those two gorgeous boys?'

'Yup. That's their mum's story, anyway – and she's sticking to it.' He winks and laughs that easy, warm laugh.

I'm glad we booked in three more sessions with him, took full advantage of their new parents discount before Jack and I become totally bankrupt. Now at least I've got this sumptuous eye candy to look forward to and dream about as we line up in the dole queue.

'Can I get you anything?' I finally remember what I'm doing here.

'If you keep me company while the boys play, yes. I'll have a pot of Earl Grey tea with fat-free soy, please.'

He pats his no doubt rock-hard abs and inhales sharply. He wanders off to the blackboard and I lumber past Jemima's skinny bottom in my bid to make Tarquin his tea.

'Who's the spunk?' asks Shosh as she wipes clean the bar for the umpteenth time today.

'Shh!'

'He can't hear over that jukebox you bought, Roxy, don't get your knickers in a twist. Who is he, anyway?'

'That's the couples counsellor,' I say as we both look longingly at him drawing animals on the blackboard.

'Married?' Shoshie sighs.

'Of course. Married with those two kids.'

'Oh,' she says, tucking the tray under her arm and putting her other hand on her hip, 'shame.'

As Tarquin approaches the table, Shoshie scuttles off and leaves me alone with him.

'So how are you and Jack getting on?' he asks when he's sat down.

'OK, I suppose,' I say.

'Sorry. I shouldn't ask out of consulting times. Sometimes it's hard to switch off. Sorry.'

'Oh no, no – don't be. You're only being polite.'

Silence descends upon us – but it's not awkward in the slightest. In fact, it's so comfortable, I feel like I've known him for ever. And just as I'm seriously thinking about grabbing his cheeks and snogging his face off, he passes me the packet of sweeteners. He takes a sip of his tea, replaces the cup in its saucer, leans back, clasps his hands behind his head and crosses his legs.

'I remember the first time I ever came here,' he says wistfully. 'With my wife, six years ago.'

'When it was the other cafe?'

'Yeah. Serenitea. Our first date.'

'Romantic?' I venture.

'After a fashion, yes.' He half smiles. 'Far too much wine, a stroll along the beach at sunset and wallop! There we were, two years later, married with twins, another one on the way, mortgaged up to the hilt, drowning in debt and planning our respective divorce parties.'

'Really?'

'Yep. Things were pretty hairy there for a while.' He smiles again, but more broadly this time.

'So I suppose you sorted things out brilliantly, being a couples counsellor and all,' I say, only a tad simperingly.

'No, no, not at all. I only specialised in couples *after* we divorced. After the ... termination.' He whispers the last bit and leans in to me, as though he's in church taking the Lord's name in vain. Then he looks up to the ceiling, waiting for a thunderbolt.

'Oh,' I say.

'Yeah. We got pregnant too soon after the twins and she couldn't take the strain of another baby on top of those two, so against my wishes, she ... Love those Deep South fans, by the way. IKEA?'

'They came with the cafe. Been here for years, probably. Maybe even when you came here with your ... '

'Ex. Yeah, maybe. Though we were too busy staring into each other's eyes, falling in love back then. Didn't think to look up or notice the furniture.'

'No, don't suppose you did.'

'So. How are you finding the counselling? My secretary tells me you booked three more in. You must be getting something out of it?'

'Yeah, we are, as a matter of fact.'

'Great,' he says, slapping both hands on his most probably damsel-in-distress-rescuingly hard, strong thighs. 'Well, I'll be back this arvo about four. You'll be packed to the rafters with punters by then, I just know it.'

'Oh, are you leaving? I thought you might like to try one of my wheat-free, gluten-free, fat-free and totally joy-free muffins,' Shoshie says, all sotto voce and dimples, just as Tarquin stands up.

'Tarquin? My business partner and co-founder of JAMM, Shoshanna. Shoshanna—'

'Tarquin, yes.' She bats her eyelids. Nearly almost curtsies as well, she's so dazzled by him and his right royal gorgeousness.

'Nice to meet you.' Tarquin beams. 'Low GI?'

'Naturally,' Shoshie says.

'Maybe later. Right now, the boys and I have got a date with some wetsuits. I'm teaching them to surf,' he says.

'Ooh.' Shoshie squirms in her apron like she's Dita Von Teese trapped in a pinny. 'I'd love to learn how to ride the waves.'

Tarquin looks slightly bemused and Shoshie's fluttering her false eyelashes so much, one's come half off and the other's starting to drip mascara down her cheek. I put my arm round her shoulders and say I think we're needed in the kitchen.

We bid Tarquin farewell for the time being and when we're safely behind the bar, we fix Shoshie's lashes in the mirror tiles.

Looking up, I see Isaac walking towards us.

'Where are you going now?' I ask him.

'Supplier. We're all out of semi-dried Tuscan tomatoes and truffle oil,' he says.

'Oh, hon?' says Shoshie, wiping her eyes with a

Kleenex. 'Would you get me some Optrex while you're out?'

'Sure, babycakes. Ooh, yes. Looks like you're getting a nasty stye in that eye.'

We both watch him in his cream linen suit, sleeves pushed up to the elbows, as he runs one hand through his badly bleached hair while the other slips his Ray-Bans on. He's singing along to the jukebox, belting out 'Hungry Like The Wolf' as he saunters off to his car and I can't help thinking he looks like a failed auditionee for *Miami Vice*. Wonder what Shoshie thinks of his look.

'Scrappy-Doo in a suit,' she says, as though she's just read my mind.

We both giggle.

'What were you doing with Tarquin just now?' I ask.

'Oh, I don't know,' she says, picking Samia up out of her pram and walking over to the baby play area. 'Trying to flirt, I suppose, but just making a big fool of myself.'

'Don't be silly – you look great,' I say.

'No, I don't!' She bends to put Samia down gently on the soft alphabet play mat and then stands up to face me, crossing her arms over her chest. 'I look ridiculous. Pathetic.'

'Rubbish!'

'Yes, that too!' She smiles. 'Oh, Rox – it's not exactly Grand Central Station in here at the moment and I've been thinking. If things don't work out with me and Isaac and he leaves me, how on earth am I going to find the courage and the will to get out there again? I don't want to be alone for the rest of my life, but I'm not sure I can do all that flirty stuff, get back in the dating game. It's just not me.'

'Course it is – you're a bit rusty, that's all.'

'Hmm. We'll see. Still, at least Tarquin was a safe guy to practise on – it's not as if he's available or anything. Is he?'

'Not sure. He's divorced, but he might have a girl-friend – or fifty. I mean, just look at him.'

We sigh in unison like a pair of swooning schoolgirls.

Another flustered woman wielding a red Phil&Teds three-wheeler bashes into a table with her front wheel.

'Let me help you,' I say, moving the table and clearing a path for her. 'Tough day?'

'Don't get me started,' she puffs. 'I just want to sit down, catch my breath for five minutes.'

'Would you like something to drink? Eat?'

'Ha! Chance'd be a fine thing. I haven't stopped all day and if it's not the baby demanding to be fed, it's my tod-dler ... Jake? Jake? JAKE! Oh God! *JAAAAAAAAKE!*'

'Is that him, over by the chalk board? Playing with the Lego?' I say calmly.

'Oh!' She slaps her right hand on her chest. 'Yes! Come here, Jake – right *now*. Sorry about that—'

'Sorry about what? One of our childminders will look after him. Don't you worry, just relax.'

'Oh, really? How much does that cost?'

'Nothing! It's all part of the service. Now, what can I get you?'

Yet another pot of chamomile tea and a plate of Oreos is ordered (a JAMM special, simple but scrummy, called The Chameo), and before you can say 'I'm knackered!' our eightieth customer is leisurely reading the paper while her baby snoozes in the pram and Jake runs Zoe and Sophie ragged.

Since lunchtime, we've been absolutely inundated with Bondi's hungry and thirsty. Some groups of mums and their kids, some mums on their own with kids in tow, several groups of women *sans* kids and quite a few clusters of ordinary people having a coffee in a cafe, their parental status unknown. So after a pretty poor start this morning, things are really starting to look up.

And the best thing is that all our customers appear to be super-satisfied when they leave. One or two have even come up and congratulated me and Shoshie on a fantastic idea, saying it's unbelievable that no one had thought of it before. They say they'll tell all their friends about it and will definitely come back, et cetera et cetera et cetera. Which makes me fairly burst with pride and smile extra widely at the next cream-crackered customer.

Who, right now, just happens to be Tarquin.

'Can't keep away, eh?' I wink at him, coming over all cocky after all the compliments we've had.

'Ha! Yes,' he says, humouring me. 'So. Where do you want me?'

I resist the temptation to say anything saucy in reply to this and show him to the table near the bar. We thought that'd be the best place for counselling sessions – far enough away from the rest of the cafe rabble, but near enough to the staff (i.e. Shoshie and me), polishing glasses behind the bar counter, to earwig. Genius.

'No one's booked in any sessions yet – but they might feel more inclined to if they can see you here, with your little laminated placard and everything, rather than expecting them to read the noticeboard as soon as they walk in.'

'Right. Well. The boys are fine to muck around with the Lego and trucks over there, are they?'

'They can even dress up in fairy and princess outfits if they want – what happens in the crèche at JAMM stays in the crèche at JAMM!' I say, proud that we're providing such useful facilities. 'In fact, they'd better get in quick, before Shoshie gets back with Joey and Gila, the terrible two.'

'Great. Could I trouble you for one of those muffins Shoshanna was trying to offload on me earlier? While I wait for the warring masses to descend on me . . .'

He flashes me that winning smile and a beam of light bounces off one of his whiter-than-white teeth, like a star-burst, so sparkly that I swear I can hear it go *ping!*

Turns out I'm not the only one to notice his Hollywood gnashers, though, because by the time I return to his table with his order, three women have pulled up chairs and they're all leaning on their elbows, chins on palms, mesmerised by whatever he's saying. Honestly, he could be reading the shipping forecast and we'd all be entranced. He's our very own lighthouse in the stormy sea of parenthood, I think to myself.

'I see the Pussycat Dolls are out on the prowl,' heh-hehs an excited, squeaky male voice next to me.

And then it hits me – the overwhelming smell of Brut 33. Who knew they still made that stuff? It makes me cough and splutter – even more so when I see it's coming from Isaac.

He's rubbing his hands together in glee as he sashays over to Tarquin's table, and when he interrupts their conversation, leaning in between two of the women, it isn't long before all three of them make their excuses and Tarquin's left sitting there by himself, reading his Kindle.

'Sorry about Isaac,' I say. 'Did the yummy mummies make any appointments for counselling – or just dates for some one-on-one?'

'They made appointments for counselling sessions with me and their other halves, as a matter of fact.' Tarquin crosses his legs and pushes his Prada glasses up with his middle finger. 'For next week.'

'That's great,' I gush.

'Yeah, it is. I'm totally surprised, I must say. But if you don't mind, I think I'll leave it for today, get the kids home and whip up a quiche for their supper.'

No, really.

'Of course, of course,' I eventually manage, once I've recovered from this latest, even more startling evidence that Tarquin is either a screaming queen, severely continental or, quite simply, the perfect man.

About five minutes after Tarquin leaves, there's a scrum by the noticeboard, with all our female customers signing up for a session with him, right next to Shoshie's nutrition notice and Super-Duper Nanny Cooper's. No one's signed up for a nutrition session yet, but there are several names scrawled under Nanny Cooper's – mine being the first in line. I can't wait to get some tips on how to deal with Joey, even if she has been marginally better since I told her about the baby.

Jack comes in briefly and picks up Joey just after six, and it's gone ten by the time the last customer leaves. It's only me and Kylie left, cleaning up and emptying the money from the registers. Well, it's mainly Kyles doing the cleaning up, to be honest, while I concentrate hard on counting the cash – and we've made an absolute fortune, if my adding up skills can be trusted. Which they can't, usually, but, in this instance, when I know both Shoshie's and my and Jack's lives depend on it, I'm being extra careful and using a calculator for good measure.

I count it all five times, just to be sure. And I'm right – we've made a motza!

And just when I'm feeling all warm and fluffy, basking in the inner glow that people get when they know they're doing something worthwhile, something noble, some-thing that really helps other people; just when I'm smiling smugly to myself, thinking we're on to such a winner here, we're going to end up millionaires and it's all down to me and Shoshie and our combined boundless brilliant ideas and astute business acumen; just when I'm feeling full of youth and vim and long-lost vitality, we get our first complaint. Or, rather, I do. And it cuts me to the core.

It's from Kylie as she's rushing out the door to catch the bus home, about the songs I spent a whole week lov-ingly – and legally, I might add – getting permission to put on our 1950s Wurlitzer jukebox.

'No wonder the place before us went bust – that music's got to go!'

'Hey!' I reply. 'I sorted all those fab eighties tunes out! And everyone loves them!'

'Everyone?' she says suspiciously. 'Everyone over forty, maybe.'

'Watch it,' I warn her.

'Why don't I access some awesome RnB for us? Something a bit more ... modern?'

'Because most modern music is total and utter rub-bish?'

'You sound like such an old ... Look. I'll prove you wrong if you just give me a chance. And what's the bet you won't be able to help yourself jiving or jitterbugging or whatever it is you old folk do?'

'Twenty bucks says I won't want to dance, just stick my

fingers in my ears!' I grin, wondering whether Kylie's noticed that old classic 'The Gambler' by Kenny Rogers has just come on softly.

'You're on!' She flashes me her perfect smile as she turns tail and runs out the door.

Chapter 15

I'm more excited than usual about going into work at the cafe today – because, finally, I'm going to get some much-needed help and guidance from our very own Super-Duper Nanny Cooper (Elizabeth to her nearest and dearest).

She has her own website, is ultra-professional, has qualifications coming out of her kazoo and even though she looks awfully stiff and over-starched in her photo, that's kind of exactly what you want in a spit-spot-sort-it-out kind of nanny, isn't it?

After reading only great things about her, glowing testimonial after near-religious-fervour glowing testimonial, I gave her a ring. As no-nonsense and businesslike as she looks, she sounds even more severe. But, after speaking to her for a few minutes, selling JAMM, she was keen to get on board. I stressed that we wouldn't be able to pay her, of course, but that she would have an endless supply of desperate families in need of her help and I think she thought it was an offer too good to refuse, not having an office of her own.

So, anyway, today's the day – my first consultation with Elizabeth. It's booked in for just after midday when she can observe how I handle Joey at a mealtime. We've cut right back on Joey's days at the pre-school now, because we're so cash-strapped. I'm not drawing a salary from JAMM yet, and Jack reckons the axe is going to fall on his neck any day now, so it's the bare necessities for our growing little family at the moment. Which means no more takeaways or sweets (well, only the JAMM leftovers, which are free – oh, the perks of being the boss!), no more ciggies for Jack and a gluten-and-everything-else-free muffin or two for Joey on Treat Fridays (we had to think of something to make up for her no longer being able to make her own challah – a kosher bread roll – at Shalom! Baby every Shabbat, which she loved).

As I walk into the cosy, orangey glow of the cafe, my heart leaps when I see how packed it is. It's the busiest it's ever been, so far. Not one table is free and Shoshie, Kylie, Isaac – even the usually slow-as-a-wet-week Luke – are running around like chooks with their heads cut off.

'*Après*-school-run rush,' pants Shoshie as she whizzes past me, holding her tray over her shoulder. 'Get your apron on and get in amongst it!'

I do as I'm told, exhilarated to hear people chatting noisily, peals of laughter periodically piercing the hot air.

Mercifully, the horrendous hardcore RnB Kylie insists on playing can barely be heard over the din, and I steady myself on the bar to stop and marvel at the mums and dads and kids who are running a-thorough-mok in our cafe. We've come up with the collective noun for mums – a frazzle – and already identified several tribes . . .

There's the Yumsters: the tables full of yummy mummies, their shiny, perfectly-coiffed hair looking like they've just stepped out of a salon, and of which they do a lot of flicking and tossing about whenever one of their number says something even vaguely amusing – or a man enters their orbit. They don't eat much – and never touch anything resembling carbohydrate (they're all wheat-intolerant, you see) – but our Diet Cokes, Evian, wines and spirits are fairly flying off the shelves thanks to them and their liquid lunches. And they do look fabulous, it has to be said – even if all you ever hear them talk about is who's had what done, whose boob job was botched and who's hosting the next to-die-for divorce party in the exclusive, super-rich part of Bondi where most of the mums from Shalom! Baby live.

Then there's the Bumsters: the hippie mums and dads, wearing Jesus sandals and tie-dyed pantaloons, reeking of pot as they casually lounge about on the chairs, only coming in out of the sun because they've got the munchies something severe and need a place to shelter from the police. I like the air of relaxedness they carry about them, it reminds you that it's not all chaos and pandemonium and that you, too, could stop to admire the view if you just took some time out of your hectic schedule to spark up some spliffs and seriously de-stress. Not that I'm into that sort of thing at all – liquor is quicker, as Dorothy Parker once said, and wine will always be my drug of choice. Still, it's good to have the Bumsters around – it's sort of like having a pocket of deep calm, a plunge pool of positivity, she'll be right and no worries in the middle of Bedlam.

Never stopping for long, but providing a steady stream of customers are the Tits, Thighs and Tumsters: the fitness freaks, all Lycra-ed up and sweaty, their hair permanently scraped back in perky ponytails – because you can pump weights and be sexy, too, you know. Or at least that's what they keep telling each other as they compare muscle definition and build up their biceps by way of some pretty nifty baby lifts. One of them, Kristin, wants to start up a running club for mums keen to rid themselves of 'their unsightly post-baby bulges' (her words, not ours) and a keep fit class for pregnant ladies who don't want their bodies to go to pot – unlike the Bumsters, who can't wait to get there.

Speaking of, there's usually a fairly hefty contingent of pregnant women around, too. Kylie's christened them the Bump Brigade – women of all ages, but mostly in their thirties and mainly in the caff on the weekends because they're still working. You can tell who's with child, even the ones who aren't showing yet, because they're all obsessed with making sure the poached and scrambled eggs are as stiff as boards so as to avoid Listeria. They're either turning their noses up at pâté and salami or running off to the loos every five minutes. It's quite hard to tell someone's pregnant when you've only got the so-called 'glow' to go by, though. The only dead giveaway clue is when you watch them carefully and see that they're constantly eyeing up the Yumsters' glasses enviously and drooling ever so slightly as the glamour pusses put away their umpteenth Pinot Grigio of the day.

Jack really likes the Token Dads, though he objects strongly to the word 'token': 'Why can't we just call them the Dishy Dads or the Stay-at-Home Heroes? Something to make them sound a little less . . . reluctant and useless? A little less like a trophy or an ornament?'

In answer to this, and a nod to how majorly exhausted and old these guys look, we're considering a change of title: Dads Army. They prance about flitting from table to table, chatting up the mums while their BabyBjörns proudly show off their progeny. Not that I blame them – I'd hang around JAMM, too, if I were a bloke – an endless sea of women cooing over your child and admiring you and your courage simply for being here and not at work/the pub/somewhere else entirely, watching footy or playing games on your computer.

There's a small clutch of tables the Enviro-Mums favour, where they sit discussing recycling and which tree or rock they're going to chain themselves to next to ward off the bulldozers which are fast-tearing up the natural beauty of Bondi. They're like a faction of the Bumsters – or maybe it's the other way round. The two groups are definitely linked, though, because as I was racing around tables the other day, one of their number told me to slow down.

'Less haste, more speed, I know, I know,' I said.

'Less waste, more weed, darl – less waste, more weed,' said the woman clad almost entirely in purple tie-dye, sounding just like Luke – or like Dylan from *The Magic Roundabout*.

Of course, they're all closet Ummies, I often think to myself, to a greater or lesser degree, it's just that most of them don't have the guts – or, perversely enough, the *confidence* – to admit it. And some of us hide it better than others.

My favourite bunch frequenting our cafe, though, is the grandparents, the Super-Olds. Stepping up to the plate and virtually bringing up their grandchildren while the parents are at work, this lot make me fill up. It's like they're having the most fun out of everyone, all care and no responsibility. And they're so lovely, sitting at the quieter end of the cafe, smiling adoringly at their grandchildren as they sip their wine or beer (no requests for Horlicks so far), grateful for a bit of a break. And even though a lot of the Super-Olds are doing the parenting thing for the second time, just when they thought it was safe to become selfish again, they still maintain that their main role is that of grandparent – and it is their right, their job, in fact, to spoil those kids rotten. And good on 'em, I say. Because without them and the kids, we'd never sell any cakes and hot chocolates and assorted other sweet treats – everyone else is far too calorie-conscious.

Of course, Anita's been a regular fixture once she found out that JAMM was reasonably priced and that stacks of men of all ages visited the place. As a result, her dance card is always full, she has no shortage of dates and she can get all her flirting in (poor Luke has been on the receiving end of more than his fair share of bum pinches, but he always good-naturedly laughs it off and flirts right back with her) while she catches up with all her old mates as well as being with Joey heaps. In between the cackling and the bony-handed bum-pinching, she and her pals talk breathlessly about the latest debate on Gransnet, the brilliance of our permanent pensioner discounts on sherry, Pimm's, Campari and Liebfraumilch, and gossip about who's stepping out with whom and who needs to up their dose of Viagra. Kylie often teases me about joining their number, given my love of music that came out before she was born.

On days like this, it seems that the place has an almost village feel to it, like a real community. And looking at all these different people with different stresses and strains, all coming together under one roof to get the recognition and respite they deserve and, indeed, desperately *need* in order to carry on – well, it makes me proud. Makes me feel like we've created a home, a haven, a safe sanctuary for our whole new extended family.

As I'm standing there, admiring our handiwork, Joey runs into me and wraps her arms around my knees. She's sobbing.

'What's wrong, flower?' I ask, stroking her Shirley-Temple-gone-berserk locks.

'That boy hit me!' She sniffs and points to a couple of little boys playing around the wigwam in the kids' corner. One of their mums is there too, laughing away as if all is right with the world, which makes me mad.

I drop to my knees (as much as my tummy will allow – sometimes I forget that I'm twenty-seven weeks gone) and brush her fringe out of her red, wet eyes. She throws her arms around my neck and howls into my shoulder. I feel her pain, so I stand up, grab hold of her hand and march purposefully over to the scene of the alleged crime.

'He did it, Mummy! He hit me!' Joey says, pointing at a particularly snotty-nosed little boy.

The mum – obviously this boy's mum – stands, pulling herself up to her full height of six-foot-a-million, and puts her hand on her hip, jutting out over the top of Juicy Couture pink velour tracksuit pants. She flicks her dead-straight (probably naturally) hair back over one shoulder, purses her plump, Pete-Burns lips and looks down at me as she says:

'Oh, for God's sake – he's a boy! Boys will be boys – he's only bloody playing.'

I'm seriously considering nutting her right then and there, but, let's face it, my forehead only comes up level to her sharp, angular hips, so it'd be *me* who'd need the stitches. And I've never really been one for violence or even acting tough – I'm a lover, not a fighter. Even if Jack would scoff and say it was definitely the other way round.

So anyway, I'm standing there, totally flummoxed by what this woman's said, mouth agape, when Shoshie flies past me, tray held high overhead and says, sing-song style, without moving her lips, never letting her smile slip:

'Customer's always right, remember!'

Hmm.

She's got a point, though – Shoshie, that is, not the smug supermodel – so I smile sweetly and whisk a battered and bruised Joey away from the teepee and on to my lap in front of Elizabeth. Who is no doubt going to have a right go at me for not standing up for Joey just now, I think, so I open with:

'Did you see that? Normally I'd have had a rational discussion with that lady about the rights and wrongs of play and probably opened up a discourse on playground etiquette—'

'I've been watching you, Roxane,' Elizabeth says flatly. And a little bit scarily, too, if you want the truth.

An embarrassed 'Um' is all I can muster by way of a

reply. 'I thought you were only going to observe us together at a mealtime ...'

'I think I've seen enough,' she says and heaves a huge sigh.

'I don't *want* lunch,' says a recalcitrant Joey, right on cue, and wriggles off my lap. 'I want *play*!'

I try to tug her back, but Elizabeth looks me dead in the eye and shakes her head from side to side slowly.

I let Joey go and hold my breath, waiting for Elizabeth to totally assassinate my parenting character.

'Let's cut to the chase, shall we? You'll have another baby to deal with soon, so you need to get your house in order. Fast.'

'I know, I know—'

'Please, Roxane.' Elizabeth cuts me off. 'My time here is limited. Let me tell you what I think the problem is and then you may speak. OK?'

I nod my head, suitably chastened and silenced. Super-Duper? Super-Schoolmarm, more like. She's talking to me as though *I'm* the child.

'Now,' she goes on, consulting her notes, 'Josephine will soon have to adapt her techniques, her up-till-now failsafe ways of getting everything she wants.'

Elizabeth pauses for breath. The intro to Wham!'s 'Everything She Wants' starts up in my head. The 12-inch version. Which reminds me – I've *got* to get Kylie's hideous music off the CD player, and put that jukebox back on. *Concentrate, concentrate. This is important.*

'Josephine has a tendency to dominate the family. Her voice is always heard, her wants are invariably instantly met and she is never expected to wait. It is not fair on her and not fair on you,' says Elizabeth.

'Now you're talking,' I say, feeling relieved that she sounds almost as if she's on my side.

'Yes, I am. Do let me finish, please!' She huffs. 'What both you and Josephine need now is for her to learn to respect you. And she will if she sees that you are in control of her in a positive, supportive, learning way. We call that discipline.'

'Ah,' I say. 'I don't know about that. I'm not really into punishing her. I don't want to break her spirit or anything.'

'It's not about breaking her spirit, it's about breaking bad habits and giving her a blueprint for life. She is a child and should not be burdened with reasoning through decisions for you.'

'But I never know what the right thing to do is,' I interrupt. 'So I often ask her. She's usually right, after all.'

'Yes, you do tend to defer to her rather a lot. But you are her *mother*. You are the adult, *you* are the boss. It may not show, but it matters to her enormously – you are her world. But do not panic – you will soon gain the confidence to know your decisions are the right ones. And Josephine will begin to respect you as she should.'

'Gor – sounds like the impossible dream to me.' I raise my eyebrows.

'What's impossible is the current situation. You can't go on like this – and neither can she – especially with another one on the way. You just won't be able to cope with a baby and Josephine throwing tantrums to get her way. Do not discuss things with her, do not engage her in reasoned dialogue and try not to take it personally. She is *not* throwing tantrums to get at you, to make you sad or because she doesn't like you. She's a four-year-old—'

'Three-and-a-half, actually.'

Elizabeth shoots me evils and purses her lips.

'She's a *little girl* used to getting her own way. But you can bend her to your will and make her a more pleasant, reliable, respectful, polite and well-mannered young member of society.'

Ooh. That last bit jars with me a little – sounds like I'll be sending her off to some kind of borstal or boot camp or something. Basic training for automatons; replicants. I'm not sure I like the sound of this any more.

But before I have a chance to object, Elizabeth dives into her Mary Poppins carpet bag and whips out a poster-sized laminated piece of thin cardboard which has lines drawn all over it, like a big piece of graph paper.

'And how do we do that?' she asks, laying the cardboard flat out on the table. 'With careful, judicious use of The Sticker Chart.'

It all goes quiet in the cafe as she says those last three little words and I get the uneasy feeling that everyone's eyes are suddenly upon us. The clanging of pots and pans stops and we hear a solitary knife dropping on the stone floor in the kitchen. Even Kylie's so-called music comes to a halt and when I look over at kids' corner, they're all staring back at me, a wall of innocent, captivated, slack-jawed faces. There's silence for about a minute, as though someone's taken the pin out of a grenade and the only thing we can all do now is wait – wait for the inevitable fatal explosion.

I look around, perplexed, and see the tables of mums and dads and grandparents all craning their necks in a bid to get a look at what's on our tabletop. And then . . .

'STICKERS!' the kids scream en masse, and start running towards us.

'CHART!' the adults chorus, as the sound of chairs being scraped back on stripped floorboards fills the air.

There's a mad rush as the hordes scramble to our table.

Elizabeth nods in a rather self-satisfied way and says:

'Never fails. You have to learn to talk to Josephine in a language she understands. And when she doesn't do what you tell her to do, punish her by taking away a star or a smiley face or whatever stickers you use. Simple.'

'Is that chart for me, Mummy?' says a breathless Joey, jostling for pole position with all the other kids next to the shiny chart. 'Are they *my* stickers?'

Elizabeth closes her eyes and nods this time, in a flagrant show of complete and utter know-it-all-smugness.

'Yes, Josephine. If you are polite to Mummy and you're a good girl, then you can put the stickers in their rightful place.'

'Well, I've heard time and time again that sticker charts can work wonders,' says one of the Yumsters.

'Didn't work with our Harmony,' chimes in one of the slow-talking Bumsters. 'Course she's far too intelligent and free-thinking. You can't box her in, pigeon-hole her, tie her down to strict routines and schedules. Nope, just like me, I suppose – you can't tie us down.'

The crowd discusses the pros and cons of chartage amongst themselves and, after about five minutes of heated debate, disperses.

When we're alone again, I tell Elizabeth what I think the column headings on our chart should be.

'I was polite to Mummy and didn't talk back; I apologised to Mummy when I was naughty; I didn't throw tantrums when I didn't get what I wanted; I did most of what Mummy told me to do all day; I stayed in my own bed all night and I went to the toilet when I needed to in the middle of the night.'

Elizabeth looks appalled.

'No. No, no, no.' She shakes her head. 'You've just given her a list of things to do that will wind you up! And it's all far too negative—'

'What does farty negative mean, Mummy?' Joey giggles.

'Tell her calmly and firmly not to interrupt, you're

having a conversation with me,' Elizabeth coaches me, her eyes never leaving mine.

'Joey? I'm talking to Elizabeth, now, so please don't interrupt.'

'But Mummy! She said farty!'

'No, she didn't,' I can't help but smile as I look down at Joey, 'she said *far too*.'

'En-*gay*-ging,' sing-songs Elizabeth, rolling her eyes to the ceiling fans and sighing. 'You're engaging with her. Tell her what's what and move on. Remember who's in charge?' Her Aussie inflection, going up at the end of her sentence, makes me think she's asking me.

'No. Who?' I ask, innocently enough, I think.

'That wasn't a question,' snorts Elizabeth. 'Oh, never mind. Let's look at the chart, quickly, shall we? My suggestions for column headings are right there ...'

I peer at this chart and down the left-hand side are the days of the week. Across the top are categories like '6.30 a.m., out of bed nicely'; 'Asked Mummy's permission to get down from the table'; and 'Bath, bed, story and lights-out, 7.30 p.m. sharp'.

'If each box has a sticker for a job well done in it, at the end of seven days of being a really good girl, Mummy will give you a treat,' says Elizabeth to Joey, who's nearly wetting herself with excitement.

'Mummy will fall off her seat with surprise, you mean,' I splutter.

Joey looks at me, wounded. Elizabeth shakes her head and tuts disapprovingly.

'No, no, what I mean is—'

'I'll leave you two to it.' Elizabeth stands up. 'Check in with me next week and we'll assess your progress, see if we need to re-evaluate. Good luck, Josephine.'

I linger wiping down a table so I can listen in on a conversation at the next table about which films these women want to see on our first film night.

'*Cocoon*,' says a radiant-looking Super-Old. 'Or *Calendar Girls*. Or, even better, *Travelling North* – a top Aussie film for the older generation.'

'You sound like a movie poster,' counters a Yumster. 'What about *Motherhood*? With Uma Thurman in it?'

'How about *The Bridges of Madison County*?' suggests an older Yumster, polishing off a large glass of Pinot Noir.

'Oh, yes, Clint Eastwood – my hero,' swoons Anita.

'And Meryl – how great is she? I'll watch anything with her in it.' The Yumster nods.

'*Heartburn*,' says Shoshie, sidling up to me and looking longingly at Isaac who, in turn, is staring at Kylie's bum.

'*Julie & Julia*,' I say. 'Meryl's brilliant in that. She and Stanley Tucci make the best couple – so romantic, so loving, with such a lust for life.'

'She slices through a lobster in that movie, doesn't she?' offers Shoshie.

'Yeah. Not as great as the lobster bit in *Annie Hall*, mind ... ' I say reflectively.

'Tea?' asks Shoshie.

'God, yes!' I yawn, and and make a beeline for the plate of brownies sitting on top of the bar. Chef made a batch earlier today – from his favourite Nigella recipe. 'What time is it, anyway?'

'Nearly nine. Why?'

'Oh no! I'm supposed to be fasting! I shouldn't have let anything pass my lips since eight – I've got the two-hour gestational diabetes test first thing tomorrow morning.'

'Are you at risk?'

'All preggos over thirty-five are, according to the hospital. There's no history of it in my family, so I'll probably be fine. I'm not bothered. But after this brownie, that's it – nothing more for me until I'm back here tomorrow. Apart from, perhaps, that teeny-tiny last slice of carrot cake, there. Seems such a waste to just throw it out – especially seeing as it's so delicioso, as Dora would say. And it's more a sliver than a slice, really, isn't it, Shosh? Shosh?'

I look around for Shoshie, but can't see her anywhere. A few seconds later, however, I can hear her. Loud and clear. Having an almighty row with Isaac out the back.

'Who *is* she?' screams Shoshie as a plate smashes.

I can't hear Isaac's quiet, mumbled reply, but then Shoshie bellows:

'There's more than one? Who are *they*, then? Tell me! Right now!'

Again, I have no idea what Isaac says, but, unbeknownst to her, Shoshie fills me in – and the rest of the cafe – when she yells:

'THE LUXURY FOODS MANAGER AND A COUPLE OF SALESGIRLS AT THE CASH AND CARRY? A *couple* of salesgirls? Oh, Isaac! How could you?'

I smile nervously at the women talking about films and mutter something about hot-blooded, passionate chefs as I make my way out the back.

'Are you guys OK?' I ask dumbly.

Isaac puts his cream linen jacket around Shoshie's shoulders and shushes her sobbing. Shoshie shrugs the jacket off and it falls to the floor.

'We'll be fine, thanks, Roxy,' says Isaac, stooping to pick up his jacket and dusting it down. 'I'm going to take Shoshanna home now, though. You right to lock up?'

He looks pleadingly at me, before putting his arm around Shoshie's waist and steering her homeward. For a moment, I almost feel sorry for him.

They look a right pair from the back, like Stephen Merchant and Ricky Gervais – one ridiculously tall and the other super-short in comparison.

God knows what Shoshie sees in him. God knows what the female half of Sydney's catering world sees in him.

'Of course,' I say. 'Ring me, will you, Shosh? When you get a sec?'

But she doesn't answer me, just storms off, the ineffectual Isaac trotting after her, trying to keep up with her, saying: 'But, babes, it was just sex, it didn't *mean* anything. I *love* you. Babes? *Babes?*' he squeals, breaking into a run.

Chapter 16

I've got to go to the hospital this lunchtime, to see the diabetic controller and get the results of my test, which, the teenager on the phone said, 'were a little high'. Just like the squeal emitted from my lips when she went on to say, after she checked my age: 'We're sorry, but you have gestational— I said, SORRY, BUT YOU HAVE GESTATIONAL DIABETES, DEAR!' as though I was deaf.

Must be a mistake. I mean, diabetes? Me? I'm not *that* overweight – it's all baby! And I'm only forty-two – hardly the ancient old crone they make you feel like with all that talk of the extra risks that go along with being a raddled old hag. Including, it would seem, becoming hard of hearing.

Jack's insisting on taking the whole day off so he can work from home and look after Joey. As if you can do both. Honestly, I've told him a kerzillion times that you can't work and do Joey, but does he listen? Does he heck.

But the weird thing is, he's not even doing this because

I've begged him to, as would usually have been the case. Normally I have to plead with him to take Joey just so I can have a bath – which is where I do most of my thinking, these days. And daydreaming about my fantasy family life, in which I always have:

a) the time to catch up with friends
b) the time and money to regularly pamper myself with wonderful massages and facials and
c) the time, money and *chutzpah* to run away and fly off to Acapulco when it all gets too much (that'll be every day between five and seven-thirty p.m., then).

As I'm getting ready to run out the door (to the cafe, not Acapulco, worst luck), it becomes clear that Jack hasn't got the first clue about Joey's new regime and The Sticker Chart.

'What's all this?' he asks in passing, seeing Joey sitting on the kitchen floor as we discuss her behaviour so far this morning. She was brilliant at staying in her own bed all night (amazing) and getting up at six-thirty a.m. without any trouble whatsoever (unlike her poor, bleary-eyed mother). With my permission, amid my gushing proclamations of how proud I am of her, she delightedly puts a spongy sunflower sticker in the box under the first heading for the day.

'The Chart!' Joey and I say in unison.

'Silly Daddy,' I add, wrinkling my nose up at Joey and giggling.

'How am I supposed to know?' Jack sounds a tad annoyed.

Briefly I feel sorry for him – because while I'm all of a sudden a rising star in Joey's galaxy, Jack's always been the sun around which she's orbited. He's not used to seeing Joey and me getting along so well – and he must feel, even if it's only a teensy bit, as though the pedestal he's been standing on for such a long time is being ever so slightly whipped out from under his feet, only for me to be stepping up on to it, waving gleefully to my adoring fan and smiling apologetically to the vanquished, the bronze medallist: him.

Then again, he's never voiced anything even remotely resembling those feelings. And if he never tells me how he's feeling, even when I ask him point blank, how am I supposed to have a clue? His silence merely forces me to make it up, putting myself in his place, asking myself how I'd feel in his situation. I haven't the faintest idea what he's *really* thinking.

No, hang on, two days ago, when we did the exercise Tarquin set us, he told me he'd stubbed his toe while he was hopping about in the morning, trying to get his motorbike boots on. He says this hurt him a lot; he felt pain. And he said that, as a result, he thought he was a bit of a pillock. Yep, that was his feeling and thought for the day.

Blood out of a stone, I tell you.

Anyway, I fill Jack in on what Elizabeth said, bandying

words like 'discipline' and 'consequences' and 'routine' and 'boundaries' about like billy-o.

'Hmm. Sounds a bit strict. I'm not sure about all this regimenting a little kid's behaviour – I don't want us to break her spirit,' Jack says warily.

'*Her* spirit? What about *my* flippin' spirit?' I reply, annoyed that he isn't immediately supportive of anything that will make my life with Joey easier. 'Anyway, we won't – she'll be just as lovely and feisty and fun and smart, we'll break some of her bad habits, that's all.'

Joey, jumping up and down beside me, tugs at my fingers and says, 'Stickers! Tell Daddy about the *stickers*!'

'Right.' I defer to her, as per usual, and do what she tells me to do.

'Righty-ho,' says Jack breezily when I've finished. It's almost as if he's blissfully unaware of the brilliant strategist he'll be dealing with.

'Did you hear anything I just said?' I ask him.

'Every word.' He sighs.

'But did you *listen* to any of it?'

He closes his eyes, looks like he's meditating, searching for inner calm or something, and doesn't say a word. It's an expression he's been working with for quite some months now, and I've seen it many, many times. I'm slowly starting to understand Jack's unspoken, silent language, and I think this look, roughly translated, means something like, *God, give me strength!*

I purse my lips and let it go.

For once I read the situation accurately and don't push any further, having learned my lesson last week. He did something nice for me, like letting me watch *How to Look Good Naked* when the cricket was on, and I stupidly commented on it.

'Oh, you're being nice,' I'd said, grinning and feeling all warm and fuzzy for the first time in a million years.

It was a short-lived feeling.

'God, don't say that!' he snapped, frowning.

'Why?' I asked, confused.

'Because it sounds like I'm never nice, like I'm normally a right nasty bastard. But I'm not. I bend over backwards for this family every day!'

And *I'm* the one with the raging hormones, the one supposed to swing wildly from mood to mood.

Anyway, as you can imagine, I decided I'd keep my own counsel from that moment on, mentally noting the slight change in rules for dealing with Jack thus:

* Most of the time, you *do* have to state the bleeding obvious to him, like: 'You're driving too fast'; 'Put another chilli in that and neither Joey nor me will be able to eat it'; 'It's so boring going through the instructions for Sky Plus – couldn't you just do the decent thing and sort it out for me?'
* But don't, whatever you do, go around pointing out his chivalrous/romantic/almost human behaviour – he'll take it as a backhanded compliment, as

though you're damning him with faint praise. The
twonk.

Maybe he thinks such acts of kindness are unmanly. Or, as
soon as you vocally acknowledge something like that, it's
out there and, as a result, rendered somehow invalid. And
maybe he's right. Maybe some things are best left unsaid.

Now, Jack slowly unfurrows his brow. I smile back.

'Sorry about that,' he says. 'But it'd be a big treat for all
of us, a real bonus, if we could just start being a bit more
pleasant to each other.'

I nod.

'We'll get there, Rox,' he says, looking down at me
almost like he used to, with warmth and affection twinkling in his eyes. 'We just need to appreciate each other
more. We're both doing a great job – you at home and me,
hopefully, in work, bringing home the bacon.'

'But I'll be bringing home some bacon, too, soon,' I say,
slightly irked that he doesn't acknowledge the cafe and
the hard toil I put in there. 'Not as much as you, I know,
but in time it could really be a growing concern.'

Jack sharply sucks in some air and thins his big
lips. Then he looks at the floor, concentrating hard, and
pretends to pick something off his tongue. Honestly.
Sometimes it's just like talking to a baby. So, in true mum-
style, I try to figure out what he's thinking, what he wants,
going by the physical signs he's displaying, reading his
face. Toying with his mouth – is he hungry? Closing his

eyes – tired? He pinches his tongue between his thumb and his forefinger and ... A-ha! Got it. Bloke-code deciphered. This is him holding his tongue, isn't it? God! Men are so *literal*, aren't they?

'Counselling next week, yeah?' he finally says, exhaling deeply, sounding exhausted with the effort of not saying anything.

'Yeah, course. Actually,' I go on, amazed by how the mere act of smiling can make you feel so much warmer towards someone, 'if you wanted to have a bit of a rest this morning, I could take Joey with me to the caff and you could come and pick her up later, before I go to the hospital.'

Despite the fact Jack's my age, there's obviously no problem with *his* hearing.

'That'd be *fantastic*,' he says, quick as a flash, and blows us both continuous kisses as he backs out into our bedroom, where he'll no doubt play some ridiculous computer game until his fingers bleed.

As I unlock the big glass doors and walk into JAMM, I trip up on the usual pile of bills and flyers and bend down to pick them up. It's the same old boring stuff and I chuck it on what we call the Post Office Tower by the antique cash register – Isaac's pile of mail that he never opens.

But then this month's *Bonzer Bondi Bugle*, the free local rag, drops to the floor and Joey picks it up for me, in a fit of helpfulness, the like I've not seen for ... for ever, really.

231

'Oh, thanks, gorgey.' I take my hand from the small of my back that I've been rubbing and accept her offering. 'Not that there's ever anything even remotely interesting ...' I mumble as I look through the mini magazine, flicking from the de rigueur beauty salon coupons to an interview with local celebrity Toni Collette, to restaurant and cafe reviews.

And that's where my eyes suddenly feel as if they're going to bulge right out of their sockets and I might hyperventilate, my breathing's so shallow.

'Jo ... Jo ... There's a rev ... JAMM ... a rev—'

'Mummy? Is it the baby? Is it coming? THE BABY'S COMING! DAAAAADDY!'

Joey spins around on the spot, like she's seen me do a million times, and screams, 'What do I do? WHAT DO I DO?'

'Calm down, for a kick-off.' I stifle a giggle. 'Just ignore me and my slight, um, overreaction. Mummy's fine, nothing's happening. I'm just a little excited, that's all. Our cafe got its first ever review!'

Joey's mouth turns down at this, her eyes following suit. She lets her arms hang limply at her sides, hunches her back and lets out a desultory, disappointed, but still ever-so-slightly irritating, whiny, 'Owwwwww. I want the baby to come nowwww ...'

'Got ages yet,' I say, distracted by the review, and let my bum slowly descend on to one of the banquette seats so I can read the small type properly. It must be for a younger audience, this mag, because the type's so minuscule, anyone over the age of thirty would have to whip out their Miss Marple magnifying glass if they wanted to have a quick squiz. I improvise and hold the magazine out in front of me, looking down my nose and squinting, opening my mouth the way I do when I'm putting on mascara, pulling the mag in, then holding it out again, until I can just about make out what it says:

SOUTH BONDI SURFIE CJ REPORTS ON:

JUST ANOTHER MANIC MUM-DAY – LICENSED CAFE

TOP OF DIDGERIDOO DRIVE, JUST BEFORE THE BEND INTO RIDGEY DIDGE ROAD

Me and my girlfriend Doreen used to love going to this place, high on the hill overlooking the beach, before it became the No. 1 family hangout. Back then, it was a great place to grab a snack and a smoothie while you were waiting for the waves or it was just too hot on the sand.

But now?

Now it seems that if you're under twenty-five and don't have

233

kids in tow, you're pretty much persona non grata in here. Took me ages to get served while the waiter took his time making sure the pregnant bird at the table next to me was comfortable. Then, just as I thought he was going to get my order to the kitchen, he stuffed his notebook in his apron and ran after two little girls who were making a bid for freedom, away from the kids' Lego and chalk board area. He got a real hero's welcome when he came back into the cafe, one girl in either arm. Even got a kiss from their mums and one of their particularly grateful grandmothers, too. When I did finally get my Surf 'n' Turf pizza, I've got to say that it was … awesome. Bloody yummy. Waaay better than the tucker you used to get here.

Put it this way, if you like screaming babies and toddlers running amuck around your table; the toxic smell of baby poo overpowering the aroma of your prawns and Peroni and the bouquet of your chick's Chardy; having to shout to be heard over mothers yelling at their equally loud, annoying kids; incessant eighties music and The Bangles on a loop, you're gonna love this!

The pros: Yummy food, yummy mummies

The cons: Always packed, hard to get a seat

9/10

So they can't spell *amok*, and it reinforces my idea that the whole mag's aimed at twenty-five-year-old childless locals, but it's a great review.

I stand up and go to the bar, looking for a green highlighter pen, about to *explode* with pride, when I hear someone else coming through the front doors. It's Shoshanna.

'Shoshie! How are you? Where have you been for the past couple of weeks? I've been worried sick!'

'Hey, Rox.' She sniffs, taking off her massively over-sized sunnies. 'I've been staying at Mum's – sorry I've been a bit incommunicado.'

'Gor, that's all right – I know you had more … urgent matters to mull over. Coffee?'

'Yes, please. Jemima's not here yet and I'm not sure I like her coffee that much, anyway. Have we got any Nescafé?'

'Course we do. I don't drink coffee, so I haven't a clue about what Jemima makes, but a lot of the customers are asking for Nescafé specifically, lately, too. Isaac's just done a massive order – oops. Sorry. The I word.'

'That's OK. Bound to happen.' She half smiles. 'We're, er … we're still together, you know.'

'You *are*?' I'm shocked. 'After all that hellness with the cash and carry girls?'

'Ha!' she scoffs weakly. 'And the rest.'

'Are you OK?'

'Yeah, suppose so.' She coughs. 'I moved back into the marital home two nights ago.'

'I don't understand.' I shake my head. 'What kind of hold has he got over you, Shosh? It's like he's your guru and you're in a cult or something.'

'I know, I know.' She reaches into her handbag and pulls out a Kleenex. 'It's the cult of family, I suppose. I can't leave him because of the kids. They'd never forgive me if I took them away from their daddy. Because despite how horrible he is to me, they love him to bits and he *is* a good father …'

I consider this, my nose screwed up at the thought of Shoshie being held captive by a short, linen-suit-loving, Brut-33-splashing, fake-tan-applying, poor excuse for a man. I can't help myself and say:

'It's none of my business, and I'm probably speaking way out of turn here – but surely it's worse for those two girls and their senses of self-worth, self-esteem, not to mention their expectations of how relationships work, to witness you taking Isaac back time and time again, even though he can't keep his willy to himself. He's deluded! Thinks he's a cross between Hugh Hefner and Don Johnson. And it can't be doing your confidence any good, either, Shosh. You're thin and gaunt and just when you start getting your identity back, regaining all that confidence as the cafe starts becoming a roaring success, he steps in and ... and tries to shag everything that moves in it.'

I take a deep breath. Shosh studies the ground.

'The Boys of Summer' comes on the jukebox and I narrow my eyes meaningfully and sing along when Don Henley sings:

Don't look back, you can never look back ...

It's not the first time I've taken timely tips and learned important life lessons from cheesy eighties chart hits, let me tell you. Now maybe Shoshanna will see the light with the help of the medium of music, too.

'You're right,' she says, finally looking me in the eye, 'it is none of your business.'

I'm stunned. To the power of a hundred.

'But—'

'Look, Roxy, I've made my decision and I'm sticking with it. He's happy, the girls are happy and I'm … I'm going to do the right thing and stay with him.'

'But—'

'No, Rox, please. You're not making this any easier. Can we just talk about something else? Like the cafe?'

I bite my lip and then show her the *Bugle* review. We both laugh at CJ's description of the place and thank our lucky stars that it was a rave review in the end – because now we've been validated. We've done exactly what we set out to do: create a place just for us, a haven for stressed-out mums who aren't welcome anywhere else. We're floating on air as we talk about Chesterfields and coffee tables and the eclectic mix of mismatching chairs we still covet for our coffee shop. Which, of course, unfortunately plonks us right back into God-that-Isaac's-so-crap territory again. And I thought *I* was totally disorganised.

'Still,' I say, looking on the bright side, 'Isaac's slackness is giving me heaps of practice. By the time this baby arrives, my organisational skills will be so finely honed, I bet it'll come out saluting, standing to attention and saying, "Sir! Yes, Mum, Sir!"'

Shosh smiles at the thought.

'Honestly, Shosh, I'm so glad you're back. This is the best job I've had, *ever*, and you're my favourite colleague ever and the cafe's doing so well, it's always so packed. It won't be long before we can start paying ourselves a wage, I reckon, judging by the daily takings.'

'It's just the best fun, too, isn't it?' Shoshie really brightens up now. 'I missed it while I was away. It's weird, but this place feels more like home to me now than my actual home. And you know what?'

'What?' I ask eagerly, sitting on my hands.

'I reckon it's time we treated ourselves for once. We're always pampering all the other mums in Bondi – but what about us?'

'Yeah! But what? I'm pregnant, probably with diabetes – what could we possibly eat that's even remotely treaty?'

'One of my flour-free, low-sugar, guilt-less, totally taste-and-satisfaction-compromised apple and pear crumbles!' She raises her fist and punches the sky in victory.

And then clocks my face falling to the floor in disappointment.

'Well, when do you find out for sure about the diabetes?' she asks.

'Lunchtime today. Why?'

'Because that gives us plenty of time to drown some brownies in an ocean of hot, fat-full, crammed-with-sugar, lousy-with-carbs creamy custard, of course!'

I beam at her, pat my tum and lick my lips. No wonder she's my new best friend.

It's one of those absolutely perfect, gorgeous afternoons – all deep-blue sky, bright, warm sunshine, with a hint of a breeze in the air. Just the kind of day that makes you want to sit outside the front of a cafe or restaurant in a floaty floral number and oversized sunnies, sipping chilled white wine for hours, laughing and chatting with good friends and whiling away the day in a haze of happiness and several sneaky cigarettes.

That's what this sort of weather makes me want to do, anyway: must be a hangover from the good ol' days, when that was my idea of heaven. The best fun you could have, I used to think, was getting a little bit tiddly with friends, knowing you were going to be up until the wee smalls *having fun* – not up all night trying to soothe a screaming baby, only to be harassed by a tantrumming toddler during daylight hours. Those were the days – no cares, no responsibilities, just good times, good sofas and good takeaways to help you get over those inevitable horror hangovers.

But I've just returned from the hospital where they confirmed I have gestational diabetes. Which is a bit of a bummer, but at least maybe I'll lose some weight now I'm forced to for the health of my unborn child. I can't wait till I've had her (it must be a her – Joey's convinced it's a girl, and she's usually right about everything) – I'll be quaffing champagne and sharing cigars with the surgeons as soon as she's out. Because I'm definitely having a caesarean – Joey was big and an emergency caesarean and they say second babies are even bigger, so I'm not going to take any chances this time. And I'll be prepared when the designated day comes, for a calm, non-traumatic, blink-and-you'll-miss-it, pain-free caesarean. No worries, as they say round here.

'Hello? Can I help you?' comes a voice out of nowhere.

I come to, woken from my daydream, and a well-coiffed woman with large sunglasses on top of her head comes into focus. I must have been staring at her all this time without even knowing it, I was so lost in thought.

I'm standing there like a lemon, under the awning out the front of JAMM, tray under my arm, eyes welling up as I picture my newborn being handed to me, the sound of waves crashing in my ears.

'Sorry,' I say, shaking my head in an effort to regain full consciousness, 'I'm supposed to ask *you* that, aren't I? What can I get you?'

'That's all right,' she says, brushing her highlighted fringe out of her eyes. 'I'll have another glass of the Dalwhinnie, please. Another large one.'

Her dead-straight blonde hair frames a pretty face and I note she's done her make up so well, so as to look au naturel, that I can't help thinking she couldn't *possibly* have kids, she's so groomed and together. Which makes me wonder what she's doing here.

But then I spy the tell-tale sign of recent motherhood on the right puff shoulder of her thin, charcoal-grey cardie – a dead giveaway for the new mum indulging in some me-time – a creamy white-coloured patch of baby sick.

'A fine choice,' I say, licking my suddenly dry lips. 'Coming right up.'

Kylie must have taken her order the first time round, because I don't remember her, even though she's in my zone. Or maybe I did, but I've been on autopilot ever since my hospital appointment, so she could have landed on our awning in a UFO and I wouldn't have noticed. I've been so busy trying to take in all the gestational diabetes information the diabetic controller gave me.

I'm still trying to get my head around the idea that you should have low-fat everything (fat blocks the absorption of insulin into the cells, apparently) – so no fat, but aspartame- and saccharine-filled yoghurts, reduced fat (i.e. refined and processed to within an inch of its life) cheese, and margarine instead of butter. Which is really strange because I've been wolfing down the butter, thinking it's the best thing for the baby, despite the fat content, because it's not overly processed with countless e-numbers and fake flavourings and colourings. But no. When you've got gestational diabetes, butter's a bad boy not worth flirting with. Not that you can have much bread with your polyunsaturated, one-element-away-from-being-plastic margarine, anyway. Unless it's soy and linseed bread – and even then, only two slices a day (max) with some protein like a hard-boiled egg or some ham.

Carbs are dead to me now, I say to myself over and over, as the diabetic controller's words sink in and I start to finally accept that muffins, brownies, cheesecakes and all things sugary and yummy have got to go.

Luckily, though, it's not all doom and gloom. On the bright side, I must have *some* carbohydrate (crucial for the baby's brain development) in my diet – and, really, there is much joy to be had from three tablespoons of chickpeas or lentils in a dressing-less salad. Or so the controller assures me.

I'm not quite convinced about that, but needs must, I suppose, so I'm up for it. And I've got to do at least thirty minutes power-walking every day, too, to help keep my sugar levels down. The worst bit is I have to inject insulin into the top of my fleshy thigh every night for the rest of the pregnancy. Myself. Every night. For the next eleven weeks.

As I walk inside, I tell myself that eleven weeks isn't all that long – and, as I catch sight of my pudgy cheeks in the glass door, I realise that I'm still a mass of ambiguity about it all, like yin and yang: half of me is overjoyed and excited and fizzing over with anticipation and the other half wants to run away screaming, or shake my head and laugh when I wake up to find it was all a bad dream.

I rack my brain, looking for a positive somewhere in all this. I scan the room. Nothing comes to mind at first, but then ... BANG! I know!

I can feel myself starting to lose weight. Yep, as I watch tables full of happy punters tucking into blueberry cheesecake, devouring plates full of pasta and chips, carbo-loading to the max, sending their blood sugar levels soaring, I smack my lips and hazard a guess that I've probably lost about five pounds since this morning's custard caper already. In drool.

Chapter 17

'First thing I want to talk about this morning, everybody,' says Chef, standing at the head of a long table, 'is the catering for Shalom! Baby's Mother's Day party today.'

'Woohoo!' I clap.

'Yep, there'll be plenty of protein for you, Roxy – smoked salmon, low-fat cottage cheese – and loads of other kosher goodies. I'm even making a special batch of challah for Joey. I know how much she misses it.'

'Oh, Chef, you're a star.' I grin at him as, bizarrely, my mouth starts watering at the thought of low-fat cottage cheese.

It's seven-thirty a.m. and we're having a quick staff catch-up before we open our doors to the hungry hordes.

'Brilliant.' Isaac nods. 'This is our first outside catering job and we definitely want it to go without a hitch. If this goes well – which I'm sure it will – the possibilities for JAMM and catering to the outside world are endless.'

'Obviously,' I say, 'Shosh and I will be attending this

do – so, Kylie and Luke, I'm sorry, but will you be able to handle things on your own?'

'Aw,' drawls Luke, 'I've got something to say, everyone.'

He stands up sleepily, one tail of his black cotton shirt hanging out over the hip of his black jeans. His sleeves are rolled up and his skateboard shoes are scuffed, but supercool. He smiles hesitantly and says, 'I'm outy, dudes.'

'What?' we chorus.

'I'm offski, outta here,' he explains.

I feel the panic rising. What will we do for a slow but cute pair of hands now? How will Kylie cope on her own? Whose bum will Anita pinch and slap playfully?

'Yeah, it's been on the cards for a while. Me and an old mate are gonna get back to Nimbin. We're gonna jump in the Kombi, surf up the coast and then get back to our roots at the commune. It's been doing my head in, living in the city. Yeah.'

'Oh, Luke.' I feel a stab of sadness. He's been so nice to have around, his easy charm winning us all over.

'Nothing we can do or say to make you change your mind?' Shosh asks.

'Excluding a pay rise, naturally.' Isaac laughs meanly.

'Nah. Me mind's made up. I wanna go home.'

'Fair enough,' I say, hauling myself up to give Luke a maternal hug. 'When are you thinking of going?'

'This arvo.' He yawns.

'I think you'll find, Luke, your contract states that you

must give a week's notice . . . ' I hear Isaac say, but quickly tune out when my mobile rings and I step outside to answer it.

'Roxy?' a small, squeaky voice asks.

'Yes,' I reply.

'Troy here, Troy from You Beaut Bank? I think we may have a problem.'

Slowly I wander underneath the awning, staring at the ground, as Troy tells me that so far, in the eight weeks since we got our loan, not one red cent has been paid back to the bank.

'You're kidding!' I say, not believing my ears.

'Never about money, no,' he says. 'This is deadly serious.'

'But we've been open for six weeks and our takings have been phenomenal,' I go on. 'I cash up every night, put the money in the safe deposit box and Isaac banks it all the next morning. We've got the You Beaut repayments on direct debit, so there must be some mistake.'

'Unfortunately, Roxy, this is no mistake. The bank took a big enough risk with JAMM as it is – but when we see not one bean of repayment in two months . . . and not even a phone call to explain your situation and try to come to some sort of an arrangement, well, I'm sorry, but I have no other option than to repossess everything in the cafe. I'm going to have to seize your assets.'

'WHAT?' I squeal. 'But—'

'I'm really sorry, Roxy. I so wanted it to work out for you, I really did, but now—'

'No! You can't do that!' My heart starts racing and I fan my face as I feel red heat pricking my cheeks. 'Not yet. Can you give us some time? Time to find out what's happened? Pay you what we owe you?'

'Unfortunately it's not up to me,' Troy says softly. 'Head office is on my back.'

'Can you give us a week? Just one lousy week to sort this out?'

'I'm sorry, I—'

'What would your mother say, Troy?' I stamp my foot. 'She loves this cafe. She and her friends are always in here, boasting about you, saying what a good boy you are and how lovely you are and how you're the real human face of banking blah-di-blah-di-blah. What would your mum say if she could hear you now, hmm? You should be ashamed of yourself!'

The phone crackles a bit in the silence and I wonder if I went too far, got too personal.

'One week, Roxy. I give you one week.'

I flip my phone closed and narrow my eyes. Back inside, heading straight in Isaac's diminutive direction, I bend down and whisper/growl in his ear, 'Quick word. In private.'

He looks up at me, all startled and jumpy. Just as he stands, a deep voice booms, like Brian Blessed's just entered the building:

'Where do you think you're going, Silverman?'

There, in the corridor coming in from the back alley, stands the man-mountain that is our landlord, Malcolm.

'Ah, um . . .' Isaac's eyes dart to Shoshie's, he brings his hands up to prayer position and whimpers as he looks pleadingly at her, then at me, and then he runs, his little legs becoming a blur, right out the front doors. All that remains is his peach linen jacket on the back of the chair and the lingering odour of last millennium's Brut 33.

No one else moves. It's like we've all been put on pause, while Isaac was fast-forwarded to that Benny Hill music. And we stay this way for ages, brows furrowing and unfurrowing, swapping looks of bemusement and excitement. Finally, the landlord stomps over to the table, making the whole room shake and making me fear for the floorboards.

'Hasn't paid the rent for eight weeks,' he bellows. 'And I lent him money for the start-up, not to mention throwing in all the equipment. I mean, just look at that beautiful Wurlitzer. Still works a treat, playing the greatest hits of the best musical decade ever.'

Kylie and Luke swap furtive glances and snigger.

'What about the deal you cut with him?' I ask, getting more and more confused. 'Rent-free for the first three months, reduced rate for the second three—'

'What deal? There was never any deal!' God, he's so shouty, he's really quite scary. It's like feeling the wrath of King Triton in *The Little Mermaid*. No wonder Ariel ran away. Swam away, whatever.

'All I asked was for my daughter to be given a job and the rent to be paid on time. That's all. Knew I shouldn't have trusted him. He was always so full of it back in the Dubbo Dubbo days, what made me think he'd have changed?'

His daughter? Who on earth's his daughter?

'Would you like something to eat, something to drink?' Kylie asks, standing up and smoothing down her skin-tight black pencil skirt. Her bump looks magnificent these days and she can't help but show it off.

'If it's no trouble.' He softens at the sight of Kylie blooming.

'Not a problem – that's what we're here for, after all. But would Nescafé be OK? Our barista's caught in traffic and she's running late—'

'No, she bloody isn't.' He smiles and sits down in Isaac's chair, looking like a giant about to crush a seat made out of toothpicks. 'I know because she still lives at home with me, her dad. And she won't be coming in again, she's quit. Not that that's any great loss to the cafe, I'm sure. Can't make a decent cup of coffee to save her life.'

We all smile, relieved that he's not going to huff and puff and blow us all away, and Shoshanna leaps up to close the front doors and hang up the closed sign.

Then she sits down next to the landlord, placing her hands in front of her on the table.

'How can we make this up to you, Malcolm?' she asks, sucking in her cheeks to reveal bones so sharp you could cut cheese on them. All of a sudden, gone is the downtrodden, unhappy wife and – POW! – in her stead is a go-getting, confident businesswoman.

'Well, if it isn't the lovely Shoshanna.' Malcolm beams.

'Anything – within reason ... We'll do anything to keep these premises,' says Shoshie.

'Pay the rent on time for starters,' he says, shifting in his seat to face Shoshie. 'It's $500 a week, plus the eight weeks you owe me.'

'How about $500 a week starting now? And maybe, as a favour to an old, reliable friend, you'll waive the weeks we owe?'

Malcolm chuckles, his belly wobbling underneath his Ralph Lauren yachting casual polo shirt.

'Never could say no to you, Shoshie. Or my missus – she loves this place. She's always in here with her cronies, whingeing about their hubbies. Better here than in my ear, I say.'

He pauses and looks around, taking in the ambience. All eyes stay firmly fixed on his. Finally, after about one seemingly never-ending minute, Malcolm smiles, lighting up the place, and speaks.

'OK. It's a deal.'

Our collective relief is palpable.

'On one condition, though ... ' He trails off, looking Shoshie squarely in the eye. 'Promise me you'll ditch that loser Isaac, will you? Never was good enough for you. Don't know what you ever saw in him.'

Couldn't've said it better myself.

Shoshie smiles enigmatically, showing off her cheek-bones again, and blushes like mad.

With this, Malcolm stands up, tucks his shirt into his trousers, thus puffing out his chest, and salutes the table.

'Nice doing business with you,' he calls out as he disappears down the corridor leading to the back alley.

'Whoa!' Luke laughs.

'Indeed,' I mutter, wondering what surprises the rest of the day has in store for us.

We scatter about like cockroaches on a dark kitchen bench when the light's just been turned on, saying goodbye to Luke, getting ready to let the customers in and putting the final touches on Chef's Mother's Day platters.

We're so frantically busy, we haven't even got time to mention the morning's events until Shosh and I are walking to Shalom! Baby for the Mother's Day do.

The guilt I feel about leaving the cafe in its time of desperate need hangs heavy in my heart as Shoshanna and I walk side by side in silence. But I'd feel even worse if I didn't make it to Joey's Mother's Day party. I argue with myself about what is the right thing to do:

Business Me: You should be at work.

Mummy Me: No, you should be with Joey.

Business Me: You should be scaring up custom and making a hefty profit – you owe it to the mums of Bondi. And the bank.

Mummy Me: Sod the bank, Joey should come first. Always.

'I can't believe we came so close to losing the cafe,' says Shoshanna, finally shutting up my internal dialogue.

'It's worse than you think, too,' I say, and tell Shosh what Troy told me on the phone.

'That explains the receipts,' she says solemnly.

'Hmm?'

'The receipts for jewellery that've been falling out of his trouser pockets lately. For his girlfriends at the cash and carry and assorted suppliers – definitely none of it was for me. Opals, gold, emeralds, silver . . . '

'He must've been skimming thousands upon thousands off the top of our profits,' I say, still having trouble with taking it in. I'm furious.

'Skimming? Shovelling, more like,' Shosh answers me.

'But a week, Shosh! That's all we've got to figure out a way to save JAMM!'

She shakes her head.

'What? Don't you think we can do it?' I ask.

'Of course I think we can do it – although I haven't got the faintest idea how. I just can't believe it took *me* so long. Took me so insanely, stupidly long to see Isaac for exactly what he is.'

'Which is?'

'A lying, cheating, spineless, badly dressed . . . '

'Embezzling, fraudulent . . . '

'Greasy-haired, toilet-freshener-smelling . . . '

We link arms and laugh at how ridiculous a human being Isaac really is.

'Honestly, I feel like I've had my eyes prised open. Like I've only just woken up.'

'You were only doing what was best for your family, Shosh – what you thought was right for the girls.'

'Well, no more. He is out of our lives for good. If I ever see him again, I swear I'll—'

'I don't think he'll be showing his face round here again for a while.' I sigh, relieved at the thought. 'He'd be far too scared he'd bump into Malcolm.'

'He better be,' says Shosh through thinning lips. 'Oh, Rox – what are we going to do?'

'I dunno,' I answer, casting my eyes groundwards, unable to look up. 'I just don't know.'

'Get another loan?' she suggests.

'What? And drown in even deeper debt? No. We're going to have to think of something much cleverer than that.'

We unlink arms and trudge our downhearted way through the backstreets of Bondi until we reach Shalom! Baby.

By the time we get there, Chef's platters are looking fabulous, adorning the tables in the big room. There are so many familiar faces here, JAMM being the preferred hangout for the post- and pre-school-run mums and when I spy my gorgeous little girl, I waddle straight up to her.

'Why are you late? Mummy! You're always late!' she cries as soon as she sees me.

'I'm not, darling, I'm not late – we're right on time.' I talk fast, hoping she doesn't go off on one now. Not here, not now – not after the shocker of a morning I've just had.

'You *are* late! All the other mummies have been here for aaages!'

There's no point arguing the toss with Joey, so I try to accentuate the positive.

'But look what Mummy's been doing – making food for everyone here for Mother's Day! Yay!'

She doesn't flinch, the food doesn't sway her – but her eyes fix on the side of my head.

'What?' I say, raising my hand, ever-hopeful for a sign of good luck. 'Has a seagull pooed on my hair?'

'No, Mummy, *no*!' She leaps up and pulls my hand away. 'Keep still or the ladybird will fly away.'

And with the deft touch of a born naturalist, she gets up on her tiptoes and carefully extricates said ladybird. As she comes down off her toes, she beams at her cupped hands.

'Ooh, it's good luck for a ladybird to fly on to you, you know.' I smile and then, under my breath, say, 'And we're going to need every last drop of luck we can get our hands on this week.'

Joey carefully puts the ladybird into an old ice cream container with leaves and twigs and grass in it and then darts straight over to the challah.

I scan the kids' artwork on the walls, searching for my

girl's name. And there, next to Gila's, is Joey's crayon-drawn picture of me where I am, amazingly, depicted as super-thin, a real matchstick mummy. This makes me smile and convinces me that kids' drawings are better than Photoshop for a fat girl with a fragile ego.

Next to the picture is a questionnaire the kids have filled out about their mums (with the help of the teachers, obviously). Apparently, according to Joey, my favourite food is salad. My favourite drink is water and my favourite TV show is – even I stifle a yawn as I read it – the news.

I look around, a bit embarrassed: I mean, am I the most boring mum in the universe or what?

At least Joey's happy. For now, anyway. I watch her tucking into the treats on the table, jostling with Gila for who gets the last Smarties cookie and laughing hysterically.

Closing my eyes, I turn my face to the ceiling and mutter: 'Please, cosmos or universe, please help us keep our cafe dream alive.'

I pull out my phone to take a picture of Joey looking so happy, and see I've missed a call from Jack. I quickly call him back and tell him all about Troy and Isaac and Malcolm and how Isaac ran away and how we've only got one week before we'll be evicted and closed down (deep breath in) and how Luke resigned and Jemima quit and how Shoshanna saved our bacon with the landlord, but now we're a general manager down and the bank's on our back and ...

'I'll be right there,' he says heroically and hangs up.

I close my phone and look at it, flummoxed by Jack's response.

Then Leah, the pre-school boss, rounds up all the kids at the front of the room and they sing a song – half in Hebrew, half in English – about how their mums are their special friends and so beautiful and such good fun to play with. There's not a dry eye in the house once they've finished, and while I'm dabbing my eyes and blowing my nose, I feel a tap on my shoulder and turn round.

'I'm sorry, sorry to bother you, but I couldn't help overhear your phone conversation just now and I ... were you talking about Just Another Manic Mum-Day? The cafe?'

'Ah, yes, yes. I was.'

'But it cawn't close,' she says in her thick South African accent. 'It's the bist thing to ever happen to us.'

'I know. But times are tough and we can't afford to pay the childminders and the waiting staff and Chef and ourselves, as well as pay the bank, the rent, the suppliers—'

'Piffle!'

'Excuse me?'

'Flimsy excuses! You simply *must* keep that cafe going. You *cawn't* close. It's our only shelter from the storm. You know, like it says on the sandwich board out the front.'

'Yeah, I know, but—'

The woman puts her hand up to silence me and looks cross. She leaves the room and paces up and down outside for a few minutes. She's deep in thought, staring at the

256

grass beneath her feet, when suddenly she looks up and fixes me in her sights. She smiles broadly, marches back inside and says, as she brushes past me, 'Mum Power. Why didn't I think of this before?'

'Gather round, ladies!' she yells, clapping her hands. 'Just Another Manic Mum-Day, everyone's favourite cafe, is in financial trouble. If we don't band together and do something, it will no longer exist. They can't afford to pay the childminders any more – and we can't let that happen, can we?'

'*No!*' comes the resounding chorus.

Shosh joins me, mouthing, 'What on earth's going on?' and raising her eyebrows at me.

I splay my hands out in the international gesture for 'I haven't the foggiest.'

'So what can we do?'

'Pay them ourselves when we use their services?' calls out one mum.

'But they need to be guaranteed pay every day – they can't hang around on an ad hoc basis,' the main mum snaps back.

Much murmuring ensues. Arms cross and uncross. Index fingers are put up to lips to tell children to be quiet and a sea of eyes stares at the ceiling, squinting as if shielding themselves from bright sunlight.

The room is deathly quiet as the manic mums pause for reflection. At last, I can hear myself think, and I, too, search my brain for a solution to our cafe crisis.

I glance over at Shoshie. She shakes her head at me in disappointment as her eyes well up. I study the alphabet floor tiles and swear that far off I can hear a death knell sounding. And it's getting closer and louder with every passing second.

'Why don't we form a co-op?' comes a heartfelt cry from the back of the room.

'Go on,' says the leader of the pack, exhaling with relief, as she nods and smiles at me.

'We all pay a nominal rate every week to keep the essential services going – pastries, childminders, alcohol supplies – and make sure we tip generously every day. Most of us can afford it and it would be a tragedy if we lost the cafe.'

'How much is a nominal amount?' I ask carefully.

'From each according to their means to each according to their needs,' the little voice from the back says to raucous applause.

'We could make a contribution box – we have plenty of cardboard and sticky-back plastic here!' shouts Leah.

'Or we could do a direct debit into JAMM's account every month. Say, $200 each? Sounds like a bargain to me!' comes a voice from the rowdy throng of mums on a roll.

My brain feels like it's about to explode as I try to do my sums. Let's see. If only ten mums put in $200 every month that would make ... That'd be $2000 straight away! And that would be the rent paid right then and there!

'Yeah!' comes another excited voice. 'I spend more than that on shoes and facials every month, but this is for an even *better* cause.'

'And *so* much more a sound investment,' yells the voice who came up with the whole co-op idea. 'An investment in ourselves, our kids and all of our futures!'

There's rapturous applause, whoops and wolf whistles. And I can't believe my ears.

'Problem solved – too easy!' says the main mum, sauntering over to Shoshie and me. 'My name's Tracey-Lee, by the way. And I've been wondering ... I'm in furniture and I've got some old Chesterfields in storage – about four, if I remember correctly. Would you like me to donate them to the cafe? I have some coffee tables and lovely art deco lamps too that I just can't shift. Would you be interested?'

Shosh and I stand there with our mouths wide open, nodding like Churchill dogs.

'Do me one favour, though?' says Tracey-Lee. 'Re-train that barista, will you? I have to ask for Nescafé to avoid her so-called coffee.'

'Ooh, yes,' says a mum standing next to Tracey-Lee. 'It really is the most God-awful sludge.'

'Like muddy ditch water!' shouts out the voice from the back. 'But more bitter!'

'Lucky for you we don't go there for the coffee,' smiles Tracey-Lee. 'But you'd be even more of a success if mums knew they could get a decent cup.'

'Your wish is our command!' I wink at Shoshie.

'What say we all get over there now and get this whole co-op thing in motion?' Shosh softly claps her hands and does a little jump off the floor.

'Let's go, then, ladies!' yells Tracey-Lee.

We kiss our kids goodbye and spill out of Shalom! Baby, hundreds of us – slight exaggeration, sorry, more like forty of us – walking down the middle of the road, cars beeping us from behind, a swarm, no, a *frazzle*, of doggedly determined mums bent on saving the best cafe in the world.

Cantering every few steps to keep up with Tracey-Lee and Shoshie, right up the front, it occurs to me that we must look like the formidable, dancing formation of women in that old Pat Benatar music video for 'Love is a Battlefield' – but a bit less prostitute-y and tarty. And raggedy. And not quite as in sync with each other, as graceful with our moves. And we're not clicking our fingers as we bend low, looking tough, shimmying our shoulders in time to the bass. And we're not going to sort this mess out with a dance-off. Because, well, I don't know about the rest of them, but my joints are a bit stiff these days, sometimes seizing up at the most inopportune moments, so, I'm sorry, but any kind of dancing in my condition is really out of the question for now.

But apart from that ...

The frazzle storms (well, wanders, to be more accurate) back into JAMM, and when Jack sees me, he marches straight over, strutting like he's an older, tubbier, greyer Richard Gere in *An Officer and a Gentleman*. He grabs me by the elbow, wheels me round and waltzes me through the kitchen and out the back where Kylie's chatting to Chef, who's sneaking a cigarette.

'Just five minutes, boss,' he says.

'That's OK,' I reply, a tad discombobulated by Jack's presence and masterful manoeuvring of myself outside.

'Come on, Chef,' says Kylie. 'Can't you see these two want to be alone?'

She winks at me and leads a slightly miffed Chef back inside. He throws his half-smoked ciggie into the small sardine can full of dark orange water and old dog ends and it hisses, no doubt echoing his feelings about having his break cut short.

'What's going on? Why aren't you at work?' I say, knitting my brow.

'Good question.' He grins. 'I'm glad you asked me that. Now. Sit down, will you?'

I sit on the blue plastic crate that Chef's just deserted and start to get really rather worried. Has someone died? Is Jack in some sort of trouble?

Jack sits on the yellow plastic crate next to me, rubbing his hands up and down his thighs, alternately looking cross one second and exultant the next.

'You know how a few weeks ago I told you there were going to be redundancies made at work? And how because I was the last one in, I'd most probably be the first one out?'

I nod, searching his eyes for some sort of clue, but only finding slightly bloodshot peepers behind his John Lennon glasses. Which only makes me think it really is time he got some new, more stylish bins – like those rimless, bendy ones. *Should've gone to Specsavers*, I can't help but say to myself just as he begins to speak again.

'Well, that was my way of testing the water, to see how you'd react. Fact is, they *did* make me redundant. The day we had that discussion. I've been unemployed for quite a few weeks now.'

Now it's he who's studying my eyes, trying to gauge my reaction, gird his loins ready to either run for the hills or wrap his arms around me.

'But you've been leaving early, in your suit, every morning—'

'I know,' he says softly, looking down at his feet. 'I didn't want you to twig. Wanted to pretend I was still in gainful employment, still able to be the sole provider if this harebrained cafe scheme of yours went totally belly-up.'

'Which it hasn't, may I remind you.' I sniff. 'In fact, it's gone brilliantly, right from the off. Well, apart from today . . .'

Jack hangs his head and stares at the ground, looking suitably ashamed.

I put my arm across his wide shoulders, marvelling at how firm and strong they feel under my fleshy arm. I haven't felt any part of Jack's body for such a long time, it almost comes as a shock, how different it feels to my own – all taut and ripply and ... *manly*, for want of a better word.

'Rox?' He looks up warily.

'Hmm?' I reply, lost in thoughts of his sexy athletic swimmer's body – even if it is covered with a fine layer of middle-age spread and there's more hair on his bum cheeks than there is on his head. He may be the personification of a balding-and-running-to-podge mid-life crisis, but he's *my* balding-and-running-to-podge mid-life crisis.

'I managed to save some money while I was working, just in case, which is good – it'll keep us afloat for another few weeks. And I haven't signed on for the dole because ... well, I've got a proposition for you. A work idea.'

'Oh God, what is it? Running motorbike tours across Australia for the fat and forty set? Reclaim your inner rebel on the road to Gundagai?'

'That's not a bad idea, Rox, but no, that's not what I had in mind.'

He draws a deep breath, holds it for a second and then blurts it out.

'I want to take Isaac's place as manager, in charge of the money, the suppliers, the staff and the general running of the place. You and Shosh will still be the main forces behind JAMM, but I want to be a part of it, too. Really make a go of it, fully turn it into the great family business it should have been all along.'

He's all out of puff, but doesn't inhale, merely holds his breath again, anxiously.

I smile smugly and wait until he turns a lighter shade of puce before I speak.

'Ah . . . so! You want to be a part of JAMM now, do you? Now that you have no other choice, it doesn't look so silly, does it? Now the little woman who's a dunce with figures might be on to something, right? And you want a piece of the action, hmm?'

'Please don't make this any harder than it already is, Roxy.'

'All right, all right.' I smile at him. 'I'll have to consult Shoshie first, but I'm sure she'll be fine with it.'

'You know, this place is packed from the moment you open the doors till closing time – both you and I as well as Shosh should be able to receive a really decent wage,' Jack says.

'Yep, Isaac was really doing a number on us. Turns out, he was paying himself a whopping great salary, getting backhanders from luxury food suppliers—'

'And *front*-handers, too,' Jack adds, smirking.

'And basically ripping the cafe off to the tune of thousands.'

'But don't you see, Rox? I can fix it! And now you won't be hoeing into all the cakes and pies and—'

'Watch it,' I say slowly, narrowing my eyes.

'Look,' he laughs, 'JAMM's been a massive success, so as far as I can see, you should – *we* should – all be getting our fair share of the profits while still being able to afford to supply all the great things that make it so wonderful: its USPs.'

'Its *whats*?'

'USPs. Unique Selling Points.'

'Oh. Right. And you can sort this out for us, can you?'

'Well, could you? Or Shosh?'

'Um. No. But maybe the co-op could?'

'Well, there you go. What? What co-op?'

'All the patrons of JAMM are going to club together and put what money they can into the kitty. And now we don't have to pay Luke or Jemima, either, that should help keep the costs down. I can pick up the shortfall from Luke and ... '

'Maybe we don't need a barista, as such, at all.' Jack strokes his chin thoughtfully. 'I'm sure I could master that machine, even though it looks pretty old and dangerous what with all that steam and hissing and hot pipes every-where.'

I hear Tarquin laughing loudly inside. Instantly, an image of George Clooney comes into my head. In the Nespresso ads.

'What else?' I murmur dreamily.

'Hmm?'

'Nothing. Hey! Why don't we just get a Nespresso machine and be done with it?'

'No! We must have real, fantastic, talk-of-the-town, best-on-the-beach coffee,' Jack says, slapping his thigh.

'We'll need to find the best barista in Bondi. We've got to be hot on everything, Rox, if we're to build on our success, really grow the business.'

It's like he's already thought about the coffee issue – like he really means business and won't leave anything to chance.

'You know, Rox, with me at the helm, we really could take JAMM viral.'

'Ooh. That doesn't sound good.'

'It is, though. It's computer geek talk for something really good – like global.'

'Whatever it means, you could certainly set up the website and e-newsletter, being the IT whizz that you are. I've been meaning to do it for eons, it's been on my list for—'

'Consider it done. And I promise I'll fix up the cash register keys – get rid of all those pounds and shillings and halfpennies . . .'

'You will? It's been the bane of my life, that old thing. I'm bad enough with numbers as it is, but, well, talk about confusing—'

'Anyway, anyway, anyway – what do you say, Rox? I know I can do it – and there's bugger-all else out there for me, I've looked.'

I don't know. Could be a surefire recipe for disaster, working together, living together, trying to be half-decent parents together, bickering like brother and sister together, trying just to *stay* together . . . Then again, it could be just what we need to bring us closer. It might be nice having Jack around all day with me and Joey – and, if he can fix the cash register and turn the cafe's fortunes around and really make us millionaires, well then. Bit of a no-brainer, really.

'Oh, go on.'

'Really?'

'Yeah. Save us from insolvency or bankruptcy or getting the receivers in or going completely bust or Troy repossessing everything we own or whatever it is that happens when you've made a right pig's ear of a cafe.'

'It's not your fault – it was all Isaac's doing. Now! When do I start?' Jack grins, clapping his hands and rubbing them together to show his eagerness.

'Right away,' I say, trying to get up from my crate but going nowhere fast, grunting in a most unrefined manner with the effort.

'Let me help you, madam,' says Jack, coming over all chivalrous and helping me up. 'And I can take some of the burden off you, as well. You know, you really should be slowing down a bit, now.'

'If you want to share some of the burden, we've got a kids' party on next week. Will you help out with that?'

'Course! Weddings, parties, anything . . . '

I give him ten minutes, I think to myself, shaking my head and smirking at his ignorance. Having rarely taken Joey to any of her friends' parties, he hasn't got the faintest clue what he's in for.

*

We walk back inside and see the party's in full swing.

All the mums from Shalom! Baby are huddled around a big long table, squealing and shouting at each other, quaffing champagne.

Shoshie's laughing with Tarquin and waves when she spies me and Jack. 'Here's to me, you and JAMM,' she says, darting behind the bar, grabbing a bottle of champagne and popping the cork.

'Ah, Shosh, before you get totally trolleyed, I've got something to ask you. Would you excuse us for a sec, Tarquin?'

'Of course, of course. Take your time. I'll wait here and admire the splendid view.'

I guide Shoshie into the loos and give her the news.

'Jack's been made redundant and he's desperate to take over Isaac's place here at JAMM and I've already said yes sort of and—'

'Great idea. Brilliant. He'll be wonderful, I just know it. Now, can we get out of this toilet, please? There's a rather tasty man waiting for me out there!'

Shosh nearly knocks me down on to the tiled floor, she's in such a hurry to get out and back to Tarquin. I heave a huge sigh, wishing I could have some champers.

I look in the bathroom mirror front-on and muss up my hair. Not bad – but not straight, shiny and sleek like I wish it was. I turn side-on and ... *whoa!* I am huge! Even losing a couple of kilos cannot disguise that fact. And what's the bet it's *not* all baby? What's the bet that once she's out, I'll be tucking my empty, fleshy, flubbery tummy into my control knickers for the rest of my life? Never again able to get Spanx over my knees?

Oops. I've done it again, haven't I? I've let negativity take over what is, in fact, a purely positive moment. All this constantly being upbeat is harder than it looks!

Let it go, Rox, go with the flow. So your hair's curly? Some people pay squillions to get that look. And you're pregnant, not fat – the gift of life is yours, you lucky bugger! Now get out there and enjoy!

The scene that greets me as I walk down the steps from the bathroom to the cafe makes my heart sing.

Shoshanna, Tarquin and Jack are all now sitting at one of our best tables, grinning and chinking their champagne flutes together.

'Here's to our new fantastic partner!' Shosh nods to Jack, raising her glass.

'Hear, hear!' cheers Tarquin.

'Care to join us?'

'Love to, but can't,' I say. 'Got to pick up Joey and Gila.'

'Why don't I do that for you, babe? You sit down and take it easy,' smiles Jack.

'No, no,' I shake my head. 'Thanks for the offer, but I want to go. I have to do the walk, anyway.'

'We'll save you some for when the baby's born,' says

Shosh, leaning over the back of her chair and shouting: 'Kyles? Can we have another bottle of Veuve over here asap?'

I excuse myself and go outside to limber up under the awning. I pull my heel up to my bum to stretch my hamstring and feel an overwhelming rush of joy.

There's the co-op; Jack; Shoshie getting over Isaac and his hideous Miami Vice jackets and sleazy Scrappy-Doo ways, about to hook up any minute with the delectable Tarquin; me actually looking forward to the walk … I mean, can things *get* any better?

Usually, I'd be asking myself whether things could get any worse! Normally, I wouldn't remember that a ladybird landing on you is good luck – I didn't believe in luck. Thought it was all mystic cobblers, a way for charlatans to make money out of the desperate. But now I'm not so sure. In fact, I'm starting to think that maybe – just *maybe* – there might be something in this whole cosmos, planets aligning luck lark.

'It's become a co-op now,' I say breathlessly down the phone to Troy as I trudge along the dry, exceedingly-difficult-to-walk-on sand. 'And I think it's just what we need to save the cafe.'

'I know,' he says.

Gor – how fast does word travel in this neck of the woods?

'How could you *possibly* know?' I ask, wondering

whether bankers have secret societies, like masons, one of their number having infiltrated the JAMM posse or something.

'Well, whose idea was the co-op?' He answers my question with another question.

'I don't know – one of the Shalom! Baby mums. I recognised the voice, but couldn't see who it was and I've been trying to—'

'Not just any old mum,' he says. 'That was *my* mum!'

'*Your* mum?'

'Yep. The one and only. She helps out at the pre-school sometimes.'

'But a co-op? Such a community-minded thing to think of, and you're ... well ...'

'I know. She and my dad and my sister are the socialists in the family and I'm the black sheep, the only capitalist pig among us.'

'But she's so proud of you. Always singing your praises.'

'She's my mum, I guess – she loves me no matter what.'

'Quite right, too.' I grin. 'Talk about expect the unexpected, eh?'

'And what did I say about family and business?' He chortles.

'So what do you think? Reckon it'll save us?'

'I reckon it's awesome,' he says. 'With that kind of financial and moral support, you'll be back on your feet in no time. Just promise me you'll open the co-op account with You Beaut and we'll all come out of this winners.'

'Done.' I scuttle up the nearest ramp, back on to the asphalt promenade, relieved to be back on solid ground again. God, that dry sand is *impossible*.

As I close my phone, Jasmine Lucy, my old friend from uni, jogs up, stopping me in my tracks.

'Haven't seen you for yonks,' she says. 'How's it all going?'

'Great,' I say. 'Walk with me? I've got gestational diabetes.'

'I knew it!' She squeals as she turns round and slows to my pace. 'I mean, I knew you were pregnant, that day we bumped into each other on the beach. It was a new moon that evening, wasn't it? And you were a miserable old cynic.'

'Yeah, well . . . '

'But you went home and did some New Moon Wishing that night, didn't you?' she asks, as though she already knows the answer.

'How did you . . .?'

She smiles that enigmatic smile of hers and hooks her arm through mine, making me walk a little bit faster.

'You seem so different, Roxy – happier, more open to ideas, practically brimming over with positivity.'

'I do?'

'Oh, yes. You're really *going places*, Roxy. You mark my words.'

As we walk, Jasmine talks about her business and our

cafe and the possibility of marrying the two, maybe giving her a permanent spot in the cafe, like Tarquin and Elizabeth have, where she can do horoscopes.

'What a brilliant idea,' I sigh as we walk off into the sunset.

Chapter 18

We've been flitting about the cafe like blue-arsed flies, blowing up balloons, placing party hats, streamers, banners, fairy bread, sausage rolls, bowls of Smarties, cupcakes and mini Mars bars, Bounties and Twixes on a couple of tables pushed together to create one big one. There are to be twelve kids plus the guest of honour, the birthday boy, at this table, and I'm girding my loins.

First off, the mum, Victoria, walks in and inspects our handiwork.

'Looks great,' she says, 'Thanks for putting this on for us – especially at such short notice. Everywhere else was booked up, must be kids' birthday party season.'

I inwardly groan at the thought.

'Even the place we had last year was full, they said,' she goes on, sitting down at the head of the table, 'but we just walked past it on our way here and it was completely empty.'

I'm not surprised at this. Victoria's son, Harry, has a

reputation round these parts as being a destructive force, respectful of nothing and no one, a real piece of work and a right pain: a nightmare to have in your eatery, by all accounts. And I thought about turning them away, because this kid's got some serious form, but Shoshanna reminded me that we're all about the mums here at JAMM – and anything we can do to lighten the load and make things a bit easier is morally incumbent upon us to actually *do*.

Victoria and Harry have only been here once or twice before, at least that I've seen – and Zoe and Sophie are so professional, so adept at handling troublesome kids, that I don't recall anything horrendous happening at all. But I *do* remember Harry – because he's got this enormous adult nose sprawled across his little five-year-old face. Honestly, it's like a joke nose attached to a pair of plastic, lens-less glasses.

Jack rushes up to join us at the party table and introduces himself to Victoria, still tying the apron strings of his half-pinny, like the ones waiters in French restaurants wear. Rather dashing it is, too.

'Jack, m'lady.' He sounds bunged up, doing quite a good impression of Parker from *Thunderbirds*. 'At your service.'

He bows theatrically before her and she looks enchanted, letting a delighted 'Ooh' escape her lips.

'God! What the hell is that?' I look up, hearing a horrifically loud whining sound. It's hideous, almost inhuman.

'Sounds like Harry.' Victoria swells with pride.

'Happy birthday to MEEEEEEEEE! Happy birthday to MEEEEEEEEEE. HAPPY BIRRRRRRRRTHDAY to meee-eee. HAPPY BIRTHDAY TO ME!'

He's coming in like a dive bomber, holding his super-hero cape behind him and running faster and faster, zigzagging through the tables with his head down, in the general direction of his seated mum until – CRASH! – he bumps right into Jack's leg and looks up at him.

'Ooomph! Whoa there, boy. Hoo – that's a lot of nose for a little boy,' Jack's saying to him, transfixed by the poor lad's prominent proboscis.

'Noise, *noise*,' I butt in. 'That's a lot of *noise* for such a little boy.' My false laugh gets better every day, dealing with the more loathsome toddlers and their more-often-than-not completely blinkered parents. And my fake smile is up to Olympic standard, I think, as I glance down at Harry's mum, who's looking up at us crossly.

'Jack's a little dyslexic.' I chortle, studying Victoria's face for signs of massive schnozzery – but finding none. She's got one of those infuriatingly perfect small ski-jumps.

Only ten other kids show up (*only* ten? What am I saying?), so we rope Joey in to make up the numbers – which she doesn't try to wriggle out of, there being loads of fairy bread triangles on offer.

The first hour of this two-hour marathon passes without

a hitch, due to kids' amazing capacities for shoving any kind of sweet treat going down their necks.

'Easy peasy,' whispers Jack to me, looking smug as he piles his tray high with more chocolate milkshakes for the boisterous boys and girls. Credit where credit's due, he does seem to be handling these kids with aplomb, I must admit.

But when it's time for pass the parcel, the tired, over-excited sugar junkies really start to put the self-proclaimed 'Jack of all trades' to the test.

'Right! Listen up, everybody!' Jack claps his hands together and tries to make eye contact with the kids.

'It's now time for pass the parcel! And then it's time to go, which is sad – but don't forget your goody-bag on the way out.'

The *Sesame Street* music plays while all the kids sit in a circle, each one grabbing and tugging the parcel out of their neighbour's recalcitrant hands. And before too long there are rivers of tears.

'I don't WANT a Kinder Egg!' cries one, disappointed with the prize they won after unwrapping the parcel.

'The music stopped when *I* had it!' whinges another. 'She snatched it off ME!'

'He was holding on to it for AGES! You're supposed to PASS it, not wait till the music stops. NOT FAIR,' wails a third.

Most of the kids are crying now – pass the parcel being infamous for causing strops and rows at kids' parties – and those who aren't are looking devious and sneaky by the party table.

'I HATE pass the parcel. It's for GIRLS!' shouts Harry, getting up off the floor, reaching for a pink cupcake from the table and taking a tiny bite.

'YUCK!' He spits his mouthful out on the floor. 'Girls like pink and they're FUCKING IDIOTS!'

I look up from the glasses I'm drying behind the bar, totally shocked – as is the rest of the cafe. Tables of mums and even the kids in the crèche stare at the raucous party, agog. And just as Victoria's making her way to her rebel son, muttering something about not using that kind of language in public, he launches the cupcake at Jack. Quite a good shot, it is, too, smashing straight on to Jack's cheek.

'Hey!' protests Jack, as a handful of Smarties whizzes past his ear. 'Now stop that, kids! That stuff's for eating, not throwing—' and he ducks to avoid a mini Bounty bar flying towards his forehead.

Suddenly it's on, like an all-in bar room brawl in the Wild West. Squeals of delight mingle with shrieks of terror as fairy bread gets thrown about with gay abandon, girls rub blue cupcakes into boys' faces, boys rub pink ones into girls' faces, Harry stamps Smarties into the floor-boards and sausage-roll-carrying party hats get thrown around like American footballs. It's mayhem.

No mothers seem to be forthcoming to tell their child to behave, dragging them away for a good telling-off. In fact, all adults seem to have deserted the scene. Even Jack's tiptoeing away, skulking about on the periphery.

'JACK!' I yell at his fast-disappearing back. 'Do something! *Quick!*'

And then someone lets off the fire extinguisher.

Kids and tables, chairs and floorboards – everything's covered in a white frothy foam. And a shocked silence descends over the deafening throng.

'Sometimes it's the only way.' Jack grins, blowing the froth off the black cone of the extinguisher, like a sharp shooter might blow the gunsmoke away from his Smith & Wesson after accurately disposing of some varmint.

Then the laughter starts up as all the kids roll around in the foam.

'Owwww! Muuum! You're hurting me! And I want my goody-bag. NOW!' Harry howls as Victoria carts him off by the ear.

And finally, one by one, the kids get collected by their parents and the clean-up can begin.

'Again, again!' cries Joey, wiping a glob of foam from her eye.

'No, no – that was Daddy's crowd-control tactics,' I say. 'Wasn't supposed to be the indoor party equivalent of a bouncy castle or a trampoline.'

'What does equilavernament mean?' Joey splutters foam from her lips.

'It means you've got to go and get changed, get ready for school this arvo,' says Jack.

'No! I want to stay here!' She clings to my leg.

'Sweet, you've got to go to school this afternoon,' I implore her.

'But why?'

'Because if you don't you'll miss Gila and Rachel and Hannah ... '

'But if I go, I'll miss you.'

I'm stunned. Until I realise it's probably just another cunning ruse by that mini mastermind, another brilliant way to get around me and get exactly what she wants. Still, quite nice to hear, I admit it. I look at Jack in slack-jawed astonishment.

'Have you been drinking, Joey? Been sneaking behind the bar while our backs were turned?' he teases her.

'Pink milk!' She shrieks, the sugar still coursing through her veins. 'I'll go if I can have some more pink milk.'

The negotiations, the deal-brokering, the diplomatic walking on eggshells and careful phrasing – *now* Jack will be able to see how hard it is, how exhausting it is, day after day, to engage in high-level crisis talks with Joey every few hours.

'Done.' He smiles. 'Get your coat and I'll buy you some pink milk on the way.'

Joey yelps with joy and runs off to get her coat, just as a triangle of fairy bread falls from the ceiling.

'So is it going to be you and Tarquin ganging up on me again? And can you not walk *quite* so fast? I am heavily pregnant here, in case you hadn't noticed.'

Jack and I are walking up Ridgey Didge Road, the steep climb to Tarquin's office at Bondi Junction, for another session.

'Sorry,' he says, slowing his pace somewhat. 'Thought you were all fit as a fiddle and up for fast-walking these days.'

'I am! Well, at the right time and place – this road's too steep for me. I nearly had a conniption when Shoshanna and I walked up here a few months ago.'

'Speaking of,' he says, brightening, 'she seems so much happier since she gave that loser the Spanish archer, doesn't she?'

'What's a Spanish archer?'

'El Bow.' He chortles.

'Yeah,' I pant. He's slowed down a tad, but not enough for my liking – i.e. we're still moving. 'He was *such* a dick. She's so much better off without him.'

'Oh, totally.' He nods emphatically. 'She can do so much better. She's gorgeous, smart – great with kids—'

'Ooh!' I grab the right side of my stomach.

'What? What's wrong?' Jack asks, turning round and walking back towards me. 'Are you OK? Is it the baby? What's *wrong*?'

'Hooh,' I breathe out slowly, 'it's OK, calm down. Just a big kick, that's all.'

'Are you sure?'

'Yes, I'm sure.' I smile at his concern. 'Now we better get a shift on. Don't want to be late and miss our time slot.'

As it turns out, though, Tarquin's not even there when we arrive at his office. Ten minutes of *Scientific American* is enough for one day, I think to myself, but, just as I'm about to suggest we reschedule, in bursts Tarquin, all flushed and flustered.

'I'm so sorry I'm late,' he huffs at us and his receptionist, 'I'll just get my messages and—'

He stops in front of his office door and reads the Post-it notes his receptionist has handed to him. His smile virtually takes over his whole face as he flicks through, his grin getting wider and wider with every slip of paper.

'Ha! Well! Yes! Just got back from seeing the lovely Shoshanna at your wonderful cafe. And she's already left me a couple of messages!'

He clears his throat and straightens his shoulders.

'Ahem. Right. Do come in, the pair of you, don't mind the mess, just sit down, make yourselves at home and, ah, let's jump in, shall we? Dive in where we left off last time I saw you together.'

'Seems like such a long time ago – I mean, the last time we saw you in a professional capacity.' I ease into patient mode.

'Together, yes – but I saw Jack on his own a week or two ago, didn't I, Jack? Jack?'

Jack's looking totally guilty.

'Uh-oh.' Tarquin takes a sharp breath in. 'Confidential, right? Sorry, Jack.'

'Eh? So you've come to see Tarquin by yourself? Without me?'

'Now, Roxy,' says Tarquin in his best soothing tones, 'it's good for you two as a couple to have some individual counselling every now and again. It could really help you come together in the long run.'

'Come on, Rox,' chimes in Jack. 'I'm only doing this for the two of us. For you, mainly. Do you really think I want to spend valuable drinking time gazing at my navel?'

'So,' Tarquin interrupts, pointing his right index finger to the ceiling, 'how have you been going with that homework I set you?'

We speak simultaneously:

'Rubbish,' I say flatly.

'Great,' chirps Jack. 'I think we're really making some progress.'

'We've only done it *twice* – and each time it's ended up in an argument. Don't you remember?' I try to jog Jack's selective memory. 'We're just so different!'

'I think what's important to remember here is that we're *supposed* to be different. We're *supposed* to see things differently,' says Tarquin slowly. 'The two sexes are very different animals. What we're trying to do is *understand* these differences so that we complement each other and don't misinterpret what the other's doing or saying in certain stressful situations.'

Both Jack and I nod.

'Let's crack on, shall we?' Tarquin sits up in his chair, placing his desert boots firmly on the floor. He knits his fingers together and places them on his lap, palms-up. 'How are you sleeping?'

'Who's sleeping?' I reply.

'Yeah, it's not good at our place,' agrees Jack. 'The backpackers upstairs are dropping Es all night, every night. Or smoking crystal meth or whatever – Joey keeps getting up and coming into our bed and it's making zombies out of us all.'

'And what with me being so big and lumbery and uncomfortable at the moment, I think I'm averaging, ooh, half an hour's sleep every night? *Max.*'

'Right. That's no good – it's no wonder you're a little skittish with each other. But right now's the time to tackle this, before the baby comes and completely robs you of any shut-eye!' Tarquin looks all chuffed with himself as he says the last bit, like it's the best part of having a new baby, the thing you most look forward to.

'We're not that skittish any more,' Jack says proudly, putting his arm round me. 'I think we're getting on pretty well lately.'

I jump a tiny bit at his touch and turn to study his face. Because all of a sudden he feels, sounds and looks quite a bit different to me.

His grip on my shoulder feels gentle, but stronger; his voice has gone down a few octaves and sounds much more confident. And those twinkling eyes! He looks so much younger, somehow. And really rather handsome. I can't quite place him, but he reminds me of someone . . .

I reach my hand out to Jack's and we hold hands, resting in his lap.

'Roxane? Do you agree?'

'Yes, yes, I do,' I say. 'Since Jack started at the cafe, I suppose, things have been quite different between us.'

'Once I'd been made redundant, I was beside myself with worry about money and you and Joey and the baby – and the cafe idea seemed so far-fetched, so unlikely, that I guess I was panicking. I didn't know what to do.'

'God, I wish you'd told me,' I say, turning in my seat to face him. 'Imagine! All that ill-feeling and tension could have simply been swept away out of our lives if you'd only talked to me, rather than zooming off on your bike, going smoking and drinking.'

'I never drink and drive and I don't smoke any more – haven't for ages. Anyway, you're just jealous because you can't do either of them at the moment.' Jack laughs.

I consider this for a second and come to the conclusion that he may, in part, be right.

He squeezes my hand and we smile at each other. All is quiet for a few minutes as we ponder what's just been said. And then Tarquin crosses his legs, straightens the notepad on his knees, looks at the floor, smiling, and breaks the silence.

'We're all works in progress, remember,' he says. 'Jack working at the cafe with you will continue to reap huge benefits for your relationship, I assure you—'

'Yeah!' I say. 'There's no escape now, Jack – you won't be able to get away when I want to chat!'

'You reckon?' He grins, like I've just thrown down the gauntlet and he's accepted my challenge. 'Thank God that caff just gets busier and busier . . . '

'Very good, very good,' resumes Tarquin. 'Now, where was I? Oh, yes. I wanted to point out that you are not alone and that having children puts an *enormous* strain on the adult relationship, of that there is no doubt. You'll always love the kiddies like crazy, but your relationship with each other may be the weakest link.'

At this, he tries to wink, like Anne Robinson – but he looks so awkward, both Jack and I can't help but smile. Tarquin brings his fist up to his mouth, coughs a bit and carries on.

'A few months ago, you both thought that the other one was the problem, correct?'

Jack and I both nod. Spookily in time.

'And while this was somewhat true, to a certain extent, what is 100% guaranteed, and what is now coming to fruition, is that you, the pair of you together, are really *the solution*, too.'

Maybe I'm on the verge of a massive mood swing, but I'm starting to think that perhaps Tarquin might not know his arse from his Spanish archer.

'This will become clear in time,' Tarquin goes on. 'But right now, in the interim, as a part of the process, I have another solution for you – or, at least, a step on the pathway to the solution. It's a way to help you two start trusting each other again. Falling in love with each other again.'

Jack and I swap glances, raise our respective eyebrows and wait to hear what's in store for us. Tarquin looks like an excited schoolboy who's just been given a puppy.

'If Jack isn't as talkative as you'd like, Roxy – and Roxy isn't as upbeat as you'd like, Jack, maybe it's time for some *non-verbal communication*.' He winks again.

'Now you're talking!' Jack licks his lips hungrily.

'Maybe you're ready to try . . . '

Jack and I inch up to the edge of our seats in anticipation.

'Ballroom dancing!' Tarquin rises out of his chair.

I don't know who groans louder, Jack or me, but we both do, slumping back into our chairs simultaneously. And once we realise that we both think the idea is ridiculous – that we actually agree on something *again* – we collapse into hysterics.

Chapter 19

'Would it be OK?' asks Kylie, who's standing next to me as we both look up at the big cork noticeboard.

'Would what be OK?' I counter.

'The breastfeeding class I'm going to set up. The notice for it – there, right in front of you? You're looking straight at it.'

I'm staring at the noticeboard, but I'm not seeing anything, not taking in much at all. I have to admit, I'm really quite dozy this morning – I walked across the road when the red man was flashing and I nearly got skittled by the 380 bus, winding its way down Didgeridoo Drive along the beach. Luckily, the bus driver beeped at me, waking me up and forcing me to run – well, making me break into a tidy trot for a few little leaps, to be more precise.

'Phil's going to do it with me. It's a two-tiered approach, really – he's going to advise and counsel the guys, help them help their girlfriends and wives, and I'm going to help the women.'

I look at Kyles. She's getting bigger by the day.

'Sounds like a great idea, Kyles. How long to go now?'

'Fourteen weeks,' she says, proudly rubbing her tummy.

'Gor – not long. How exciting.' I wearily smile.

'I know!' She does a little jump and claps her hands together, just like Joey does.

'So how's your family taking it now?'

'They still don't know.' She stops clapping and thrusts her hands into her apron's big front pocket. 'They think I've gone away on a long holiday, cruising the Med. They agreed it'd give me time to think about what I want to do now that Maverick's history.'

'I see. And Phil?'

'He's been great, just awesome.' She grins again. 'You know I moved in with him? Well, he's taking care of absolutely everything: back massages, foot massages, and he makes me tea early every morning – decaf, of course! – and sets my clothes out for the day. He pays for my bus pass every month, he comes with me to every scan at the hospital – even just the routine appointments, he's there!'

'Sounds amazing,' I say, opening my eyes so wide I can almost feel the wrinkles in my forehead carving their way through my flesh.

'Yeah. He is.'

We both stand there, smiling dreamily, Kylie patting her belly for a few minutes until she eventually breaks the, quite literally, pregnant pause.

'What do you think of the name?'

'Name? You didn't tell me you knew your baby's sex!'

'No! Not the *baby's* name – the name of the breast-feeding class!'

'Oh!' I shake my head at my idiocy and look back up to the noticeboard.

LACTATION, LACTATION, LACTATION!
with Kylie and Phil

Join us on the most amazing journey of your lives and learn how to breastfeed your baby or even help your baby mama breastfeed.

That's right!

Girls? Come with me and we'll sort these suckers out. Guys? Go with Phil to find out what all the fuss is about and how you can help your partner get to grips with those lovely lady lumps – for the benefit of your beautiful, bouncing baby!

'Ha! Awesome,' I finally manage, once I've squinted and peered at the noticeboard like the old lady I'm fast becoming. 'But what does Phil know about it?'

'Nothing! Neither do I – that's the beauty of our plan,' she squeaks, jumping again. 'We'll all be finding our way in the dark together. Look, four couples have already signed up – a few Yumsters and a couple of Bumsters, too. It's going to be a blast!'

'You betcha,' I agree. Well. Who am I to burst the kid's bubble? If she wants to think it's all easy and natural and fun and bereft of frustration and fear and panic, then let her. She'll find out soon enough.

'And Elizabeth is going to help us out if we need it, which is awesome,.'

'Brilliant.' I sigh.

'Oh, and Rox?'

'Hmm?'

'Phil's turned really serious about his baking now and wondered whether JAMM would stock his pastries. I know they're sometimes bigger sellers than the coffees and teas here and you've tried his pastries before and you loved them and he says he'll give them to you for a massive discount – he's just after a bit of exposure, really, and we all know how fantastic mums are for spreading the word when they really like something . . .'

'And breathe, Kyles.' I smile. 'Yeah, course – his stuff is so delicious – what a great idea. I'll have to check with Shoshie first, but I'm sure she'll love it. Going out with a baker, eh? You've hit the jackpot there, kiddo.'

'I know. And guess what he's going to call his business? You'll never guess. It's . . . wait for it, wait for it: Phil-O Pastries. Phil-O – get it? Like Filo, but *Phil*-O.'

I look at her blankly.

'Get it? Phil-O. Like *filo* pastry. Don't you get it?'

'Yeah, I get it,' I say. 'But Phil's last name is Nelson. It doesn't start with an O. There's no O.'

'Yeah, I know.' She giggles. 'But Phil-N Pastry didn't have the same ring to it.'

I laugh lazily and turn round just in time to see Elizabeth marching towards me.

'Morning.' I sigh.

'Good morning, Roxane,' she replies. 'I have a client in a few minutes, but I wanted to check with you and see how you were doing with the sticker chart.'

'Oh,' I sigh again. 'good, good. Although I do feel like I'm micro-managing Joey a bit, like I'm a full-on control freak.'

'That's as may be.' She clasps her book closer to her ample matronly bosom. 'But is young Josephine behaving?'

I'd walked her to pre-school this morning, before I was nearly knocked over by the 380, and she was as good as gold. Neither of us had anything even remotely approaching a meltdown. And when it comes to getting in and out of the bath, sleeping in her own bed, eating most of her dinner, asking for permission to get down from the table, saying please and thank you . . . she's, well, perfect.

'Yes, yes, she is,' I admit. 'But I'm concerned that some of her personality's gone AWOL. Maybe all this discipline, rationing of treats and praying to the Sticker God has made her a little robotic.'

'You'll be so glad of that robot when you've had your little one. How long to go now?'

'Nine weeks. If she comes on time.'

'It's a girl, is it?'

'Without a doubt.' I smile.

'I imagine you'll be doing the CLB as soon as you can, hmm?'

'The what?'

'The Contented Little Baby routines,' she says tersely, tapping her book and offering it to me. 'Gina Ford. Love her or hate her, her plan works.'

'Oh God, I haven't even thought about—'

'Well, you'd better start thinking – quick smart. You'll be exhausted after the birth, you'll want to get the infant sleeping through as quickly as possible, I expect.'

'This one's coming out the sunroof, so I may not be quite as tired as—'

'A caesar, you mean?'

I nod.

'Even more reason to get the baby settled as soon as you can. And don't think for a second you'll be any less tired than someone who's gone through labour. You'll be having a major operation and will take time to heal. Last thing you need is a recalcitrant child and a wakeful new-born.'

'Yes, yes.' I frown. 'I must remember, at my next appointment, to beg and plead and make sure I'm getting my caesarean. I don't want to ever, ever, *ever* feel contractions again.'

Elizabeth purses her lips, raises her eyebrows and turns to walk towards her table. Obviously dismissed, I wander over to the glasses and start polishing them with a tea towel, while staring out at the bright sunlight drenching the footpath in front of the cafe.

I'm so tired today, I barely even notice I'm talking out loud when I mumble something about being too old and too weary.

'You *are* a bit of a plonker.' Jack sniggers as he sorts out the float in the vintage cash register.

'Am I? Do you really think we're too old to be going through all this again? Is this the dumbest thing we've ever done?' I ask, looking down at my belly that's been so big for so long, I can't remember what my feet look like.

'Don't be ridiculous,' he scoffs. 'Everything's going to be fine, just fine. If we can keep on being nice to each other, we'll get through it relatively unscathed.'

'So you're glad it's happening? You wouldn't change it?'

'No, silly,' he says, ruffling my hair. 'But I tell you one thing I *would* change . . .'

'What?'

'That bloody Bangles song on high rotation in here – it blasts out of the speakers every two minutes!'

'But it's all part of a cunning marketing plan—'

'I think we get it, Rox. Your point's been made. Now, get off your lazy backside and source some more music!'

All this eschewing carbs and power walking for at least half an hour every day is all fine and well – and, in Bondi, everyone's so young and fit and good-looking, you're almost *shamed* into a punishing fitness routine if you want to live here. But it can get a little tedious, the constant chatter about weighty issues.

So, as you can guess, after an hour of talking about how many carbs there are in lentils, and whether you need fructose for good brain function or not, Shoshie and I turn our attentions to the kids and menfolk in our lives.

'How's it going with your littlies, as my gran used to say?' I ask. 'Is Gila still being … sometimes, as, um, aggressive to—'

'Oh! No, not any more. She's a little angel! Never lays a hand on her baby sister – unless it's to stroke her cheek.'

'Really?'

'Yep. Super-Duper Nanny Cooper sorted us out on that front. Turns out, she was positively rabid with jealousy.'

'Elizabeth?'

'No! Gila. But, with Elizabeth guiding and advising me, I instigated "special time" with just me and her and, ever since, she's been a little darling.'

'That's great,' I say.

'To tell you the truth, I think what really turned it around for Gila was seeing me be decisive, booting Isaac out and getting on with my own life again. Being happy for once. Genuinely happy.'

Shosh smiles at me and we both look around the cafe, taking in the buzz.

'Speaking of happy, where is our mastermind of a new

295

manager?' she asks, looking behind her, through to the kitchen.

'He's gone to sort some business out at home, he says.' I jerk my head in the direction of the big glass doors.

'And how are you feeling?'

'OK,' I say. 'Tired today, though. A bit up and down, mood-wise. You know, the usual.'

'Yeah, you do swing about a bit with those moods,' she says tentatively.

'I do?'

'Yeah, you do.'

'Oh, I know I do. I'd just hoped you hadn't noticed. When Jack told me the other night that I was up and down like a yo-yo, I snapped and yelled at him to at least try to not be so patronising.'

'And what did he say?'

'He said: "Ooh, that's a big word for such a little girl!"'

Shoshie chuckles.

'At least you two have a laugh together. Isaac and I never really shared a sense of humour. It's almost sad, in a way. I mean, that was the best he could do, he'd given the most he could muster to me and the girls – he just couldn't manage any more, or anything better.'

We ponder this for a few seconds.

'It's barely even painful now – just embarrassing.' At this, she starts blushing madly and batting her eyelashes.

'What's wrong, Shosh? Is he here? If he is, I'll ...'

But, of course, it's not Isaac who's just rocked up: it's loverboy Tarquin. And he's grinning like the cat who got the cream.

They lock arms and drift away to a cosy table where they can gaze at each other and the sunset, and, as I watch the sun fading through the plate glass wall, I see before me a vision in black leather.

Silently, he moves towards me, the sunlight putting him in silhouette – a particularly masculine silhouette, I might add, all broad shoulders and nipped-in waist atop muscular thighs and calves swathed in ... in ... are they motorbike boots?

Then it dawns on me that the man in black leather is wearing a motorbike helmet, too – could he be here to rob us? Steal the day's takings from the cash register?

Or has he come to ravage me? Is it some sexy stranger come to whisk me away on his bike for a raunchy interlude, having his wicked way with me on the soft sand as nearby the waves crash on to shore?

Or am I dreaming again?

'Phew, it's hot in here,' I say in my best sultry voice, fanning my face as I watch this fine specimen take off his helmet, making what little hair he has on the back of his head stick up, like a punk monk.

And then he speaks.

'It's your hormones, darl,' says Jack. 'I'm not hot.'

At this precise point in time, I beg to differ. And, just like that, it comes to me in a flash! Yes! *That's* who he's been reminding me of lately – the younger Jack I met and fell in love with all those years ago!

'What are you doing in all your bike gear?' I ask.

'Just rode the bike down here – someone's coming to look at it this evening. I'm selling it. To prove to you how serious I am about JAMM – and you and the kids.'

'Really?'

'Really.' He grins. 'Reckon I'll get a tidy sum for it, too.'

'Oh, Jack – but you love that bike!'

'True. But not as much as I love you. And I don't need it any more. *And* we can't afford it. If the guy wants the gear, too, our coffers will be looking pretty healthy this month. So, what do you say?'

'Can't you hang on to the leathers?' I say, casting my eyes over their finery. 'Just in case you need them sometime later down the track, when we're in the money and the kids have grown up and we can afford a bike again . . .?'

'Hadn't considered that. Good thinking, Rox. Are you sure you're feeling OK?'

'I am rather warm,' I say, breathing much more heavily than usual. 'Must be the baby.'

Yeah. *That*. And the fact that I've suddenly got the raging horn. And all because the lady loves a lad in leather. It's quite reassuring, in a way, to know that I can still dredge up those saucy feelings. I'd never admit it to Jack, of course, but cor blimey, guv – how sexy does he look in all that gear? In a really clichéd way ... but, hey! Who knew?

'Listen, Rox – I think it's time we launched our range of weaning foods. How about I get some costings and talk it through with Jack? I'll work on a snappy name for it, too. Something catchy,' says Shosh.

'I thought we could call it Just Another Manic Mum-Day All-Organic Baby Food,' I say.

'Hmm. Bit boring. I was thinking something more along the lines of: The Manic Mum's No-Panic Organics. Or: Just Another Panic-Free Kids' Meal. Or just: Manic Organix, with an x. You know, I can see the ad: Teatime panic? Grab Manic Organix! Or something ...'

'That's brilliant, Shosh!' I gush.

'Maybe ... As long as it's something that matches our well-thought-out ethos.'

We both giggle – JAMM may be a lot of things, but well-thought-out it most definitely is not.

At least, that's what I always think. But, looking around me now, I see a fully functioning cafe that's raking in the cash and providing a real sanctuary for the stressed and exhausted families out there who may not be able to afford a two-week holiday in Mustique or somewhere equally exotic, but they can stretch to a piece of Phil's divine Death By Chocolate cake and a bevvie of their choice.

Some families even make a weekly trip to JAMM for

dinner – Wednesday evening being our busiest and breaking up the drudgery of the working week.

During the day, it's mainly women and their kids. Jasmine does a roaring trade on Tuesdays (regardless of whether it's a new moon or not) and come Saturday and Sunday daytimes, the weekend dads descend upon us so they can read the paper, muck around on their laptops while their kids play, safe in the knowledge that they're being closely supervised and that they're in safe hands.

Friday and Saturday nights seem to be either girls' nights out or date nights for single parents (like lovers Tarquin and Shoshie, for instance, who are often found these days sipping wine and staring into each other's eyes, egged on by the warm glow of candlelight), and the film nights are proving really popular for those of us who want a break and to get away from the house, but don't want to go boozing and can't afford the hefty price of cinema tickets.

In fact, this cafe – JAMM to its nearest and dearest – is a fantastic success story just waiting to be told, now I think about it. What's the bet the *Financial Times* will be calling for an interview any day now?

Chapter 20

'Roxane?' says an unfamiliar voice.

I spin round, only to come face to face with a most impressive bust. With my nose teetering dangerously, embarrassingly, close to this person's cleavage, I quickly look up, thus knocking my chin against one of her, um, knockers, step back and say: 'Uh, sorry about that. Yes, hello, I'm Roxane.'

I hear a plate drop in the kitchen and look to see Chef and Jack staring at the Amazonian figure in front of me.

'Jack, my love?' I say, putting the back of my right hand up to my chin and exaggeratedly using it to force my mouth shut.

Neither Jack nor Chef move a muscle. Just drool a bit more.

'Hi! I'm Rooby – that's Rooby with an "ooh", not a "ewe" – as in kanga-*roo*,' the vision says in its posh British accent.

'I know!' I say, my neck starting to ache from all the

craning it's doing. 'I recognise you from an interview you did once . . .'

'I've wanted to meet you for ages and now, finally, here you are!'

'*You've* wanted to meet *me*?'

'Could we sit down?' she asks, as though it's an imposition.

'Yes, please!' I giggle, rubbing my neck. 'Let's get things on a bit more of a level playing field.'

'Yes, yes, of course – sorry! I often forget how tall I am!'

Jack appears at Rooby's side and puts his hand ever so gently on the small of her back, guiding her to the table nearest the bar.

'This way, ladies,' he says, his voice several octaves lower than usual.

'Thank you,' says Rooby, sitting down elegantly and taking the menu from Jack.

'Yes, thank you,' I say. 'That'll be all for now.'

He's lost in her eyes. He's got his head cocked to one side and he's come over all dreamy and fluttery of eyelash.

'Jack? Jack, *dear*?' I say, kicking his ankle with my foot.

'Hmm? What? Yes, yes – just give us a shout if you need anything. Anything at all.'

He shuffles off, the new leather still stiff – just like its owner, I hazard a guess.

'I've been a fan of yours for ages,' Rooby gushes.

'*Me?*' I recoil. 'Why?'

'Well, you started the Pissed-Off Parents Club back in the UK, didn't you? Bold move. I'd just had our first child, our daughter, She, and I was desperate to talk about how my life had changed. My husband, Giles – Giles Somerset? You may have heard of him?'

Heard of him? He's only in the news all the time and on the telly in some new cooking show or showing terrorists how to stop eating junk food or somesuch! He's a mega-wealthy celebrity chef – and our very own Chef's hero.

I look up at Chef in the kitchen and see he hasn't moved in the last five minutes.

'Yes, of course—'

'He wasn't around much when She was a baby and I really needed to talk to someone, to offload. So when I heard about the Pissed-Off Parents Club in Riverside and several villages in Berkshire, I raced to set up my own chapter. In West Hampstead!'

'I know! I read all about it on the Pissed-Off Parents Club website!'

I steal another lightning-fast glance at her boobs, take in her square shoulders, slender upper arms and flat stomach all wrapped up in a flirty, flouncy floral frock and it makes me screw up my nose involuntarily.

'Really?' she snorts, sounding like a horse.

'Can I just ask – is She short for Sheba?'

'No. It's English for "she" – like, you know how the French have Elle? I thought I'd strike a blow for the Brits and the English language and call her She. It's feminine and lovely. Don't you think?'

'Oh, definitely. You have a boy, too, don't you? What's his name again?'

'Homme. Like the French for "man" – but with an English lilt to it, so I make sure everyone stresses the "h". *Homme.*'

I'd never call a boy Homme, stressing the 'h' or otherwise. Can you imagine it? The other kids'd tease him mercilessly. And have branded him Homme-oh-sexual by the time he was two.

'Great name,' says Jack, appearing out of nowhere.

'Poo-wee,' I wave my hand in front of my nose, 'who's just tipped a whole bottle of aftershave all over themselves?'

'Can I get you anything, madam?' Jack directs this at Rooby.

'Oh! Just water with ice and a slice for me,' says Rooby.

'Same for me, Easy Rider,' I say, and shake my head at Jack's cack-handed attempts at chivalry.

'Your wish is my command,' he says, heading off back to the kitchen.

'Isn't he lovely?' says Rooby.

'He's a doll,' I say. 'He's my husband, Jack.'

'Compliments of the chef,' says Jack when he returns,

304

smoothly placing a plate of Turkish bread, olives, houmous and semi-sundried tomatoes in front of Rooby and plonking down a glass of tap water in front of me.

She scoops up a wodge of houmous with her little finger and sucks on it. I imagine Chef and Jack nearly wetting themselves at the sight.

'Oh no,' she says, 'don't like that houmous. He's put come in there.'

I spit my water out.

'*What?*'

'Come in. The houmous.'

'I'm sure he hasn't, there must be some mistake.'

'Nope – there's definitely some come in there.'

'God, I'm awfully sorry – Chef!'

'At your service,' says a beaming Chef, at the side of our table faster than you can say: 'You're sacked!'

'What did you put in this houmous?' I ask, appalled, disgusted and just about to be incandescent with rage.

'Tahini, lemon juice, chick peas, salt, cumin—'

'Queue-min ... is that how you say it?' Rooby giggles.

'Cumin! Not *come in*! Ha!' I guffaw.

'Oops. I've never been sure how to pronounce that one – no wonder Giles won't let me read out the specials at his restaurant, I'm always doing things like that! What am I like?'

And she starts snorting again, making Chef nearly fall over himself, he's laughing so hard.

'Sorry about that,' I say crossly, trying to shoo Chef away with my head, surreptitiously jerking it in the direction of the kitchen.

'Anyway,' Rooby clears her throat, 'when I read on KiddingAround that you were launching a cafe called Just Another Manic Mum-Day in Sydney, I just *knew* that I had to come and see it for myself. I *knew* I was destined to one day be a part of it.'

'You saw that ad? On KiddingAround.com.au? The website?'

'Yes!'

So someone *did* actually read that site! We once had A Real, Genuine, Bona Fide Reader! I can't believe it. Bet Kylie won't, either, when I tell her.

'Awesome,' I say, the ghosts of Maverick still haunting my speech.

'It certainly is,' she squeals. 'And now, seeing you here, seeing what you've done, I know I'm doing the right thing.'

'And that is . . .?'

'To ask you to come back over to London with me and help me set up the London arm of the operation. I want to take it to the next level, make it into a franchise.'

I can't speak.

'I want you to see to all the details, like in which suburb to set the first one up – Hampstead? Chiswick? You decide. Basically, I want to be your business partner and expand the JAMM empire, take it global. How does that sound to you?'

I still can't speak. All I can manage is to open and shut my mouth, like a fish, in an effort to try and form the word 'Why?'

'Why? Well, I'm sick of Giles always being the noble one, the one who's going to save the world, while the little woman stays at home and pushes babies out year after year. Not that I don't love him to pieces, don't get me wrong, it's just that now it's my turn. Time I gave something back, you know?'

'Wow.' I finally regain the power of speech. 'How?'

'Obviously, I'll be the face of JAMM, the beauty, if you like. And you, well, you can be the brains.'

'Obviously,' Jack and Chef chorus, leaning over the bar, their chins cupped in the palms of their grubby little hands.

'That's enough from the cheap seats.' I smile at them.

'But we'll have to act fast,' Rooby goes on. 'And you'll only need to be in situ for two weeks or so, and then you can come back here and have your baby. I want this all in train and happening before Giles opens his third bistro in a couple of months. It's in Tower Hamlets – "Bringing good food to bad boroughs". That's his slogan.'

She stands up, grabs the handles of her Balenciaga handbag, slings it over her shoulder and hands me a card.

'Here's my number. Do call me as soon as you can and let me know – I'll be leaving in two days, can't hang around.'

Looking down at me, she softens and says:

'Oh, Roxy, I just know this is going to be big. Really big. Please say you'll do it. Say you're in – please say you'll be my partner.'

And as she wafts her way through the tables and chairs, floating outside on a cloud of serious gorgeousness, I'm suddenly plunged back into reality with a big, fat bump.

'Talk about fragrant,' says a misty-eyed Jack.

'I think I'm in love,' says Chef, putting one hand on his chest and reaching his other arm out to where she was only moments ago standing.

'Pull yourselves together,' I say. 'And, um, *God*. Think it's time for an emergency staff meeting or what?'

Trying to track Shoshie down or get her on her own these days is nigh on impossible. Eventually I do manage to locate my elusive partner – she's gazing out at the stars blinking over the beach, just across the road from JAMM, with Tarquin snuggled in, right by her side, of course.

'Shosh?' I tap her on the shoulder.

'Hmm?' she murmurs, lost in love.

'I think we should have a staff meeting – you know, keep everyone up to speed. Remember how Troy told us to always keep the staff in the loop?'

'What? Now?' she says slowly, like she's nearly asleep.

'Yeah. But first I need to talk to you. No offence, Tarq, but preferably alone.'

'No worries,' says Tarquin. 'Time I was off. Got some serious thinking to do tonight myself.'

I watch them smooch like teenagers (i.e. for what feels like twenty minutes, without coming up for air) and, finally, they say farewell. Shosh crosses the road with me and we start clearing up after the last customers.

'What's up?' she asks.

'Well . . . ' I take a deep breath. 'Rooby Somerset, Giles Somerset's wife—'

'Ooh I love him! He's so cute – and so caring. He's my hero!' she squeals.

'Yeah, his wife came to see me today. She wants to open up a JAMM in the UK. London, most probably. And she wants me to go over there with her to sort out the premises. In two days' time.'

'She *what*?' Shosh knits her eyebrows.

'I know – I haven't said yes yet. I wanted to check with you.'

'She wants to set up the first JAMM franchise?'

'Yep! And she's got money to burn and contacts galore and talk about profile – she's so famous, the publicity we'll get will send our profits soaring.'

Shosh doesn't speak, but her mouth drops open as her eyes jump from my left one to my right one, my left one to my right one, in sheer disbelief.

'Shosh? Are you OK?'

'Just feel a bit dizzy, that's all,' she says carefully. 'Think I need to sit down.'

I put my hand on her shoulder and guide her into one of the wicker chairs.

After a short while, she looks up at me and smiles.

'I don't believe it,' she says slowly. 'I mustn't have heard you correctly. Tell me again!'

I repeat myself and she asks me to do it two more times. And a third.

'Shosh! What do you think?'

'I think it's awesome! I'm so totally stoked! And I think you were right to discuss it with me first – but I definitely think you should go. You know London, you're the one who's been missing it and ... and ...'

'And what?'

'And I don't want to be anywhere else but here at the moment. Don't think I could bear not seeing Tar. Even for just one day.'

'Really?'

'Yep. We've got it bad, Rox.'

'Oh, Shosh, that's wonderful!'

'Yeah, thanks. I know!'

'And now with the cafe going global, I mean – how lucky are we?'

'We are two lucky ladies, that's for sure.' Shoshie smiles. She stands up and I go round the table to help her.

'Let's fill the troops in on everything once we've finished clearing up, shall we?' she says. 'But can I do the talking? I mean, love the bones of you, Rox, but you do go on a bit and I'd really like to get home before midnight tonight, if that's all right with you.'

'Cheeky moo,' I say, scooping up two wine glasses between my index and middle fingers.

Chapter 21

'You can't go gallivanting off to London – you're thirty-five weeks pregnant!'

'But Joey was nine days late, this one's bound to be the same – and anyway, it's only for two weeks. I'll be back before you know it.'

'No,' Jack shakes his head, 'it's too much of a risk.'

'The hospital and the diabetic controller are fine with it – they're writing me a note,' I reply.

Please don't put up too much opposition to this, Jack, I plead to myself. I mean, I've got to go! Two weeks back in the UK? I could stay at Mum and Dad's place in Paddington while they're away working in Sweden and I could get up to Bath, spend some much-needed one-on-one time with poor old Charlie ...

'Nope.' Jack's still shaking his head, smiling. 'No, it just won't do. Tell you what, I'll go. Just me and Booby Rooby!'

'Ha!' is all I can say.

'What's so crazy about that?' He smirks, knowing full well.

'You've got to stay here and get the business back on track. You're going great guns, finally making JAMM into a profitable enterprise, managing the co-op mums, et cetera et cetera. Don't blow it now.'

'But—'

'Anyway, *you're* the one who wanted to come out here in the first place, bask in the sunshine, see your mum, escape from the cold – I'm the one who's missing it back there. And Charlie. Not to mention all those great pubs with roaring fires and big, woolly jumpers and autumn ...'

'Seriously, Rox – what about the baby?'

'I *am* being serious. And the baby will be OK – as if I'd put her or myself in any jeopardy. Honestly, Rooby checked with Kanga Air and they're fine with it as long as you have a doctor's note, so ...'

'Pulled some strings, did she?'

'Probably – but what's wrong with that? Oh, Jack – this could be the thing to really send JAMM up into the stratosphere. Give it a real virus.'

'Send it viral, you mean,' he snorts.

'Yeah, that's what I said.'

'We'll talk about it later – right now I've got to get over to Penrith and see a supplier for those Nespresso pods.'

'Jose*phine*!' I stop, bringing our walk to an abrupt halt just before we get to The Galah. 'I've said no, I mean no, and that is my final answer. No!'

'But I wanna come to London, too.' She starts to cry. 'Why can't I come?'

'Sweetheart,' I bend down as best I can and try to kneel on the footpath, sitting back on my haunches, 'it'll be very boring, just Rooby and me looking for a place to set up another cafe. You'll miss your friends – Gila and all the gang – if you come with me.'

'But I'll miss you if you go without me.' She sniffs, her turquoise-blue eyes awash with tears.

'Come on.' I drag myself up. 'We'll be late for pre-school if we don't get a shift on.'

We take about ten slow steps and, just as we're smack-dab in the middle of the footpath out the front of The Galah, the area packed with tradies having their first beers and cigarettes of the day, Joey sees her chance and takes it. With the vim and vigour I thought was reserved only for the getting of Caramello Koalas and Cornettos, she drops my hand, stops dead in her tracks and screams:

'Don't leave me here, Mummy!'

I whip my head round, confused, wondering where that banshee shriek has come from. I focus on Joey just as she falls to her knees and brings her chin into her chest.

'*Pleeeeeease*, Mummy! Leh-heh-heh-heh-het me go with you!'

'Joey, honey,' I whisper, rapidly waddling over to her.

'Take me with you, *pleeeeeease!*'

'Sweetheart, I—'

'You ruin my life!' She sobs, giving me a clue as to how

314

our conversations are going to go once we hit the adolescent years.

'Ga'arn! Take her with you, you big meanie!' calls out one of the tradies.

'Here she is again, Mother of the bloody Year!' shouts another.

'Mum on the run, more like!' barks a third.

'Some people shouldn't be allowed to have kids,' the barmaid sneers as she picks up some empties.

I try to ignore them and concentrate on my seriously upset little girl.

'Babe, it's *work*. I'd love to take you with me, but I can't.'

'You cawn't,' Joey says, sounding more South African than Tony Greig, 'or you WON'T?'

A hush descends over the tradies and, even though I'm not looking, I can tell they're all craning their necks in a bid to see more clearly the latest contretemps between their favourite performing mother and daughter.

As I'm dithering about, sweeping Joey's hair out of her eyes, unsure as to whether she really just said she'd miss me or whether I was imagining it, the mumbling starts over where the tradies are. Unfortunately, I can't hear exactly what the usually rowdy throng is saying in its entirety, but, luckily, for the benefit of us hard-of-hearing older mothers, they shout out a few choice words and phrases in amongst the low rumbling of their rough voices:

'Mumble, mumble, WORKING MOTHERS, mutter, mutter, SLAVES TO MONEY, NOT THEIR KIDS, rhubarb, rhubarb, CRYING SHAME, blah blah, PRIORITIES ALL WRONG, grumble, growl, ANYONE GOT THE NUMBER FOR SOCIAL SERVICES?'

Joey looks at me with her puppy-dog eyes and pouts, a solitary, plump tear tumbling down her cheek. I take a long, slow, deep breath in and, unable to take any more public shaming from the morally outraged tradies, I give up and wave the metaphorical white flag.

'All right, darling.' I smile, defeated. 'You can come with me.'

Joey beams and squeals as she throws her arms around me. As I stumble back slightly with the full force of her jubilation, I hear a few whoops of victory and schooner glasses chinking together in celebratory cheers coming from the tradies. It feels a tad embarrassing to be so derided out the front of The Galah once again, but it also feels good to give in, to give Joey what she wants – on my terms, of course. After all, *I'm* the adult in this relationship, the one who calls the shots. Oh, yes – I am *definitely* the one in total control here.

I stride over towards Shoshie, who's grinning like a lunatic, staring off into the middle distance.

'Shosh, I better tell Rooby that everything's cool for us to go to London tomorrow, then.'

'Hmm? Sorry? I was miles away. What did you say?'

'We're off tomorrow, Joey and I. With Rooby Somerset. Are you OK?'

'Yeah, fine.' She sniffs, looks up and, tentatively, twitchily moves her lips into an almost-smile. Her cheeks are shiny and wet with tears.

I put my hands on her shoulders and look into her big, excited eyes.

'Shoshie? What's wrong? Do you want to go? I'm so sorry. Please, don't cry. You go.'

She lowers her eyes again and flings her arms around my neck.

'Oh, Roxy!' she blubs. 'I can't go!'

'Shh. Yes, you can. Jack and I will look after things here; you go and have a break, have a good time. You can leave the kids with us, if you like.'

I shudder momentarily when I finish uttering those last words. 'Ah – if you promise you'll only go for two weeks, that is!' I add.

'I can't go, Roxy,' she sobs into my ear, her words sounding heavy with the thick saliva of the truly distraught crier, 'because I'm pre-heh-heh-heh-heh-gnant!'

Flaming Nora.

'Make way, make way – lady with a baby,' I want to say, as we weave through the punters and past Kylie, who's also looking like she's going to pop any minute, out to the back where the plastic milk crates sit amid the butts of a thousand ciggies. But, of course, I don't, I just grab Shoshie's hand and lead her out there in silence.

'Sit down,' I say, in my best calm and soothing yet also authoritative voice, while I remain standing.

Shoshie's so discombobulated, she does as she's told.

'How far gone are you?'

'This is my seventh week, I think. I'm going to go for an early scan as soon as I can get over the shock and call my obstetrician.'

'You have an obstetrician?'

'Of course.' She sniffs, wiping her nose with an already sodden, shredded Kleenex. 'And a gynaecologist. And a paediatrician for the kids. Don't you?'

'No. But anyway. Who's the daddy?'

'That's just it, Roxy.' Her face crumples up again and, as she dissolves into tears, I can just about make out that she's saying:

'I don't know whether it's Isaac's or Tar-har-har-quin's!'

'OK, OK – calm down, Shosh, calm down. Getting hysterical won't help anyone,' I say, coming over all good-girl-scout, unflappable, reassuring and comforting.

Shoshie looks up at me, confused and begging for help. Instead, all she gets is: 'Bloody hell – what are you going to do?'

'I dunno!'

I rub her shaking shoulders as she cries her eyes out. Which takes quite a long time, actually. All those tears must have been building up what with all the stress about Isaac, the daily nightmare of juggling two kids and then finally falling for a decent bloke and hoping to regain some semblance of her former self – and now this. Talk about a whirlwind. No wonder she's bawling, now she's got bonkers hormones to deal with as well. Poor Shoshie. What rubbish timing.

After about ten minutes, she stops, blows her nose, wipes her mascara from under her eyes and says, 'Hooh! I needed that. Coffee?'

We go back inside and, while I tuck into a hot pot of Earl Grey with skimmed milk and Splenda, Shoshie knocks back a double espresso.

'I know, I know – caffeine yadda yadda yadda – but my need is greater at the moment,' she says, battling with her already-oversized guilt gland.

'Don't tell anyone yet, OK?' she says. 'For all the usual reasons and then some.'

'Course I won't,' I say, wondering whether I'll get a chance to tell Jack before we leave or, indeed, whether I'll even *remember* this bombshell amidst all the mental listage that's constantly going on in my head.

'So, you see, as much as I'd love to go for a quick jolly off to the UK, I am, quite literally, up the spout on this occasion.' She laughs.

Then we both spy Tarquin sauntering our way.

'G'day, gorgeous.' He grins on approach.

'G'day!' I say, as if he was addressing me.

He kisses Shoshie's forehead and she gazes at him adoringly, like most of the other women in the cafe, if truth be told.

'I got your message and came as soon as I could,' he says to Shoshie. 'Are you feeling any better?'

'So you already know?' I ask Tarquin, puzzled.

'Know what?'

Shoshie administers a swift kick to my shins under the table.

'That, ah, that, um, you're going to have to look after Shosh for me for a few weeks – I'm off to London to extend the JAMM brand!'

'No, I didn't know that.' He smiles, his long dimples creasing his cheeks beautifully. 'How wonderful! Are Jack and Joey going with you?'

'Nope. Jack isn't – it'll be just me and Joey.'

'Uh-huh ... good idea. I like it. Could be just what the pair of you need, a little time away from each other. Might be just the ticket to bring you guys closer together, give you some breathing space before the bub's born.'

I hadn't thought of it in that way at all, but, now he mentions it, maybe it is a good idea in that respect.

'So the cafe's going international now, is it?' Tarquin says, looking from me to Shoshie, from Shoshie to me.

'You betcha,' I say, rummaging about in my bag by my feet. 'Where's that mobile, I can never ... find ... ah! Hello?'

'Roxy? It's me, Rooby.'

I look at Shosh and we widen our eyes at each other briefly, before I wander off, out to the front of the cafe where the reception's better.

'Hiya, Rooby! How are you?'

'Good, good. And yourself?'

'Fine, yep, good.'

'Enough chit-chat. What's it going to be? Are you with me or agin me?'

'With, with, WITH!' I shout unnecessarily.

'All right, all right! No need to yell.' She giggles girlishly, sounding a lot like Joey. Which reminds me ...

'Sorry about that, I'm just so excited. But I have to tell you something, Rooby.'

'Yes?' she says, sounding worried.

'Joey's coming with me – my daughter. She's three-and-a-half, so you'll have to book an extra seat, I'm afraid.'

'Is that all? That's great! But, oh, damn! First class is all full for the flight tomorrow – would business be OK? At least we'd all be slumming it in business together ... ' She sounds truly apologetic.

'Oh, well,' I splutter, trying to sound disappointed while my left arm punches the air with joy, 'I suppose it'll just have to do.'

Chapter 22

'Got everything?' asks Jack for the umpteenth time.

He's standing at our front door, having already put Joey's suitcase into the boot of the car, holding mine in one hand and the door open with his foot. He's been waiting there for the past, ooh, I dunno, ten minutes or so, while I get myself and Joey and all our stuff ready for tonight's journey to the other side of the world.

'Shh! Let me think!' I continue mumbling my mental list to myself. 'Now I'll have to start at the beginning again!'

And then, in my head, I hear my mum's dulcet tones, nagging me to remember:

* Your blood glucose test strips, darling – a crucial part of your testing kit
* And, oh! I know you don't like them, but you can't do without those little needles either, sweetie
* Nor the whatsit that looks like a pen that you jab

into the top of your leg every night to administer
the correct dose of insulin

* Speaking of: insulin itself – enough for two weeks.
  If there's an emergency, you'll always be able to get
  more over there, I'm sure
* Now, have you got your passport?
* Joey's passport?
* Joey's QV bath oil, QV cream and Cetaphil non-
  soap for her sensitive eczema-prone skin – as well
  as her lipsalves?
* And your mobile phone? Even though, you know,
  you could save an absolute fortune and get a Tesco
  temporary one while you're there . . .
* Makeup. Another must-pack. It's so important to
  make the effort, sweetheart – especially now, when
  you look so . . . *tired*
* Still on personal hygiene, darling, *do* pack a pair of
  scissors and some tweezers for some deforestation
  of the hag hairs during the trip
* What else? There's definitely something else
  you've forgotten, definitely something very, very
  important . . . Your hospital notes! But where the
  hell are they? Hmm? I mean, really, Roxane! Lord
  knows why you find it so impossible to get
  organised . . .

I look on the kitchen table and pick up several different
piles of stuff. I swear this is where I last saw them, buried

under an Annabel Karmel cookbook and an empty diet yoghurt carton with the spoon still sticking out of it.

'Are you looking for your hospital folder, Mummy? Here it is. By Daddy's com-pew-dah.'

Who needs to get organised when I've got my own little walking talking concertina-file sorting everything out for me?

'Thanks, sweetheart. And I think you mean com-pew-*ter*. Make sure you say the t. Com-pew-*ter*.'

'Com-pew-*dah*.' She flashes me a wry smile.

Sitting in the car on a packed motorway (Jack's driving, naturally – with my anxiety attacks and uncanny knack for getting lost, I figured we'd save time and, probably, several *lives* if he was at the wheel), my mind starts racing and I go through my list again – this time without Mum's voice, but now with added fear and panic, knowing full well that it's far too late to go back for anything if I've forgotten it.

I suddenly slam my foot on the imaginary brake in the passenger's footwell.

'The Chart! I forgot Joey's Chart! FARK!'

'No, you didn't,' comes the sweet little chipmunk-voice from the back. 'It's in the boot. In my suitcase.'

'Oh! Yes, yes. You're right.' I bring my hand up to my chest and sigh with relief.

'I'm always right!' she announces.

'Darling – what *would* I do without you?' I say, genuinely meaning it.

'I don't know,' Joey replies, also really meaning it.

'Neither do I.' Awkwardly I try to turn round and reach out to ruffle her hair, but settle on a smile and a tapping of her foot, thanks to the big belly in the way.

'You might say "fark" more if I wasn't here.' She grins, knowing she's being naughty.

'That's enough,' says Jack, giggling. 'Mummy and Daddy never say that rude word any more, do we, Mummy?'

'But Mummy just did. I heard her. So did you, Daddy – don't tell fibs.'

'Well, yes, *technically* she did, but that was a slip-up. Normally, she—'

'Normally she says "fuck"!' yelps a delighted Joey.

Jack gasps.

'No, I don't! Honest! A flipping or a flaming or, at worst, a *fark* – but never a—'

'Mummy, that's not true! When you scraped the car coming out of the driveway, you said it then,' Joey sings like a canary.

'You *what*?' Jack looks horrified.

'I didn't! I said "fudge" or something—'

'Not the swearing, you ... you scraped the car? And you didn't even tell me?'

'No one was hurt – both Joey and I were fine – and I got it fixed at the Girls Torque smash repairs as quick as a flash, so I didn't—'

'How could you not tell me?' He's incensed. 'And how much did it cost?'

'Only . . . about a thousand dollars.'

Jack goes red and his eyes look like they're about to pop out of his head.

'One thousand dollars? *Only* a thousand bucks?'

I turn round and flash Joey my wide-eyed uh-oh-I-think-I'm-in-trouble look and she laughs her high-pitched excited laugh and, totally deadpan, says:

'I think I'm in trouble, Mummy. I've just had an accident.'

'I want Daddy!' Joey bellows as I drag her around the food court in the Sydney Airport departure lounge.

'Well, you've got me for the next two weeks and so . . . Joey? You will *be quiet* and we will *enjoy the whole experience together*!'

'But I want Daddy!' she yells.

I hold her wrist even tighter as she goes limp and drops to her knees. Exasperated, I look up and see a NO WORRIES CURRIES sign beckoning us inside, the industrial fans seducing us with the smell of sweet spices.

'How about a mild korma and rice? You love rice. Would you like some chicken korma and rice?'

'I DON'T like to eat ANIMALS,' she shouts through clenched teeth.

'Since when?' I ask, even though I should know better than to try to engage her in rational adult conversation.

'Too spicy for me!'

'OK . . . how about some fruit? You love apples. And

pears. There's a fruit shop just over there. Let's go and see what we can find.'

I pull her along, her pale-pink tights getting grubbier by the second, her fairy wings intermittently scraping the filthy floor. We carry on like this, passing the iPhone shop called HOW DO YOU LIKE THEM APPS? and draw up in front of a little stall with SHE'LL BE APPLES emblazoned across the top.

'Right. Here we are. What would you like?' I say to a red-faced Joey, who's looking so hard-done by, the man serving the fruit looks at me and shakes his head, muttering something about some people not being fit to be parents.

'HATE fruit!' she wails. 'BOR-*RING*!'

I acquiesce. 'What do you want, then? You find it and I'll buy it for you. Go on. I'll walk behind you.'

Miraculously, the thought of this – me letting her go her own way, forging ahead with her grown up independence – brightens her up a bit. And before I can say, 'You capricious little—', she's off, purposefully marching straight towards a sushi bar called RAW-IN-TRADE.

Lured by Hello Kitty dolls and assorted Japanese kitsch, Joey strides into the place, climbs up on to one of the stools and picks a plate of sashimi off the conveyor belt slowly gliding past her.

In typical interfering, fussy-Mum mode, I put the dish straight back on the conveyor belt and tell her she won't like it.

In typical teenage-rebellion style, she grabs the plate back off the belt and takes off the see-through lid.

'Are you sure, Joey?'

But she doesn't answer me. She's too busy cracking the wooden chopsticks apart and pouring some soy sauce over the two bits of raw salmon draped over two clumps of yummy-looking sushi rice. My mouth starts to water a little, it being yonks since I've indulged in any rice – I mean, one bite of that and my blood sugar levels would hit the roof.

'Not too much soy sauce, sweetheart,' I nag, pushing her pouring hand away from her plate.

'Mu-um,' she groans and expertly grabs the morsels with her chopsticks, shovelling them into her mouth.

She chews, swallows and barely comes up for air before she's shoving the second bit of sashimi down her throat.

'Liked that, did you? Yumbo?'

She nods her head emphatically while she's still chewing and pulls another identical plate of raw fish and rice off the belt.

She polishes that one off in seconds flat, then a further two plates of prawns and rice. She starts to slow down somewhat and makes a play for one last plate – something fried and crispy and stuffed with I-haven't-got-a-clue-what.

She scoffs it down in no time.

'It's like crisps!' she says through a mouthful and starts laughing uncontrollably.

'Careful,' I say, 'you don't want to inhale a bit of that and choke.'

She looks at me like I'm a Grade-A handbrake, rolls her eyes to the ceiling and carries on munching.

A couple of minutes later, she pushes the empty plate away and announces that she's finished.

'Wow,' I say, truly amazed. 'You ate all that? With chop-sticks?'

'You see, Mummy,' she says, using her newfound oh-so-slightly-irritatingly-smug tone, 'I eat everything on my plate if I like it. You always give me too much stuff I don't like.'

And there endeth the lesson.

Joey's fast asleep, stretched out in her own little pod of luxury, wrapped up in a duvet so light yet so warm, I just want to snuggle up to her and hug her tight. She's got a smile on her face, even though she's in a deep, still sleep, and she looks more content and comfortable than I've seen her in a long time.

This business class is amazing. Awesome, even, you might say. There's real stainless steel cutlery to eat with and the hostesses even dish out your meal on to your plate, like posh waitresses who know silver service. There's space for your bump, your legs – you can even walk around without giving every other passenger the Spanish archer in your wake.

It's light up here and heaps quieter than back in cattle

329

class. If money were no object, I'd fly business class whenever I set foot on a plane. I mean, luxury, peace and quiet? On a twenty-one-hour flight? With a nearly-four-year-old kid? I must be dreaming.

'But I'm not,' I say out loud, pinching my left forearm just to make sure.

I reach for my bag and plunge my hand bravely into its depths, dodging unused nappies, wipes, spare pairs of Joey's knickers and trousers, searching for the New Moon List I did in Bondi all those months ago.

My hand comes back up for air with supermarket receipts, hair elastics, bobby pins, five- and twenty-cent pieces and a couple of yellow Jelly Babies in it and I sigh. But then I remember I put it in the inside pocket, the one with the zip that I haven't opened since.

'What you got there?' comes Rooby's voice from over the aisle, as she puts down her Kindle. She told me she just can't put *The Secret* and *The Law of Attraction* down. I guess she was wrong.

'Oh, just a list.' I smile, embarrassed.

'A wish list?' she probes.

'Of sorts,' I answer. 'It's a New Moon Wish List. Even though I'm not usually into that sort of thing.'

She thanks the hostess who's just brought her another G&T. 'Any of it come true yet?'

'Um, not much of it, no,' I scan the list desperate to read something next to which I can put a mental tick.

'Don't worry, it will. Eventually.' She smiles. 'The first

time I ever did it, I asked for the love of my life to appear.'

'And he did?'

'No, not immediately. But I was doing a lot of meditation at the time, as well, so I had a lot of quiet and a lot of hours to focus, clear my head of all the chaos and really zone in on what was most important to me.'

'What happened?'

'I asked the cosmos for a sign, anything, *something* to reassure me that there was someone for me out there. Someone who was perfect for me.'

'And what did the cosmos say?' I stifle a titter.

'Giles.'

'It said "Giles"? The cosmos spoke to you? What did it sound like?'

'It's hard to explain – it wasn't a man's voice, exactly, but it was clear and it spoke directly to me with the name Giles.'

'Wow,' I say.

'If you've been doing New Moon Wishing or cosmic ordering a lot, it will have spoken to you, too. It's just whether you've been in a good enough place, a quiet enough place, to hear it. Have you heard anything?'

'Nope.' I shake my head, images of seagulls and hot dogs flashing into my mind. 'I might have seen a sign or two, though. Mind you, I only did it the once. I just never seem to get the time.'

'Are you sure you haven't heard anything?'

'Pretty sure . . .'

'It just so happened that when I asked for something big, the cosmos answered with something equally big. But it can say anything when it speaks – and may not sound like you imagine it would.'

'Well, maybe I *have* heard the cosmos speak to me. When I've been making lists. But all it ever said was "Buy milk" or "Find list". And, come to think of it, it sounds just like my mum.'

Rooby laughs. 'If you take up meditation, too, you'll hear the cosmos loud and clear.'

I look back down at the piece of paper and mentally place a tentative tick after 'Get Organised', despite what Mum/the cosmos might say. So I didn't get skinny, so what? I got pregnant. And I've seen no action whatsoever (with Jack or anyone else for that matter) since that fateful night . . . but I *did* get my dream job running JAMM, and for that I will be eternally grateful.

And now, here I am, flying business class to London, where we will take steps to expand our cafe empire and I, personally, will get to see whether I think we'd all be better off back in Blighty or whether we should stay happy and on top form Down Under.

'Where,' I wonder aloud, 'will we end up calling home?' I nod slowly to myself, hoping that this trip will culminate in one of those light-bulb moments, one of those epiphanies that people talk about.

'Would now be a good time to try to meditate?' I smile,

shuffling about in my seat a bit more and closing my eyes.

'Perfect,' slurs Rooby. 'Now, in order to connect, really engage with the universe and yourself, just close – yes, that's it – just close your eyes. Empty your mind of the clutter and noise of your everyday life and try to think of nothingness: white space, calm, cool, contentment. Just be. Ju-u-u-st relax. And ... zzzzzzzzzzzzzz.'

I open one eye to look over at her and see whether she's meditating or has simply passed out and I gather it's the latter, considering her head's resting on her left shoulder and there's a tiny bit of drool pooling at the corner of her open mouth.

A hostess bends down to take her glass – her real glass, I might add – away, and, as she closes the curtains, going back into the galley, I can hear her colleague say:

'So is she mad? Or just pissed?'

It's the flying, you see. For all Rooby's grace and coolness, long-haul trips give her the screaming abdabs, she says, and the only way she can deal with it is by taking Xanax with gin and sleeping.

I feel strangely protective of Rooby, though, and want to inform the hostesses that she is neither (well, maybe she is a tad tiddly) – if they must know, she's actually quite the inspiration.

And so with the cabin quiet – save for the muted sound of the engines roaring – I close my eyes once more and give this meditation lark a go.

Let's see ... empty your mind ...

I can't. It's chockers with thoughts of Joey, the impending baby, Jack, the cafe, the UK arm of Operation JAMM, Charlie, Shoshie, Tarquin, Elizabeth and Jasmine going round and round in my head.

'Ah, it's useless,' I mutter, sitting up straighter in my seat. 'I can't even be quiet when I'm trying to meditate – no wonder Jack gets the hump with my endless chuntering on. I think I finally know how he feels.'

The baby issues a sharp, swift kick to my groin as if to say, 'Shut up and let us all get some shut-eye!' so I turn over on to my side, finding myself in the most comfortable position *ever*, and slowly succumb to sleep.

Chapter 23

Charlie and Rose are milling about the front doors to Bath Spa station when Joey and I get through the ticket barriers.

There are screams and shrieks, squeals and hugs, bumps colliding and all-round merriment as we're reunited with my best friend and her ten-year-old daughter.

I well up as I tell Charlie how worried I've been about her and how desperate I've been to see her face to face. She gives me an extra-big hug and assures me she's fine and has, in fact, never felt better.

'But you've been so scared about being pregnant! And then the whole John thing – '

'No, Rox, I'm good. Really. Everything's great. I'm in a much better place, honestly. Please don't worry – let's just concentrate on having some fun now. OK?'

Within seconds it feels like we've never left each other's side – we fall into the same old easy, comfortable patter and banter and, before we know it, we've driven up hill and down dale until we're there, parked out the front of Charlie's fantastic, beautiful, absolutely wonderful four-storey Georgian townhouse.

'Don't worry,' Charlie says as she helps Rose clamber out of the back seat, 'we can walk to the kerb from here!'

I just about wet myself laughing, as does Charlie, while Rose and Joey swap withering looks.

Rose puts her arm round Joey and says, 'Come on, let's go to my room. I've got some great Darcey Bussell ballerina books I think you might like.'

Joey looks up at her adoringly and beams all over her face.

'Hasn't Rose changed?' I say to Charlie as we walk inside.

'I know!' Charlie squeaks. 'One day she's all guitars and football and wanting to be a boy and the next, sometime round her tenth birthday, she finally wants to wear a dress. A pink one at that!'

Unable to hide the pride in her voice, Charlie shoots me an ever-so-slightly embarrassed look.

'I know it's not the most amazing thing in the world, but with nine years of her looking and behaving exactly like her dad, to finally have some acknowledgement that she's a girl and she wants to look a bit more like me, well, it's nice. I felt cheated for a long time, missing out on that whole daughter mini-me thing. You know, like you've got with Joey.'

'Eh?' I grunt as I put our bags down and give Charlie's front room the once-over.

It's still all high ceilings and smooth brown leather sofas, earthy, creamy-coloured velvet curtains and Farrow & Ball adorning every wall. Despite Charlie's disastrous love life she's always kept an immaculate home – always with the latest styles and trends, always with the big names and expensive brands. It's like something out of *Livingetc* magazine, and I feel a tiny twinge of surprise.

Everything else in Charlie's life has changed – she's pregnant when she swore she'd never have any more kids after Rose, for a start. And now my once-slim, bordering-on-bony friend is now magnificently rotund. I used to always be able to count on her to have a roll-up dangling from her lips and a glass of something dark red and alcoholic in her skeletal hand – but now she's all shortbread and muffins and huge mugs of comfortingly sweet milky tea.

'Put the kettle on, Rox. And help yourself to some shortbread or whatever you fancy – Rose and I have been baking for days in preparation for your visit. I'm just popping to the loo,' Charlie shouts as she clomps up the stairs.

I sit and then slide down into my preferred slumped position on Charlie's couch, picking up one of the magazines she's carefully fanned out on her coffee table.

It's *Positive Parenting!* (hardly the designer label title I'd expect from Charlie), the magazine I worked for all those years ago when I lived in London.

337

The picture of the baby on the cover makes me smile and feel all gooey inside. I flip the pages and feel myself being sucked into that magazine fantasy world, where every baby is gorgeous and constantly smiling or asleep, where every adoring mummy is tall, skinny and about twenty-four years old, where every image you see – whether it's selling a baby product or illustrating a feature – makes you feel fat, frumpy and a failure in comparison.

I snap the magazine shut when Charlie waddles into the room.

'I never thought I'd see the day when you'd be buying baby mags.' I lock my fingers together and rest my arms on my belly.

'I know,' she grins, 'but I've got right into it this time. And I've forgotten all the stuff you need to know – it being a hundred years since I had Rose – and isn't the cover baby so cute?'

'Yeah,' I say warily, wondering what's happened to the Charlie I used to know and love – cynical, sarcastic and caustic. What have they done to her?

'Not long for you now.' She nods in the direction of my sizeable mound.

'Yep – three more weeks and I'll be having my scheduled caesarean at Randwick Hospital in Sydney.'

'Ooh – I'm in no hurry for this to end. I love being pregnant this time.' She rubs her tummy and smiles contentedly at it. 'Last time, with Rose, I knew I was with the

338

wrong man and I hated what the pregnancy was doing to my figure. But this time, I don't give a toss about the man – whether he stays or goes – and I love all the changes my body's going through. It's amazing, really, and so unlike me, but I absolutely *love* eating whatever the hell I want, whenever the hell I want it – and not having to choke myself on cigarettes all day, every day, just to keep myself from eating. It's liberating, you know?'

'Wish I did.' I sigh. 'I've got to be careful with the old diabetes now – sugar and carbs are pretty much the enemy – which means, as yummy as they look, I can't indulge in any of your biscuits. Promise you'll send some over to me so I can binge to my heart's content once the baby's out?'

'Course,' she says through a mouthful of chunky crumbs. 'When are you going back?'

'Eight days. I'll be thirty-eight weeks then. Kanga Air did Rooby a favour letting me fly at this late stage in the pregnancy, and next week is absolutely my last chance to go back.'

'Well, you don't still want to move back to London, do you? Not now it's getting colder and the nights are drawing in.' She smiles, crunching down on a whole new piece of shortbread.

'No, no.' I shake my head. 'Not London, no. Rooby, Joey and I did a reccy the other day of potential locations for the cafe and even though we were driving through all my favourite haunts, revisiting my old stomping grounds,

I felt a strange disconnect. I didn't want to leap out the car and revel in a trip down memory lane; I didn't want to have a go at reliving the good old days – I felt detached, like an outsider. There was no pull for me at all. I didn't feel any pangs of longing for those days or people or places – just a strange indifference.'

'About time.' Charlie clucks. 'I mean, a lot's changed since we were twenty-five running around London with not a care in the world. And thank God for that! We're completely different people now, I hope. Look at what we've both got and what we both have to look forward to. I wouldn't go back to being twenty-five again if you paid me.'

'Nah, me neither.' I screw up my nose. 'Well, maybe if you paid me a few million. Oh, I don't know – don't know where I want to live any more. Jack says that wherever we are – Joey, the baby and me – that's his home.'

'Aw, that's nice.' Charlie looks surprised. 'I mean, it's a lovely sentiment – didn't know Jack had it in him.'

'I know. It is rather a nice thought . . .'

'So what's she like, anyway?'

'Rooby? She's all right, as it goes – bit of a fruit loop, but no more than the rest of us. You know, one minute she's this giggly, silly, dumb model, and the next, she's all profit margins and deficits and serious-faced business.'

'She's so beautiful,' Charlie says.

'Yeah. She is. But she wasn't always so blessed. I mean, she's always *looked* amazing, I'm sure, but she told me she grew up in total poverty with her alcoholic mother and physically abusive stepdad. She left home when she was fifteen and got a job at an estate agent's in Elephant & Castle. Met Giles a few years later and – bang! – the dirt was gone.'

'Nightmare. The parents, I mean, not meeting Giles.' Charlie shakes her head. 'Just goes to show, you can never tell what hellness someone's been through, even if their life appears to be so charmed.'

'Rooby says we're all a work in progress. And it's not what happens to you that makes you who you are, but how you deal with it. She reckons that without her meditation and New Moon Wishing and positive thinking, she probably wouldn't be alive today. She says our lives are the result of our thoughts, whether we're awake or asleep. So if you want something badly enough and believe that you will get it then you will. Fill your heart and your mind with positivity and good things will come to you—'

'Who does she think she is, Oprah Winfrey?' Charlie sniffs. 'What a load of celebrity *balls*. They really do spout a load of old twaddle. Have you met Giles?'

'No. Sounds like a lovely guy from what Rooby says – a genuinely caring philanthropist hero. Bit too busy for her liking, though: doesn't spend enough time with Rooby and the kids, from what I can gather.'

'So selfish!' Charlie giggles. 'Men, eh? Who needs 'em?'

I smile and shiver at the chilling thought of being permanently without Jack.

'Are you cold?' asks Charlie. 'Feels almost balmy to me – must be in comparison to Sydney, though?'

'Maybe. I'm constantly boiling over there, telling Joey to take off her coatigan all the time—'

'Coatigan?'

'Yeah, it's this long, woolly cardigan that's almost like a coat . . .'

'Normally mums are trying to get their kids' woollies on, not pulling them off.'

'I know – poor thing's always shivering, her teeth chattering while her mum sweats for Britain.'

'Rose!' Charlie yells. 'Come down here and light the fire for us, please?'

'OK, Mummy,' comes the obedient, resigned reply from upstairs.

Watch and learn, Joey, watch and learn.

'You've got her well trained.' I smile, hearing the thud of two kids come running down the stairs.

'I know – great, isn't it? Course it's all to do with bribery. Last time she lit the fire only because I promised I'd paint her nails for her.'

Rose and Joey fly through the door, panting, and when I look at Joey, I gasp. She's got eyeshadow, blush, lipstick and mascara all over her face and is grinning like a lunatic, her nose in the air. She looks like Robert Smith, The Cure's pale-faced frontman. Or Michael Keaton in *Beetlejuice* – all black kohl around her eyes and smeared-off, bright-red lipstick.

342

'Mummy? Do you like my makeup?'

'Lovely.' I smile.

Charlie laughs and Rose looks proud of her handiwork.

'Once they start mixing with other kids, you can't control them any more – your influence starts fading faster than fake tan,' says Charlie proudly, as though that's a good thing. 'But, at least now, instead of worrying about sprained metatarsals and teeth getting knocked out, the only thing that's going to keep me awake at night is worrying where my Touche Eclat's got to!'

Rose giggles and busies herself ripping up newspaper and scrunching it into balls, encouraging Joey to do the same. They carefully arrange the kindling on top of the newspaper mountain and then Rose gently pushes Joey back towards me, explaining that fire is dangerous and she should never get too close lest she get burned.

'Speaking of tans,' Charlie goes on, 'you're looking extremely St Tropez, I must say.'

'Totally by accident,' I say. 'It's because I have to do a thirty-minute walk every day and usually forget my hat and sunscreen, even though it's winter over there.'

'You're letting your hair go curly, too, I see,' notes Charlie. 'It's gorgeous! Especially with all those natural blonde highlights from the sun.'

'Mummy's straighteners broke.' Joey grins.

'And I haven't got the time,' I add. 'I can't be arsed with all that drying, then straightening ... and, weirdly enough, I don't mind it curly.'

Joey shrieks with delight and launches herself at me, trying to wrap her arms all the way around me in a huge hug.

'I'm so surprised to see you looking all sun-kissed and bronzed, knowing how you feel about sun and the beach. I've always imagined you and Joey in Bondi head-to-toe in black high-necked, sand-sweeping Victorian dresses, your pale faces kept in the shade by your paper parasols, like Holly Hunter and her daughter in *The Piano*.'

I laugh at the picture she paints.

Charlie motions for me to get up and I follow her into the kitchen. She sets about organising a teapot and big mugs and even a little jug of milk with a bowl of sugar on a tray.

I ferret about in my handbag for my sweeteners and ask whether it's skimmed milk – which, of course, it's not, but I figure I'll take the risk of the full-fat milk and just cross my fingers that my blood sugar levels don't go soaring thanks to the fat and the lactose.

'Hey!' Charlie says. 'If you ever decide to open a JAMM here in Bath, bagsy I get to work in it!'

'Well, waitressing *is* where the money's at – told you being a property lawyer was a waste of time and you'd never amount to anything,' I tease her.

She smiles and says, 'Do you think maybe Jack's grown up a little bit, too, since you went to Oz?'

'He certainly got right into the whole counselling thing, so maybe he has grown up – on the inside, anyway. But

344

there's something about warm weather that makes normally quite sensible, sane – even suave, on occasion – men like Jack dress as if they're overgrown schoolboys. It's hideous. Forty-year-olds cavorting about in shorts and "hilarious" slogan T-shirts ... and Jesus sandals! If you're lucky, without socks. I mean, really! It's like wherever you turn, there's Tweedledum gurning back at you. Quite unsettling.'

'Right!' she says, picking up the overloaded tray. 'Let's get this little lot by the fire and cosy up!'

We meander back into the front room.

'In fact,' I carry on, 'if Jack ever wore, say, a dark chunky knit jumper and long trousers, with a nice, thick, heavy navy pea coat slung over his shoulder ... hmm. Because if I could feel attracted to him again in that way, in that uncontrollable animal lust way, then you never know, we might even end up having sex again. With each other. In this lifetime.'

'Haven't you two ...?'

'Not since the night of the conception, no.' I'm inwardly shocked at the great length of time that's elapsed since we last shagged and pull Joey towards me. 'But, you know, being pregnant and all not only wreaks havoc with your desire to get at it, but the fundamental impracticalities of it, too. Don't you reckon? You must have found the same thing – particularly with relations between you and John turning somewhat rather frosty lately?'

'Nope,' she says, throwing me one of her wicked,

sneaky smiles. 'We've been at it like rabbits ever since the first night we met.'

I should've known that'd be the case. Charlie's always been mad for a bunk-up, no matter what's been going on emotionally. Maybe not so much has changed, after all.

'Well, we *were* at it constantly ... before he left for good.'

'Really? For good?' I open my eyes and mouth wide with surprise. 'Oh, Charlie! I'm so sorry.'

'Don't be – I'm fine. It's all fine. I couldn't bear his incessant wittering on about not wanting to deal with a newborn again at his age, yadda yadda yadda. I'm over it now – no, really. *He can go his own way ...* ' She sings that last bit, like in that Fleetwood Mac song. 'Do what he wants. And if he doesn't want me, I'm totally fine with it. I've got everything I need right here with my two girls.'

Rose smiles up at her mum and hands her a small jar of dark metallic-blue nail varnish.

'You know yours is a girl? For sure?' I raise my eyebrows.

'Oh yeah – that's one of the first things I found out. Don't you know what yours is?'

'It's a girl,' says Joey authoritatively.

'We *think* it's a girl,' I correct her.

'I bet you can't wait for your baby sister to be born.' Charlie addresses Joey, who's delighted to be involved in a proper big girls' conversation.

'We'll be able to play princesses and fairies together.' Joey nods.

'Have you got any Bratz dolls?' Charlie asks.

I mime the internationally recognised signal for 'Shut up!' by pretending my forefinger is a knife and slitting my throat.

'What are Bratz dolls, Mummy?' asks Joey.

Charlie laughs, placing professional toe spacers between Rose's toes and starting to brush the viscous liquid on to her nails.

Joey's mesmerised by this but eventually looks up at me, almost as though she's checking it's OK she witness such big girl things.

Charlie flashes me that evil smirk again and says, 'Would you like to come shopping with me, Joey?'

Joey can hardly contain herself and jumps, quite literally, for joy, as she moves closer to Charlie, like she's magnetised and Joey can't resist her pull.

I scratch my head and come to the conclusion that resistance is futile – and if you can't beat 'em, you might as well join 'em.

'Shall I do your nails, Joey?' I ask her.

'Yes, yes, YES!' screams Joey.

Charlie and Rose chuckle at Joey's exuberance. And I'm just thinking what a lovely, warm mother–daughter scene this is when Charlie speaks:

'Hey!' She beams. 'It's a bit like *Beaches*, this, isn't it?'

'Yeah,' I say wistfully. 'No! Hang on! Who's Bette Midler here?'

Charlie throws me a look that says, 'You have to ask?'

and I groan. 'You are, of course – you're short and you've got curly hair!' Charlie guffaws.

'I suppose you're Barbara Hershey, then? All dark hair and plump lips,' I say, sounding a tad envious.

Charlie puckers up and plants a big smacker on Rose's perfect pout.

Joey watches Charlie and Rose and then bounds over to me, nearly strangling me as she hugs me tightly, kissing me.

It's as though she's in competition with Rose for who can be the loveliest to her mum, and I inwardly declare Joey the winner when she looks me straight in the eye, grinning when she says:

'You are *awesome*, Mummy!'

Chapter 24

My mobile says it's eleven a.m. in Bath, so that makes it eight p.m. in Sydney. I've managed to pull my jet-lagged self together a bit, washed my face and brushed my wiry, curly hair into some sort of decent shape and now I'm ready to Skype the cafe.

I can't wait to see Jack's lovely face – extra olivey with his tan, the wrinkles around his twinkling eyes, his salt and pepper hair (what there is of it) making him look distinguished and handsome. A silver fox, to be sure.

Shoshie answers the call and I picture the laptop sitting on the corner of the bar bench, Shosh on the tall stool. It's noisy in there tonight, but not with the normal sound of punters clinking glasses and laughing – more with the sleazy sound of modern RnB. Rihanna's warbling on about whether her boyfriend is 'big enough' and wondering out loud whether he can, indeed, 'get it up'. It sounds like some dodgy nightclub run by Snoop Dogg and I half expect to see Kylie pole dancing in the background.

'Roxy!' Shoshie shrieks. 'How are you? *Where* are you?'

'I'm in Bath, staying at my best mate Charlie's place,' I say, looking eagerly over Shoshanna's shoulder to see any sign of the wonderful Jack.

'Oh! We miss you! Gila's in bed at Mum's now – she'll be so annoyed she missed Joey. Is she there? Or is she in bed, too?'

'It's morning here – she's gone out shopping with Charlie and her daughter.'

'Shopping? I thought Joey hated shopping,' she says, looking puzzled.

'Not any more, she doesn't. Anyway, it might have been a massive case of transference, that. I'm the one who's not all that keen on shopping. As a hobby, I mean,' I admit.

'Ha! I knew it! You miserable old bag.' She grins her warm, welcoming, happy grin. 'How's business? Found a place for JAMM yet?'

'Not yet. We're going back to London for another reccy before we leave, though.'

'And how's your bump? You must be just about to drop!'

'Nah, plenty of time. There've been no signs of the baby engaging or anything yet – no mucous plugs popping out, nothing untoward at all. But, hey! Speaking of babies … how are *you*?'

'Shh.' She puts her forefinger up to her pouting lips and leans into the laptop, whispering. 'I'm going to have a

CVS soon and from that they'll be able to match the DNA to Gila or ... the *unknown quantity*.'

'Unknown ...?'

'Shh! Tarquin, hello, my love! Look, it's Roxy. Beaming to us all the way from sunny Bath!'

Shoshanna reaches out to bring Tarquin into the fold and I'm momentarily taken aback by how smashing-looking he really is. My eyes dart to the right corner of the screen to check myself out in all my semi-pixelated glory and it's quite disconcerting, actually, seeing yourself like that.

'Hiya.' Tarquin waves with one hand – one manly, tanned, rough-hewn hand. Tarquin's hands have always made a big impression on me. Ha! Chance'd be a fine thing, I think to myself.

'Hey there, Tarquin. Is Jack around?'

'I'm fine – thanks for asking!' He smiles. 'Sorry to disappoint you, but he's not here, no. As a matter of fact, I'm just on my way to meet him at the Tea Gardens in Bondi Junction.'

'You're meeting him for a cup of tea? At a rival cafe? Blimey – things have changed more than I thought!'

'The Tea Gardens is a pub, silly. I've been meeting him there a couple of times a week for quite a while now.'

'Ah,' the penny drops, 'no wonder counselling's worked for him – if chatting involves several pints of ale, he can talk the hind legs off a donkey!'

'Yeah. Once you get him started, there's really no stopping him. He's a good guy, you know, Roxy. And he loves

351

you very much. I hope it works out for you two, I do. Great couple. And I hope I've been of some help, not that I'm really any good at this stuff any more ...'

Tarquin looks to his left and down at the floor.

'What? What do you mean? You're brilliant! And you've helped immensely. If it wasn't for you, we'd probably be divorced by now!'

'Thanks for saying that, Roxy,' he looks up again, 'but my heart's just not in it any more. I always felt like a fraud, which I kind of was – keep it under your hat, but I only read *Men Are from Mars, Women Are from Venus* a couple of times to get my degree over the internet, simple as that. I was acting, playing a part, being how I thought a marriage counsellor should be ... I never really felt that conflict resolution was a strong point for me and—'

'Well, ballroom dancing's not going to solve any major problems,' I cut him off as I begin to feel a little bit cheated. I mean, really. A degree off the internet? The cheeky sod!

'Heh heh heh,' he chortles. 'Yes, well, that was a little leftfield of me, I admit. Hopefully it was only a temporary lapse of reason and sound judgement.'

He smiles at Shoshanna, standing close by his side, and I think to myself how good they look together – love's young(ish) dream.

'And I'm in too good a place myself at the moment.' He kisses Shoshie's cheek. 'So I can't be doing with tears and tantrums and he said this and she said that and you started

352

it and I hate you and I never liked your hair or whatever. I don't know whether you noticed, but in our last session I was a bit off, I was finding it extremely difficult to concentrate. Particularly on the negative aspects of a relationship when I feel so good, so happy, so *positive*.'

Shosh repays the favour and plants a big, lingering kiss on Tarquin's handsome cheek.

'I'm thinking of starting up a surf school right here at the cafe – what do you think?' he goes on. 'Something dads and their lads can do together or separately. I know how much I get out of it, doing it with my boys, the bonding between the sets out there on the ocean ... '

He trails off and I notice someone behind him, waving furiously at me.

I peer at the laptop, unable to make out who exactly the face behind Tarquin's is, even though it seems eerily familiar.

'Who's that behind you, Tarq?' I ask.

'It's Super-Duper Nanny Cooper!' Shoshie cries.

Sure enough, it's our very own *Supernanny*, Elizabeth. But she looks so different – her specs are off, her makeup's heavily applied, her long hair's flowing free and I'm expecting her to purr – rather than speak – any second now. She's seriously going for hardcore sexy and sultry and her severe demeanour of yore has all but vanished.

'I didn't recognise you, Elizabeth! You look so, so ... '

'I know,' she says huskily, tossing her fabulously auburn mane about like a racehorse. 'Thought an image revamp was way overdue. And it's so much easier to maintain than the daily laundered and pressed business suits. Not to mention the skyrocketing price of new glasses every time I broke a pair, which was often. And that bun was a killer – the headache I'd have after a full day of that, I can't tell you.'

'Wow.' I'm agog.

'Very liberating, I must say.' She stops flinging her 'do about and fixes me with beady eyes. 'Now, how are you and young Joey getting on?'

'Good, good,' I reply, not feeling the sense of panic I used to at her interrogations. Thank God for the millions of miles between us. And her makeover. 'Overall, pretty good.'

'Remembering that you're the boss? Giving her boundaries? Tell, don't ask! And—'

Shosh gently elbows Elizabeth to the side of the screen.

'I think you've got a client, Liz.' She nods to Elizabeth's regular table.

'Oh! Yes.' Elizabeth turns to profile, licks her lips, pats her hair, smooths down her figure-hugging dress and saunters away off-screen.

Shosh leans into the camera and whispers:

'There's a dishy single dad who's having a nightmare with his four-year-old daughter. He sees Elizabeth a lot and I think there's some chemistry there.' She shrugs her shoulders and winks at me.

'That's amazing – how different does *she* look? Still sounds a bit scary, mind,' I say.

'She can't help it,' agrees Shoshie. 'Just like this marvellous young lady here ... ' She throws one arm to the side, hooks her hand on to a pregnant bump and then reels it into full view of the screen.

It's Kylie.

'Kyles!' I yelp. 'How on earth *are* you?'

'Great, boss, great!' She beams. 'Lactation, Lactation, Lactation classes are nearly full and Jack's going to take Phil on part-time as a co-manager.'

'Hang on.' I gasp. 'Phil? As in Phil-O Pastry?'

'That's the fella.' Kylie giggles, rubbing her tummy. 'Oh, Roxy, it's going to be so good having him work here while I look after the baby. I feel good about everything now – he even came with me and held my hand when I told my olds.'

'And ...?' Shoshie eggs Kylie on to say something more.

'And ... and, God, I can hardly say it, it's so unbelievable ... '

'Say it!' Shosh and I both scream at the same time.

'He's asked me to marry him.' Kylie breathes out. 'And I said yes!'

'Oh.' I cock my head to one side and pull my clasped hands up to my mouth, as if in prayer. 'That's fantastic, Kyles. Huge congratulations.'

Kylie thrusts her hand at the laptop's camera and I'm

nearly blinded by the megawatts bouncing off her ring finger.

'Twenty-four carats!' she squeals.

'Fabulous,' I reply. Because what else can you say to that?

And then the sound of porn sex, all moaning and groaning and sharp intakes of breath from the song playing from the stereo (for it is definitely not one of the Wurlitzer's eighties tracks), gets too much for me.

'What the hell's going on over there?' I demand, putting my hands over my ears. 'Not exactly age-appropriate tunes, Kyles!'

Kylie looks sheepishly at me and gets up, disappearing from view.

And suddenly it goes quiet again. I take my hands from my ears and stop frowning.

Shoshie looks up to where I know the jukebox is and smiles, nodding. Then the familiar tinkling piano of 'Manic Monday', our collective favourite tune, kicks in and it's as though a whole cafe is singing as one.

Shoshie sings along for a bit and then picks up the laptop, jerkily walking me to behind the bar.

'You've got to see this,' I can hear her say, the computer camera firmly focused on her crotch.

'No, thanks!' I splutter.

She turns the camera away from her body and a framed poster hanging on the bar wall comes into view.

'What is it?' I ask.

Shoshie puts the computer on her shoulder, like a boombox, and steps back to let the full glory of the poster fill the screen.

'It's our review! From the *Bugle*!' I squeal in delight.

'You better believe it, kid,' says Shoshie. 'Jack got it blown up and framed. See the fluoro-green highlighter on the good bits?'

'Yeah! God, that's great!'

'That's Jack for you.'

'Yeah,' I agree. 'That's Jack. For me.'

Chapter 25

Charlie's lent me her automatic Saab Convertible and Joey and I are driving back from the local convenience store where we've bought loads of salad and gestational-diabetes-friendly food for us to make for dinner. It's our last night in Bath before Charlie drives us back to London tomorrow.

So while Charlie's off watching Rose play netball, Joey and I are going to prepare a feast. My mouth starts watering as I think about it and I realise I haven't eaten anything for a while.

'I am starving, sweetie,' I say to Joey in the back seat. 'Now, while I start to get the dinner ready, you must have your bath, OK?'

'Noy,' comes the defiant reply in her *Kath & Kim* Aussie accent.

'Yes, Joey, you will have your bath. I don't want any tantrums about it either.'

'Noy,' she says again, giggling.

I manoeuvre the car up one narrow steep street and slowly turn right into the next.

'Joey? You do as Mummy tells you, right?'

Silence.

'I'm in charge here, so you do as Mummy tells you, right?'

'Noy, I doyn't,' she says matter-of-factly.

'Well, you should, missy.'

'Noy, *you* should, miss!' She grins.

It's hard enough weaving in and out of these old narrow streets with cars parked up and down either side of them, without having to jump through verbal hoops with Joey as well.

'Promise me you'll have a bath when we get back to Auntie Charlie's, OK?' There's a tiny bit of a whine in my voice.

'*Promise me you'll—*' Joey mimics me with a big whine.

'You'll have a bath when we get home, Joey,' I almost snap.

'Noy! I woyn't!' she declares.

'Yes, you will!'

'Noy, I WOYN'T!' she shouts.

'Yes, you WILL!' I smile at her wonky accent. 'And it's "no", like in "snow" – not "noy".'

There's silence for a second, so I add, for good measure:

'And don't talk back to me, young lady.'

'And DOYN'T talk back to me, old lady!' she mocks me, pushing me just a tad too far.

'JOSEPHINE!' I bark, losing a bit of my voice as I do so.

And then I . . . I don't know. I just completely lose it.

Either my blood sugar levels have dropped lower than a Blue-tongued Lizard's belly or I'm having a massive panic attack. Whichever way, something's going horribly wrong. My legs go to jelly, I get all hot, my vision starts to go, everything's turning black and somehow, in my distress and confusion, I manage to put the car into reverse.

The next thing I know, we're rolling all the way back down the road, bouncing up and down, both Joey and I screaming, the smell of crushed lettuce filling my nostrils. Then there's a loud crash and it feels like someone's smashed into the back of us, like we're in bumper cars.

We come to a halt and when I open my eyes, the first thing I see is steam hissing out of the Saab's bonnet. I crack my neck as I whip my head round, looking over my left shoulder at Joey.

'Sweetie? Are you OK? Does anything hurt?' I croak at her.

'Noy. I'm OK,' she says, eyes wide with excitement.

'Are you sure?' I try to undo my seatbelt, so I can get out of the car and pull Joey out of there, too, lest it does a Hollywood crash and bursts into flames.

But just as I'm grappling with my seatbelt, my mobile, buried deep in my handbag, sitting on the passenger seat, rings. Joey gets her belt off quick as a flash and holds on to my headrest with her right arm while she shoves her left

360

hand into my handbag, surfacing with said phone. She gives it to me.

'Hello? Hello?' I squeak, sounding like a guilty teenager getting caught coming home at dawn, voice box sacrificed to the Gods of Party and several packets of Marlboro Lights.

'Hey, gorgeous!' shouts Jack. 'What's happening? You been smoking or something?'

'Um, ah ...' I look at Joey for inspiration. She stares back at me, bouncing on the back seat as if we're eagerly awaiting another go on a rollercoaster. She's grinning like a mad thing.

'Er, I, ah ... we ...' God, it's like amateur yodelling night.

'Go on, spit it out!' Jack laughs.

'We've just been to the, ah, the supermarket.'

'Don't think I can bear the excitement,' he says. 'Is Joey there? Put her on for a sec, will you?'

I nod to Joey and widen my eyes in the hopes she'll understand what this look means. I can't take any chances, though, so I put my palm over the receiver as I hand her the phone and whisper:

'Don't say anything about what just happened, Joey. Please. It'll only worry Daddy and scare him. Talk about fairies or rainbows, just don't mention—'

'WE JUST HAD A CRASH, DADDY!' Joey squeals in delight as she snatches the mobile from me.

I roll my eyes to the roof of the car.

And only then do I notice a small crowd milling about outside. Their voices are muffled but they look concerned as they cock their heads to the side and stare at us, like we're aliens who've just fallen to earth and now we're trapped inside our UFO. I smile warily. One kind-faced old man pulls open my door and says:

'Don't move, love. Stay right where you are. The ambulance is on its way, should be here any minute . . . '

'YES! MUMMY CRASHED GOING BACKWARDS!' Joey screams.

I shake my head from side to side and shoot her my furious, you-don't-wanna-mess-with-me look, putting my index finger up to my lips in a futile attempt to get her to shut up.

'Ew, YUCK!' comes her reply into the mobile's mouth-piece. 'Mummy's doing a big wee!'

I look down at my lap and see my skirt totally sodden, a puddle at my feet. There's water gushing out of me and streaming down my legs.

'Oh my God,' I groan. 'It's not wee, it's water.'

'THERE'S WAR-DAH COMING OUT OF MUMMY!'

'Not war-*dah*, Joey, war-*ter*. Say the t, so it's war-*ter*. OK? War . . . *TAAAAAAAAAAAAAAARGH!*'

Chapter 26

Three days later

It's somewhere round about two in the morning and I'm in bed with the baby. We're softly lit by the maternity ward's calm, warm, middle-of-the-night dim-orange glow and I'm so happy, I feel as if my heart's going to pop.

It's almost completely quiet, save for the soothing tones of mums trying to comfort their newborns, whose weak cries belie how forceful and strong those bellows will become in only a few short weeks.

The baby has latched on perfectly, so the midwife just told me, and I'm feeling ever so slightly, pleasantly drunk. That's Voltarol and morphine for you, I say to myself, and smile. And maybe it's the hormones, too, the delicious buzz you get from bringing a new life into the world.

Whatever it is, it's terrific. I want to feel like this forever, smothering his little head in kisses, the pair of us staying in whatever position sleep descends upon us, stuck to each other and stuck with each other for life. For dear life.

Joey's fast asleep on the fold-up bed next to me, exhausted from tending to my every need, helping the midwives and cooing over her brand new baby brother.

I stare lovingly at her and then the baby, Joey and then the baby again. But I can only really move my eyes, my neck's kind of fixed in place by the neck brace.

Suddenly I hear raised voices at the nurses' station and then heavy footsteps approaching my shared room.

I look up just as my curtain flies back, revealing a soaking wet overgrown schoolboy in shorts and an I'M WITH STUPID T-shirt, carrying a bunch of bedraggled flowers.

It's Jack, shivering and pale, but grinning.

'Hi, honey – I'm home!' he splutters through the raindrops falling from his forehead on to his lips. 'I got here as quickly as I could, Rox – are you OK?'

'I'm sorry, Roxy, I did try to stop him,' says the flustered midwife, peering round Jack's sodden form.

'It's OK,' I whisper, beaming. 'He's the dad.'

The midwife looks him up and down disapprovingly, tuts and closes the curtain around us.

'You couldn't text?' I ask.

'I raced out the door the minute I heard you screaming on the phone. I panicked and forgot my mobile – look at me! I didn't even change or pack anything – I ran all the way up Ridgey Didge Road to Bondi Junction to get a taxi to the airport!'

I consider this, picturing it in my mind's eye, and let out a giggle. Which just makes my neck hurt.

'Rox!' he goes on, getting exasperated. 'I've felt totally lost for the last two days … I didn't know whether you and Joey were OK, whether the baby was OK, whether my family was—'

The baby stirs and lets out a tiny, sweet squawk.

Jack's gaze falls from me to the baby and he steps closer to us, dropping to his knees in the space between Joey's fold-out bed and my hospital bed. He extends a wet hand, complete with one or two daisy petals, to the baby's head.

'I'm sorry I'm late, little one,' he whispers, his thick voice making me swoon. Or maybe that's the drugs.

He picks the baby up and perches on the side of the bed, gazing into his son's barely-open eyes.

'Thought of any names yet?' he asks.

'Zephyr,' I say, trying to sound like a small, warm wind.

'What? Like the monkey in *Babar*? No way!' he says, getting excited. 'What about Jackson? Like Jack's-son. Geddit? *Jackson*,' he brays.

'Hmm. Bit obvious,' I counter. 'Why don't we call him To Be Announced – TBA for short – until we can agree and decide?'

I shift slightly to make more room for Jack as I reach out for Zephyr/Jackson/TBA. Jack hands me the baby and reorganises himself on the bed, incapable of taking his eyes off TBA snuggling into my right side.

Both of us luxuriate in the warmth and joy of the moment, wide-eyed with contentment, transfixed by our beautiful baby boy.

Until, a few minutes later, I realise I need more room to arrange the pillows so I can feed TBA, so Jack carefully gets up, sorts out the pillows for me and gets under the covers on Joey's bed. She mumbles 'Daddy!' in her sleep and the next thing you know, they're both flat-out, snoring softly as they spoon.

I crane my neck, oblivious to the pain, so I can gaze at them a little bit longer, their smiles fixed and their bodies still, their breathing perfectly in sync. And I can't get the smile off my face.

So Jack and I aren't two twenty-five-year-olds romping around in a meadow, chasing each other until we fall under a shady willow tree, holding buttercups underneath each other's chins and snogging to Rod Stewart tunes. So what if the dappled sunshine doesn't highlight our sharp cheekbones at every turn, like the models in that Rels 'R' Us ad? And who cares that our two kids aren't white-blonde twins from the land of Timotei? Because you know what? We're real. A real family. With real ups and downs, real triumphs and disappointments, real good times and real bad times, real chaos and clutter and utter exhaustion. We're a real, knackered family – not some fake advert, a cliché seventies image of what love looks like. And that's just fine with me. In fact, it's perfect.

I watch Jack and Joey sleeping soundly for what seems like hours, until I notice TBA's rooting, desperate for a feed.

I manage to get him latched on and after a few minutes

he stops sucking and falls into that delicious-looking, almost drunken sleep that newborn babies full of milk do.

I sigh contentedly and carefully look around the cubicle. But all I can see, all that's in focus, is my family. Everything else – the flowers, the cards, the balloons, the other women and their babies – is a blur. It's like all of a sudden, no one and nothing else matters.

I'm the only one in the whole room who's awake now. But I don't feel alone – far from it. In fact, I think I'd go so far as to say I've never felt quite this *un*alone in my life: so together, so surrounded by love, so full and satisfied and complete – like I really *belong*. It's as though the final, missing piece of the puzzle is in place at long last and I feel … at home. As it slowly dawns on me, I imagine a light bulb suspended over my head, switching on, beaming out a bright light, and I start to giggle, able to see, to really *feel* what Jack means when he says that home is wherever we are.

Because that's what it's all about, isn't it? I mean, I get it. Finally, I *get* it. It's about family. It's about home. It's about your family *being* your home.

And it's about time.

Glossary

Following are some words and phrases with which you may be unfamiliar, and their definitions. Also, a handy guide to their usage in an everyday Australian context, as one might encounter when conversing with the locals.

Caramello Koala (noun): Chocolate-covered caramel confectionery in the shape of a small, smiling cartoon koala wearing dungarees. Exceedingly handy for bribing small children to do your bidding. As in: 'Bring me that cask of red in the fridge, would you, Junior? Oh, and if you eat all your spinach, you can have a Caramello Koala.'

Cop an optic (phrase, colloquial): Ordering someone to lay eyes upon something, usually something you can't afford to miss, the sight is so amazing. As in: 'Cop an optic on the unbearable tightness of that surfie's bum in those Speedos!'

Drongo (noun): A dolt, a simpleton, a stupid person. As in: 'What kind of drongo do you think I am? I'm not gonna eat spinach for nothin' or no one!'

Fugs (adjective): Contraction of the word 'fugly' which, in itself, is the marriage of two words (why say two when one will do?) – 'f***ing' and 'ugly' to describe the looks of someone extremely aesthetically displeasing. As in: 'He's got a great personality – really sweet and funny and nice. I know it's wrong to the power of a hundred, but I just can't get over the fact he's so full-on *fugs*!'

Got tickets on himself (phrase, colloquial): Someone who is arrogant, conceited. Someone who thinks they're better than everyone else, too cocky for their own good. As in: 'He hasn't just got tickets on himself, he's got a whole season's pass!'

How do you like them apps? (phrase, colloquial): Possibly borrowed from the Seppos (Septic Tanks = Yanks), this is usually used as a rhetorical question, assuming 'them apps' (short for apples – or, in the case of the iPhone/iPad shop at Sydney Airport, applications) are pretty great. As in: 'I got you the new Just Another Manic Mum-Day app for your iPad for your birthday. How do you like *them* apps?'

Make a motza (phrase, colloquial): To coin it in, to make a mint. To earn an absolute fortune and become

369

exceedingly wealthy; obscenely rich. As in: 'The lottery is *not* a tax on the stupid – it's a surefire way to make a motza! Eventually.'

Olds (collective noun): One's parents, one's mother and father. As in: 'I'd love to go out with you tonight, Darryl, but my olds won't let me. Well, it is a week-night – and they say as long as I live under their roof, I have to live by their rules. I know I'm thirty-four and a company director, but I can't afford to move out of home just yet – have you seen how high the rents are in Sydney these days?'

Pash (verb): To snog: to French kiss; to engage in passionate kissing, often involving tongues. Usually only used (and done) by twenty-year-olds and under. As in: 'We had a pash behind the bike sheds, but then Mrs Mackenzie caught us and now I'm on detention for two weeks!'

Root, rooting, rooted (verb): To root – to have sex. Rooting – to be in the act of having sex, or what a baby does when trying to suckle at its mother's breast (not to be confused). Rooted – broken, no longer working, exhausted, totally ruined. Can also be used as a noun. As in: 'Yeah, he's all-right-looking, but I wouldn't bother if I were you – word has it he's a dud root.'

Rousing on someone, to rouse (verb): To tell someone off, get on their back about something and have a right go at them. As in: 'Mum was really rousing on me about eating too many Caramello Koalas, reckons I ate two at a time the other day. I said I only had one and she should lay off the Cask Red because it's making her see double.'

She'll be apples (phrase, colloquial): Everything is going to be OK; everything is going to work out just fine. As in: 'So after ten years of the worst drought in Australian history, we're now suffering under the crushing weight of floods and the whole region is in a state of emergency. But she'll be right, mate. She'll be apples, no worries.'

Squiz (verb): To take a look at, to have a gander at, to cop an optic on. To take a squiz at something is to study it closely. As in: 'Take a squiz at me lottery numbers, would ya, love? Can't find me glasses.'

Stoked (adjective): Very happy, enthusiastically pleased, extremely chuffed. As in: 'Jeez, I'm stoked!'

Tacker (noun): Usually prefaced with the word 'little'. A small person, a child, an infant, someone under the age of twelve. As in: 'Poor little tacker, she's been crying all the way home from the beach – shop's only gone and run out of Caramello Koalas again.'

Tanty (noun): Short for temper tantrum. An endearing term usually reserved for children's bad behaviour or, indeed, when adults are acting childishly. As in: 'Don't chuck a tanty, it was only a pash. It's not like we were *rooting* or anything.'

Tradies (noun): Tradesmen; men in the plumbing, building or electrical trades. As in: 'I may be a tradie but I'm not a complete drongo – I'm making a motza fixing your blocked dunny!'

Undies (noun): Pants, knickers, undergarments. As in: 'I'm so over these undies – take a squiz at the perished elastic!'

Acknowledgements

First of all, I'd like to thank Rebecca Saunders – the best editor in town – without whose invaluable help and encouragement, this would be a very different novel indeed. Huge thanks are due, too, to my fabulous agent, Rowan Lawton. Thank you to my fantastic copy-editor Emma Stonex, Hannah Hargrave and everyone at Little, Brown. And I'd also like to thank Jane Costello and Carmen Reid for saying nice things about *The Pissed-Off Parents Club*.

Susan Penn-Turrall gets a massive thanks from me for always going above and beyond the call of duty as a friend. Thanks too to Aideen Clarke, Yasmin Boland, Emma Kelly, Ann Eley, Fiona 'Milque' Sandiford, Maria Kontis, Raphael and Odette Kapferer as well as the Bondi Trattoria. I'd also like to say a special thanks to Lesley and Tracey-Lee Schneier at Hug-A-Bub nursery and pre-school, as well as Jacqui Cameron and all the 2011 Year K mums at Rose Bay Public School for being wonderfully supportive and kind.

Thank you Nick Heyward, Terry Hall, Jo Brand, Emma Kennedy, Steve Coogan, Rob Brydon, Ruth Jones, Miranda Hart, Cold Chisel, Andrew Ridgeley and George Michael. Gigantic thanks to Bruce and Roland Kapferer – gentlemen, scholars and quite simply always the best company for a Silly Saturday movie marathon. Sammi and Maxi Eley deserve an extra special thank you for being magnificent, as does Jon for his buoyant sense of humour, ever-present as we lurch from crisis to catastrophe, his unending support, boundless generosity and general all-round nice guy-ness.

But most of all, the biggest thanks ever must go to Judith Kapferer – the warmest, wisest, wittiest, most knowledgeable, most beautiful woman I've ever been lucky enough to know.

Also by Mink Elliott

THE PI**ED-OFF PARENTS CLUB

First-time mum Roxy feels perennially ticked off. She and her partner Jack have left London for a new life in the village of Riverside, with their ten-month-old daughter Joey. But their new house resembles a building site and Roxy is struggling to cope with parenthood. With no family or friends to turn to for help, Roxy sets up a club in order to meet like-minded parents, and so begins The Pissed-Off Parents Club.

Hilarious and refreshingly original, this is a story telling it like it is – for mums and dads of all descriptions.

'Mink Elliott's funny, feisty debut novel is perfect light-relief for anyone finding new parenthood less than easy-peasy'
Jane Costello

978-0-7515-4339-1

Other bestselling titles available by mail

☐ The Pi**ed-Off Parents Club   Mink Elliott   £6.99

The prices shown above are correct at time of going to press. However, the publishers reserve the right to increase prices on covers from those previously advertised, without further notice.

———————————————— sphere ————————————————

Please allow for postage and packing: **Free UK delivery**.
Europe: add 25% of retail price; Rest of World: 45% of retail price.

To order any of the above or any other Sphere titles, please call our credit card orderline or fill in this coupon and send/fax it to:

Sphere, PO Box 121, Kettering, Northants NN14 4ZQ
Fax: 01832 733076   Tel: 01832 737526
Email: aspenhouse@FSBDial.co.uk

☐ I enclose a UK bank cheque made payable to Sphere for £ . . . .
☐ Please charge £ . . . . to my Visa/Delta/Maestro

Expiry Date ☐☐☐☐   Maestro Issue No. ☐☐

NAME (BLOCK LETTERS please) . . . .
ADDRESS . . . .
. . . .
. . . .
Postcode . . . . Telephone . . . .
Signature . . . .

Please allow 28 days for delivery within the UK. Offer subject to price and availability.